She'll find more than redemption in the arms of her Highland lord.

A ghost stepped out of the shadows.

Suddenly, she barreled into a solid chest jacketed in fine wool. Two arms reached out to steady her, but her momentum toppled them both to the dusty stone floor.

Dark blue eyes the color of a Highland night stared up at her.

For a long moment, she stared back, horrified and transfixed. She could feel his heart thudding below her, and the solidness of his body against hers.

"You're not a ghost," Jean said breathlessly.

"I am not," he said in a clipped English accent.

He grabbed both her wrists, pushed up and rolled with her.

A second later their positions were reversed and she was pinned beneath him.

A Scandalous Scot

KAREN RANNEY

AVON
An Imprint of HarperCollinsPublishers

AVON BOOKS
An Imprint of HarperCollins*Publishers*
10 East 53rd Street
New York, New York 10022–5299

Copyright © 2012 by Karen Ranney
ISBN 978–0–06–202779–5
www.avonromance.com

First Avon Books mass market printing: July 2012

Avon Trademark Reg. U.S. Pat. Off. and in Other Countries, Marca Registrada, Hecho en U.S.A.
HarperCollins® is a registered trademark of HarperCollins Publishers.

Printed in the U.S.A.

10 9 8 7 6 5 4 3 2 1

To Heather Griffis
Just because

A
Scandalous Scot

Chapter 1

Ballindair, Scotland
Summer 1860

RULES FOR STAFF: *When being addressed, stand quiet with your hands folded together in front of you.*

Jean MacDonald dropped down behind a dusty bureau, wrapping her arms around her knees. Silence was a necessary requirement for seeing a ghost. So was patience. She'd been patient for the last year. All she'd learned in that time was that this business of ghosts was a delicate one.

According to the other maids who claimed to have seen him, the Herald had no qualms about appearing even in daylight. A handsome soldier, clad in kilt and shirt with a set of pipes slung over his shoulder, he didn't announce death as much as change.

The Green Lady wasn't supposed to be that difficult to find, either, since she was reputed to appear in the coldest spot in a room.

She had yet to see either of them.

Nor had she seen the French Nun, but no one had. That ghost was proving to be elusive. Was it because the nun still felt shame, even a hundred years later?

Jean yawned, clamped her hand over her mouth and shivered with fatigue.

Her aunt, Ballindair's housekeeper, had set them all to working like dervishes this past week. The Earl of Denbleigh himself was due to visit in ten days. Although Ballindair was normally spotless and perfect, she insisted that the entire castle be cleaned again. All the chandeliers, ornate picture frames, urns, and silly little statues of posing shepherdesses and dogs that really didn't look like dogs had to be dusted over and over again. All the ornate furniture must be treated with a special beeswax and turpentine mixture. All the fireplaces must be blackened, even though that chore had recently been done, and the shiny andirons polished still further. The floors were scrubbed, then buffed using a lamb's wool pad, until Jean could see her face in the dark oak boards, and each of the carpets brushed and beaten until her arms ached.

Her knees were abraded and her hands swollen and red. She'd worked as hard as any of the others—except, perhaps, for one person. Her sister, Catriona, had the ability to escape everyone's watchful eye.

Jean sometimes thought that Catriona believed she served the world simply by looking beautiful. Perhaps she did, at that. Most people stopped and stared when first viewing her. Catriona had bright golden hair, and eyes a deep blue, a color Jean had never seen in another. In addition, Catriona was dainty and delicate, unlike her own too tall frame.

Even the Presbyterian minister, sermonizing on the evils of the flesh, had allowed his gaze to linger on Catriona during Sunday services. Before they left for church the next week, Aunt Mary had given all the maids a stern lecture on comportment. Catriona only smiled sweetly, as if not realizing the admonishment had been pointedly directed at her.

What would it be like to have a man fall at her feet? Or to have a man stare at her across the room? That had happened on a great many occasions when they lived in Inverness, but the attention was always on Catriona and never on her.

She sighed. What a waste of time to think about such things, especially since it was doubtful she'd ever attract any man's attention, being a maid at Ballindair.

Tomorrow they were to start cleaning this very suite. When all the work was done, her aunt would have the rooms locked, just to make certain all stayed in readiness for the earl.

Tonight was the last opportunity she'd have to see the French Nun. Since the nun was rumored to haunt the Laird's Tower more than any other place at Ballindair, she couldn't overlook this chance to see the ghost.

She lay her head back against the wall, grateful the floor was hard. At least she was in no danger of falling asleep. To be a little more comfortable, she untied her shoes and set them to the side, wiggling her toes in pleasure.

Why was the earl coming back now?

"He had business in England," Aunt Mary had said. "He was a representative peer for Scotland at Parliament."

Evidently, no longer.

What her aunt hadn't said was that the earl had disgraced himself, and was returning to Scotland like a fox going to ground. Jean had only learned that through the Laird's Lug—a cunningly designed tube in the wall leading to the Clan Hall. She hadn't meant to eavesdrop, truly. But when Mr. Seath and her aunt were talking and the earl's name was mentioned, it had been impossible to turn away and pretend an interest in dusting the painting of a long-dead person.

"Why ever did he do it?" Mrs. MacDonald asked. "Why

couldn't he let the situation stand as it was? He wouldn't have been the first man to endure that kind of behavior."

"He has his pride."

"Too much of it, I'm thinking," she said. "If he damages the reputation of the MacCraig family for it."

The two of them had moved away, leaving Jean wishing she knew more. What had the Earl of Denbleigh done?

After five years away he was finally coming home to Ballindair. Why hadn't he returned in all that time? Was it because he preferred London to his own country?

She much preferred Ballindair to Inverness. Inverness was filled with memory. Here, at least, her recollections were only a year old.

The past had a way of creeping into her mind like the mist over Loch Tullie. First, you couldn't see your feet, then your legs, and before you knew it you were enveloped in a neck high cloud. She'd learned never to consciously remember Inverness. Or, if memories slipped up on her unawares, to run from them as quickly as she could.

Ti tak the bree wi the barm. One of her mother's sayings: to take the rough with the smooth. The past had been rough.

The life of a maid couldn't be said to be smooth, not with all the rules to learn and tasks to master. Her time was regulated from dawn until two hours after dinner, when she was expected to return to her room, prepare herself for bed, and go instantly to sleep. No daydreams were allowed, or dreams, either. Sleep was only a restorative, to ensure that Ballindair had an eager and rested staff.

Leaning back, she glanced at light filtering through the emerald curtains. In the Highlands the sky didn't darken until nearly midnight. Earlier, she hadn't needed a candle when she left her room—against the rules—and crept through the castle to the tower.

Moving a few inches to the left, she studied the Chamber

of State, the old name for the suite of rooms: bedroom, sitting room, and bathing chamber occupied by the Earls of Denbleigh.

The four-poster bed was heavily carved, with a headboard inscribed with the earl's crest—an eagle with outstretched wings holding a cluster of thistles—and dominated the dais on which it sat. The bed had been made in Scotland; that much she knew from her instructions. Her aunt insisted that each of the maids learned not only how to clean Ballindair, but also the history of every room, the better to appreciate the value of those items entrusted to their care.

A secretary and chair sat opposite the bed, with a large fireplace on the adjacent wall. The bureau behind which she was hiding was the match to an armoire, both pieces festooned with curlicues and crafted from the same cherrywood as the bed. The room was spacious enough to accommodate a round table in the corner, along with two chairs and a small settee beside which stood a table and lamp.

The entire lower floor of their house in Inverness could have fit comfortably within this chamber.

No, thoughts like that would only lead to tears.

Yet wasn't it normal to feel the past so strongly when she was waiting for a ghost? Didn't a ghost belong to the past? Didn't ghosts wander through the present because of sins they'd committed, or wishes left unfulfilled, or longings that would not let them pass into eternity?

Would she be a ghost one day? Would people study her life the way she'd pored over the book, *The Famous Ghosts of Ballindair*? Would they speak of her in low voices, pity coloring their words? *Poor, dear Jean, plain as milk. Died alone and single, of course.* What man would want her?

There she was again, thinking of a man's attentions. Just as she was aware of Catriona's beauty, she was conscious of her own appearance.

Her face lacked any distinction at all, being an oval shape. Her eyes were brown and average, and always looked too large for her face. Her mouth was average. Her chin neither jutted out nor receded. Her nose was neither too long nor petite. Her forehead was neither too high nor too short. She was simply average and regrettably indistinct—plain as milk.

In addition to lacking her sister's looks, she also possessed a mind that was a constant source of irritation to some people. Even after the wisest woman in the room subsided into silence, she kept asking questions.

"Is 'why' your favorite word?" Catriona asked once.

"Why shouldn't I want to know?" she'd responded. "Have you no curiosity about the world?"

Catriona only shook her head and moved away, dusting the bric-a-brac on the mantel with a desultory sway of the feather duster.

"What does it matter what you discover? It doesn't change your circumstances or make them better."

Granted, the world had been a difficult place for both of them in the last two years, but surely Catriona had more hope than that.

When she'd said as much, her sister laughed.

"Hope is just another name for wishing, Jean. Wishing never made anything better."

"If you don't have hope, Catriona," she said, "what do you have?"

Catriona had smiled. "You have the world as it is. And you must make do with it."

At that moment her younger sister seemed so old and worn that she had been silenced.

At least they had a roof over their heads and food to eat. During that last month in Inverness, she'd doubted they would survive. Hunger had been one of those constants like sunrise and sunset. If she was awake, she was hungry.

Then the letter had come from their aunt, offering them both positions as maids at Ballindair. Catriona was sent to tend to the public rooms, while she had been designated a general maid. She'd had to learn a great deal about the workings of a large home when her only experience was a small house of seven rooms.

Circumstances change. You must adapt. You have to accept certain realities about life. On that she agreed with Catriona.

She hadn't the education to be a governess. She lacked fluency in French and she was abysmal at watercolors. Her alternatives were few: become a bedewoman, a licensed beggar, or allow her sister to become a wealthy man's mistress. More than one man had hinted at an arrangement with Catriona.

At least being a maid was a decent occupation.

When they came to Ballindair a year ago, she had a choice: bemoan what had happened to them or accept her new life. She'd grown tired of grief, of worry and despair, so she took up her aunt's lessons in earnest, deciding to become the very best maid she could be. She'd taken pride in each task given her, learned as much as she could, and tried to become a valuable addition to the castle staff.

Along the way she found nuggets of joy in each day, like the sight of a flower in bloom, the breadth and depth of the night sky, or the flicker of a candle flame.

The book she'd borrowed from Ballindair's library was one of those nuggets, leading to her interest in three of the castle ghosts: the Herald, the Green Lady, and the French Nun.

That interest was why she was here in the middle of the night, trying to find the ghost of a woman whose life had been, in contrast, so much worse than hers.

At least, so far.

* * *

"The thing is to decide what to do with the rest of your life," Andrew Prender said. "Since you've surrendered your position at Parliament."

"I didn't surrender my position," Morgan said. "I was asked to give it up for the good of Scotland." The last part of that sentence was the hardest to say and tasted like bile on his tongue.

Andrew waved a gloved hand in the air as if to dismiss his banishment.

"They'll come around."

They wouldn't come around. He was a scandal. He, Morgan MacCraig, 9th Earl of Denbleigh, was a detriment to his fellow Scottish peers. His father had been the Keeper of the Great Seal of Scotland, while his son was a disgrace.

He hadn't been prepared for the reaction of his friends. People he'd thought would understand had turned their backs on him. More than once he'd greeted another man at an event, someone who suddenly found the floor, the ceiling, or the opposite wall of great interest. Even those whose opinions didn't matter to him pretended he was invisible. No one curried his favor any longer. He'd become a social and political pariah.

Only Andrew had remained a friend, even going so far as attaching himself to him and expressing a sudden and fervent desire to accompany him home to the Highlands.

They'd traveled by train to Inverness, and from there in a carriage his steward had arranged. When he'd questioned the driver how he knew they were arriving on that particular train, the man just tipped his hat and grinned.

"I've instructions to wait for you, Your Lordship. However long that might be."

Morgan's eyebrows rose. "Even at dawn?"

"Whenever the train comes in, Your Lordship."

"I'm not due for another ten days."

That made the man grin even more. "Your father had a habit of always arriving early. Mr. Seath, sir, thought you might do the same. Besides, sir, you're the MacCraig of Ballindair."

He'd felt absurdly grateful for the man's comment, the first sign of anything other than disgust he'd received in months. He nodded, entering the carriage and remaining silent for a while. Andrew was content enough to leave him to his thoughts until the last hour. As the sun rose, so did Andrew's curiosity.

He'd known better than to try to change Andrew's mind about coming with him to Scotland. Once Andrew was set on a course, nothing could alter it. Their friendship had begun as boys at school. Together, they had suffered privations and admitted their homesickness to each other.

Andrew's father had been a wealthy merchant, Morgan's father a hero of Scotland. Hell, he'd even died a hero, attempting to save a child after his ship sank off the Isle of Man. Andrew's father had expired in his bed, but both men left their sons a well-funded legacy.

Sometimes, especially recently, Morgan thought he'd much rather have Andrew's life. His friend dabbled at anything he wished—painting was his newest interest—and once bored, found something else to pursue.

A trait he carried over to women, his most important occupation.

The Duchess of Montrose had once told him that Andrew was the perfect companion, even married as he was. His wife kept to his country estate, leaving Andrew to the pleasures of London.

Andrew's handsome face always bore a pleasant expression. He even smiled in his dreams, an observation Morgan had made when they shared a cold and comfortless room at school. Andrew listened intently, told a great jest, and made each woman believe she was the only object of his affection.

Rumors about his equipage, spoken in tittering whispers, were true.

"God gave me another few inches there," Andrew once told him, "to make up for my lack of stature."

"How are you going to deal at Ballindair?" Morgan asked him now. "Without one of your lovelies on your arm?"

"I'm not skirt chasing on this trip. I'm merely enjoying a little taste of Scotland with a friend," Andrew replied. "I've brought along my paints, and I'll capture your bucolic scenery on canvas."

Morgan smiled. "It's not exactly bucolic," he said. "It will take your breath away. Nothing like your England with your hazy air and rolling hills. The Highlands demand your attention. Summon it. Pull your eyes to the mountain's summit, make you gasp at the sight of the lochs."

"Spoken like a true Scotsman, for all you've been an expatriate for the last five years."

Andrew's comment might have been correct, but he didn't have to like it. Morgan turned away, his attention on the view.

His heartbeat quickened at the sight of the hills in front of him. An Englishman would call them mountains, but a Scot knew they were only nubs, nothing like Ben Nevis or Ben Macdui and the rest of the Grampians.

"You didn't answer," Andrew said. "What are you going to do with yourself now?"

"That's the question, isn't it?"

For most of his adult life, he'd done his duty to the family at the distilleries bearing his name. He'd acted in every capacity, working his way up through the ranks until he understood everything about making whiskey. Not for him the indolent occupations of his friends.

Five years ago that had changed. He'd become the 9th Earl

of Denbleigh, with all the duties attendant to the position. At first he was woefully inept at the job, but he'd learned quickly.

Now, scandal hung onto his coattails with tenacious fingers.

He couldn't go back to politics. He was unwelcome both in London and Edinburgh. He couldn't even go back to work at the distilleries. He'd handpicked and approved every single one of his managers. Dismissing one simply because he was bored and needed purpose hardly seemed proper.

What the hell was he going to do with the rest of his life?

"Then tell me why Ballindair, at least," Andrew said.

"It's far enough away that they won't gossip about me. If they do, I don't have to hear it."

Andrew's mouth quirked in a half smile.

"Gossip has always followed you, Morgan. You're cryptic, which only makes people curious. The more curious people are, the more they speculate among themselves."

"I've never found it necessary to concern myself with the actions of my fellow man," he said.

Andrew's smile broadened. "That's because you're also an independent bastard. You really don't care about other people."

Since the Countess of Denbleigh had screamed that same accusation at him numerous times, Morgan turned and studied the Scottish morning.

Instead of the broom and rocks, he saw the face of his wife. A beauty, a magnificent porcelain goddess come to life, and as cold as a statue. Except, of course, to any man but him. He pushed away thoughts of Lillian. She didn't deserve any of his attention, especially now.

The noise of the carriage wheels on the macadam road was a constant, comforting sound. The whistling cry of a curlew made him smile, reminding him of days he'd spent walking through the moor.

Ahead lay the MacCraig Bog. As a boy, he'd been fascinated by tales of his ancestors, the Murderous MacCraigs, who lured their enemies into the bog and watched, gleefully, as they were trapped. His family wasn't a hardy group but they'd been bloodthirsty.

They were no longer thought of as the Murderous MacCraigs, but as a family who worked to protect and defend Scotland and on whom great honor had been bestowed.

His father had been a representative peer and Keeper of the Great Seal of Scotland on three occasions. Thomas MacCraig had been invested as a Fellow in the Royal Society, praised for his mathematical genius, and sought after for his cogent advice.

A damn hard individual to emulate.

Even as a father he had been perfect. Thomas made time for him, took him fishing and boating on the Spey. They'd climbed the hills around Ballindair, and at the peak sat and viewed the scene before them. Sometimes they'd eaten their lunch as the carpet of broom colored their world yellow.

His breath caught as he remembered the smell of peat, the melody of burred voices and rolling laughter. He recalled the cold, the bite of it against his skin and his teeth as he grinned. A large warm hand pressed down on his head, ruffling his hair. A voice called him laddie, an appellation he hadn't heard since his boyhood.

He knew why this homecoming was more difficult than any other. This was the first time he'd been home since his father's death, and he did so in disgrace.

His father had imbued in him three things: an intense love of his country, a sense of his own purpose, and the desire to live an honorable life.

How many times had he been told people would be watching him because he'd be the Earl of Denbleigh? People would be matching their behavior to his. He'd be an example to those who depended on the MacCraigs. All Scotland, and perhaps the world, would see him as the embodiment of what they'd become: no longer the Murderous MacCraigs, but honorable men.

Morgan was the fulcrum on which his family's reputation balanced.

Yet he'd willingly destroyed everything with a few strokes of a pen.

What would his father have said? He might have remarked: *You could do nothing less, son.* But he doubted it. His imagination furnished his father standing before him, his voice a deep baritone, the frown on his face leaving no doubt of his feelings.

In the hundreds of years since the first MacCraig planted his sword in the ground and claimed this land, no one has shamed the family to the degree you've managed.

The 8th Earl of Denbleigh, however, was dead. In his place was Morgan, 9th earl and disgrace of the family.

"Good God, Morgan. Is that Ballindair?"

He turned his head to see Andrew's gaze intent on the approach to his home.

The castle stood in the middle of four hundred fifty acres of woodland and farmland and was constructed of beige stone that, in certain light, appeared white. Built in an H configuration, Ballindair had a large rectangular main structure flanked by two smaller wings, each ending in a large tower whose tops looked like upside down funnels, painted black.

Two *laigh biggins*—low buildings—sat behind the castle and contained workrooms and stables. In addition to formal gardens, a walled terrace led down to the River Tullie, before it descended past Strath Dalross and the MacCraig Forest to join the River Spey.

Once he arrived, the flag of the MacCraigs would fly on the right front tower—the Laird's Tower—to indicate he was in residence. A conceit his father had picked up from the Queen.

"You told me about the castle, of course," Andrew was saying, "but I'd no idea the thing was so bloody huge. And damn impressive."

"It's home," he said, hoping to cut off his friend's rhapsodic comments.

Along the approach to Ballindair, he could envision a line of his ancestors, all MacCraig lairds, feet braced apart and planted in the earth, cudgels at the ready, facing him in censure.

Damn it all.

"It's magnificent," Andrew was saying. "When was it built?"

"Fourteenth century, thereabouts."

The first stones had been laid in the Year of Our Lord, thirteen hundred twenty-six. As the only surviving child of the earl, he'd been required to memorize every fact about Ballindair.

Andrew sent him a sideways look. "It isn't easy for you, is it?"

"Coming home?" He forced a smile to his face. "It's just a place."

Not just a place. Ballindair was the scene of his family's honor, where their history began, and the citadel of their pride. Coming home was the single most difficult experience of his life to date, and given everything he'd endured in the last two years, that was an admission.

But one he'd never make to another living soul.

Chapter 2

RULES FOR STAFF: *When being addressed, do not look away, but keep your attention on the person speaking.*

Jean blinked until her eyes cleared, staring at the slatted back of the bureau. The French Nun hadn't come. Instead, she'd fallen asleep propped against the wall in the earl's bedchamber.

Oh, dear God. No. Dear God, no.

She slid on her shoes, tied them, then stood, walking to the window and pushing open the curtains. She didn't need a clock to tell her she'd overslept. The morning sun was bright in the sky.

Panic clawed its way up her throat.

She raced from the room, across the hall, and down the curved steps, her feet flying as fast as her thoughts.

What excuse could she give her aunt? What could she possibly say?

A ghost stepped out of the shadows. Just when she didn't

have time, she saw a ghost, one who stood in front of her and nearly dared her to ignore him.

She couldn't stop to admire him now.

Instead of moving through him, or the ghost stepping aside, she collided with a solid chest jacketed in fine wool. Two arms reached out to steady her, but her momentum toppled them both to the dusty stone floor, Jean landing on top.

Dark blue eyes the color of a Highland night stared up at her.

For a long moment she stared back, horrified and transfixed. She could feel his heart thudding below her, and the solidity of his body against hers.

"You're not a ghost," she said breathlessly.

"I am not," he said in a clipped English accent.

He grabbed both her wrists, pushed up and rolled with her.

A second later their positions were reversed and she was pinned beneath him. The savagery of his look made her pause for a moment before she began pushing at his chest. Not very successfully as it turned out, since he was still holding her wrists and didn't seem inclined to budge.

"Will you let me go?"

He might not be a ghost, but he was definitely a stranger. She twisted her wrists. He had her firmly caught.

"Will you let me up?" she asked, meeting his scowl with a frown of her own.

"Morgan, you really should let her go," a man said, humor in his tone.

She glanced up to find another stranger standing there, smiling at both of them.

A voice—the very last voice she wanted to hear—said, "What is going on here?"

Oh dear.

Jean closed her eyes, chided herself for her lack of courage, then forced herself to look up. Standing next to the stranger was her aunt, a look of shock on her face. Three maids, one of them Catriona, stood behind the housekeeper, each looking entirely too interested in the scene.

The stranger released her wrists, got to his feet and began to dust himself off.

Her aunt abruptly sank into a curtsy. "Your Lordship, we didn't expect you for a number of days."

Your Lordship? Jean's heart plummeted to her feet. For an instant she was light-headed. She knew better than to faint—no one would revive her. Worse, she'd probably receive a lecture for littering the floor.

Standing, she shook out her skirt. Perhaps she was still asleep behind the bureau and this was just a dream. A quick look at her aunt's face proved that to be a lie.

"What are you doing, Jean?" her aunt asked, looking straight at her.

She tried to answer, to form the words, but the ability to speak had abruptly disappeared.

"I believe the girl ran into him," the second man said, grinning. "They both went down rather spectacularly."

Her aunt glanced at her again. Jean nodded. There, she could nod at least.

"Your Lordship, I apologize most humbly for the behavior of my maid," her aunt said.

"If this is the way you train your maids in decorum," he said, brushing at his dusty sleeves, "I fear for the state of my home."

Her aunt flushed, before again curtsying, so low that Jean feared she would not be able to rise again, given her girth.

"She will be suitably punished, Your Lordship."

Oh dear.

Her aunt turned to her. "What are you even doing here, Jean?"

What should she say? What could she say?

She took a deep breath, faced them all, and lied. "I thought to get a start on the cleaning," she said. "I knew what a monumental task was before us."

God whispered in her conscience, and her stomach soured as she spoke. Or perhaps her incipient nausea was simply because her aunt was staring straight through her, eyes searching for the truth.

Jean managed a weak smile, but it had no effect on Aunt Mary's intent look.

She glanced over at the earl. His eyes were narrowed, his lips thinned. His face seemed hewn from a block of wood—a block of angry wood.

The situation called for a bit of subservience.

"Forgive me, Your Lordship," she said, curtsying. "I should have been more careful."

He didn't say a word, the loathsome cur. Nor did his expression ease.

Neither did her aunt's, but now there was a look on her face that Jean didn't like one bit. Compassion was rarely evident in the housekeeper's expression, but it was there now, as if Aunt Mary were apologizing in advance for having to release her from her position at Ballindair.

If she had to leave, what would happen to her?

She stared down at the floor, frozen by the thought.

"Since your maid is so conscientious, can I assume my suite is ready?" the earl asked.

Jean glanced up. At Aunt Mary's look, she shook her head.

"Not yet, sir, but it shall be shortly," the housekeeper said. "May I offer you some refreshments? Breakfast, perhaps?"

Jean's stomach rumbled at that moment, loud enough that the other maids giggled, even Catriona. The blond man smiled, but the earl looked as if the sign of her hunger was another mark against her. Her aunt just sighed.

"Do you feed your maids, Mrs. MacDonald?"

"Yes, Your Lordship."

He studied Jean, as if seeking out more flaws. She faced him resolutely. If he meant to shame her, then he was two years too late. If he meant to discover all her transgressions, then he'd better have a ledger handy. She had a great many of them to be recorded.

After a long, speechless moment, he headed for the door, his companion at his side.

At the doorway, however, he turned. "Who did you think I was?" he asked, looking at her. "Which ghost?"

"The Herald," she said. "But you didn't have pipes."

He only nodded.

As he left, she had the oddest thought that they'd had a secret conversation, one no one else understood.

"Get up there and clean, Jean," her aunt said. "You're acting as daft as a yett on a windy day. Be about your tasks, and we'll talk later."

Then, with a wave of her hand, she was out the door, after the earl and his companion, leaving the four maids staring at each other.

Jean turned, leading the way back up the curving steps and wishing she had the courage to put toads in the Earl of Denbleigh's bed.

"Did you see her?" Andrew said. "What a glorious creature!"

Morgan glanced over at his friend. "I thought her plain and without merit."

Andrew sent him an incredulous look. "Didn't you see her eyes? I've never seen blue eyes like that."

"They're brown."

"Not the mouse," Andrew said. "The other maid. The glorious one with blond hair."

"And blue eyes." Evidently, there would be some occupation for Andrew at Ballindair. "Leave my maids alone," the earl said.

Andrew smiled. "You want her for yourself," he said.

"Good God, no."

He was done with women for a while. He wanted nothing to do with them. He didn't want to be in their company. He didn't want to hear them speak. He didn't even want to see one. Especially Mrs. MacDonald, who was following him at a winded pace.

Resigned, he stopped and faced the housekeeper. Before she could begin an involved apology, he said, "Would you send word to Mr. Seath I've arrived, Mrs. MacDonald. I'd like to speak to him as soon as possible."

Fear spread over her face, and he should have reassured her his meeting with his steward had nothing to do with her performance—or lack of it. But he remained silent, wishing she would do the same.

It was not to be.

"Forgive me, Your Lordship, we were told you were not to arrive for a matter of days," she said, wringing her hands. "Otherwise, I would have had everything in readiness."

"Forgive *me*, Mrs. MacDonald, for failing to advise you of my plans."

The woman paled. He felt the bite of his conscience, not to mention the sensation that all the MacCraigs lined up on the moor below were uttering curses for his lack of care of a kinsman.

A MacDonald or not, he thought, she was employed at Ballindair. That made her his responsibility and a member of his clan. Besides, he hated one woman, but not *this* woman.

"I was wrong not to send you word," he said, to her obvious surprise. "No doubt the early hour is the reason for my poor mood. If you could provide my friend with breakfast, I'd be grateful."

"Of course," she said, smiling. "Of course. If you'll follow me."

He stepped aside to let her pass, not commenting that he still knew the location of the dining room. Instead, he kept silent, following the woman like a trained sheep, all the while ignoring Andrew's smile.

"Isn't he the most handsome man you've ever seen?" Catriona said, after the men were gone.

Sally and Susan, the other maids, tittered.

Jean turned to look at her sister. "Are you daft? He's a pompous prig. Or didn't you notice how he looked at all of us?"

Catriona smiled. "You'd just knocked him down, Jean. That gave him a right to be angry. But even angry, the man is a handsome devil."

Devil was right.

"His companion was more pleasing," Jean said, remembering the blond-haired man.

"He's short," Catriona said, dismissing him. "The earl, however, is tall, with the most wonderful broad shoulders. Don't you think so?"

"I didn't notice," she said, beginning to mount the steps.

"Did you notice his eyes? They were as blue as mine."

"They're darker." She'd been close enough to see the black ring around them.

Sally and Susan whispered among themselves. No doubt they, too, were transfixed by the Earl of Denbleigh's appearance.

She held her tongue, but it wasn't easy.

At the first landing she turned to Sally. The woman had been at Ballindair for two decades, and despite her age, was one of the best workers.

"Which room do you want?" she asked, deferring to the older woman.

"Susan and I will take the sitting room," Sally said. "You and Catriona can clean the earl's bedchamber."

Susan smiled brightly at that, and Jean knew why. The earl would notice the condition of the bedchamber before the sitting room. If the room wasn't cleaned perfectly, she'd be in even more disfavor with her aunt, not to mention the earl.

She nodded, reaching for a bucket containing their supplies, and entered the room, Catriona beside her, empty-handed.

"I don't care what you say," Catriona said. "I think he's the most handsome man I've ever seen."

She didn't want to discuss the earl's appearance. What good was a handsome exterior when the man had an arrogant character? Or when he viewed others with contempt?

She was as good as the Earl of Denbleigh. He'd been born into the role. She'd been thrust into hers, but she'd done her best not to shame herself, while he'd evidently tarnished his title.

How dare he, of all people, judge her with a glance?

She noticed she hadn't pushed the bureau back into place. She did so now as Catriona went to the armoire and opened it, obviously disappointed to find it empty. The earl's trunks had arrived a week ago and were piled on the landing outside, but no one had the keys. None of the drawers Catriona opened held anything but a few sachets, the scent of sandalwood wafting through the air.

"Have you finished your inventory?" Jean asked. "Are you ready to work now?"

Catriona shrugged.

They would need to shake out the draperies at both the windows and the bed, fluff the mattress, dust, and clean the floors. Even with the two of them working, Jean wasn't sure how long it would take them to finish.

When she said as much, Catriona answered, "I'd rather not work at all."

Her honesty brought a smile to Jean's lips.

"I'll start on the furniture if you'll take down the bed hangings," she said.

The world might forgive Catriona anything because of her beauty, but Jean knew she wasn't so fortunate. She'd already broken so many rules—rules the maids had to memorize—she'd be lucky to escape without being punished.

She balled up a rag and began to wipe down the bureau behind which she'd sat the previous night. Her stomach rumbled again, and Catriona laughed.

"You missed a wonderful breakfast," her sister said, engaged in unhooking the draperies from their rod. "Scones with butter, and rashers."

Jean ignored the words, just as she ignored her hunger, and set about finishing the dusting. Once that task was done, she moved to the bed.

After pulling off the sheets, she dragged the mattress toward her and shook it vigorously. With Catriona's help, she turned the mattress, then plumped it back into place. Before sweeping the floor, she tucked the bottom valance out of the way.

Catriona opened the window, grabbed one end of the bed curtains and, allowing the rest to hang outside, began shaking the fabric. A cloud of dust billowed back into the room.

Jean took one look at what her sister was doing and sighed. She'd have to wipe down the furniture again.

First, however, she sprinkled the spent and dried tea leaves on the carpet, rubbing them gently into the soiled spots. Only then did she use the broom she'd found in the cupboard near the stairs.

The linen press held a clean set of sheets, thickly embroidered with a pattern of thistle blossoms. After she'd dusted again, she and Catriona hung the emerald bed curtains, then made the bed.

She looked around. The furniture gleamed, the bed was freshened, and the floors were swept. The curtains at the window still needed to be aired, the windows washed, and the bathing chamber cleaned.

The Earl of Denbleigh had indeed returned.

How soon would the odious man leave?

Chapter 3

Morgan sent Andrew off to breakfast in the care of the housekeeper, but delayed his own meal in favor of a meeting with his steward.

"His office is in the north wing, Your Lordship," Mrs. MacDonald said.

He stopped himself, just barely, from commenting that he knew Ballindair better than she. His five-year absence might well prove him a liar. But, no, the steward's office was just where it had been on his last visit.

He hesitated, then knocked. When he heard Seath's voice, he pushed the door open.

The man who occupied this office had served his father before him. In the last five years, William Seath had proved invaluable, acting as gillie, tacksman, and chamberlain for Morgan. Whatever Morgan needed done, Seath did it without fanfare and with excellence.

Seath had come to London every quarter to report on Ball-indair and the estate. The last time Morgan had seen him was two months ago.

The change was startling.

Seath's Adam's apple was glaringly prominent, as well as the line of his jaw. His wrists looked frail and his jacket hung on bony shoulders. His ears, always pronounced, now stuck out from his head as if blown by a stiff breeze. The man's angular face was gaunt, and dark circles appeared beneath his bloodshot blue eyes.

What the hell had happened to Seath?

He didn't comment on the man's appearance. If Seath had wanted him to know about his health, he'd have said something. Morgan was all too conscious of the steward's privacy, having had so little of it himself the past two years.

"Have my trunks arrived?" he asked, taking a look around the room.

The steward's office was more crowded than he remembered. Shelves of books—all ledgers holding records of rents, expenditures, and other minutiae pertaining to the castle and estate—occupied two walls. The third wall held two windows with a view of the grounds, and the fourth a fireplace where a small fire was blazing.

He didn't comment that it was summer.

"Last week, Your Lordship. Will your valet be arriving shortly?"

"No," he said. "I've dismissed him."

The man had quit. He'd given Peter a letter of recommendation but doubted that his valet would use it. To do so might well tarnish Peter's chances for any position in the future. He had been the faithful servant of the Earl of Denbleigh. *That* Earl of Denbleigh. Or perhaps Peter would be sought after because of all the gossip he knew.

"Shall I interview likely candidates, Your Lordship?"

He shook his head. "I'm tired of servants hovering about me." He'd become acutely sensitive to the silent derision of his staff.

Another curse the Countess of Denbleigh had screamed at him. *You'll find yourself alone, Morgan! No one will want to be around you!*

"And your secretary, sir?"

"He won't be arriving," Morgan said.

His secretary had remained behind in London, to look after his English investments. His ancestors might have been murderous, but they'd also known their whiskey. The distilleries that bore his name were prolific, prosperous, and had all received the royal warrant. To his eternal gratitude, MacCraig whiskey was prized throughout the world.

"Will you be remaining long?" Seath asked.

"Isn't this my home?" he asked, irritation tingeing his words. He was a little tired of being treated as a visitor, an unwelcome one at that.

Yet a small voice whispered that if he'd come home more often, perhaps he'd have been welcomed with some emotion other than trepidation.

The ghost hunter hadn't been afraid of him, but then, she'd not been afraid of the Herald, either.

He turned and walked to the window, seeing the view stretching out before him and beyond to the MacCraig Forest where he'd played as a boy. Every place he looked was filled with memory.

Thick, spiny gorse blooming with yellow flowers swayed in the morning breeze as if in greeting. To his left was Loch Tullie, narrow and nearly twelve miles long. Gray-green at the shoreline, the water deepened to black in the loch's center. Near bottomless, his nurse had said, and as cold as a Murderous MacCraig's heart.

Forested islets jutted out into the loch. Places where he'd

rowed his boat under the strict and watchful eye of either his
father or his nurse. He'd wanted to stay and play, explore and
pretend, but as the only child of the Earl of Denbleigh, he was
too precious to court danger.

Now, the sun glittered on the surface of the loch, changing it to a bright triangle of mirror, an arrow's point leading
to a dense pine forest, more MacCraig land. Everywhere he
looked was his, and the thought conjured up another memory
of his father.

*'Tis a land we fought to hold, son. More than one of us
died in the service of it.*

Five years had passed since his father died and he'd
become an orphan. Strange, the word had a punch to it
even as an adult. Five years since he'd become the Earl of
Denbleigh.

Four since he'd become a bridegroom. A scant four years.

"Is there anything I can do for you, Your Lordship?" Seath
asked.

*Give me back my childhood. Keep me ten years old. Tell
me why the promise of my boyhood did not mature. Tell me
why I feel nothing but ennui and a sadness that sticks with
me like dung to my shoe. Give me a purpose to my life.*

"Nothing at all," he said, turning to face the steward.
"You've done a magnificent job. As to the length of my stay,
Ballindair has always been a family home. It's my home now."

"You won't be returning to London?"

London didn't want him. He didn't want London. Who
had truly repudiated whom? He wanted nothing to do with
the life he'd lived for the past five years, and perhaps even
longer than that.

"Tell me about Mrs. MacDonald," he said.

Seath's eyebrows arched in surprise. "The housekeeper?
Have you not met her before, Your Lordship?"

"I have," he said. "I don't remember her being as intrusive. Or as incompetent. I would've expected the Laird's Tower to have been kept in readiness for my arrival, however unexpected."

"She's been at Ballindair for eleven years, Your Lordship, and I've known her to be unfailingly competent at her job."

"Perhaps you need to reevaluate her performance," he said.

A look flitted over Seath face, but the man didn't say a word. Morgan could decipher his thoughts easily enough: Were they supposed to anticipate him every day of his five year absence?

Yes, damn it.

Mrs. MacDonald abruptly opened the door, without a knock, without any notice at all.

"Would you care to attend the Laird's Greeting now, sir?" she asked.

Had she been listening at the door?

He'd been traveling all night and now it was barely ten o'clock in the morning. He was tired, irritated, and not in the mood to charm people. When had he ever been? Even Andrew had commented on his lack of empathy for his fellow man.

When the hell had his fellow man given a flying farthing about him, especially in the last year?

His conscience murmured to notice the trembling of her hands, the jiggling of her eyes as they darted on one object after another. He made Mrs. MacDonald nervous.

The Laird's Greeting was a tradition, a duty. Each time the laird returned home from an absence of any duration, he was greeted by the staff and inhabitants of Ballindair, a tradition dating back to the Murderous MacCraigs. Since he hadn't been home in a while, it was even more important for the chore to be done now.

Morgan doubted he was going to receive any spontaneous cheers.

"Yes," he said, watching her eyes widen. Had she thought he'd decline? "I'd like to greet the staff. All of them, please. In a quarter hour's time."

She bobbed a curtsy and left the room silently.

Seath didn't say a word.

Sally popped her head into the bedchamber. "Hurry, Catriona! Mrs. MacDonald says we're to be inspected."

"Inspected?" Jean asked.

Sally's look traveled to her. "By the earl. It's the Laird's Greeting. All staff is to be assembled in ten minutes!"

Once in their room, Jean surveyed herself in the mirror over their shared bureau.

Her hair was a mess, but she gathered it up as well as she could, pinned her cap on, and changed to her only remaining clean apron. If she kept her hands together, no one would see the stains on her cuffs. Her skirt, however, was still dirty from when she'd tumbled to the floor with the earl.

Her sister, on the other hand, looked perfectly acceptable, perhaps even darling, with the lace cap atop her curls and her face a becoming shade of pink.

"Why do you think he wants to inspect us?" Catriona asked as they made their way to the front of Ballindair. "Do you think he's brought his own servants from London?" She turned worried eyes to Jean. "Do you think he means to dismiss us?"

Although she had much the same fears, Jean pinned a determined smile on her face. "Surely not," she said. "Training a new set of servants would take time."

"But they would be from London. Everyone knows London servants are better."

Catriona was forever doing that, stating "everyone knows" in an emphatic voice when Jean wasn't at all sure anyone knew anything of the sort.

What had the earl planned? Insufferable prig that he was, it was probably not going to fare them well.

On the way to the main entrance of the castle, Morgan stopped at the Great Hall. The chamber, located in the middle of the H of Ballindair, had been the meeting place for generations of MacCraigs. Now it served as a family gathering spot, the four-foot-thick walls of Ballindair rendering it cool in the summer and surprisingly warm in the snows of winter.

His grandmother had converted the Great Hall into a family space. All the weapons once arranged here had been moved to the West Tower, thereby hinting at a more peaceful past for the Murderous MacCraigs than was true.

The couches and chairs were all upholstered in the same fabric, a shade reminding him of overcooked salmon. The mahogany tables were all oversized, to compensate for the height of the ceiling. The carpet below his feet was Flemish and had been woven to his grandmother's design in a pattern of thistles and heather blossoms.

His grandmother had lived longer than her daughter, and had provided him with a large dose of maternal affection. Her death had come two years before his father's, and Morgan mourned them both deeply.

Perhaps it was better they were no longer alive, rather than see what he'd made of himself.

He moved into the Great Hall, conscious that Seath was standing directly behind him. Thankfully, the man didn't speak, allowing him a few moments of silence.

Not so, Mrs. MacDonald.

She clapped her hands at the doorway, as if he were eight years old and late for supper.

He turned and faced her, keeping his face arranged in as pleasant an aspect as he could manage. Evidently, it wasn't as friendly as he thought, because Mrs. MacDonald dropped her hands immediately and sank into a fulsome curtsy.

He wished she'd quit doing that.

"The staff is ready for the greeting, Your Lordship," she said.

Should he wave her off like an Asian potentate? Or smile, which would no doubt frighten her just a little? The choice was taken from him by Seath, who nodded and said, "Very well, Mrs. MacDonald. We'll be with you shortly."

She nodded and disappeared again. Perhaps he should insist Seath remain beside him as a way to keep the housekeeper at bay.

He turned to the steward. "How many staff do we have now?" For the life of him, he couldn't remember. Had he ever known?

"Sixty-three, Your Lordship."

"And the number of maids?" he asked. A strange question, evidently, from Seath's look.

"Seventeen, Your Lordship. Would you like to know their rankings?"

"I think not," he said, striding to the doorway.

What had made him ask that question? What did he care if he employed two scullery maids or four? Did it matter the number of upper floor maids? As long as he didn't have to be bothered with the ghost hunter, he'd be content.

Jean, that was her name.

The staff was arranged in the front courtyard, spread out in a semicircle in front of the main entrance. The archway leading to the courtyard beckoned to him: come away, come away. Be a boy again and escape to the hills, the river, the woods.

Instead, he turned to greet Mrs. MacDonald, who curtsied yet again.

Seath, no doubt sensing his irritation, stepped forward and took command of the introductions. Bless the man.

Andrew wandered out of the front entrance, sauntering

over to them with a smile on his face. Andrew was amused by a great many things, and no doubt this ceremony would serve as fodder for his cutting remarks later.

He ignored Andrew, intent on Seath's introductions. In the next few minutes, Morgan learned that Ballindair employed a dozen very tall young men as footmen, gardeners, and stable boys. Two cooks and a number of undercooks provided all the meals. Females outnumbered the males, and all of them, regardless of their station, looked terrified of him.

Was he that much of an ogre?

He stopped in front of the ghost hunter. She was staring down at the drive, her heightened color the only indication she was aware of him. She held her hands tightly together in front of her. If she trembled, he saw no evidence of it. Her apron was spotless and the little white lace cap on her brown hair was a new addition to her uniform.

What a little wren she was.

The girl next to her, however, was her opposite in every way. Her hair was blond, her eyes blue. She was as petite as the wren was tall. Her shoulders didn't slump, and when he looked at her, she glanced back cheekily. A smile curved her lips and reached her eyes.

"Have you worked here long?" he asked.

"A year, Your Lordship," she said. Her voice was laced with honey, low and inviting, and rich with a teasing burr.

"Where are you from?"

"From Inverness, Your Lordship. Both my sister and I," she added, glancing toward the wren.

"The MacDonald sisters," the housekeeper said, stepping forward. "Very good workers, all in all, Your Lordship. Once again, I apologize for the events of this morning."

"Sisters?" he asked, ignoring the woman, and addressing the question to the blonde. "With the same father and mother?"

The wren's face reddened further, but the blonde thought his comment a delightful jest. A burbling little laugh escaped her before she placed her fingers over her lips. She curtsied, with more grace than he'd seen today.

"Yes, Your Lordship," she said, smiling again, and revealing white, even teeth. "We had the same father and the same mother."

"I see," he said, and moved down the line.

He'd have to watch out for her. The girl was a tart.

The ghost hunter's stomach rumbled loud enough to be heard. He turned back to Mrs. MacDonald, her bitten lips an indication that she'd heard as well.

"Have you not yet fed her, Mrs. MacDonald?"

"There wasn't time, Your Lordship."

The wren stared back at him, frowning.

"Feed her," he said, moving back to greet the last of his staff.

He could feel the wren's glare between his shoulders.

Jean wanted to hit the Earl of Denbleigh. Slap him, perhaps. Or pummel him in his stomach. Not that he'd feel it.

The man looked fit, as if he ate bricks for breakfast and boxed for the love of it. He was probably here because no one could tolerate him in London. Or the whole of England, perhaps, for all he sounded like an Englishman.

Begone, you arrogant Scot. Traipse northward to your roots. Let Scotland deal with you for a while.

Had his wife said those very words to him?

"Where's the Countess of Denbleigh?" she whispered to Catriona.

The earl stopped.

Everything else stopped as well. Jean's heart seemed to skip a few beats.

His shoulders were squared, his back rigid. The man's

entire demeanor was that of a statue. If she didn't know better, she'd have thought him made of bronze.

Except bronze didn't move, turn, and face her. A statue would not look at her as he did now, with nothingness on his face. No, even a statue had an expression.

Her curtsy was so clumsily done she was off balance. Rather than land on her derriere, she pitched forward, her palms coming to rest on the gravel of the courtyard.

Look up, Jean.

She didn't want to look up. She wanted to claw at the surface beneath her fingernails and dive into the hole she created.

A year later—because that's how long it seemed—she forced herself to meet the earl's eyes.

He wasn't looking at her at all. In fact, he'd turned again, finishing up his inspection. Instead, his friend was there, his face wreathed in laughter.

She was happy he found her humiliation amusing.

"Get up, you silly girl," her aunt said, before scurrying to follow the departing earl.

Catriona was laughing as well, a hand pressed over her mouth to stifle her merriment. Her own sister wasn't helping matters. When Jean attempted to stand, the heel of her shoe got caught in her skirt hem and she tripped again.

She finally stood, brushing her skirts back into shape, annoyed that her pristine white apron had dust on its hem.

Her stomach rumbled once more, a sound that made Catriona giggle again.

She sent an annoyed look toward her sister, but Catriona was smiling at the blond man, the two of them exchanging a look of glee.

The wren had been the only one courageous enough to say what the rest of them were thinking.

But he hadn't answered her. What the hell could he say? Nothing that would bring honor to his name. He was the laird, the earl, the one to carry his family's banner forward. As the Earl of Denbleigh, it was incumbent on him to marry, sire a child, and form a dynasty.

All he'd done was blacken the reputation of the MacCraigs again.

He winna rive his faither's bunnet.

His nurse's voice, speaking from his childhood. He will never fill his father's shoes.

He carved a smile onto his face and went about his task of greeting the rest of the staff of Ballindair.

Chapter 4

After the inspection, Jean retreated to the kitchen and grabbed a bridie from the oven to quiet her rumbling stomach.

Catriona was laughing, the sound carrying through the crowded kitchen. No one paid any attention to Jean, a normal occurrence, and one for which she was grateful now. The less anyone said about the inspection, the better.

Her aunt, however, noticed her immediately, and headed in her direction. For a moment Jean debated escaping from the kitchen, but she was going to have to answer for her behavior sooner or later.

Being Mrs. MacDonald's niece meant no preferential treatment. If anything, she was under more pressure to perform. She wasn't Catriona. She didn't have the ability to smile and charm everyone. She was just plain Jean, mostly invisible to the rest of the staff, unless she made a mistake.

As her aunt approached, Jean bobbed a little curtsy of respect. A little groveling would go a very long way in this situation.

"How could you, Jean?" Aunt Mary said, keeping her voice low. "I've never been so humiliated in my entire life."

"I'm sorry, Aunt."

"Have you no idea what could happen if the earl takes a disliking to you? I couldn't save you then, Jean. And for the sake of your poor mother, I've done all I could."

Jean nodded, left with no other recourse than to stare at the floor, feeling shame wash over her. It was true, her aunt had saved them when they'd had nowhere else to turn. Aunt Mary had ensured that she and Catriona had a roof over their heads and food to eat. Granted, the position of maid was not one to which she'd aspired, but it was decent, honorable work.

If she felt too much a prisoner at times, that was a defect of her character, and not her aunt's fault.

"Did you finish the earl's suite?"

"There was no time," she said. "We were called to the Laird's Greeting. But I was on my way back now."

Worry fled from her aunt's face to be replaced by irritation.

"Then be off with you. Go and finish. Who else do you need?"

Most of Ballindair's staff was now milling about the kitchen, the subject of their conversation the abrupt arrival of the Earl of Denbleigh, and how his presence might affect them. Despite the fact that the future was uncertain, she still heard words of approval about the earl's bearing, appearance, and smile.

Had they nothing better to do?

Jean's gaze slid over Catriona. No, her sister would go on

and on about all the earl's attributes to the exclusion of anything else, including working. She chose two older women: Betty and Nell.

"We should be able to get the work done with the three of us," she said.

"Be as fast as you can, Jean," her aunt said. "I've no wish to be dressed down by the earl again today."

Instead of asking her why she had been at the end of the earl's temper, Jean kept her mouth shut, bobbed a curtsy, grabbed another bridie, and waited as the housekeeper spoke to the two women she'd chosen.

Where was the odious earl now? As long as he hadn't yet retreated to his suite. And if he was there? She would simply have to ignore him. People never noticed servants anyway. They were invisible little creatures like ghosts, moving things around, dusting, making life amenable for those who could afford to pay them.

Evidently, the Earl of Denbleigh was wealthy. Too bad he was a pauper when it came to manners or decency.

She stepped into the storage room, grabbed another bucket, a stack of rags, a jar of ashes and one of dried tea leaves, and a small metal pot of French polish. Since she couldn't remember if the maid's closet in the Laird's Tower contained any brushes, she took a few of those as well.

Betty and Nell followed her down the back hall, silent as she turned right toward the Laird's Tower.

"We have the sitting room to finish," she said. "As well as the bath chamber."

The other two merely nodded. If they had any curiosity about their tasks, they didn't question her. They spoke softly between themselves, not including her in the conversation. She was often treated that way. Those who didn't know of her relationship to Mrs. MacDonald merely considered her an alien, an import from Inverness. Those who did know that she was the housekeeper's niece rarely shared any information with her for fear she'd tattle.

Catriona, however, was treated differently. Her sister was so lovely the younger maids sought her advice on hair and skin care. The footmen, as well as the stable boys, eyed Catriona in a way that was supposed to be surreptitious and was, instead, only cow-eyed and silly.

She knew she shouldn't begrudge Catriona her appearance. Instead, she should concentrate on the task ahead.

This area of the castle was airy and lovely. The corridor was wide and well lit from the windows spaced at intervals between the main part of the structure and the tower.

The carpet beneath her feet was an emerald so deep it appeared black in the shadows. She felt as if she were walking atop an enchanted moor, one sprinkled from time to time with golden curlicues and the MacCraig crest and eagle.

Occasionally, a nook broke up the long line of wall, displaying some beautiful work of art. Being a maid had spoiled her. Once, she might have been able to pass the small statue of a Greek athlete with an appreciative glance. Now, she noted the dust collecting on the shoulders of the figure, and reminded herself to clean it on her way back to the kitchen.

Although Ballindair was several centuries old, there was no musty scent of cold stone or lingering dust about it. Instead, the rooms were freshened by her aunt's potpourri. Even here, in this long corridor, she could smell the scent of roses.

The ceilings were painted in little tin squares, scenes depicting the greatness of the MacCraigs over the generations.

They'd been known as the Murderous MacCraigs, that much she'd learned from the steward, a man who reminded her of her father in earlier times. Not one of the paintings depicted a murder. However, most of them were of war, and a few were of court scenes, no doubt in Edinburgh, or perhaps London.

Had the Earl of Denbleigh left his wife in London?

No one had answered her question.

Or had the earl been guilty of even more heinous acts than desertion? Had he killed the poor woman?

Could she be working for a murderer? But if he'd murdered his wife, surely everyone would know. That kind of secret was not easily kept. She knew that all too well.

On the landing outside the Laird's Suite, she waited for Betty and Nell.

In the last hour the earl's trunks had been moved inside the sitting room. Was she supposed to put away his things? Surely, he had servants to care for him? Of course he did. The Earl of Denbleigh wouldn't know how to function on his own. No doubt someone had to dress him.

"I'll finish the sitting room," she said, "if you'll take the bathing chamber."

"It's a small space, isn't it?" Nell asked. "I'm thinking it'd be better for one person. You could do it just as well." She reached into the bucket Jean carried and pulled out a few rags and the French polish. "We'll be doing the polishing, I'm thinking."

With that, the two women began to work, ignoring her.

Jean shrugged, took the bucket and made her way to the bathing chamber. They all knew cleaning the bathing chamber was harder work than polishing.

She pushed open the door, intent on getting this task done so she could return to the kitchen for a proper meal. What a shame the earl couldn't have remained in London with his wife.

Where *was* his wife?

And wasn't anyone else curious?

Chapter 5

RULES FOR STAFF: *If asked a question, provide an answer in a low, respectful, voice.*

Morgan hadn't seen Andrew for hours.

He was only too aware he'd been an abysmal host, and hoped Mrs. MacDonald had seen to his friend's comfort.

After a walk through Ballindair, he'd returned to his suite to find the air filled with the scent of polish and everything gleaming in the afternoon sunlight.

Dressing was more complicated than when his valet had been with him. He'd forgotten to give someone the key to unpack his trunks. Secondly, his garments were in woeful need of attention.

He finally found something presentable to wear, making a mental note to have someone take the rest of his garments to be ironed.

A few hours after his inspection of the servants, he was walking through the corridor leading from the tower to the main part of Ballindair. He could remember running through this exact corridor every Sunday morning, eager to reach his father. On Sundays, after church, they went fishing, or boating, or a dozen other occupations designed by his father to keep him happy. On Sundays the Earl of Denbleigh wasn't bothered by his secretary or his correspondence.

On those days, no one chastised Morgan not to run. Or whispered to him to lower his voice. He was allowed to be ebullient and wild, the future laird with the spirit of the Mac-Craig clan in his laughter.

Now, his footsteps were measured, his temperament solemn. He didn't want to be in this corridor, fighting memory. Perhaps because his companion was guilt. He'd not acquitted himself well in his adult life. Had his father realized it? Had his staff?

Where's the Countess of Denbleigh? Even here, he heard the wren's words.

"Good evening, Your Lordship," a voice called.

He glanced up to find himself facing a maid, the one who'd interested Andrew so much. The wren's sister—Catriona, wasn't it?

"Yes?"

"May I assist you, Your Lordship?"

What a remarkably melodious voice she had.

"I'm not lost," he said.

She smiled, revealing lovely white teeth, as well as a dimple to the left of her mouth.

"Of course not, Your Lordship." Her curtsy was gracefully executed. "I merely wished to be of assistance."

Even though her pose was perfectly demure, her eyes twinkled at him. She wore a spotless white apron over her blue uniform dress. Her shoes were polished, her blond hair had been artfully braided and peeked beneath her lace cap, and she smelled of rosewater and soap.

The top of her head barely came to his shoulder, unlike her sister, who was a tall, gangly thing. In terms of beauty, Catriona was easily the match of the women of London.

He was no longer the boy he'd been, or the naive young man off to London. Instead, he doubted everything, challenged all he heard and most of what he saw. If he'd been that boy, he would have seen her actions as innocent. He knew better, and a part of him grieved for the world-weary man he'd become.

No one else was in the corridor; there wasn't a reason for anyone to be there, unless it was to ensure that the gaslights were lit. She'd been waiting for him, that was easy to see.

He disliked being waylaid, especially by women. Most especially by women who wanted more from him than a chance to be of service.

"No," he said. "I don't require anything."

She allowed her face to fall into an expression of disappointment, just for a moment, before smiling brightly again.

"I'm Catriona," she said.

"I haven't forgotten your name," he said.

Irritation danced across her face. Evidently, Catriona was used to affecting a man with her smile. Did she run the male staff in circles?

She was beautiful, charming, and no doubt filled with the knowledge of her own allure. He knew her type well. He'd been married to a woman similar to Catriona.

Did she realize her tactics were wasted on him?

Catriona folded her hands together in front of her and smirked. No doubt the gesture was meant to be a demure smile, but she didn't look the innocent type.

When she showed no signs of giving way, he stepped to one side.

"Which guest room is Mr. Prender in?" he asked.

"I believe Mrs. MacDonald has put him in the Green Suite, Your Lordship," she said, curtsying once more.

Was he supposed to note the trimness of her ankles, the swanlike grace of her neck, as well as the dancing light in her arresting blue eyes? Very well, he noted all three, and was so supremely unimpressed he didn't even bother to thank her for the information.

He made his way to the second floor without encountering another maid. Some of the staff disappeared into the woodwork, since several closets were concealed along the wainscoting. More than once he saw the door softly close as he walked past.

His knock was answered immediately by a smiling Andrew, who looked disappointed at the sight of him.

"Were you expecting someone else?" Morgan asked. "A certain blond maid?"

Andrew only laughed.

The last thing he wanted was a domestic crisis. Andrew was more than capable of planting his seed in any available garden, witness the number of children in London with his distinctive nose. Not to mention his own brood safely ensconced in the country with his wife of ten years.

Yet anything he might say to Andrew would be answered with a smile and some jest. Andrew was an unrepentant hedonist, with the wealth to do exactly as he wished.

On the way to the dining room, Morgan pointed out several items of interest—the sword used by the first Earl of Denbleigh, the carpet loomed and installed before the Queen's visit, and the plaster relief in the entranceway.

Andrew nodded, said all the obligatory guest remarks, but his attention was halfhearted.

Dinner was a desultory affair. Granted, the food was superb, equal to anything he had tasted in Edinburgh or Inverness. His cook, thank God, was Scottish and not English. He could only salute the difference. The salmon, alone, was worth returning to Ballindair.

He and Andrew didn't speak often, and he noted his friend was drinking more of his dinner than he was eating it.

"You should pace yourself on the MacCraig whiskey," he said. "That single malt will put you under the table."

Andrew only nodded, took another sip from the etched crystal, then set the glass down. He waved at the footman stationed at the door, and a moment later the man had taken his plate and replenished his glass.

"What is it?" Morgan asked. "You've been uncharacteristically quiet. I can always count on your cutting wit. Unless, of course, you've found everything to your satisfaction. I doubt that's the case."

"I've been thinking about Lillian," Andrew said.

Morgan stiffened.

"Oh? And why would you be thinking of Lillian?"

"She's the reason you're here, isn't she? After five years?"

"It hasn't been five years since I've been back in Scotland," Morgan said.

"But the first time you've been back to Ballindair," Andrew countered.

Morgan clenched his glass tighter in one hand, looked straight at Andrew and said, "You might as well tell me. Why is Lillian on your mind?"

"I regret I ever said anything," Andrew said. "If I hadn't, you'd still be married, still in London."

"Did you think I didn't know?"

Andrew looked surprised.

Morgan took a sip. "You weren't the only friend to come to me and report my wife was having an affair. Or another affair. It got to the point I couldn't enter a room without wondering how many of the men there she'd bedded."

"Do you still hate her?"

Morgan sat back, studying his friend. "Why, exactly, are you so concerned about Lillian? I divorced her, Andrew. I didn't kill her."

"No, but you wanted to."

For a long moment Morgan didn't say a word. Slowly, he took another sip of his whiskey, then answered his friend.

"Perhaps I did, once. She survived my murderous impulses, however."

"Marriage is actually very calming," Andrew said.

"I've never found it to be so."

"Perhaps, one day, you'll marry again."

"Not bloody likely," Morgan said. "I never want to repeat that experience."

"My own wife is a dear sweet soul."

"Your wife is a broodmare," Morgan said.

Andrew didn't take offense. In fact, he only smiled proudly, no doubt reflecting on his five children, none of whom he saw very often. One day he would be faced with all of them grown. Morgan knew he wouldn't be surprised if his friend took the males off clubbing and the females to one of his many mistresses for advice on dress and manners.

"Is that why you're here, Andrew?" he asked, keeping a check on his temper. "To make sure I'm no longer angry? Time has done that. I no longer care what Lillian does, with whom she sleeps, where, or how. It's none of my concern."

Andrew studied the liquor in his glass, took a sip, then said, "She's here, even though she isn't here."

Morgan smiled, genuinely amused. "Lillian never came to Ballindair. Scotland was beneath her. But, I will agree, as long as my solicitor sends me correspondence, it's impossible to completely forget her."

Andrew looked surprised.

Before the other man could ask, Morgan said, "She wants

the Paris house, and despite the fact that we're no longer married, she thinks that repeated demands will make me change my mind."

"Really? Why not give it to her?"

Morgan's good humor vanished. "Because she's not getting another thing belonging to me," he said. "She took my reputation, I'll be damned if she gets anything else."

He stood, nodded at Andrew, and left the room, unwilling to discuss his marriage or Lillian any further. Sometimes, the boundaries of friendship needed to remain strictly in place.

Mary MacDonald hesitated at the entrance to the kitchen.

Could this day have been any more disastrous? What had Jean been thinking? Not only had she been terribly afraid that she wouldn't be able to save her niece, but her own position might be in danger.

Jean, sensible, hard-working Jean, had acted completely out of character.

What was she going to do about this situation? Other than counsel Jean on how to act as a proper maid, she didn't know what else to do. She couldn't even go to the earl and ask for a little compassion for the girl. What would she say? *Your Lordship, she's had a terrible time of it. They both have. Please overlook her utter stupidity.*

No, he'd want to know about the girls' past. God forbid anyone should discover it.

For the first time, Mary wished she'd taken Mr. Seath into her confidence. She'd been afraid the steward would forbid her to hire her nieces. The actions of their father had been horrible, true, but neither Jean nor Catriona had inherited any of his tendencies.

Now, foolishness, that was another thing entirely.

Look at Jean, back to being her silent self, sitting with the other maids but not speaking. More than once she'd tried to advise her niece about such things.

"You must try to get along with them, Jean."

"I do, Aunt. We just have nothing in common. No one wants to discuss books or things I'm thinking."

"Can you not try to find common ground? Catriona seems to do well enough."

"I am not Catriona, Aunt," the girl had said, getting that mulish look.

No, she wasn't. Life would be so much easier for Jean if she were more like Catriona. Everyone liked Catriona, sought her advice and laughed at her jests. Jean just sat there like a mound of overcooked cabbage.

Today was the only time she'd acted differently, and it had been with a shocking lack of decorum.

Mary moved away from the doorway, knowing she couldn't solve the problem tonight. Instead, she sought her suite of rooms, where she could close the door on Ballindair and all its problems.

Chapter 6

Morgan couldn't sleep, especially after Andrew's comments about Lillian. Perhaps he should thank his friend. For months, no one had mentioned his wife, but her presence had been felt nonetheless.

At his last meeting with Lillian, he'd been able to let her words flow over him like water. A few of the droplets, however, had the effect of acid on his skin.

"You're the most hideously boring man I've ever known, Morgan. A pity, since you don't look exceptionally boring. You're quite a handsome man. But it's a well wrought package containing nothing of any interest."

He hadn't known what to say to that remark so he remained silent. A judicious approach to his wife's verbal assault.

"You're so bloody gentlemanly. There's a time to be a

gentleman and a time to be something else more exciting."

"A satyr?" he asked.

"Even a mythical creature would be better than you."

"You surprise me, Lillian. I didn't know you even knew the meaning of the word. So it's my fault you went from one bed to another, is that it, my dear?"

"I didn't always need a bed, Morgan, something you might have once considered." Her smile was mocking, her beautiful, heart-shaped face twisted into a mask of derision.

"Because I was exceptionally boring," he said, pushing back his rage, "you were forced to seek out the company of other men."

"Yes!"

Her blond hair swung from one side to another. For this confrontation, she'd chosen her attire carefully, a peignoir set no doubt from Paris. Of the palest yellow silk, to better set off her beauty.

Was it a last, desperate, attempt to seduce him? He was so far from being seduced he might as well be in the Canary Islands.

Where, exactly, had their marriage faltered? The only fortunate aspect of the entire union was they'd had no children. If Lillian had borne him a child, he would have doubted its paternity.

At last count, Andrew had five children. And him? Nary a one. No progeny to inherit the earldom. No boy to take fishing or little girl to capture his heart.

It was just as well.

One less person to shoulder his dishonor.

Catriona made a sound in her sleep. A murmur of pleasure that had the effect of annoying Jean tremendously. Was she dreaming of the Earl of Denbleigh?

Jean was heartily tired of hearing about the man.

Catriona sighed again, and Jean placed the pillow over her head. If the Earl of Denbleigh was as wealthy as he was rumored to be, surely he could purchase better pillows. Something made in London, perhaps, and hinting of lavender, as the pillows on his own bed. These were thin and lumpy and smelled of mildewed hay. Of course, if she had any time at all, she would have stuffed the pillow herself, choosing pine needles or dried flowers.

She would add it to her list of chores to be done when she had a free moment.

Catriona murmured again. Jean threw off the pillow and sat up on the edge of the bed, staring across the small room. If she woke Catriona, she would be subjected to a barrage of complaints. Better to simply fall asleep herself, nature's way of tolerating the intolerable.

Except, of course, she'd been abed for two hours and hadn't slept yet.

She leaned back against the wall, her legs straight out in front of her. The cotton nightgown had been well laundered. In fact, it was over three years old and was a bit higher on the calves than it should be. It fit Catriona perfectly, but made Jean feel like a poor child who'd outgrown her donated attire.

After several minutes of staring at her sister—an action that had no effect on Catriona's pleased murmurs, Jean stood.

She knew better than to leave the room in her nightgown and wrapper, so she donned the uniform she'd worn today, dispensing with any stays. She looked proper enough. During the day, she kept her corset as loose as she could, in order to give herself room to move while she worked.

Who decided that a woman had to be so tightly confined when she was reaching, stretching, bending, and pulling all day? If she were a society matron, she could see herself sitting on a sofa doing nothing but needlework or reading, perhaps, staring into the fire considering how she might spend her millions of pounds. As a maid, a corset was a torture device.

She sat and laced her uncomfortable shoes, wishing she had money to have a new pair made. Something soft in kid leather, perhaps. A pair of shoes that didn't encourage the bulges on her feet and hurt her heels by the time the day was done.

Her dress was a little too long now that she wasn't wearing a petticoat, but who would see?

She left the room, closing the door quietly behind her. For a moment she stood with her back to the door, looking left, then right. Only women slept on this floor. Some of the men slept above them, in the attics. A few of the more muscular footmen occupied small rooms on the ground floor, the better to guard the treasures of the MacCraigs. Not that any family known for their murderous ancestry truly needed extra guards.

The Earl of Denbleigh might well be a throwback to an earlier time. She could easily see him running someone through, if not with an actual weapon, then the sharpness of his gaze.

Odious man.

Jean waited, but no one stirred, not even when she walked down the corridor. The floorboards creaked, the gas lamps sputtered. Was night ever truly silent?

The housekeeper's suite of rooms was at the end of the women's corridor. Aunt Mary had the hearing of a curious cat. Consequently, she felt like a mouse as she crept in front of the door, praying it wouldn't suddenly open.

She couldn't sleep, but that didn't mean she was allowed to roam around Ballindair as if she were family.

Aunt Mary had still not questioned her as to her true purpose in the Laird's Tower last night. Jean knew her aunt hadn't believed the story of wanting to get an early start on cleaning.

If her circumstances changed, if she ever moved back to Inverness, if she ever became a wife and mother, she would never again take for granted the cleanliness of her surroundings. She would thank her servants—should she be fortunate enough to be able to afford any—every day, and appreciate their work without reservation.

Why hadn't she noticed those things earlier?

The same reason she hadn't noticed her father's acute sorrow at her mother's illness.

So many things were better seen through the prism of the past. What would she see about herself, looking back five years from now? Would she chide herself for being foolish and sad occasionally? Would she ridicule herself for being curious about ghosts? No one else at Ballindair wanted to know. Instead, they treated the ghosts as if they were a necessary nuisance, and any encounter with them was to be avoided, not sought.

She slipped down to the back stairs, her destination a place she knew well. At the doorway, she hesitated. Tall, mullioned windows, rising to the ceiling, summoned the sun on even the dreariest day and illuminated the paintings along the far wall. Now, the Highland night had given way to darkness, and only moonlight entered, bathing the space in a bluish white light. Two benches sat in the middle of the room. A few ornamental urns were placed between each tall window.

The wood floor was highly polished and echoed her footsteps, the sound announcing her presence in the Long Gallery.

The maids had been industrious here, too. Twin smells of French polish and vinegar hung heavy in the air. The curtains had evidently been taken down to be brushed.

She'd cleaned the Long Gallery herself more than once. The portraits, now only blurs of shadows in gilt frames, were to be dusted with care so as not to damage the canvases.

Some of them were old, she knew, having listen to her aunt's lecture.

In daylight, she'd studied the faces of the men and women of Clan MacCraig, amazed that all the men were handsome and tall, and all the women beautiful.

Suddenly, she felt as if something had pressed against her chest, a hand, a sensation. Abruptly, she stopped, wrapped her arms around herself and stood silent and attentive.

Even though it was the middle of summer, the Long Gallery was chilly. As she watched, a shadow coalesced. Was it a ghost?

She took a step back, and as she did so, chided herself for her cowardice.

Something was there. Something made a sound, almost a breath. She shivered, wishing she'd brought her shawl, and took a resolute step forward.

The French Nun was rumored to appear only to single women, and although it didn't specifically say so in the book she'd read, she had the impression the ghost only appeared to warn them of the perils of losing their virtue.

What a pity Catriona wasn't here.

She fisted her hands and pressed them against her stomach, forcing herself to breathe.

At times, she felt as insubstantial as a ghost, as invisible. Perhaps that's why she wished to see one, to prove to herself that she, too, existed. Although not as vivacious as Catriona or as beautiful, she still mattered, if only to herself.

"Do you have anything to say to me?" Jean asked softly. "Any advice?"

She dropped her arms, hands clenched at her sides.

"Will you speak with me?" she said to the amorphous shape. "I've waited so very long to see you."

Jean took one more step forward.

"Can you not find peace?"

"Not if you are forever haranguing me," the Earl of Denbleigh said, stepping out of the shadows.

She bit her lips against a scream, and pressed her hand flat against her bodice. Her heart felt as if it was leaping right out of her chest.

Several long minutes later she tilted her chin up and faced the shadow of the Earl of Denbleigh.

"I do apologize, Your Lordship," she said.

"You thought me a ghost again," he said.

She nodded, then realized he couldn't see her. "Yes," she said. "I did."

"Perhaps I am."

The comment startled her. From his position, he was standing in front of the portraits, one of them his father. Did he miss him?

Curiosity she shouldn't have felt.

"Why are you such a resolute ghost hunter, Jean?" he asked.

She didn't know what surprised her the most: that he'd posed the question in such an amicable tone or that he remembered her name.

She wished she could see him.

"I don't know what you mean," she said.

He made a sound of disparagement, as if he knew she was playing for time and didn't know how to answer him.

"Why do you seek out the ghosts of Ballindair?"

"I'm sorry for disturbing you," she said, stepping backward, as though he were king and she a lowly subject leaving the room.

"You needn't leave," he said.

Curiosity kept her in place.

"My old nurse used to say there were ghosts aplenty at Ballindair, one for every season or mood. I've never seen one."

She didn't tell him her efforts had been in vain as well.

When he remained silent, she said, "I think they show themselves when they want, not when we wish."

"When I was a boy, I used to believe the ghosts would come to me, because I was to be laird."

The confidence surprised her.

She no longer retreated. Instead, she stood where she was, half the room between them. Neither of them spoke forcefully. The hour encouraged a tone just above a whisper.

His shadow suddenly moved, and she wondered if he was coming closer.

"I'm not certain I ever saw one, either," she said. "I think, sometimes, we see what we want to see."

His laugh startled her. "Indeed, you're correct in that. Do you really want to see ghosts, Jean?"

How did she answer that question?

"Sometimes," she said. "At other times, I wonder if I have the courage."

"Yet, you still seek them out. Why?"

She turned, gripping her skirts as she walked to a window. If it were daylight, she'd see the approach to the castle. The long expanse of lawn was perfectly manicured. How could it be anything else? This was Ballindair, the jewel of the Highlands.

"Must you know the answer to everything?" she heard herself say.

Of course, why try to salvage her position after this ruinous day? He already thought her a foolish girl, given to rash and reckless behavior, and now a dolt, to believe in ghosts.

"Is my question intrusive?"

Yes, because it surprised her. Yes, because she hadn't thought him the type of man to be interested in anyone other than himself. Yes, because she didn't know how to answer him, the second time he'd confounded her in a few minutes.

He didn't say anything, the moments stretching between them.

"I look for ghosts because it gives me something to be interested in other than my own life," she said.

There, in reparation for her rudeness, she'd given him the truth.

"An admirable feat, if indeed it does that. Escaping from one's life would be pleasant from time to time."

Was there no end to surprises from the earl this night?

She turned her head, wishing he would step into the moonlight, but he remained in the shadows. Perhaps she'd found a ghost and he was the Earl of Denbleigh, conjured up from confusion, interest, and a little loneliness. Perhaps he wasn't there at all, but only a shadow who talked to her as if they were equals.

"How does one go about this ghost seeking of yours?" he asked.

She fisted her hands in her skirts.

"One remains very quiet," she said softly. "And waits."

"Why here?"

Did she dare give him the truth again?

"Because hardly anyone comes here at night," she said. "I reasoned if anyone inhabited the Long Gallery, it would be a ghost."

"Would you like me to leave?"

She smiled. How very gentlemanly he was behaving, and how foolish as well. She was his maid.

She turned and walked back to the door.

"Where are you going?"

She tossed a remark over her shoulder. "You're the Earl of Denbleigh, the MacCraig. It's not for you to leave."

"Perhaps it was the ghost who left, because we weren't quiet enough."

She turned and faced him, startled to see he'd emerged

from the shadows and was standing in a pool of moonlight. His white shirt glowed, his black trousers merging with the night. His face was pale and unsmiling. He might well have truly been a ghost at that moment, one whose face was carefully expressionless.

Why did the Earl of Denbleigh guard his emotions?

She was foolish to stand there, without her petticoat and corset. But she hadn't thought to talk to him like this. Or share confidences of a ghostly nature. She should be abed, but the temptation to learn more about the Earl of Denbleigh was so great she remained where she was.

A moment later she moved to sit on a bench in the middle of the room.

"What ghosts were you hoping to find here?" he asked.

Should she tell him about the French Nun? Did he know his family's history? Instead of responding, she asked a question. "When you were a little boy, did you ever go hunting for ghosts?"

His chuckle was warm, surprisingly rendering him human and approachable.

"As a matter of fact," he said, "I did. But my activities were reserved for the West Tower."

Where all the weapons from the past were stored. All the knives, swords, and cudgels the Murderous MacCraigs had accumulated over the years.

"And you never saw a ghost there? Not even the Herald?" The Herald was renowned for his ability to warn the Mac-Craigs of momentous events.

"Not even the Herald," he said.

"Do you think they see us?" she asked. "Ghosts? Do you think the reason we don't see them all that much is because they don't wish it?"

He turned his head to study her.

"Let's pretend ghosts are real," he said, startling her.

"You don't think they are?"

"I don't know what I think," he admitted. "But let's pretend ghosts are real. Why wouldn't they want to appear before us?"

"Because it's painful."

He didn't say anything for a moment. "Painful?" he finally asked.

"Perhaps they remember being alive, and being around the living reminds them of life."

"You've given some thought about this."

She nodded.

"Perhaps they can only see certain people, such as relatives or friends or loved ones," she said.

"Or," he said, adding to her list, "they only appear to those who wish to see them. Otherwise, they'd frighten people."

She shook her head again. "I don't think so. Sarah, one of the maids, won't go near the East Tower. She swears the Green Lady came to her when she was cleaning the chapel. Sarah most definitely did not wish to see a ghost."

"The Green Lady?"

She glanced over at him.

"She was confined to her chamber when her father discovered she'd planned to run away with her love. It's said she lived there alone for three years until she couldn't bear it anymore and threw herself out the window."

He didn't say anything again.

When he still didn't speak after several long moments, she said, "But Sarah is a little flighty and may have only imagined seeing her."

He turned his head again. "Do people think you're flighty, for wanting to see a ghost?"

She smiled, more to herself than to him, because he couldn't see her.

"Yes," she said.

Every single member of the staff at Ballindair thought she was more than flighty. They thought her a little barmy. Catriona had spread the tale, thinking it a great jest.

She loved her sister, but there were times when Catriona tried her patience.

"How many ghosts do you know about?" he asked.

"Twelve," she said. "But the only ones I'm truly interested in are the Herald, the Green Lady, and the French Nun."

"I wanted to see the first earl," he said. "He was reputed to be quite a swaggering figure."

He had a bit of swagger about him as well, but that was a comment she wisely didn't make.

For a few long moments they didn't speak, simply listening to the silence. Ballindair was so large, so filled with people, it was unusual to find any peaceful spot. The moonlight streaming into the gallery anointed this a hallowed place. Here, ghosts might walk with mortal man, and even stop to tell a tale or two.

"The French Nun," she found herself saying, "fell madly in love with the 2nd Earl of Denbleigh."

He glanced at her again. She wished she'd taken more care with her hair, rather than just tossing her night braid over her shoulder.

"She'd already taken her vows when she met him, of course. Nor did she want to fall in love. At least, that's what the book on Ballindair's ghosts says. But she left her convent in France and traveled to Scotland because none of her letters had been answered, and she was worried for him."

He didn't speak, which was just as well. How did she tell him the rest of the story, or did he know it?

She continued, pushing through a barrier of reluctance. If he chided her afterward for saying things about his ancestors, then she would just simply have to accept the rebuke.

"When she arrived at Ballindair, it was to find her love had married. She was ill from the journey, and the laird took her in, of course, but she died not long afterward."

"Where did she die?"

He already knew or he wouldn't have asked.

"The North Tower."

"The Laird's Tower," he said.

She nodded, then reminded herself he couldn't see her in the darkness. "The very same."

"So that's what you were doing there," he said.

What had she done? She was certain to be dismissed now.

He surprised her again by only saying, "Not an honorable man, the second earl, was he?"

She knew better than to agree. She wasn't about to insult her employer's ancestor.

"My father was an honorable man," he said, and the words sounded wistful.

"I'm sorry about his death," she said. "It's difficult to lose a parent."

"Have you lost your father?"

She stood, knowing the time had come to leave him. She wanted to say something to indicate her gratitude. For a few moments he'd treated her with kindness. For a space of time they'd been strangers in the darkness, sharing a little of themselves. He hadn't been an earl, and she hadn't been a maid.

But now it was time for them to slip back into their respective roles.

"Good night, Your Lordship," she said, and escaped before he could say anything else, or question her further.

As she left him, she realized she hadn't asked about his wife. An omission that troubled her all the way back to her room.

Chapter 7

RULES FOR STAFF: *Never laugh or giggle in the presence of others, or incite others to do so.*

His night had been dreamless, and when Morgan awoke, he felt more refreshed than he had in months.

He lay looking at the dawn sky creep in through the curtains he'd opened before retiring. For once, he wasn't thinking of all the things he needed to do or the people he had to meet, or to avoid, as the case might be.

His valet wasn't there to give him a disapproving glance. Nor did he have an angry wife marching into his bedchamber and demanding all sorts of things, from a new wardrobe to his concession that he was an idiot, a fool, and a cold, callous bastard.

The birds sang, the morning mist was burned away by a rapturous sun, and he was blessedly alone.

He lay in the bed his father had occupied, which he realized didn't concern him at all. Perhaps he should have returned home earlier.

The encounter the night before slid into his mind. He'd never expected to have a conversation with a maid about ghosts. He'd almost told her about his childhood, how magical and enchanted it seemed now, looking back. Had she had a similar upbringing?

And why the hell did he want to know?

Was he so damn lonely he would seek out the company of a maid? Next, he'd be taking tea with the housekeeper.

He dismissed the little wren from his mind with some difficulty, but he did it nonetheless, intent on his first full day at home.

She was the most beautiful woman Andrew had seen in a very long time, and London was filled with beautiful women, most of whom were well aware of their appearance.

If he had any occupation at all, he was a professional connoisseur of women. He courted them. He flattered them. He was thoroughly appreciative of all their physical attributes.

He loved the smell of women, the curve of their necks, the supple grace of their arms, the mystery of their bodice as it curved and hid, protected and promised. He loved the way they walked, a simple, enchanting sway of hips.

He'd spent enough time talking to women to know the state of their minds. Most women simply wanted to be appreciated. He could certainly do that, just as he was now, watching the blonde as she cleaned a parlor on the first floor. The Ruby Room, he thought it was called.

Andrew had the perfect ploy. He would confess he was lost, and she would put her duster down, smile at him and give him all her attention. From that moment it would be nothing at all to get her into his bed. Strange, he hadn't had a maid before. He'd spent all this time with women of the peerage. He had the money to interest them and to give them baubles when the affair was done.

He wondered if that bodice of hers was real, or simply padding.

"I'm hopelessly lost," he said, leaning up against the door-jamb.

To his surprise, she ignored him. No, she did more than ignore him; she turned her back on him.

"Did you not hear me?" he asked, strolling into the room.

"You're not lost," she said.

What a lovely voice she had, a complement to her appearance.

Her eyes were a shade of blue he'd only seen in the sky. Or perhaps in the Mediterranean, near the Costa Brava in Spain, to be exact. And her hair, that glorious blond hair. He wanted to paint her, but doing so would test the limits of his talent.

"What makes you think I'm not lost?" he asked.

She wiped the table with a rag, missing several spots. But she didn't look overly concerned about her chore. What a pity she was a maid. What an utter waste of her attributes.

She turned, fisting the rag in one hand. Her chin tilted up arrogantly.

"Begging your pardon, sir," she said, dipping into a curtsy. "How may I assist you?"

Her eyes were twinkling, and for a moment there was perfect communion between them. She knew he was interested. He knew she was a flirt and a tease.

She smiled then, twin dimples appearing on her milky white cheeks. What a glorious female she was.

With her smile, his intention to remain without female companionship on this trip to Scotland abruptly disappeared.

He had to have her.

"I was off to paint some of your scenery," he said. "I'd rather paint you instead."

She bestowed on him a throaty chuckle, less a sound of

amusement than one of seduction. Damned if he wasn't intrigued, even as she turned and deliberately walked away.

That morning, Jean had been assigned to the scullery. That afternoon, she was a messenger for Aunt Mary, traipsing back and forth between the stable, the outer buildings, and back to Ballindair. She hadn't seen anyone, which was exactly what she'd wanted.

Just when she was certain her aunt meant to walk her to death, she was sent to the laundry. She couldn't decide which was worse, the scullery with its eternal smell of onions, or the boiling kettles of steam and lye-based soap.

The women who worked in the laundry were a garrulous sort, forever talking about one subject or another, their conversations centering around family, babies, and womanly ailments. From their talk, she could expect dire things to happen if she ever bore a child, grew old, or drank a certain type of tea.

But at least they weren't discussing the Earl of Denbleigh. Catriona was still doing that. He was the first thing she mentioned in the morning and the last thing she spoke about before saying her prayers and finally, blessedly, going to sleep.

"You use the stick, the long one," Sarah said, pointing to the kettle. "Not the short one. You'll be burning yourself for sure."

Jean took the long stick, stirring it into the boiling kettle and using the strength of her entire body to fish out a soapy sheet. Sarah lay another stick underneath the material. Together, the two women began to walk in opposite directions around the kettle until enough of the soapy water was squeezed out of the sheet so it could be dropped into a barrel of clean rinse water.

Two shorter sticks were used to fish out the rinsed sheet

and twist it until it was nearly dry. Only then could she hang it on the nearby line, and start on another sheet. So far today she'd washed twenty sheets, a multitude of pillowcases, towels, rags, and dishcloths.

Her back ached and the muscles in her arms were screaming with pain.

Thank heavens they only washed the flat items on Monday. Tomorrow they would start on clothing. Wednesday they'd iron. Thursday they would stack, fold, and return the sheets to the presses for inspection by the housekeeper. She didn't know what Friday held in store.

Would she survive until Friday?

She was given a respite to go and eat the noon meal, following the other women into the kitchen. In some great houses, she'd been told, there was a room set aside just for the servants. But Ballindair's kitchen was cavernous, and there was more than enough room for all of the women to sit and eat even while Cook and her helpers were bustling about preparing food for the earl and his guest. The male staff normally ate an hour earlier, but all of them took their dinner together.

"He's a bold adventurer," Catriona was saying as Jean sat next to her sister.

"The earl?" Jean asked.

"No, His Lordship's friend," she said, turning to her. "He waylaid me while I was working. He was a terrible bother."

Jean sent a sidelong look to her sister. She'd wager Catriona used the encounter to explain why she hadn't finished her tasks.

"Tell us again what he told you," a woman from the laundry said.

Catriona smiled. " 'You're a picture of beauty, you are,' he said. 'I'd like to preserve you for all time. I must paint you.' "

A girl laughed. "What did you say?"

Catriona tossed her head. "I told him I wasn't interested." She propped her chin on her hand. "Now, if His Lordship wanted to paint me, I wouldn't mind."

Jean kept her mouth shut, hoping one of the older women would chide Catriona for her behavior. Instead, the head laundress laughed and said, "I'd be a party to that myself."

"I think he's the most handsome man I've ever seen," Catriona was saying.

"Is he staying long?" asked one of the laundry girls.

Catriona shrugged. "If he wasn't planning it, perhaps he could be convinced."

Someone giggled. No doubt it was Barbara. She was the giggling sort, always laughing at something.

The meal today was colcannon, one of her favorite dishes, but Jean wasn't hungry. She put down the fork, picked it up again, staring at the plate. If she didn't eat, she'd be back to having a grumbling stomach. With more determination than hunger, she ate a few bites, trying to concentrate on her food rather than the conversation swirling around her.

A girl was asking about hair, how she could replicate Catriona's shiny locks.

"Vinegar," her sister said. "Mix it with the rinse water, and your hair will shine, too."

Catriona was once again reigning as Queen of the Table. Maids and laundresses—some of whom had been at Ballindair for an age—were listening carefully to her sister's conversation.

Now she was going on and on about how the earl wanted to smile at her during the Laird's Greeting. "Of course, doing so wouldn't have been proper under the circumstances," she said.

Jean sent a quick glance toward her. The demurely coy look Catriona wore was one she had often practiced in front of the mirror.

"He did seek me out again, to locate his friend," she said.

"Why didn't he ask the housekeeper?" Jean asked.

Nine women turned their heads to look at her. Jean kept her attention on her sister. Unlike Catriona, she didn't like being the center of attention, but curiosity—and perhaps irritation—had made her speak.

Catriona shrugged again. "Who knows the male mind?"

Was her sister never going to learn? Attracting male admirers was one thing, if they'd still been who they were two years ago. After all, choosing a husband among eager suitors was what the marriage mart was all about. But it wasn't two years ago, and Catriona was now a maid. Flirting was against the rules, especially flirting with the Earl of Denbleigh. None of the nine women seemed to remember that.

"What did he say?" one of the younger maids asked. "When he sought you out?"

Catriona sat up taller, her shoulders back, thereby accentuating her bosom. "He must have remembered my name," she said, sending a smile toward the questioner. "And just wanted to foster the acquaintance."

Most of the women looked rapturous at that comment. Two of the older women, however, were frowning. A sign that not everyone thought Catriona was acting correctly.

All one of them had to do was seek out their aunt. Or, worse, tell the steward about Catriona's behavior.

"His eyes are blue, the most beautiful blue, like the deep waters of a loch."

She'd never known her sister to be so eloquent.

"And his shoulders. He must drive his tailor to distraction. Or dance divinely."

How Catriona had made the mental leap from the man's shoulders to his footwork, she didn't know. Nor did she ask. She wasn't going to encourage her sister.

"Do you think it will get cooler soon?" Jean asked.

Not one person paid any attention to her.

"I think it feels more like autumn each day," she said.

"Do you think he'll have parties here?" one of the girls asked. Longing laced her voice. "I should so like to see a party."

"Perhaps I should hint about it to him," Catriona said.

If Jean wasn't mistaken, her sister was batting her eyelashes, no doubt in practice for addressing the earl again.

More than one person at the table laughed in delight. Had everyone lost their minds?

The Earl of Denbleigh wasn't going to pay any attention to a maid, even one as lovely as Catriona. He was going to stay at Ballindair as long as it was convenient for him, and while he was here he would act in his normal manner. He wasn't going to be swayed by blond hair and pretty blue eyes. He wasn't going to act differently than he'd always acted. He was going to be the same person, and that person was never going to forget that he was an earl and Catriona was a maid.

Even if Catriona pretended to forget it.

Suddenly, everyone was intent on their lunch, and without even looking, Jean knew Aunt Mary had entered the room.

"Catriona," her aunt said, "your hair is not acceptable. Leave the table now and take care of the matter."

As housekeeper, Aunt Mary wanted all the women to braid their hair and wear their caps to provide a similar appearance. Catriona had sulked about the rule for days, and attempted to shirk it at every opportunity.

Now, her sister looked as if she wanted to argue, but at the last moment only nodded and stood. Jean hoped she would obey Aunt Mary's dictates. People watched to make sure the two of them weren't being treated with any preference.

"Once you've tidied yourself, take His Lordship some fresh toweling and tins of soap."

Catriona's expression turned from sullen to gleeful so quickly that Jean's heart sank.

She stood up. "I'll go, Mrs. MacDonald," she said, sending a look to her aunt, and hoping the older woman understood.

The very last thing she wanted was for Catriona to be alone with the earl. After days of comments about his looks and bearing, her sister had as much as announced her attraction to the man. She wasn't exactly sure what Catriona would do to advance the earl's interest, but knowing her, it would be something.

Catriona was sometimes vastly improper. She flirted outrageously, and with her gaze, she promised what morals and propriety forbade her to deliver.

Aunt Mary frowned at her, a look only half as irritated as Catriona's quick glance.

"Please, Mrs. MacDonald," Jean said. "I feel as if I need to make reparations for my actions."

"The earl is with Mr. Seath, I believe."

And if he wasn't? If Catriona was somehow left alone with him? She feared for her sister's reputation.

"Please." Must she beg? Very well, she would, in front of all these women, if necessary.

Her aunt must have read some of her desperation, because she finally nodded.

Ignoring Catriona's fulminating look, Jean gathered up the linen Aunt Mary gave her, along with the tins of soap inscribed with the earl's crest—an eagle painted with one eye staring at her—and left the room.

Once at the Laird's Tower, she placed the two tins atop the stack of toweling just below her chin and fumbled with the latch on the door. The earl's trunks were arranged in front of the armoire, which made her wonder if someone had unpacked for him.

Entering the sitting room slowly, she balanced the towels

as far as the table beside a chair before they tumbled to the floor. She bent to retrieve a washcloth and stood once again, only to be faced with the Earl of Denbleigh himself.

He wasn't with Mr. Seath. He was standing there naked.

Naked.

Her heart skipped a beat, then started thumping loudly. Was she breathing? She took a halting breath just to prove she could.

He just stood there, unmoving, as she stared.

She steadied herself by reaching out one hand and gripping the back of the chair.

He didn't turn, walk away, or cover himself with his hands.

She didn't scream, run from the room, or close her eyes.

He didn't say a word.

She couldn't speak.

A maidenly woman would have looked away, but she couldn't do that, either. Instead, she stood there, eyes fixed on him.

Tall, broad-shouldered, he looked fashioned after the statue in the corridor. Except he was larger, a Highlander of old, the width of his shoulders and the layered muscles of his chest tapering to a flat stomach and lean hips. His well-developed legs attested to his strength and made her wonder if he was, somehow, transplanted from the past, when the Murderous MacCraigs often went into battle. His black hair was damp, the ends curling.

The sight of him was more than a woman, even a virgin, could take.

Move, Jean.

Close your eyes, Jean.

Should she say something? No, she should turn around and simply walk out. That's what she should do. But her feet wouldn't move. There, she was breathing a little more. But her eyes refused to look away. Never in all her life had she ever seen a sight as arresting as the Earl of Denbleigh naked.

Her father's medical texts had been forbidden her, but that hadn't stopped her from taking a peek at the books when he wasn't around. She'd occasionally been startled. A few times she'd been horrified. But if she'd seen anything like the earl illustrated, she might have been tempted to tear out the page and hide it beneath her pillow.

Was this lust? Or was she just feeling appreciative for the wonder of God's creation?

That's it. She was simply being devout.

Turn around, Jean. Turn around. Or at least curtsy. Do something! Stop staring at the man.

Once, she'd happened onto a stable boy who was sluicing himself with water from the trough. Then, she'd been aghast at the sight of his scrawny naked chest, burnt by the sun.

This man wasn't scrawny. Nor was he an object of pity.

Later she'd think about how frightened and distant she felt at the same time. And how the roof of her mouth had been so dry her tongue stuck to it. That's the only reason she didn't say anything to him, of course.

"Have you seen enough?" he finally said, making no effort to cover any of his parts.

Instead, he placed his fists on his hips and turned slowly, giving her a long and unrestrained look at his magnificent backside.

Her heart pounded even harder.

He was as beautiful from the back as he was from the front.

When he turned to face her again, that masculine organ of his, once flaccid, was firmer, somehow. As she watched, it grew, rising out of its nest of hair, abandoning its stance of pointing at the floor, quivering as if sensing her.

Was it sentient?

She took a step back, startled by its curiosity.

"Well? Have I satisfied your curiosity? Or is there anything else you'd like to see? Not that there is anything else for you to see."

"I—" What on earth should she say? Had she suddenly lost the ability to speak?

She took another step backward, wondering if she should curtsy at this particular moment. Could she manage a curtsy? Her hands were trembling. Her entire body was trembling.

Perhaps she'd become ill suddenly.

Could that explain the weak feeling in her knees?

In all the education from her parents, in all her in-depth study of the duties of a maid, no one had ever explained the proper etiquette when faced with a naked earl.

Catriona would know. Catriona would flirt and act coy and maidenly.

Thank God she was here instead of Catriona.

Jean's lips were numb.

She could not force them into a smile. They wouldn't go that way. She felt her mouth move into this odd little grimace to one side.

He would think she was repulsed.

Wouldn't a virgin be repulsed? Horrified, certainly. She did need to leave, and quickly. Before she lost her position. She'd already lost her virtue. Not in the actual sense, of course, but she was nowhere near as innocent as she'd been a scant five minutes earlier.

His organ stretched even farther, growing harder, and pointing at her like a one-eyed serpent.

She had the strangest compulsion to reach out and touch it. Her hand opened and closed, wanting to grab it, fist it, hold it in admiration of its beauty.

What could she possibly say?

Your Lordship, it's quite astounding.

Did women ever talk about such things?

She could feel the warmth of her cheeks, knowing she should have left the very instant she realized he was naked, instead of studying him as if he were a dusty statue.

Taking a step back, she hit the door, reached back and opened it with one hand. She garbled something, starting with, "Your Lordship, I'm sorry," and ended up with a squeak and a couple of pants before sputtering to a halt.

She pointed toward the tins of soap with a shaking hand, still unable to speak.

At least she'd stopped looking at his snake.

Her nose was hot.

Her lips were trembling, and she felt as if she was going to cry at any moment. Instead, she wanted to put her apron over her head and just disappear.

She'd give anything to be a ghost at the moment.

Turning, she rushed out of the sitting room, flying down the stairs. Instead of taking the corridor back to the main part of the castle, she ducked beneath the stairs, heading for a wooden door consisting of thick, weathered planks banded with iron. She removed the bar, placing it against the curved wall, then escaped into the private garden drenched in the afternoon sun.

Her aunt had instructed her never to use the Laird's Garden, since it was strictly for the use of the Earl of Denbleigh and his family. But she didn't want to meet anyone right now. Besides, what was one more infraction? The last two days had been filled with them.

The garden had been tended to recently, in preparation for the earl's return. The stone bench sat along a curved walk glittering with oyster shells.

She sat on the bench, wrapping her arms around her body. Her face was flaming and her hands were still shaking.

Dear God, what was she to do? What could she do?

She was going to be dismissed for certain now. If, by

chance, some miracle prevented that, she'd ask her aunt to assign her to a different part of the castle, so she wouldn't come in contact with the earl ever again. She'd gladly work in the laundry, rather than see the Earl of Denbleigh. She'd dissolve in a pool of humiliation and embarrassment.

But, oh, he was a fine specimen of man.

She drew herself up, horrified at her thought. Who was she to be lusting after the earl? If that's what it was. She'd never had much experience with lust. Attraction, certainly, but she'd never witnessed a man standing naked before her with no sense of embarrassment.

In fact, the earl had looked decidedly proud of himself. Arrogant even in his nakedness.

The very first thing she should do is forget the entire episode. Dismiss it from her mind. Eradicate it, even if it was very difficult.

Especially since she could see him even when she closed her eyes.

She should concentrate on other thoughts—such as how she was to survive these two horrible days without losing her position.

The very last thing she should be thinking about was the Earl of Denbleigh, naked or clothed.

Chapter 8

Whenever he'd disobeyed an order or was guilty of some infraction, Morgan had been called to the library and made to stand in front of his father's acres-wide carved desk. Rumor had it the desk had been crafted in France, a gift of one branch of the MacCraigs. Remembering Jean's story of the French Nun, he wondered now if the desk had some connection.

He'd never been punished for his misdeeds. Instead, he'd had to explain himself in detail. If there was discipline meted out, his nurse was the one to switch him.

What explanations had he given in this exact spot? He'd wanted to explore, rather than study his letters. He didn't want to come to supper as much as he wanted to collect frogs. And he wanted scones and biscuits more than he'd wanted anything.

Back then Cook had taken credit for his growing height, and the fact by the time he'd turned thirteen he could look his father in the eye.

Standing there, all those years, had been a lesson in itself. How to keep his pride and at the same time be humble enough to admit his mistakes.

He moved around the desk and sat in his father's chair, half expecting to be chastised for doing so. He stood again, walked to the windows and threw open the drapes, letting the Highland night into the room. Despite the hour, the sky showed no sign of darkening, and wouldn't until near midnight.

The air was rife with the scent of leather, sandalwood, and tobacco, the same scents that had been there all those years ago.

He returned to the desk, sat, and surveyed his father's library. This time, not with the viewpoint of a penitent, but as the Earl Denbleigh.

If the circumstances were altered, and he was fortunate enough to have progeny in the future, would he send for his son to stand before this desk? Would he make the boy stand there until he finished with his work, then slowly put down his pen, look up, and survey him with grave disapproval?

Morgan would have been more comfortable with a beating than his father's disappointment.

He'd wanted to be like his father, more than anyone else. The man was beloved by everyone, a hero in Scotland, a statesman, a man renowned for his honor and wisdom. After Morgan's mother had died at his birth, his father never remarried. Nor had he kept a mistress. If he had female companionship, the world—and Morgan—didn't know of it.

Morgan had watched his father with an eye to being just like him.

As a boy he'd even tried to emulate his father's walk, gestures, and way of speaking. He followed behind his father, listening as he'd given instructions, making mental notes of the way the man stood, arms folded, feet apart. On those mornings when they walked through Ballindair, he learned a great deal. To always talk to others with dignity. To speak only the truth or withhold it when provident, but never lie. To value those possessions you held in trust, and think not only of your forebearers, but those who will come after you.

When he cried at the death of his beloved dog, his father had bent down and whispered in his ear, "Toughen up, lad."

Morgan had taken the comment to heart. No one ever saw him cry after that, regardless of the provocation. He learned how to be stoic. He could experience a number of emotions without anyone knowing.

Except for lust. He'd been blindsided by lust.

The disaster that had become his life began innocently enough at a house party hosted by the Duke of Blankenship. He'd found himself supremely bored. The hunting was good, and the horseflesh was magnificent. But he'd much rather have been at home, in his library, working on a new proposal before the House of Lords, than standing and watching the dancing.

He'd hired a dancing master two years earlier, someone who was reputed to be an excellent teacher. Perhaps he was a lost cause, because the Frenchman—Monsieur Doran— declared him incapable of learning. He was told that he had neither the grace nor the patience for dancing.

Therefore, he had carefully avoided all occasions such as the house party, and would have left had the Duke of Blankenship not indicated a desire to talk to him about the new Poor Law.

"Are you alone?"

He had turned, then, to find himself facing Lillian Carstairs, a beauty of the past two seasons. Lillian was not, rumor had it, eager to be married. Four suitors had gone to her father, and all of them had been rebuffed.

Little had he known her father was holding out for a richer man.

That night, her dress had been pale green and she wore emeralds at her throat and ears. Her blond hair was upswept, with ribbons the same color of her dress woven through the curls.

"I'm not alone now," he said.

Her smile was doing something to his stomach.

Her heart-shaped face was dominated by warm brown eyes and a mouth perhaps too large for conventional beauty.

Lillian was gloriously created, with high, full breasts, wide hips, and a narrow waist. Her creamy shoulders were revealed as often as possible, as were the plump tops of those fulsome breasts.

She was lust personified, and her smile hinted she knew it only too well.

The fact that she'd singled him out should have been a warning. Perhaps he'd been arrogant in those days, or simply lonely.

For whatever reason, he'd found himself captivated by Lillian Carstairs, and the next night sought out a secluded alcove and kissed her. He should have noted her eagerness on that occasion. She hadn't been horrified by his actions. Nor was she over the next two months, when he'd kissed her more often.

When he offered for her hand, he was greeted with open arms by both the father and the daughter.

Another warning, one as telling as his wedding night.

Although his experience with women hadn't been excessive, Morgan knew his wife wasn't a virgin. But by then he'd been well and truly snared, diving into the emotion of love as he did all things, with enthusiasm and intensity.

How long had it taken him to realize he wasn't loved in return? Was it the conversation when Lillian had expressed a distaste for the idea of bearing a child? Or was it at his first suspicion that she was not faithful?

Toward the end of two miserable years of marriage, he'd sought out each of the four men who preceded him in idiotic adoration of Lillian Carstairs. One by one the men confirmed what he'd suspected.

She had seduced each one.

Strange, he was the only one with whom she'd been circumspect. But his fortune no doubt played a part in her portrayal of innocence. A fortune she'd not, blessedly, been able to decimate, however much she attempted it. When Lillian wasn't shopping, or being unfaithful, she was giving money to her father. A thoroughly dislikable minor baron, whose sole claim to any achievement was that his only child was now a countess.

Now, Morgan wondered why he was giving so much thought to the past, and realized it was because he was home again. Perhaps his father's shade required penance.

He stared down at the top of his father's desk, empty but for an oil lamp to the right and a leather-edged blotter taking up the middle.

What was he going to do with the rest of his life? Sit here day after day, thinking about the past? Insist on measuring himself against some unseen ruler, and always coming up short?

He couldn't involve himself in politics any longer. He'd become a pariah, a social disgrace. He was unfit for the company of others, not because of his own morals, but because he'd been unwilling to accept the lack of morals from his wife.

Why, then, did he feel as if he were paying the price?

Should he have continued to be cuckolded by Lillian? He

would no doubt be looked at with pity, clapped on the shoulder by men with compassion in their eyes. People would stop talking about his wife when he walked into the room. Or whisper behind his back.

All in all, he preferred being a pariah.

That didn't mean, however, he had a plan for his life.

Between his steward and his father's long-range plans, Ballindair was running smoothly, hardly requiring his intervention. The distilleries could do with a visit from time to time, but didn't need his daily interference.

He had no other occupations to speak of—work had been his solace and his ambition. He'd enjoyed being elected to represent Scotland at Parliament, thinking himself following in his father's footsteps.

Maybe he should take up painting like Andrew, traipsing around the countryside with his leather satchel of paints and brushes, for the sole purpose of staring fixedly at an object in order to replicate it on canvas.

Where was the sense in that?

He didn't want to see a landscape as viewed by another man. Nor was he enamored of those portraits he'd seen exhibited in London. All the subjects had dead eyes. For that very reason, he'd gone to the gallery the night before, to view his father's portrait himself.

The artist had been more talented than some he'd seen. His father looked on the verge of smiling. Or laughing, perhaps, as he was always doing.

Why shouldn't he be happy? People considered him a hero. He was forever being lauded by one person or another. Books had been written featuring the most famous of all the Murderous MacCraigs. Except, of course, Thomas Mac-Craig had single-handedly forced the world to forget that appellation.

Morgan had almost spoken to the portrait. Why, to beg

his father's forgiveness? What would his father have said? No doubt something like: *Toughen up, lad.*

"What is wrong with you?" Catriona asked as they undressed.

Jean only shook her head.

Her sister, clad only in her corset and shift, turned to look at her.

"Something has happened, Jean," she said, hands on her hips. "Tell me what it is. Everyone knows something's going to happen. You've learned something, haven't you? Tell me. Are we being dismissed?"

Jean shook her head again. "I haven't learned anything."

"I don't mind the mystery, as long as it doesn't affect me."

Jean looked at her sister. That comment was so true she was startled. Was Catriona becoming more self-aware? Frankly, she doubted it. Catriona was the center of her world, and anyone else just an orbiting body. No one else was as important to Catriona as Catriona was to herself.

"I shouldn't be talking to you anyway," her sister said, tossing her hair. "You were very mean earlier." She went back to her undressing, then stopped and stared at her.

"Was the earl there?"

Jean blinked several times, wishing words would come to her mind.

"When?" she finally asked.

"When you took the towels and soap to him."

"No."

Lies didn't come easily, but she wasn't about to tell Catriona the truth in this instance.

Sometimes she wished she could confide in her sister. Catriona could be a source of comfort, instead of just aggravation. Now, especially, she wished she had someone to whom she could say: "I saw the earl nude. I saw him naked.

Not only did I see him naked, but I stood there and stared at him while he was naked. I didn't turn away. I didn't scream. I didn't faint. I didn't run out of the room until much later. I simply stared, appalled." Her sense of fairness asserted itself as she imagined what she would say, and she added, "No, not quite appalled. Fascinated."

Those words would go with her to the grave. She would never, ever tell anyone what she'd done, or how she felt about it.

But was it entirely normal for the picture of him to be implanted in her mind? She didn't even have to close her eyes to see him standing there, that portion of him growing larger as she stared.

She had often chastised Catriona for flirting, but what she'd done was worse, so much worse.

Their room was small, but tonight it felt even smaller. She finished undressing on her side of the room, hoping and praying Catriona wouldn't bring up the earl again, but she was doomed to disappointment.

"I asked Aunt Mary how long he was staying, and she didn't know."

She wouldn't blame Aunt Mary for not sharing what she knew with Catriona, as her sister had no reticence. Whatever she thought, she said. And secrets? Catriona had never met a secret that wasn't worthwhile sharing—with anyone.

"Perhaps he'll return to London soon enough," she said, hoping the discussion was ended.

Catriona sighed. "I hope he stays for a very long time."

"Don't be thinking things that cannot happen, Catriona," she said. "Our stations in life have changed. We're no longer the daughters of an Inverness physician. We're maids at Ballindair."

Catriona's beautiful face twisted in a look of disgust.

"Don't you think I know, Jean? Even if I could forget for one day, you're forever reminding me."

"I don't want you to sigh over the Earl of Denbleigh. The only way he would look at you is if he wanted a mistress."

"And what would be so wrong with that?"

Aghast, Jean stared at her sister. "What are you saying?"

Catriona smiled. "Exactly what you're thinking. If he summoned me tonight, I would willingly go to his bedroom."

Jean sat down on the edge of her bed. "You can't be serious."

"Why not? We're already ruined. What man would want to marry either of us? He'd think we'd murder him in his bed."

What should she say to that comment? Regrettably, it was the truth.

"I don't want to be a maid for the rest of my life," her sister said. "If it was a choice between being a mistress or a maid, Jean, I'd gladly choose the role of mistress."

Once again Catriona managed to shock her.

"What do you know about being a mistress?"

Now, Catriona's smile was sly. "I like kissing."

Jean stood and advanced on her sister. Once in front of her, she folded her arms and glared down. "Who have you kissed?"

"Does it matter? I wanted to know what a kiss was like and I kissed someone. More than one someone."

"Was there more than kissing, Catriona?"

"You're not my mother, Jean."

Suddenly, Jean felt even older and plainer than before. Catriona might be three years her junior, but she had much greater experience in flirting and handling men. They weren't supposed to fraternize with the other staff, but more often than not a footman stepped up to assist Catriona whenever she had to carry something, or reach something, or do something she didn't want to do.

All she had to do was purse her lips, look down at the floor and sigh, and suddenly a man was there.

"Leave it alone, Catriona, please. Nothing good can come of you longing to be someone you're not."

Her sister didn't say anything in response. But her eyes twinkled, as if she were anticipating luring the Earl of Denbleigh into her bed.

Dear God, what was she going to do about her?

A refrain that kept her awake after Catriona had fallen asleep.

She was not, however, going ghost hunting. If she did, she might encounter the earl, and he was the very last person she wished to see. Ever again.

For an hour she told herself that. For an hour she was resigned to remaining awake, despite her tiredness. For an hour she was virtuous and abed.

Until she rose, donning her uniform once again.

She avoided the Long Gallery, her destination instead the library.

Chapter 9

Morgan moved from the desk, walking slowly through the shadowed room until he came to the circular iron staircase leading to the second floor of the library.

The expansion of the library had been the last renovation at Ballindair. A gift from his father to succeeding generations.

As early as he could remember, he'd been told that if he didn't produce an heir, Ballindair and his other estates would pass to a cousin. However, the Entail Amendment Act of 1848 gave him the power to petition for the restrictive fee tail to be removed. The law had served him well once; it might do so again.

His reputation was as blackened as it could be. What did a few more ashes matter?

He could see his father's planning as he ascended the steps. Each shelf radiated outward from the circular stairs, like spokes of a wheel. At the farthest point, comfortable chairs and tables with reading lamps were set. A reader didn't need to descend the staircase with his selection of books. Instead, he could read in comfort here, feeling a sense of seclusion.

He stood at the landing to the room, wondering where he would find books on Ballindair's ghosts. Strange, that his interest was incited by a maid's curiosity.

But, then, she'd been curious about a great many things, hadn't she? Especially his nakedness.

Her eyes hadn't left him for the whole time he'd stood there. Should he have apologized? Banished her from the room? Anything but stand there, letting her look her fill. Perhaps his only excuse was he'd never had a woman regard him in that way.

Every other woman of his acquaintance would've turned away, gasped, or fainted. The little wren did nothing but stare at him. He wanted to ask her if she was disappointed by the sight. If he measured up to other men of her acquaintance.

Jean had irritated him, befuddled him, intrigued and now amused him, and he'd only been home two days. He couldn't help but wonder what the following weeks would bring.

He heard a faint sound like a whisper. He hesitated, staring at the books in front of him. The noise came again, but now he recognized it. Someone had entered the library and was walking very quietly.

He doubted if ghosts cared about being overheard. Moving to the end of the bookcase, he folded his arms and waited.

The grandfather clock on the first floor of the library sounded eleven chimes, obscuring the sound of footsteps. They kept country hours at Ballindair. He had his suspicions, and as he waited, he felt a stirring of anticipation.

Since he didn't want to startle her on the stairs, he waited until Jean was on the landing and moving toward him.

Nevertheless, she made a sound like an abbreviated scream at the sight of him.

Reaching out, he grabbed her upper arms to keep her from falling. For several moments she trembled beneath his hands. He wanted, curiously, to pull her close, wrap his arms around her and just hold her until she was still and calm.

Instead, he dropped his hands, forcing himself to move several feet away.

"Forgive me," he said. "I didn't mean to startle you."

She bolted.

He went after her, grabbing her arm before she descended the steps.

"Don't go," he said, the second time he'd done so. Why couldn't he just let her go, leave him to his solitary pursuits?

Because loneliness was a damn difficult companion.

She stopped, turned around and stared at him.

"I didn't go to the Long Gallery tonight, because I thought you might be there," she said in a rush of words. "And here you are. I truly do want to avoid you. How can I do that if you're always where I am?"

"No one has ever come out and admitted they were trying to avoid me," he said. "Even though they were." God knows the last year he'd been rebuffed by more people than he could count.

"I don't want to intrude upon your privacy," she said, blushing.

Was she remembering this afternoon?

Suddenly, he was as well.

He moved back and turned, so she wouldn't see evidence of his sudden recollection.

Until returning to Ballindair, he'd had some control over his libido. After all, it had been some time since Lillian welcomed him into her bed. His wife had a way of banishing him for any infraction. He hadn't known it at the time, but she was busy juggling her many lovers. When she had time, she accommodated him.

What was it about this plain maid that intrigued him?

Perhaps it was her way of speaking directly to him, something he'd not experienced for a very long time.

"Were you ghost hunting?" he asked, glancing at her over his shoulder.

That was the wrong thing to do, to express any curiosity about her actions. He should simply have dismissed her and sent her back to her room.

"No," she said. "I wanted something to read."

Another surprise.

His wife never read, never willingly entered the library in his London home, or a bookshop. He wasn't even certain she could read.

"What kind of book does a maid read?"

"Must I be defined by my occupation?" she asked, frowning at him. "Are you forever labeled earl? What does the earl read? What does the earl eat? What does the earl do?"

"Yes," he said. "I'm almost always defined by my title."

At his words, her face carefully assumed a blank expression. He preferred her frown.

"What do you read, Jean? Novels?"

"Good God no," she said, startling him. "Why on earth would I want to read about histrionic females? They're all wandering from one disaster to another. I don't need to read about such things when my life has been the same."

She clasped her hand over her mouth and looked at him in horror, as if the words had become sentient beings, overcoming her will and escaping by themselves.

Once again she incited his curiosity. More, he wanted to smile in her presence.

"We have quite a few books on the history of the Murderous MacCraigs," he offered. "However, I'm not entirely certain that particular selection of reading material will lead to a dreamless sleep."

"I don't mind dreaming," she said. "In fact, I much prefer my dreams. In them, I'm intelligent and witty and I don't make mistakes."

"I like your mistakes," he found himself saying. "You're very honest, and that's rare to find. I should think you would cherish that quality of yours."

"I think, perhaps, you've misjudged me. I haven't been all that honest."

"Isn't honesty a good trait for a maid to have? Or have you absconded with my silver?"

She looked startled.

"I don't mean that kind of honesty," she said. "I mean the kind where you lie to yourself and tell yourself everything will be all right. Or when you talk yourself into doing something even when you know it's wrong."

"Internal honesty?" he asked, feeling the most absurd wish to smile.

She nodded.

"And how have you been internally dishonest?"

He didn't think she would answer, but she did.

"I lied to my sister. I fibbed to the housekeeper."

"Dastardly deeds."

She nodded again.

He knew it was wrong to ask, but he was somehow unable to bite back the question.

"What did you lie about?"

To his surprise, she shook her head and wouldn't speak.

"How did you come to work at Ballindair?"

She looked away, concentrating on a shelf of books. One hand reached out and touched a gilt edged spine, fingers straying over the title. Was she all that interested in animal husbandry?

With her silence came a feeling of shame. He should have been inured to that emotion, and it was curious to experience it now. But he knew, by his very position, he was coercing her to remain here.

"It's not important," he said. "I was merely making conversation."

She retreated into that irritating silence again.

"Get your damn book," he said.

She didn't.

Nor did she move. Instead, she turned her head, studying him as if he was an insect she'd never seen, some repulsive specimen that horrified her at the same time it fascinated.

"What happened to your wife?"

Of all the things she might have said, he was the least prepared for that.

"I divorced her," he said, giving her the truth. "Does that shock you?"

She didn't say anything for a moment. When she did speak, her words surprised him again.

"I wasn't raised to be a maid," she said. "It's an honorable profession, however. Anything you do well is honorable, don't you think?"

"Would you be an honorable man if you were a very good thief? Or an honorable woman if you were an accomplished harlot?"

She didn't have an answer to that.

He moved to the other side of the bookcase where he couldn't see her. His fingers trailed across the tops of the books, irritated when he found a layer of dust on them.

"Do you clean in here?" he asked.

"Not recently, no," she said, her voice low. "Mrs. Mac-Donald rotates the staff."

Did he imagine the tone of pity in her voice, as if she understood he wanted to banish her at the same time he wanted to force her to remain?

"What have you been doing recently?"

"Working in the laundry. And being a scullery maid."

"What does a scullery maid do?"

"Dispose of garbage and clean pots," she said, and now there was a note of humor in her voice. He wished he hadn't moved away from her. He would've glanced at her then, to see if there was a small smile on her lips.

"And floors, and tables, and more pots, and dishes, and silverware. And anything that needs to be cleaned. Or scrubbed."

"Is the laundry a promotion?"

"Anything is a promotion from the scullery," she said. "But before you arrived, I was an upstairs maid. The scullery and the laundry are punishment, I'm afraid."

He walked around the end of the bookcase in order to see her. "Why are you being punished?"

She smiled at him, then glanced away, her attention once more on a book. "I was unpardonably rude to a certain earl."

"Perhaps he deserved it," he said.

"Perhaps he did," she said, her smile deepening.

"Shall I speak to the housekeeper?"

Her smile abruptly disappeared. "I hope you won't, Your Lordship."

"Why not?"

"I'll be moved back to my normal duties soon enough. And if you do speak to the housekeeper, it would undermine her authority."

"Plus, she'd resent you for my interference."

She shrugged but didn't answer.

"Have I no influence even in my own home?"

"I think you have more influence than you know, Your

Lordship. People wish to please you. Everything they do is for that singular reason."

"Do you wish to please me, Jean?"

She took a step back, and he regretted the question the moment she moved. He'd frightened her, somehow. Or played lecher, more like.

How did Andrew do it? How did Andrew convince all those women he seduced that he wasn't to be feared? Would Jean have listened to him? Or believed Andrew, for that matter? He knew, suddenly, she wouldn't have been any more receptive to Andrew's blandishments than to his rusty conversation.

Was that what he was trying to do, seduce a maid? The thought brought him up short. Surely he wasn't that lonely. Or that dishonorable.

"Where is the book about the ghosts of Ballindair?" He'd get the book, then banish her, the wisest course.

"You don't believe in them," she said.

"Is it necessary to believe in something to study it?"

She tilted her head and regarded him solemnly, like the wren she was. "I think it requires an open mind, Your Lordship, to fully study something. Not a mind narrowed by suspicion and disbelief."

Now that was surprising. "Are you given to philosophy also, Jean?"

She didn't answer.

"Tell me more about the French Nun," he said. "Why does she insist on haunting Ballindair? Is it to punish the Murderous MacCraigs somehow? Inspire them to change?"

"Do you think a ghost could have altered the behavior of your ancestors?" she asked, her smile back in place.

"I don't," he said. "A cudgel, perhaps, would have had more effect."

She laughed, an odd sound in this room dedicated to contemplation and learning. The fact he'd made her laugh gave him a strange and curious warmth, as if he'd just consumed a particularly fine single malt whiskey.

"Are you seeing anyone?" he asked, abruptly curious.

She blinked at him, as if processing the question before answering it. "Seeing anyone?"

"Are you stepping out with anyone? Or are you engaged? Hell, are you married? Do I employ married maids?"

She had that look on her face again, as if she couldn't decide whether to be annoyed or insulted.

"Isn't that a very personal question, Your Lordship?"

"So was wanting to know about my wife," he said.

She folded her arms and began to tap her shoe on the floor, for all the world like his nurse when she'd been impatient with him. How many decades ago had that been?

He folded his arms as well, the two of them staring at each other in identical poses. Surprisingly, she wasn't much shorter than he. Nor did she look remotely like a maid at the moment. In fact, she had a countesslike appearance, the look on her face reminding him oddly of Lillian at her most intransigent.

However, Jean did not spark in him a desire to retaliate. Probably because he had no emotion invested in the woman. Or perhaps it was simply because he knew, in some deep part of himself, that she was in the right. He had no business asking her if she was involved with someone.

She dropped her arms first. Then he did, each of them smiling at the other. Did she wonder at their sudden amity as much as he?

"You do," she said. "Employ married maids, that is."

Would she answer his other questions? When she turned to leave him, he got his answer—no.

"Are you one of those women who wish to remain a mystery, the better to deepen her allure?"

She began to laugh in earnest as she descended the staircase. The sound of her rich and tantalizing laughter gradually faded into nothingness, as ghostly as those specters she hunted.

When Jean reached her room, her heart was still pounding, less from the possibility of being discovered outside the fourth floor at this hour than for another reason entirely.

He was divorced. A shocking thing, for a man to turn his back on his vows, to abjure his wife.

Why had he done so?

That was the reason for his return to Ballindair, then. The Earl of Denbleigh was a figure of scandal.

But he thought she was mysterious.

And womanly.

And alluring.

He'd wanted to know if she was married, or to be married, or even interested in someone. Surely that was not a question an employer normally asked?

Perhaps he was just being kind to a member of his staff. Would he have talked to anyone about books? Or about the ghosts of Ballindair?

Or was she simply guilty of thinking too highly of herself?

What a foolish girl she was.

She'd seen him, even after she'd not wanted to see him. It hadn't been dreadful at all. She'd entirely forgotten about the sight of him naked. Almost, perhaps—very well, she hadn't.

She closed the door of her room softly behind her and began to unbutton her dress.

"Where were you?" Catriona asked. "The library again? One of these days you're going to get caught, Jean."

Jean turned, her back to the door, facing the shadows surrounding her sister's bed.

"I couldn't sleep," she said. "I went to look for a book to read."

Too late, she realized she'd left the library empty-handed.

Catriona sat up, lit their lone taper, and stared at her. She didn't say anything, but her look was accusation enough.

"I couldn't find anything interesting to read," Jean said, removing her dress and hanging it on the hook beside the door. Clad only in her shift, she sat on the edge of her bed. "It's no good looking at me that way, Catriona. I've done nothing wrong."

Her sister blew out the candle. They were given only one a week, so had to be judicious in its use.

"You lecture me on propriety all the time, dear sister," Catriona said. "Yet you see nothing wrong in wandering through Ballindair at night."

Catriona was right. She'd been foolish. But sometimes she needed to be alone. Sometimes she needed to pretend her life was other than what it was. This time, she left the room when she shouldn't have, and flirted with her employer. If Catriona had behaved in such a fashion, she would've lectured her for hours.

Instead, her sister remained silent.

Jean got into bed, staring up at the dark ceiling. Her heart was still beating too fast, and a warm feeling was spreading through her, a feeling she'd never experienced, and one that troubled her more than just a little.

She reached under the bed for the book about the ghosts of Ballindair. She hadn't wanted to tell him she'd taken it from the library.

Now, she lay awake, holding the book in her arms and feeling an absurd—and forbidden—connection to the Earl of Denbleigh.

Chapter 10

RULES FOR STAFF: *Make the proper demonstrations of respect to the family. Women shall curtsy. Men shall bow.*

Every morning, just after breakfast, Aunt Mary assembled the staff and gave them their assignments for the day. As housekeeper, she believed rotating people in their tasks made for a more skilled staff and a cleaner Ballindair.

This morning, however, Aunt Mary's face was florid and her voice quavered as she spoke to the assembled maids and footmen.

"You've been shirking your duties," she said, looking at each of them in turn.

When Aunt Mary focused her gaze on Jean, she felt like crawling beneath the bench on which she sat.

What had she done now?

"His Lordship informed me this morning," her aunt said, "that the library was in deplorable condition. He stated that more than a few shelves were layered with dust."

Aunt Mary's gaze had moved to Fiona, and held steady on her. "I believe you were in charge of cleaning the library last week, Fiona. Is that not so?"

The woman paled, but nodded.

Then Jean became the object of her attention. "His Lordship specifically requested you be placed in charge of cleaning the library, Jean. Have you any idea why he would single you out?"

Catriona's indrawn breath was a warning not to look in her sister's direction. Instead, Jean studied the floor and shook her head.

"I have no choice but to accede to His Lordship's demands."

Jean sneaked a glance at her aunt's face. Evidently, the audience with the earl had not been an easy one for Aunt Mary.

"You'll take Jean's place in the laundry," the housekeeper said to Fiona. "Perhaps after you've boiled a few dozen sheets you'll begin to pay more attention to your dusting."

Jean knew everyone was looking at her, no doubt speculating why she'd been chosen by the earl. Aunt Mary continued her lecture, including admonishing each person to do his job to the best of their ability and to follow her dictates to the letter.

The lecture over, they all stood in two long lines to be inspected. Had there been a majordomo on staff, he would have been the one to examine the males. Aunt Mary did so now, rigorous and demanding with both sexes.

"Charles," she said, "go and change your neckcloth. You've spilled some jam on it."

"Sally, your hair is untidy. Your cap is askew."

"I would have you brush your jacket, Mark, before presenting yourself."

When she came to Catriona, her sister gave her a bright smile. Aunt Mary, always attuned to any hint of favoritism, only nodded to her niece.

The only public criticism her aunt gave Jean was a shake of her head, as if she despaired of ever making more of her.

Jean bit back her sigh, replacing it with a determined smile, all the while avoiding looking in Fiona's or Catriona's direction.

A few minutes later she entered the Earl of Denbleigh's library and closed her eyes, experiencing the room as she never had before today.

The air smelled musty and tinged with the scent of leather and wood. Something else tickled her nose. Opening her eyes, she turned to the wall, sniffing at the mahogany panel. Tobacco. Had the previous earl smoked a pipe? Did the present earl do so?

How silly she was, to wonder at such things.

Like the Long Gallery, this room had been a haven. When she could, she'd escaped here in the evening, well aware that it was not allowed but unable to avoid both the lure of all these wonderful books, and the blessed solitude. For a few hours she could forget that she was a maid and simply be Jean.

Over there, on the small chair in the corner, she'd read Plato. One quote was oddly apt now. "Human behavior flows from three main sources: desire, emotion, and knowledge." What, then, could she ascribe as the cause for her foolishness last night? Desire, of a certainty. She'd wanted, very much, to talk to the earl. Emotion? Loneliness, perhaps? What kind of knowledge had she possessed? She didn't know anything. Instead, she had an abundance of ignorance about her own feelings. Why had she remained awake half the night, thinking of him?

She glanced up at the iron staircase. How many times had she mounted it in violation of the rules? How many times had she slipped to the back, to the settee, spending hours engrossed in one of the books? Would she ever be able to slip from her room again and come here? Prudence dictated not. Or not as long as Morgan MacCraig was at Ballindair.

But for a few moments last night it had been a magical time. The earl had talked to her as if she wasn't a maid at all, but a person. She hadn't thought of him as her employer or the Earl of Denbleigh, only a handsome man who'd made her heart beat faster.

Being with him had reminded her of a poem she'd once read in this very room.

Sound, sound the clarion, fill the fife!
To all the sensual world proclaim,
One crowded hour of glorious life
Is worth an age without a name.

Had the minutes she'd spent with Morgan MacCraig been her time of glorious life? Oh, it had felt that way.

He'd made her feel like a woman. A female. Was it because he was so male? His collarless shirt had been opened, and she'd had the strangest compulsion to put her fingers against his throat.

The image of him naked came to her again, unbidden, and certainly forbidden.

She should recall the words of her grandmother instead. *A gowk at Yule'll no be bricht at Beltane.* A fool at Christmas would not be wise in May.

Forcing thoughts of the earl away, she grabbed a cloth and went about dusting the first bookcase. She'd been sent here with a job to do, and she would do it as well as she could.

A noise from above made her stop and listen, but before she could investigate it further, Catriona opened the library door.

"You were with the earl," her sister said, shutting the door firmly behind her.

Jean closed her eyes and prayed for patience. When she opened them, Catriona was still standing there, eyes flashing with fury. Twin spots of color on her otherwise porcelain complexion revealed the degree of her anger.

"Last night, you were with the earl. Why didn't you tell me?"

"There was nothing to tell," Jean said, directing her attention to the shelves in front of her. "We merely talked books for a few moments, and that was all."

"You talked books with the earl?" Catriona asked, frowning. "Why ever for?"

"What would you prefer we discuss, Catriona? We were here in the library."

"You didn't flirt with him?"

Aghast, she stared at her sister. "Of course not," she said, hoping her part of their conversation couldn't be construed as flirting.

She'd left the library even when she truly wanted to remain. She'd been sensible despite herself. Now, here was Catriona, being the opposite.

"Are you sure you weren't flirting?"

Jean fixed a look on her sister.

"Good," Catriona said, smoothing her palms down her dress as if to accentuate the attributes straining against the dark blue fabric.

Jean concentrated on a large book that looked old, its binding so worn it should be sent to be repaired.

"Do you know what Aunt Mary has me doing today?" Catriona asked, holding out her hands. Each fingertip was stained black. "Blacking all the fireplaces in the downstairs parlors!"

"It's better than starving, Catriona," she said, moving to another row of books and beginning to dust.

"I'm beautiful," Catriona said. "You must admit that."

She glanced at her sister.

"There's more to a woman than simple appearance, Catriona. She should have character, a loving, open heart, and the willingness to care for others."

Catriona only smiled pitying at her. "How foolish you are sometimes, Jean. A woman should have courage most of all. I've decided to become the earl's mistress."

Jean regarded her sister with a mixture of shock and irritation.

"How are you going to do that?"

"By being in his bed when he retires tonight. He won't be able to refuse me."

Jean took a step back. "You wouldn't."

"I would," Catriona said, tossing her head. "I have to. I'm destined for greater things than being a maid."

She'd promised her father to look out for her younger sister. For years she'd tried to protect Catriona. But how did she steer her sister to a bridge when Catriona was all for jumping into the river?

"You think throwing yourself at the earl is the answer? Catriona," she said, lowering her voice, "have you no pride?"

"I have a great deal of pride now, Jean. What good does it do me?" She held out her hands, wiggling her black fingers.

"Have you forgotten he's also our employer?"

"The better to secure our future, Jean," Catriona said. "He wouldn't dismiss you if I was his mistress."

Stunned, Jean couldn't think of a thing to say.

"It's the perfect plan," Catriona said. "What man could deny me?"

The question made Jean sick. Not only did it indicate Catriona's willingness to give herself to a stranger, but the very fact she could devise such a strategy made her suspect that Catriona had done this before.

Had she parlayed her appearance to her advantage here at

Ballindair? Before she could frame that question, her sister left the library.

Who would have thought a maid was Lillian's double? Catriona's hair was a slightly lighter shade, and Lillian had brown eyes, but in character they were evenly matched. Lillian, too, would not have hesitated to manipulate circumstances to her advantage. Nor would she have cared about another's opinion.

Twice he'd wanted to interrupt the two women, but he'd been so interested in Jean's response to her sister's intentions that he kept quiet. Evidently, she was shocked, enough to stand there for several moments, staring at the closed door.

Since he'd been the recipient of too many similar ploys, he could only congratulate Catriona. At least she'd been direct and honest, which was more than he could say about the women he'd met in London, several of whom had been married, bored, and looking for a little entertainment.

As he stood listening, he felt both gratified and ashamed of himself. He'd been lying in wait for Jean, but if he hadn't been, he would never have learned the extent of Catriona's plans.

He had no intention of being her victim. Besides, he didn't care for blondes anymore. Pushing aside the surprising thought that he preferred a plainer female, he watched as Jean left the library, then made his escape as well.

Chapter 11

RULES FOR STAFF: *Return all belongings to their owners on a silver salver.*

"**I**f the gal's offering herself to you," Andrew said at dinner, "you'd be a fool not to take advantage of the situation."

Andrew's unabashed pleasure in sex had been amusing at times, but it had never struck Morgan as unseemly. Perhaps Lillian's infidelity had changed him, made him view the world through the eyes of a cuckolded husband.

"She's a gorgeous creature," Andrew continued.

"She reminds me too much of Lillian," Morgan said.

"Lillian was a beautiful woman," Andrew said.

His eyes narrowed as he regarded Andrew. "Were you one of her stable?" he asked.

Knowing his friend's penchant for adultery, the question should have been asked before now.

"Do you think I would do that to a friend?" Andrew asked,

standing, and looking like an undersized, irritated rooster.

A head shorter than Morgan, Andrew nevertheless possessed some quality making him appear taller than he was. Or perhaps it was simply that people forgot his stature in light of his charm.

"If you think me capable of that, Morgan," he said, "then perhaps I shouldn't have come to Scotland."

Morgan rose as well.

"Forgive me," he said. "My only excuse is that Lillian made a fool of me. I dislike being manipulated by any woman."

"Even one as delectable as your little maid?"

"If you like her so much, trade rooms with me. You can take the opportunity to plead your case. Tell her how wealthy you are, that should do it."

One of Andrew's eyebrows rose. "Do you really think she's going to be there?"

"I'm sure of it," Morgan said. "Women like Catriona take advantage of every situation."

"I confess to being fascinated with the little blonde," Andrew said.

"You're fascinated with any woman."

"Ah, if that were only true, I'd see my wife more often."

"She's seen you at least five times," Morgan said dryly.

Andrew's laughter almost lifted the tension between them. Almost, but not quite.

"What is it, Jean?"

She turned at her aunt's approach, then went back to folding the last of the cloths and placing them on a wooden shelf. Aunt Mary insisted a maid's job was not done until they'd replaced all their supplies in their baskets or pails. That way, they could start work first thing in the morning with no delay.

Aunt Mary walked closer, waiting until the last of the maids left the storeroom.

"You've been fretting all day, and your eyes didn't leave Catriona at dinner. What's wrong?"

"Nothing, ma'am," she said.

Catriona had avoided her all day, refusing her requests to speak with her privately. At their communal meal her sister wouldn't look at her.

"Is aught amiss, Jean? Something I should know?"

Until the earl had arrived, she'd always been honest with her aunt, with everyone. Lately, however, she was awash in lies.

If Aunt Mary knew what Catriona planned, she could possibly prevent it. But then her aunt would discover that she had been in the library with the earl. There was every likelihood that, relative or not, her aunt might dismiss both of them. Her aunt's position at Ballindair was very important to her, and she wouldn't want the actions of her nieces to reflect on her.

What would the earl's reaction be? He might be so irritated by Catriona's seduction plan that he'd tell Aunt Mary to get rid of her. Or worse, he'd take Catriona as his mistress. Despite his talk of honor, he might be so charmed by her beauty that he could do nothing less.

She would dwell on that thought—and the unexpected pain of it—later. For now, she needed to answer her aunt, who was looking at her with narrowed eyes.

"No, Aunt," she said, uttering yet another lie. "Nothing's wrong."

By the time she'd finished all her work and reached their room, there was no sign of Catriona. Her brush had been moved, but nothing else looked out of place.

Please, dear God, don't let Catriona have gone to the Laird's Tower. Please, grant my sister some sanity.

She could barely breathe. Her chest felt tight, as if bands of anxiety were tightening around her.

Dear Lord, something needed to be done. She couldn't just sit here and pretend everything was fine. Catriona was about to throw her life away. Yes, her sister only thought of herself. Yes, Catriona could be annoying and small-minded. But there had been plenty of times in the past when she'd been kind and caring.

The past two years had been difficult ones, but even more so for Catriona. She'd gone from being a cosseted and spoiled, cherished physician's daughter to a servant.

Somehow, she had to rescue her sister.

Going to the Laird's Tower alone wouldn't prove wise. Look what had happened the last time she was there. She needed someone to accompany her.

Jean ran through the roster of maids and footmen. While Catriona was popular, she wasn't. A few people might assist her, but she'd have to ask them to lie. Otherwise, they'd be honor bound to report Catriona to Aunt Mary.

Only one person at Ballindair might help her and also keep silent: the earl's friend, Mr. Prender.

She straightened her cap, changed her apron for a spotless one she'd laundered herself, and brushed off the tops of her shoes with a rag. There, she looked presentable enough to go calling on a man in his bedroom.

A nervous titter escaped her.

She was doing exactly what she'd begged Catriona not to do.

What if Mr. Prender was forward with her? How would she handle that?

She would just have to chance it. Before she could talk herself out of it, Jean left the room, intent on saving her sister.

Fiona removed her lace cap, now sodden because she'd been sweating all afternoon. She pushed her hair back from her face and knew she'd have to bathe in cold water. She hadn't the energy to go and fetch hot water for herself, and the boiler pipes didn't reach the servants' floor.

It wasn't fair what Mrs. MacDonald had done, but she wasn't unduly surprised. Jean and Catriona were the housekeeper's nieces, for all they'd tried to keep the relationship as quiet as possible. Sometimes Mrs. MacDonald did go out of the way not to show any favoritism. But most of the time, like today, anyone who wasn't related to the housekeeper was punished unfairly.

She'd cleaned the library as well as one person could. She shouldn't have been taken from that task and sent to work in the laundry.

The unfairness of it all burned in her chest. More than once she'd wanted to report Catriona for dallying with a footman. Twice now she'd seen the girl in the stable loft where the lads slept. She was cutting a wide swath through Ballindair, and neither Mrs. MacDonald nor her sister, Jean, acted as if they knew.

She was so weary by the time she reached her room, she opened the door and leaned against the jamb for a moment, surveying her small, precious chamber. She had the bed, chest, and chair all to herself.

A noise made her turn her head. She watched as Jean slipped out of her room and down the back stairs. Was she as frivolous and light-skirted as her sister?

Fiona was weary enough to close the door and simply disregard what she'd seen. But after today's injustice, she closed the door behind her and followed Jean.

The earl's sitting room was empty, which suited her purposes perfectly. Catriona softly opened the door between the sitting room and the bedchamber, wishing the drapes were open. Wishing, too, the night was a moonlit one. She looked her best in moonlight.

She moved to stand at the door, listening.

A shadow moved, alerting her. The earl wasn't asleep.

She smiled.

In silence, she began to unbutton her dress. Before taking it off, however, she'd bent to untie her shoes, slipping them from her feet. Her petticoat and corset were next. Slowly, she removed her stockings.

Clad only in her shift, she moved toward the bed, stretching out one hand to touch the edge of the mattress.

The strike of the match startled her. But not as much as the man staring back at her from the earl's bed.

Mr. Prender lit the lamp and smiled at her.

"You aren't the earl," she said.

"No," he said. "I'm not. For once, I'm rather glad not to be him. He's not here, but I am."

"You should have said something earlier."

"And miss the delightful sight of you disrobing? I think not."

She stood there, clad only in her best shift, the one that had taken her hours to embroider the roses around the neckline. The fabric was threadbare, revealing every single crevice and hollow. Her breasts pressed up against the worn linen, her nipples erect.

She should put on her dress again.

But she'd never seen anything as appreciative as the look on Mr. Prender's face, almost as if he were worshiping her.

"Come," he said, leaning forward.

He placed his hand on hers, tugging gently.

"I should leave, Mr. Prender."

"Call me Andrew," he said. "I'm not the earl, but I promise you'll not find me lacking."

The lamplight caught the glint in his eyes, and the wickedness of his smile.

Catriona placed one foot on the step.

A second later she was pulled onto the bed, tumbling over the mattress.

An annoying thing, a conscience. Just when it was supposed to sleep, it popped up again, shook its tail at him and dared him to ignore it. Right at the moment the damn thing was waving at him.

He shouldn't have sent Andrew after the girl.

Andrew was a cocksman, a term he'd used to describe himself. Catriona, for all her wiles, might be an innocent still. The situation could well be like sending a fox after a particularly succulent and full-breasted young hen.

Morgan had undressed for bed and was now in the process of dressing again.

Why should he be wary of any woman's machinations after Lillian? Instead, he should've remained in his bedchamber, just bid the little maid farewell and sent her back to her room. Or visited the housekeeper and had Catriona dismissed. That would've been the better alternative to cowering here in Andrew's room.

The accommodations were equal to those in his own suite. The furniture was polished to a sheen. The mattress was firm, without lumps. The sheets had been changed this morning and still smelled of the sun, and the pillows of rosemary.

His trousers donned, he stood looking out at the Highland night. How many times had he raced through the glen in the enchanted gloaming, feeling as if God had given him those extra hours to play?

Those days felt like a thousand years ago. Had he become so jaundiced and bitter over time?

A timid knock sounded at the door. He debated whether to pull on his shirt, then another knock sounded, this one not as reticent.

He opened the door, frowning.

The little wren stood on the other side of the door, her fist upraised as if to knock again.

Persistent little bird.

"What is it?" he asked.

She stared fixedly at his bare chest, her face going from pale to bright red.

If she hadn't wanted to see him half dressed, she shouldn't have knocked on his door at this hour. But then he realized that she wouldn't have known he was here.

Had she come in search of Andrew?

She looked stricken. "I apologize, Your Lordship." She looked away, down the hall, then resolutely back at him. "This isn't your room."

Now, she frowned at him, her cheeks pink, and her eyes narrowed.

He wondered if she knew how attractive she was with her pink cheeks and her flashing brown eyes.

She looked beyond him, taking in the room with a sweeping glance.

"Is my sister here?"

"What makes you think she's here?" he asked.

"Because you're here," she said. "Why are you here?" She peered beyond him once again.

Annoyed, he stepped to the side so she could see into the sitting room.

"Would you care to examine the bedchamber as well?"

To his surprise, she ducked around him and entered the room, marching toward the bedchamber as if intent on some holy mission.

She stood at the doorway, looking in, before turning to him in confusion.

"Where is she?"

"I can assure you she isn't here."

He folded his arms over his bare chest and watched her.

The little wren was agitated. Her hands twisted together, and she was biting her bottom lip.

"Where is Mr. Prender?" she asked.

"Why do you want to know? For that matter, why are you here?"

"I was going to ask your friend to go with me to the Laird's Tower."

He remained silent. His patience was rewarded a moment later.

"My sister has some idea of becoming your mistress, Your Lordship. I thought to dissuade her."

Her honesty surprised him.

"Am I too much an ogre to approach on your own?"

"It wouldn't look right," she said. "It wouldn't be proper."

He held his hands out. "Is this proper? Being alone with me now?"

Her eyes widened and she moved quickly toward the open door.

"What were you going to do, Jean? Interrupt us? If I am, like you think, a satyr, what success do you think Andrew would have of separating us? No doubt I would've spirited your sister away to my dark dungeon and had my way with her."

She stopped in mid-flight, her shoulders straightening. She turned, her frown still in place, the look in her eyes cold, as if she judged him in that moment and found him wanting.

"I never said you were a satyr, Your Lordship. What you think of yourself is your concern. I was merely worried about my sister."

"I don't think your worry is merited," he said. "Your sister is a grasping, greedy fool who would use anything—even her beauty—to get what she wants."

"Have you such a foul opinion of all women, Your Lordship?"

"Only about those who use their bodies in an attempt to manipulate others. Yes, I do."

"And you are, of course, a perfect being."

"I'm neither satyr nor perfect, Jean."

She turned as if to go. He wanted to say something to stop her. Why, he hadn't the slightest idea. Leave her to her ghost hunting, or her sister protecting, anything but bothering him.

"Where are you going?"

"If you're here in your friend's rooms, then it's because you've switched places." She turned back, her face a study in anger. "You knew, didn't you? Why else would you be here?"

"Perhaps I did know," he said, feeling his conscience sit up and wave to him again.

No, he'd been wrong. She wasn't angry. She was about to cry. Her face paled. Her hands were clutched together so tightly he could see each individual knuckle.

Again she turned to leave. To stop her, he reached out and touched her on the shoulder.

"Where are you going?"

"To the Laird's Tower," she said, her voice sounding choked.

"How long has she been gone?"

"I don't know," she said, wrapping her arms around herself. "An hour, perhaps two. Maybe even longer."

"It might be too late," he said, as kindly as he could. "Nature has a way of speeding up these things, especially if both parties are amenable to it."

"It isn't your friend she wants," she said with some asperity. "It's you."

"It's my title," he said. "And, no doubt, my wealth."

"Of course it is," she said, a little too quickly for his peace of mind. If he had been plain Mr. MacCraig, laboring in a Glasgow factory, surely some woman would have seen his merit.

"Fine," he said, grabbing his shirt. "I'll come with you."

He was donning one sleeve when he realized something was wrong. Jean was utterly still. Not one word emerged from her.

He turned his head to see the housekeeper, accompanied by four other people, standing in the hallway, staring at him.

Not a damn thing came to mind.

He was still bare from the waist up. His shoes and socks had been removed earlier. He looked, for all the world, like someone who had just risen from his bed and donned his trousers in an act of semi-modesty. Exactly what he'd done, except his bed had not been shared.

Mrs. MacDonald's face was a thundercloud on an already dark horizon.

"This isn't what it appears," he said.

Mrs. MacDonald didn't respond either by gesture or word. He'd never been as repudiated by silence as at this moment. Not even in London had he been so thoroughly rebuffed.

"I think, madam, you misunderstand the situation," he said.

A quick desperate look from Jean silenced him. Evidently, she didn't want him to announce the reason for her presence here. She'd rather be considered a harlot than cast aspersions on Catriona.

He doubted if it would concern Catriona overmuch, as long as she achieved her aims.

Perhaps Andrew had some gentlemanly instincts and would leave the girl alone. Morgan quickly pushed that thought aside—Andrew had never demonstrated any restraint in regard to women—and directed his attention to the farce before him.

* * *

Truly, this was not happening. She was sleeping, and dreaming of a disaster that had befallen her.

From the moment the earl had returned to Ballindair, her life had changed, become a disaster of monumental proportions.

He stepped closer, reminding her that this situation was all too real.

When was he going to put on his shirt? Jean noticed that Fiona was much too interested in the earl's physique, and Aunt Mary was frowning at his bare chest.

The two footmen, David and Tom, were looking at her with more interest than they'd ever expressed. She had the feeling she'd be garnering a great deal of attention from the male staff after this debacle.

A loose woman was fair game.

She couldn't meet Aunt Mary's eyes.

"I'm waiting for an explanation," her aunt said.

What on earth should she say? The truth might make the situation worse than it was. Or could it get any worse?

She wasn't going to lie again. Silence was her only recourse, and when she lifted her eyes to her aunt, the disappointment on the other woman's face made her stomach clench.

"Go to your room, Jean," Aunt Mary said. "With your leave, of course, Your Lordship." By her words, she was indicating she knew there was an illicit relationship between Jean and the earl.

When he only nodded, it was acknowledgment of that fact.

Jean left the room, so ensnared by a lie she wondered if she'd ever cut herself free.

At the staircase, she hesitated, wondering if she should go on to the Laird's Tower. She'd already caused one disaster tonight. Let Catriona be responsible for her own actions.

Once in her room, she readied for bed, but couldn't sleep. Catriona hadn't yet returned.

When she came in, two hours later, Jean lit their taper and stared at her sister. Catriona's lips were swollen and there were two marks on her face, one at her chin and the other higher up on her cheek.

She knew, without asking—and how did anyone ask that kind of question?—that her sister was no longer virtuous. Had she ever been?

She blew out the taper without saying a word.

Chapter 12

RULES FOR STAFF: *Any staff member who notes egregious behavior or behavior in violation of these rules is honor bound to report it to the housekeeper, majordomo, or steward.*

Mary MacDonald had been employed at Ballindair for eleven years. For eleven years she'd given good service. Excellent service, some would say. She'd prided herself on the appearance of Ballindair as if it were her own home. No, more than that. As if the Queen would visit at any moment.

She'd only employed the finest young women, those with an eye to a future at Ballindair. When a maid didn't do her tasks as instructed, she was retrained. If a footman eyed the silver, he was sent to work in the stables. If she caught wind of fraternization, she stopped it immediately, ensuring the two involved knew she wouldn't tolerate any such behavior.

She had completely and totally missed the viper in her own nest.

She walked into William Seath's office and stared at the steward seated behind his desk. Whatever wasting sickness he had was not getting better. But he wouldn't speak of it, even when he returned from his visits to the physician.

"What is it, Mrs. MacDonald?" he asked.

"Nothing of import," she said, changing her mind. Jean was her problem and she'd have to figure out what to do about it on her own. "I merely came to wish you good morning."

He put down his pen, leaned back in his chair and regarded her with solemnity.

"Is it about the scene last night?"

"You know?"

He smiled, the amused expression odd on his gaunt face.

"A great many people have stopped by my office this morning, each one wishing to impart the news. Besides, I've known you all these years, and not once have you ever come to wish me good morning."

He motioned to the chair in front of the desk, and she considered it for a moment before moving to sit.

Had he always been so stubborn? Perhaps that's why he was at his desk every day, despite the fact he was ill.

She sat on the edge of the chair, placing one hand flat against the surface of the desk to steady herself.

"I've come for advice," she said. "And I don't know what to do."

Then she proceeded to tell him the whole shocking story.

Mrs. MacDonald had requested time to speak with him on this sunny afternoon. Morgan granted her a few moments, thinking she'd come to apologize for her actions the night before.

After Jean had left, Mrs. MacDonald stared him down as if he'd been guilty of assault. He was so uncomfortable, he'd deliberately not spoken, merely donned his shirt.

"Your Lordship," she'd finally said, inclining her head as if she found him beneath contempt. She turned then, and the other three followed her like ducklings down the hall.

He'd nearly slammed the door after them, thought better of it and merely closed it.

Now, Mrs. MacDonald stared down at the floor. Just when he thought the woman had come to the library to act as a statue, she looked up him, her eyes, surprisingly, brimming with tears.

"Did you know Jean was my niece, Your Lordship?"

"No, I didn't, Mrs. MacDonald. Which means, of course, Catriona is as well?"

She nodded. "I didn't share that fact with anyone, Your Lordship, but secrets have a way of being known, regardless. But I'll have none say I treat either of them differently from the rest."

He kept silent, wondering at her point.

"Jean's a good girl, Your Lordship. Anyone would have told you that. I would have no harm come to either of them, either to their persons, or to their reputation. I run a decent household at Ballindair. None of my maids are allowed to fraternize with the men employed here. Only one girl has ever left Ballindair in a family way, and it was a great shame. I'll not have it happen again."

"Nothing happened last night, Mrs. MacDonald."

But the housekeeper wasn't listening.

"How was I to know, Your Lordship, that Jean's greatest danger would come from the very man we all labor so diligently to serve?"

Now she was veering a little too close to the edge.

"That will be all, Mrs. MacDonald."

"No, sir."

"No?" he said, sitting back in his chair and folding his arms. When had he lost the respect of his staff?

When he'd appeared bare-chested with a tearful maid in Andrew's rooms.

The thought sounded as if it had been uttered in his father's voice.

"When I came to work at Ballindair, Your Lordship," Mrs. MacDonald was saying, "I was pleased beyond all measure."

"And now you don't feel the same?"

She could always be replaced, she and her troublesome nieces.

"Your father was a man well loved throughout Scotland, Your Lordship. It was a pleasure to serve him."

The inference being, of course, that it wasn't as enjoyable to be in his employ.

"Nothing happened, Mrs. MacDonald," he said. His body felt as stiff as if it were coated in iron. "Your niece's virtue is still intact, I can assure you."

She heaved a great sigh, one that stirred her plenteous bosom. Slowly, she nodded, then raised her head to look at him directly.

"You may know that, your Lordship. So might Jean. I might even come to believe it. But no one else will. From this moment on, Jean will be the subject of gossip and laughter. No good man will have her."

"A situation not of my making, Mrs. MacDonald." Damn it, he hadn't done anything. "What would you have me do, Mrs. MacDonald? Marry the chit? Make a decent woman out of her?"

Her eyes never wavered from his.

"Exactly that, Your Lordship."

"You can't be serious." He sat up straight, placing both hands on the blotter before him.

"Jean's father was a respected physician. Her mother was my sister. We have distant connections to a baron, and my great-grandfather was cousin to an earl."

"I haven't any desire to hear your ancestry, Mrs. MacDonald. It doesn't make a whit of difference to me. Are you not aware of my own history?"

"Your divorce?" she asked, whispering the word.

"Exactly."

She looked down at the floor again. "In all honesty, Your Lordship, I would have had Jean marry a man of honor, one with less shame in his past. But I don't have a choice. People will treat her differently from this moment. They'll think her without morals or dignity."

He forced a smile to his face. "Marrying me wouldn't make her less a pariah, Mrs. MacDonald, but more of one."

She drew herself up, clasped her hands in front of her, her face frozen into a frown.

"You have a title, Your Lordship. And wealth. It would go toward making her situation bearable."

Surprised at her honesty, he studied her. Was that sort of directness a family trait?

"It would make her a decent woman before the world. Anyone would excuse her actions as a sign of anticipation of the marriage. But without a marriage, she'll be labeled a slattern."

He didn't have a thing to say to that impassioned argument. Did she know about Catriona? What was the solution there? Andrew was already married.

She bent her head. "I thought you would answer as you have, Your Lordship. I know your father was a man of honor."

The inference being he wasn't. She dared too much, but it seemed she wasn't finished.

"I know reputation means nothing to you, so I've given Jean a choice, Your Lordship. To leave your employ entirely, or to seek a position at one of your other properties. Mr. Seath says I can send her to Glasgow."

She smiled, a strange expression after insulting him.

Without another word, she turned and left him. He raised his hand, as if to command her to return, then realized the housekeeper wouldn't change her words.

It was what she believed.

It was what the whole of Scotland believed. The Earl of Denbleigh was a man of dishonor. To hell with wanting some decency in his own life, and a wife who didn't tumble every man within scenting distance.

He stared at the closed door long enough to see the carved panels long after he shut his eyes. How dare his housekeeper use words like "honor" to him. How dare she imply he had to make an honest woman of Jean.

Nothing had happened. The girl would weather the storm well enough. In a few days people would forget what they'd seen.

And if they didn't?

How many times had friends turned their backs on him? How many invitations had been carefully withdrawn? How many people were suddenly not at home?

Would a society comprised of maids, footmen, and gardeners be any more forgiving? He doubted it.

Would he willingly wish that on another human being? A woman who hunted ghosts and had tried to protect her sister? *Damn it.*

Mrs. MacDonald had the temerity to address him in this room, of all rooms, where he'd stood in front of this very desk as a supplicant too many times, ready to disappoint again.

The irony of the moment wasn't lost on him.

Jean was a maid. Yet her father had been a physician. If they'd met at another time, another place, a match might have been made between them.

He didn't want to marry ever again. He didn't want to have anything to do with women. Especially one who manipulated a situation to her own advantage. But Jean hadn't, he thought.

She'd come to seek help from Andrew, not realizing they'd changed rooms.

Why the hell had he ever suggested that idiotic plan? Who was the manipulator in this situation? The housekeeper, of course, but was she pushing him to do what she considered the "honorable thing" in order to gain some kind of reward herself? Or merely to protect Jean?

Jean wasn't beautiful. She wouldn't turn men's heads. She wouldn't make a man stare at her when she walked into the room. She hunted ghosts. She read books.

Would she be faithful? That was the question, wasn't it?

No, he wasn't even going to consider it.

Chapter 13

The rain, so fine it was a mist, wet Jean's face and curled her hair.

In the spring, cheerful yellow daffodils lined the paths around Ballindair, their heads bobbing in greeting. Now, only mulch remained, and she missed the sight of the flowers. Someone had thought to place a few backless, rough hewn benches along the walk, but she ignored those in favor of approaching the edge of the pond. Herons stood in patches in the shallows, ignoring her. Feeding the pond was the River Tullie, burbling down a miniature waterfall and providing the sounds of the day.

She turned toward the west, where the sun would be if it wasn't hiding behind the clouds. The avenue here was lined with copper beech trees, their leaves shivering in the wet.

In the winter the trees would be festooned with icicles. The entire panorama of Ballindair was magical then. One winter morning she'd awakened and stared out at the frozen countryside in awe. In that moment, only months ago, she was struck speechless by the beauty before her. The despair of the past year had been erased by the sight of the crystal decorations on the trees, and the pure white snow.

On that morning, she fell in love with the castle. And, now, she had to leave.

Aunt Mary had sent her outside, to walk off her misery. She was given a choice: to move to another of the earl's properties or to try to find work elsewhere. Whatever her decision, she'd be separated from the only family she had left—Catriona and Aunt Mary. Hardly fair, since she'd done nothing wrong.

But she'd seen the look of speculation in the men's eyes that night in Mr. Prender's room, and all this week. She didn't want that kind of attention.

Nor did she want to leave Ballindair.

Jean turned and began to walk, away from Ballindair's manicured beauty and into the wilder areas around the castle, stopping only when she came to Strath Dalross.

The sky was gray, the color of an old woman's hair and her own mood. Clouds hugged the top of the mountains, as if wishing to be earthbound.

The valley was wide, the walls of earth high. Halfway up the side of the hill sat Dalross Kirk, a long rectangular building with a slate roof and a view of the village farther to her west. The lone tree was the sole living thing near the kirk. The only other neighbors were the inhabitants of the churchyard.

This bend of the river, sometimes shallow, occasionally deep, curved through the basin of the strath. Gray and black rounded boulders sat at the bend of the river, as if offering a place for a picnic—nature's banquet hall. On either side fertile ground supported both animals and crops. Or would have if the previous earl had allowed it.

She stood for a moment, closing her eyes, listening to the river tumble over the rocks, smelling the sweet scent of the heather and feeling as if her heart were being squeezed.

She turned and began to slowly walk back to Ballindair, uncomfortable within the shadow of the kirk.

Had the builders thought to place the church just so, as warning to any who would act in a sinful manner? The minister would say she'd been a sinner indeed. Perhaps not for the deeds she'd performed as much as her thoughts.

Twice now she'd seen Morgan MacCraig almost naked. Well, once naked and once half naked. Her mind had mentally stripped him of his trousers, and he was standing there just as he had that day in the bath.

What kind of woman was she? She was shameful, loose. Nor was Catriona any better. Why, then, had she been singled out as a harlot and not her sister? Everyone evidently felt the same, or they wouldn't be avoiding her with such assiduousness.

The thunder sounded like God's displeasure. Would he send a bolt of lightning to purify her? To strip thoughts of the earl from her mind?

She'd heard of a farmer once, who'd been struck by lightning and survived, but his wits had been addled from then on. Is that what God wished for her, to scrub the sight of the Earl of Denbleigh from her memory?

For a week no one had spoken to her except Catriona, and her sister's remarks were cutting. Once Catriona heard that she and the earl had been caught in a compromising position, she lost no time in letting her know exactly what she thought of all her many lectures.

The one time she'd tried to explain, Catriona cut her off.

"Oh, Jean, you will say anything now to save yourself. It's evident you had your eye on the earl from the very beginning."

Had she?

Had she been concerned about Catriona's reputation that night? Or had she wanted to keep the earl for herself?

Perhaps she deserved to be sent from Ballindair.

Were there any convents left in Scotland? Would they accept a penitent Presbyterian?

At least she'd been spared the sight of the earl for a week.

But how could she bear to leave Ballindair?

Rather than being tossed out without a job or a recommendation, she'd been given the choice to work at the great house at Dumgoyne. Not the measure of Ballindair, to be sure, but the residence of the manager of the Dumgoyne Mac-Craig Distillery. She'd be a housekeeper to a staff of seven. A promotion, Mr. Seath had told her.

She knew she hardly merited a promotion, any more than she deserved being sent from Ballindair. No more ghost hunting. No more feeling of being home, just when she needed a place to anchor herself.

No more Earl of Denbleigh.

She wrapped her cloak around her, miserable and alone.

William Seath's path had been charted from the time he was a young man and had first come to Ballindair, falling in love with the castle in a way that startled him even then. Familiarity had only encouraged his affinity for Ballindair. Over the years, he'd grown more appreciative of the original builders and architects, and those Earls of Denbleigh who had built onto the structure.

He thought of himself as a captain, of sorts, sailing the ship of Ballindair through choppy waters and onto a placid sea. Whatever needed to be done at the seat of the Earls of Denbleigh, he'd somehow accomplished.

Now he saw the horizon, and knew he would have to relinquish his tasks to a man ill-prepared for them. Morgan MacCraig didn't lack the intelligence to care for his own property. Quite the opposite. The man had a mind for weighty matters. He'd worked at the MacCraig distilleries, increasing their profits, establishing new work rules, making a name for himself as a fair and equitable employer. But then politics had taken his fancy, and they'd lost the earl to London.

William wondered if they'd ever get Morgan MacCraig back.

Soon, the earl would need to assume sole responsibility for Ballindair. So far, however, Morgan had failed in each test he'd given him. Take the figures he'd sent the man last week. Not once had the earl challenged him on the tally of the sums, even though he'd deliberately made more than one error. Not once had His Lordship asked about the expenditures. The cost of seed, for example, was outrageous. The man would throw away his entire fortune if he were not educated.

And educate him he would, even if Morgan MacCraig fought him all the way.

The day was gray, the sky the color of a pigeon's belly, the low hanging branches sodden with rain. Even the air felt wet as Morgan breathed deeply, grateful to have escaped Ballindair for the moment.

The service he'd received from his staff for the last week had been excellent, as it had been since he arrived at Ballindair. But the ever present, accusatory atmosphere was beginning to annoy him.

Mrs. MacDonald had not repeated her entreaty for him to act with honor. Nor had his steward mentioned the matter. Each person who served him did so perfectly, but he was being driven to madness by silence.

Even Andrew, the most voluble of companions, was oddly

quiet. Nor had Andrew bragged of his conquest with the little blonde once.

Truth be told, he hadn't divulged what happened in his room to Andrew, either. He'd done nothing wrong. He'd instigated nothing. All he had been guilty of, if guilt could label his actions, was avoiding Catriona. He should have simply sent her away.

Nor had he been bothered by Catriona since that night. She didn't come to his door, she didn't smile in his direction, and she didn't lie in wait for him in the corridor. In other words, life at Ballindair was damn near bucolic.

Then why was he so dissatisfied?

Twice, he'd found himself in the Long Gallery after midnight. No ghosts were there. Neither was Jean. She was nowhere to be found.

The wren had flown away.

She was leaving. That was simply idiotic. Given enough time, people would simply forget the matter.

As well as they'd forgotten his divorce?

A black-cloaked figure slipped from behind a bush, heading toward him on the graveled path. He stopped, waiting, knowing who it was before she noticed him and hesitated.

He crossed the few steps between them, wanting to ask her where she'd been for a week. Had she deliberately been hiding from him? Was she happy to be going away?

Instead, he stood in front of her and asked, "Are there any ghosts out here?"

A stupid question, and one not worthy of an answer, but he received one anyway.

"No, Your Lordship," she said, her voice low.

That was all. Just one comment, and she retreated into silence.

Bloody hell.

"You're soaked."

She didn't say anything.

"Shall I have your death of pneumonia on my conscience as well?"

He wished she'd push the cowl back so he could see her features. She was only a shadow, a ghost of herself, a wraith come to wordlessly chastise him.

"You needn't worry about me, Your Lordship. I absolve you of any responsibility for my welfare."

Had she always been so mocking?

She turned and walked some distance away, following the gravel path. The rain was coming in earnest now, the hem of her cloak dragging against the stones. He ignored his own discomfort and followed her.

"Why are you here?" he asked. "Why aren't you cleaning something?"

She turned to stare at him.

"Have you turned housekeeper now, Your Lordship? Do you truly care where all your maids are?"

He didn't know how to answer the question, since he'd only ever wondered about one maid, tart-tongued and intriguing as she was.

"I've been given the day," she said. "I'm leaving Ballindair tomorrow."

Bloody hell.

"Where are you going?"

When she told him, he frowned. "A distance away."

"I believe that's the intention, Your Lordship."

"Do you want to go?"

She walked away, and once more he followed her.

"Well?" he asked.

"I don't have a choice, Your Lordship."

"You always have a choice."

She turned to face him, pushing back her cowl. "No, Your Lordship, you don't."

"Why haven't you married?" he asked.

"Am I required to answer such personal questions?"

Her irritation pleased him, somehow. It was better than that damnable sadness of hers, which shielded her better than her rain-soaked cloak.

"In this instance, yes," he said.

She shook her head and turned away.

"Is there anyone you fancy?"

"You've asked me before, Your Lordship. The answer is the same. It's none of your concern."

Strange, but it felt like his concern.

Her hair was a jumble of curls around her face. The color on her cheeks, the mist clinging to her eyelashes, transformed her from plain to startlingly lovely. He was unprepared for her transformation.

"Your aunt says I should do the proper thing by you," he said, surprising himself by admitting that.

"What does my aunt wish you to do?"

"She hasn't told you?"

She shook her head, dislodging some of those curls. He wanted to reach over and loosen the rest of them, let them flow around her shoulders, take one and pull it until it was stretched as long as it would go, then wind it around his finger.

His experience with women, however, dictated he not touch her coiffure. Lillian had hated him to "mess her."

"What does my aunt want you to do?" she asked again.

Emotion sparkled in her brown eyes, color deepened on her cheeks.

"You've no idea?" he asked, feeling remarkably refreshed at the moment. No doubt it was the rain.

She shook her head.

He smiled. "Don't stay out too much longer. You'll grow chilled."

"Are you my keeper, Your Lordship?"

"Yes," he said slowly. "I do believe I am."

He strode to her and before she could say a word grabbed her arms, pulled her close, and placed his mouth on hers. A startled gasp was her only response. Her lips were cool, full, enchanted. He angled his head and deepened the kiss, placing his palms on either side of her jaw. Not to hold her immobile as much as to simply feel her.

If he was going to be excoriated for being devoid of honor, let it be based in fact. Let him do the very worst thing he possibly could, come upon a defenseless woman on the grounds of his estate, someone who was dependent upon him for employment. Let him kiss her until her lips grew warm and pliant, until they fell open beneath his gentle assault.

Let him pull back and stare at her in wonder.

He turned and left her while he still had some honor left.

Yet as Morgan walked away, he couldn't keep from smiling.

Chapter 14

RULES FOR STAFF: *Never, under any conditions, offer your opinion to your betters.*

Mary MacDonald was startled to see the Earl of Denbleigh standing in the doorway of the storeroom.

She motioned with one hand for the two maids with her to curtsy quickly, and did so herself.

"Your Lordship," she said, wondering why he'd sought her out.

Before she'd met with the earl, she worried that the options she and Mr. Seath had devised would be too onerous. The earl would bridle at the suggestion of marriage. Worse, Mary knew he might dismiss her, and where would she be then? Unable to help either Jean or Catriona or a score of other young maids who stood between their families and starvation.

But he hadn't dismissed her. Neither had he agreed to her shocking suggestion, leaving her no choice but to find another position for Jean. It worked out in the end, though, hadn't it?

Jean would be elevated to housekeeper, and far enough away from Ballindair that she wouldn't be a temptation for the earl.

Now he stood there, smiling amiably, but appearances weren't to be trusted. A garden snake could still strike.

"Have you a moment, Mrs. MacDonald?" he asked.

"Of course, Your Lordship."

"Then attend me in the library, if you will." He consulted his pocket watch. "In ten minutes' time."

She nodded, suddenly terrified.

"Yes, Your Lordship."

She watched as he left, took a deep breath and turned to the two maids.

"I will be checking your figures," she said. "Be sure and count correctly." The two girls nodded.

Mary went to her room as swiftly as decorum would allow, checked her collar and cuffs, patted her hair into place, and tried to lessen the red of her cheeks by use of a cold compress. After consulting her brooch watch, she made it to the library with two minutes to spare, but didn't knock until exactly ten minutes had passed.

Instead of sitting at the massive desk, the earl was pacing in front of the wall of windows. She knew better than to speak, so she stood there, her fear growing with each agitated second.

Was he going to dismiss her? Was he going to dismiss the girls? Or was he going to dismiss all of them? She had a little money put away, some savings for her old age. But it wasn't enough for a cottage, not yet.

She'd spoken her mind after a lifetime of keeping silent. Worse, she'd implied that he was lacking. She closed her eyes, said a quick prayer, and when she opened them, the earl had stopped, turned, and was regarding her with narrowed eyes.

"Where was Jean born?" he asked.

Surprised, she answered, "In Inverness, Your Lordship. She lived there all her life before coming to Ballindair."

He nodded, crossed his arms and turned away. Evidently, he preferred the view of the rainy gardens to looking at her.

She'd often done the same, especially when giving bad news to one of her staff.

Her stomach hurt. She chewed on her bottom lip, then forced herself to calm. It would do no good to let the earl know how frightened she was. She'd done what was right, what she and Mr. Seath had decided must be done.

"And her father? You said he was a physician."

Oh dear, he wasn't going to continue that line of questioning.

"Jean and Catriona's parents were fine people," she said. "She's an orphan now, though."

"Like me," he said, staring out at the view.

"Yes," she said. "If you don't mind, Your Lordship, why do you wish to know these things?"

He turned and studied her for a moment. "I should know something about my bride-to-be, don't you think?"

She wanted to weep with relief and the sudden easing of the pain in her stomach.

"You'll do the right thing, then, Your Lordship?"

He turned away again.

"I haven't the slightest idea what the right thing is, Mrs. MacDonald. You may have condemned your niece to a lifetime of misery with me."

The alternative wasn't palatable, either.

Jean had always had a level head, until the earl came home. Since then everything she'd done had been a disaster, witness the episode in Mr. Prender's room.

Sending her away might have solved one problem, but it had seemed too great a price for a foolish girl to pay.

Now, Mary could only nod, a gesture that surprisingly caused the earl to smile. Had she amused him?

"Tell your niece it will be a quick wedding. Within the week, I think."

She nodded again, beyond grateful. "Thank you, Your Lordship."

"Time will only tell, Mrs. MacDonald, if you should feel any gratitude at all."

She wondered if she should leave. For several long moments he didn't address her at all, merely stood there at the window. Just when she was about to ask him if she should retire, he turned and faced her once more.

"It is the honorable thing to do, isn't it, Mrs. MacDonald?"

She sank into as deep a curtsy as she could manage, and when she rose again, she smiled at him. "Yes, Your Lordship. It's the honorable thing to do."

"Then God help us all."

Jean wanted to run as far and as fast from Ballindair as she could. She wanted to escape, and now, before the pressure in her chest grew so fierce her heart exploded.

Instead, she stood there, the words reverberating in her ears.

"You're to marry the Earl of Denbleigh."

Had Aunt Mary actually said those words? She must have imagined them.

"Have you nothing to say?" her aunt finally asked. "You're to marry the Earl of Denbleigh."

She hadn't imagined them, then.

Jean shook her head.

Aunt Mary's smile melted into a frown.

"I'm disappointed, Jean. I would have thought you'd be pleased at the circumstances."

Jean couldn't breathe. She pressed both hands against her chest and forced herself to calm.

"He's an earl. I can't marry an earl. I'm a maid," she added, and had the most incredible urge to giggle. Was her aunt daft?

Aunt Mary advanced on her, stopping only when their skirts touched. Her frown faded, replaced by a gentle expression, her brown eyes warming.

"Jean, you're the equal of any woman he might find to marry."

She shook her head. "He's an earl, Aunt."

"He may have a title, but I'd have you marry a better man. Still, the title and his wealth will have to compensate."

"Because of his divorce?"

Her aunt looked surprised. "You knew?"

She nodded. "He told me himself."

Aunt Mary sighed. "Evidently, he did not like the way his wife behaved. There are some legal remedies for men, my dear. If a wife does not comport herself with propriety, a man can dissolve the marriage."

Confused, Jean stared at her. "What did she do?" And what guarantee was there she wouldn't do exactly the same?

Her aunt didn't answer. What she did say, however, had Jean's heart beating violently again.

"The marriage will take place in three days."

The tip of her nose was cold. What an odd feeling. She touched it with trembling fingers, then concentrated on this absurd meeting in her aunt's suite of rooms.

Her trunk was packed for her departure tomorrow. She'd been told what time to appear at the entrance to Ballindair, and a plethora of information she'd memorized and didn't need now.

"Did you hear me, Jean?"

"Is this real, Aunt?" she asked.

Her aunt gently took her arm and led her to a chair. She sat, heavily, staring at the carpet.

"You'll be married in three days' time, my dear. If you have any objections to Wednesday, please let me know now."

"I can't marry the earl," Jean said in a remarkably calm voice. She wasn't trembling at all.

Perhaps she was a ghost, and everything around her only a diorama someone had arranged for her spectral amusement.

The frown was back on her aunt's face.

"Of course you can," she said. "You must. There is no other avenue open for you, Jean."

"I was the one who went to his room, Aunt."

The frown was now a thundercloud. "Do you think I don't know that? I'm well aware of your behavior, Jean. But he is doing the honorable thing. If nothing else, this marriage will restore his tarnished honor."

"I can't marry an earl."

"You're the daughter of a respected physician and my sister. You are the equal of any woman the earl might have married and no doubt superior to the one he did."

"I have to tell him who I am. I can't marry him as Jean MacDonald."

Her aunt abruptly sat on the chair opposite Jean.

"You cannot tell him."

They looked at each other.

A moment later her aunt sat back in the chair, staring up at the ceiling as if the answer was written in the plaster.

"We are once and truly caught, then," she said. "If you don't marry him, he'll demand to know why. If we tell him, he'll dismiss the three of us."

"And if I do marry him, it won't be a true marriage."

Her aunt sat forward. "Perhaps you're wrong about that. Perhaps it doesn't matter your name as much as your person."

She blinked at her aunt, who waved her hand in the air as if to dismiss the legalities.

"It's not as if you were a man," she said. "Your name is going to change regardless. What does it matter what it is now?"

That didn't sound right, but her aunt, having decided that her name was of no importance, refused to hear differently.

"I can't be married without telling him, Aunt Mary. I can't be married as Jean MacDonald. The marriage won't be valid. I'll be engaging in sin, which is the very reason you want me to marry the earl in the first place, so people won't think I'm a sinner." A strangled giggle trembled on her lips.

Aunt Mary stood. "I am the first person to demand the truth, Jean. I've lived my life with integrity. But I'm practical as well. Because of what your father did, you and Catriona might never find a man willing to marry either of you. I believe we should consider this circumstance a blessing."

"I have to tell him."

"I took a chance putting you on Ballindair's staff, Jean. I never even informed Mr. Seath of your past. If you insist on telling the earl, he'll not go through with the marriage, and we could all be in jeopardy."

Before she could truly understand what was happening, Aunt Mary whisked her out of her suite and to the family wing, where she stood in front of a set of double doors.

"The Countess's Suite," Aunt Mary said, throwing open the doors. "You'll be the first countess to occupy it in thirty years."

Bemused, Jean followed her inside.

"Didn't the earl's wife live here?"

"She never came to Scotland."

Jean stood in the sitting room, the space feeling heavy, as if the very air disapproved of her. Her gaze noted the various blue-and-white urns, the rose upholstered sofa and chairs, the oversized mahogany tables.

Two weeks ago she'd collided with the Earl of Denbleigh, and now she was to be his bride? What kind of place was Ballindair? When she'd first seen the castle, she thought it enchanted, and perhaps it was.

She couldn't marry Morgan MacCraig.

"I'd rather go to Dumgoyne," she said.

"If you do," her aunt said, "you'll be a servant forever. Is that what you want for yourself? Think carefully, Jean."

"To be a servant, or a woman living in sin, are those my choices?"

"It was more than you had before," her aunt said. "I cannot make the decision for you, Jean. I agree that these circumstances are unusual, perhaps even shocking. But your father's actions condemned you to a half-life. This situation at least gives you a chance to live your life fully."

Without waiting for Jean's response, her aunt sailed out of the room, leaving her alone.

Jean walked to the window, pushing aside the rose patterned draperies, and stared down at the ornamental garden. If she married the earl, she'd never have to be a maid again. But, more importantly, she wouldn't have to leave Ballindair.

She'd be a wife. He'd be her husband. That magnificent, arrogant, irritating, charming, intelligent man would be her husband. Or her pretend husband.

They were a pair, weren't they? The earl who'd divorced his wife, and the maid who hid her past. Perhaps they deserved each other.

She turned and surveyed her surroundings. The tiny chamber she shared with Catriona could fit into the sitting room four times.

Some people would say the most wonderful wish of all had been granted her. A chance to change her life, even if it was based on a lie.

The painting above the fireplace, no doubt of Morgan's

mother, showed a woman with light brown hair and dark blue eyes, a smile curving her lips and her gaze brimming with happiness. What would the countess have said to her?

Go away. Who do you think you are, to become the Countess of Denbleigh?

Yet the earl was not perfect. He'd stood up in church, said his vows, then turned his back on them. Did he think to make up for betraying one set of vows by taking another or by marrying a maid?

Perhaps they were both to be faulted for considering this marriage.

"Is it true?" Catriona asked, suddenly appearing in the doorway.

Her sister was out of breath, her hair askew and her face pink. Had she learned of the news and raced up the stairs to verify it?

"Everyone says you're to be married to the earl. Is it true?"

Jean made her decision in that second. She nodded.

Catriona entered the room. "Aren't you the sly one. I gave you the idea, didn't I?" Her eyes narrowed. "And you, all prim and proper, seduced him."

Jean walked to her sister and stared her down. "Even for you, Catriona, that was an idiotic remark."

"What do you mean, even for me?"

"You haven't demonstrated your intelligence up until now. If you hadn't gone to the Laird's Tower, I wouldn't have had to seek Mr. Prender's assistance."

"Andrew never said he saw you."

"He didn't," Jean said, frustrated beyond belief with her sister. "Since when are you calling him Andrew?"

"Since you're marrying the Earl of Denbleigh."

The two of them glared at each other.

Catriona looked away a moment later. "I don't have to be

a maid any longer. There, that's all I truly wanted. However it came about, I'm happy enough."

No, Catriona would be happier if she were the one becoming a countess. Frankly, so would she. But was that entirely true? Did she want Catriona to marry the earl?

Her stomach fluttered and she pressed her hands against her waist.

"Does he know who we are?" Catriona asked, glancing toward the open door.

Jean shook her head.

Catriona nodded, as if satisfied. "I'll have to go and pick out a room," she said. "I think it should be in the family quarters, don't you? I'm going to be the Earl of Denbleigh's sister-in-law." She glanced down at herself, giving her uniform a look of hatred. "And I shall need a new wardrobe as well. Have we anyone at Ballindair who can do hair?"

She loved her sister, she truly did, but there were times when Catriona stretched her patience so thin she could read through it.

While Catriona was still planning, Jean left the room. She didn't want to see anyone or talk to anyone, or answer any questions. A few minutes later she found herself in the Long Gallery.

The day was cloudy; shadows shrouding the room. She sat on the same bench where she'd sat the night she talked to the earl.

What did she know about being a countess? For that matter, what did she know about being a wife?

What would her parents say to see her elevation to a countess?

You were raised with good manners and all the graces, my dear, her father might have said. *An earl would be blessed to have you as his wife.*

Her mother, on the other hand, would've done everything in her power to learn as much as she could about the duties of countess, and educate her for her new role.

She missed her mother dreadfully, had missed her even before her actual death. Pain had taken the gentle woman away, the constant smile turning to tight lips, and the patient understanding to stoic endurance.

Until that last year, when illness stripped her of any peaceful moments, her mother had been the spirit, and perhaps the soul, of their family.

How could she possibly act the same in this marriage? How could she see the good on even the darkest days? How could she support her husband and nurture any children that might come to them?

How could she be a wife, let alone a countess, when it was all too evident she was being used by the Earl of Denbleigh to atone for his past sins?

For that reason, and that reason alone, she was to be married. And not a real marriage, at that, which was her sin.

Was ever a bride as miserable as she?

Chapter 15

"**H**ave you lost your Scottish mind?" Andrew said, putting down his paintbrush and staring at Morgan. "You're an earl. Earls don't marry maids."

Earls don't divorce, either, but Morgan didn't make that comment.

Instead, he said, "She was employed as a maid out of necessity. Her father was an educated man and her mother comes from good stock."

"Good God, Morgan, you make her sound like a horse."

"I wouldn't be the first one to liken the marriage mart to a stable full of mares."

"Then if you have a yen to get married, go to Edinburgh, find yourself a wife there. Or London."

Andrew reached for something in his wooden box. At least the weather was allowing him to paint. The sun was a bright orb in a semicloudy day. Knowing the Highlands, it would rain again soon. Summer was accompanied by enough wet days to last them all year.

"Oh, I'm certain all the mamas would parade their virtuous young daughters in front of me," Morgan said. "God knows I would be a catch."

Andrew didn't say a word. What could he say?

He walked closer to Andrew's composition, wondering what the squiggles and lines would be when the painting was finished. He knew well enough, from past experience, not to ask.

Andrew had chosen his spot well, however. The river glinted in the distance, a shimmer of light in the vee between the hills.

"This might well be the last time I have the opportunity to marry," he said. "Besides, she's an agreeable woman."

A rather entertaining spectacle—Andrew in shock. Perhaps he should do it more often. The only other time he could remember his friend looking stunned was the day he announced his decision to divorce Lillian.

Andrew shook his head. "You can't do this," he said. "Are you ready to fall even more in society's estimation?"

"Is that even possible?"

"Is it love?" Andrew asked. "Are you in love with the girl? If that's the case, Morgan, then simply bed her and be done with it. You don't have to offer her marriage. You'll be elevating a maid to a countess."

He'd already explained Jean's background, and for Andrew to harp on the fact annoyed him. Nor was he about to confess that she fascinated him. He wanted to know how her mind worked.

She lightened him somehow, and maybe he could ask her exactly what it was about her that made him feel so free and boyish in her presence.

"My honor isn't so tarnished as to bed a woman dependent upon me for her livelihood." Morgan looked at his friend. "And I'd prefer if you left my maids alone."

Andrew's eyebrow arched. "Would you? Is that an order, Morgan? Is that how it is between us now? You, the mighty earl, giving me orders. Tell me, do I unquestioningly obey you?"

"Evidently not," Morgan said. "Is it Jean's sister? The little blonde?"

"Catriona."

At least Andrew knew the girl's name. He turned, ready to head back to Ballindair, wishing he'd not felt the need to tell Andrew of his decision.

"You're not your father, Morgan."

He glanced over his shoulder at Andrew.

"All your life, you tried to be your father. When it's obvious you're not."

"You think I need you to remind me of that?" Morgan asked, pushing down his irritation.

"Evidently. Otherwise, why would you think of doing such a thing? Why, because someone caught you with the girl in my room? You don't see anyone forcing me to marry Catriona."

"You're already married."

Andrew smiled. "Exactly. And you're an earl. All you have to do is dismiss the girl."

Morgan regarded his friend, wondering if Andrew had always been so unscrupulous, or if it was a character trait he'd only begun to notice.

"This is a stupid thing you're considering doing, Morgan. Why? All for honor? You would ruin the rest of your life for honor?"

Andrew had asked him that very same question when he first decided to divorce Lillian.

What had he answered then? Something about being able to live with himself.

People considered his father a great man. On some level, he had always known he'd never achieve the greatness of his father. No one would ever call attention to his passage on the street, or whisper that he'd been entrusted with the Great Seal of Scotland.

Yet Morgan had wanted to be able to answer this question: Have I lived my life according to a set of principles and values that do not shame me? In this case he could answer in the affirmative.

Now Andrew moved to stand in front of him. "Morgan, don't do this thing."

"You weren't this serious when I talked of divorcing Lillian," he said. He considered the other man for a moment. "Would you have divorced your wife if she'd done the same?"

From the look on his face, the question obviously surprised Andrew.

"I haven't the slightest idea," he said. "Could you have forgiven Lillian her escapades if they'd occurred with a gardener, a deliveryman, the grocer, or the butcher, rather than your friends?"

"No," he said. "Adultery is adultery, Andrew."

Andrew laughed.

"What happened between you and the blonde?" Morgan asked, the first time he'd ever questioned him about one of his conquests.

"It's an interesting adventure," Andrew said. "Let's leave it at that."

Another first, since Andrew normally bragged about positions, stamina, and the noises his partner made, not to mention the gratitude they expressed afterward.

He couldn't help but wonder if both MacDonald women were proving to be more fascinating than the females of London.

"Stand straight, Jean," Aunt Mary said. "Or the fit will be all wrong."

Jean kept her arms raised out to her sides as she'd been instructed. She stared straight ahead, her gaze fixed on the far wall, the better to ignore the other people in the room.

To judge from her expression, the seamstress, whose talents ran to curtains and clothing for the staff, was agonizing over the pale yellow dress she was fitting. Her aunt was frowning, and two of the maids in training were staring, wide-eyed, at Jean. She'd shared meals and learned to make French polish with them. Now she was a stranger.

She was standing on a large ottoman, elevated some two feet above the onlookers, being fitted for the dress she was to wear at her wedding. And a great many other occasions, she fervently hoped. All this effort, and all this material, should not go to waste for simply one wearing.

When she'd ventured the thought to Aunt Mary, the older woman fixed her with a stern look.

"You're no longer a maid, Jean," she'd said. "You'll be the Countess of Denbleigh, and expected to dress as such."

She nodded, unwilling to continue the conversation in front of the others.

For the last two days, she'd vacillated from thinking this marriage might be a good thing to knowing it would be a disaster. She couldn't marry the earl.

Oh, she knew her etiquette well enough. There were books galore that could teach her how to comport herself. But how did one talk to an earl? Was she supposed to have an extensive knowledge of politics? Know a foreign language? Or be witty?

She was to have her own suite of rooms, a new wardrobe, a new title. A new life, one seemingly without purpose or duty.

An example was the sitting room of her new suite. Two maids had spent a whole day industriously cleaning, and now the room was spotless and shining. She hadn't been allowed to do a thing to help.

In fact, she hadn't done anything for two days now but read. Once, she'd dreamed of having time to read all the books she wished, but now she felt absurdly guilty.

"His Lordship expects you to dine with him tonight," Aunt Mary said.

Jean glanced down at her aunt.

She couldn't eat dinner with the earl. She couldn't marry the earl. She certainly couldn't bed the earl.

"I believe Mr. Prender will be in attendance," Aunt Mary continued. "That will make it less difficult for you."

Would it? Instead of facing just one sophisticated person, she was going to face two. Mr. Prender had a way of smirking at everyone, indicating his barely veiled contempt. But telling the earl she disliked his friend intensely was hardly a way to start a marriage, was it?

Perhaps her misery had something to do with her sister. Catriona hadn't spoken to her for two days. She wasn't here now, and Catriona hadn't shared any of her meals with her. Instead, she was ensconced in the guest room she'd picked, playing at being a guest at Ballindair.

Catriona was going to be a problem.

"Can I lower my arms yet?" she asked.

The seamstress, pins in mouth, nodded, and a few minutes later one of the girls helped her down from the ottoman.

Jean sighed, and went to ready herself for dinner, feeling as enthusiastic about the occasion as scrubbing a dozen chamber pots.

Chapter 16

Jean entered the formal dining room, or the Queen's Dining Room, as it was called, renamed after Queen Victoria's visit to Ballindair as the guest of the 8th earl.

The room had been redecorated in honor of that visit. The MacCraig eagle was embroidered on the cushions of the crimson upholstered dining chairs. A rectangular rug covered most of the floor, its background loomed in the same deep red, the pattern one of thistles surrounding the MacCraig clan crest. Crimson draperies adorned the floor-to-ceiling high windows, six of them revealing a view of the glen and beyond, to the river.

Aunt Mary told her the Queen had complimented the earl on Ballindair's magnificence as well as his stewardship of the land. She'd signed the guest book, adding her comments that she'd never seen such a lovely setting as Ballindair, or one more representative of the beauty of Scotland.

Mr. Seath had the key to the glass case containing the guest book. If she became countess, she'd be able to unlock it, hold the volume in her hands and marvel that she was touching something the Queen had signed.

Neither the earl nor Mr. Prender were in the dining room when she arrived. Aleck, the footman, stood behind the chair at the head of the table. There was another place setting at the other end, and she guessed she was supposed to sit there. She guessed rightly, because Aleck came and pulled the chair out for her.

She'd known him ever since coming to Ballindair, but he didn't smile or acknowledge her in any way. Instead, he fetched her a goblet of red wine, for which she smiled in thanks. He then moved back to his position behind the earl's chair.

Was she supposed to instruct him in some fashion? She suspected she wasn't supposed to talk to him. Was she supposed to pretend he wasn't there? She was evidently invisible to him, since he looked right through her as if she were glass.

She sat in the dress she'd borrowed from her aunt, swiftly altered by the same seamstress who'd appeared so worried about her wedding gown. Although it had white lace cuffs and collar, the dark blue color reminded her of her maid's uniform.

Was she supposed to talk at dinner? Or would she even be given an opportunity to converse? If she was expected to add to the conversation, what would she say? She knew little of politics, and nothing at all about life in London. She was certainly not going to discuss Inverness. Perhaps she should simply ask questions and allow the men to answer them.

At home, her father and mother had discussed his patients sometimes, and treatments he'd advised. When her mother had proposed an opinion, her father listened with great interest. More than once he'd given her mother praise for her insight.

She doubted the earl would be pleased by her recitation of the symptoms and treatment of gout.

Was a countess allowed to speak her mind? Or must she forever be invisible, like a maid?

She knew what her aunt was doing. Aunt Mary thought this was the perfect opportunity for her to have some security in life. Who would marry her, otherwise, knowing who she was?

How did she dissuade the earl from marrying her without telling him the truth?

She took a sip of wine and wished Aleck would go away. As the earl's soon-to-be bride, did she have the power to dismiss him with a flick of her hand? What if she tried, and he remained stubbornly there? Or worse, what if she did so and he left the room, only to regale those in the kitchen with tales of her arrogance?

The jumble of silverware wasn't all that confusing, thanks to her mother's tutelage. Work from the outside toward the plate. But what did she use that odd shaped spoon for? She'd simply have to watch the gentlemen to ensure she didn't make any mistakes.

She knew the earl was coming because Aleck suddenly snapped to attention. Turning her head slowly, she watched as he approached the table. Mr. Prender wasn't in sight.

"Forgive my tardiness," he said.

"You can't marry me," she said, blurting out the words.

He waved toward Aleck, who promptly disappeared. Perhaps she'd imagined him and he'd only been a ghost.

"Good evening to you, too, Jean," he said, sitting at the head of the table and unfolding his napkin.

"You're an earl. I'm a maid."

"Thank you for explaining that," he said.

She needed to convince him that he'd made a mistake. Then, she could obtain another position away from Ballindair, and he'd never have to know who she really was. That way, her aunt and Catriona would both be safe, and free to continue their employment.

But her plan wasn't going to work if he refused to listen to her.

"Have you ever heard the tale of Cinderella?" he asked.

She shook her head.

"Cendrillon ou la petite pantoufle de verre," he said. "'Cinderella, or the Little Glass Slipper,' written by Charles Perrault nearly two hundred years ago."

"I don't speak French," she said.

"Pity. It's the tale of a girl who was forced into being a maid by circumstance. She ends up attracting the attention of a prince."

"Did he marry her?"

"I believe he did, and they lived happily ever after."

"What rot."

His laughter surprised her.

"I thought all women were romantics at heart."

She'd seen the effect of deep and abiding love. If nothing else, it was frightening.

Another quick flick of his fingers and they were being served by magically appearing servants. She'd never had to serve, being a maid of all work, but she admired both the dexterity and the silence of the girls who flitted around the table.

"Will Mr. Prender not be joining us?" she asked.

"I've asked him not to," he said. "It's the perfect opportunity to get to know my bride."

She couldn't help it; she flinched. That word—bride—had all sorts of connotations, none of which she wanted to think about at the moment.

"Why a little glass slipper?" she asked, desperate for something to say. "Your story."

"Evidently, the heroine dresses as a princess but leaves a

slipper behind, and the prince travels through the countryside trying to fit it to a variety of women."

She stared at him. "Didn't he recognize her? Wouldn't he have noticed her face? Or was he always staring at her feet?"

He laughed again, which made her flush.

"Perhaps he only saw the trappings," he said. "And not the woman."

"I doubt they lived happily ever after," she said. "If he couldn't remember what she looked like."

He put down his silverware, placed his hands on the arms of the chair and regarded her. His scrutiny lasted a good two minutes, during which she debated whether to continue eating her dinner or put down her fork and return his stare. The decision was made for her by the sudden cramping of her stomach. She couldn't eat as long as he was studying her.

She put her silverware down, sat back in the same pose as he and forced herself to meet his eyes.

"You need to find someone of your own rank, Your Lordship. Someone who would be thrilled to be a countess. Someone who will be content enough to be defined by her rank."

"Do you remember everything I say?"

She didn't look away. "Yes."

"You're recommending I find someone who would throw rose petals down wherever I walked. Or kiss my boots, perhaps."

"Now is not the time to jest," she said, irritated at him. "I am serious, Your Lordship."

"My name is Morgan."

She couldn't do that either. To the day her mother died, whenever she referred to her husband, especially to her daughters, she called him "Mister." Perhaps in the seclusion of their bedroom they addressed each other by their first names, but she doubted they would do so in a dining room suddenly crowded with people. Two footmen stood at opposite sides of the room, and a maid hovered near the door. Why? Just in case the earl needed something? Could he not do for himself?

"You surprise me, Jean. I never thought to be more egalitarian than my wife."

Panic danced through her. "I'm not your wife. Not yet, anyway. Not at all, if you would only come to your senses, Your Lordship."

He glanced at the servants in warning, made another gesture with his hand, and the room was suddenly empty but for the two of them. How had he learned those things? Was he taught the care and handling of servants from boyhood? She'd never been trained in how to obey an earl's unspoken commands.

She closed her eyes, minded her temper, and wished she could convince him. The best thing for her would be for him to allow her to leave Ballindair and take the housekeeper position at Dumgoyne. That way, she'd never feel this conflict. She'd never worry about lying to him. Or be concerned he'd dismiss her sister and her aunt on hearing the truth.

"Would you tell me your objections?" he asked. "Perhaps you can convince me. Or I can convince you otherwise."

Incredulously, she stared at him. "You mean for us to debate?"

He shrugged. "Why not? I've debated weighty matters in Parliament."

"What could possibly be more weighty than your marriage? If it's miserable, you'll be miserable for the rest of your days."

Too soon, she remembered his divorce. Her face flamed, heat traveling up her cheeks to her temples.

He abandoned all pretense of eating, sat back and studied her again.

She held up one finger. "I am not of sufficient rank to marry you." She tapped the second finger. "I'm not well-traveled. I've only lived in Inverness and Ballindair."

Holding up the third finger, she said, "I don't speak French."

The fourth finger was reserved for another comment. "I do not like gatherings of any sort. A large group of people makes me shy."

Number five couldn't be spoken aloud, but it was the most compelling of all. She was not Jean MacDonald.

He nodded, which gave her some hope, but then he said, "You entertain me. Number one." He held up the second finger. "I don't require a wife who's well-traveled. I would hope you wouldn't be 'well-traveled' until after our marriage."

"I was speaking of visiting other places, Your Lordship," she said, mildly affronted.

"I wasn't." His third finger rose. "I don't require my wife speak French. What on earth made you think so?"

"That's one of the requirements for being a governess. If I can't even meet the requirements of being a governess, what makes you think I meet the requirements of being a countess?"

"My decision, that's what."

Arrogant man.

He began to smile, which silenced any comment she might've made. He did have a lovely smile.

"What was number four?" he asked, waving his fingers at her.

"I don't like groups of people."

"Finally, a circumstance on which we agree. We shall have to keep any of our entertainments to a reasonable number, say six?"

He was not going to let her out of this marriage. He had a skewed sense of honor and he was going to save her from circumstances. She sat back and stared at him, realizing she was well and truly trapped.

This was terrible.

She had to tell him the truth. But if she told him the truth, he would certainly repudiate her. And Catriona. And Aunt Mary.

There was nothing to do but marry the Earl of Denbleigh.

Morgan had expected Jean to be effusively grateful. He'd never thought she might want to talk him out of marrying her. He'd expected a more demure Jean, one intimidated by his rank and his wealth. Instead, she'd sat and argued with him like a Jesuit priest.

The dinner hadn't lasted long. In fact, she'd even claimed a stomach upset, something none of the women of his acquaintance would have ever said.

He'd asked the housekeeper to have Cook prepare her favorite dishes. He'd had roses cut from the garden. The room was thick with the perfume of them. Not once had she noticed. Instead, she'd been intent on convincing him she wasn't suitable enough to be his wife.

What was strange was not only that Jean was reluctant to marry him, but that he was suddenly anticipating it more than he expected.

Tomorrow, the little wren would be a countess.

Chapter 17

RULES FOR STAFF: *Keep a few paces behind your betters if required to aid them in any fashion.*

Perhaps she was wrong.

Perhaps she hadn't thought this through well enough.

Perhaps she was worried unnecessarily.

Early the next morning, before she was to be dressed and prepared for her wedding, Jean slipped out the back stairs, down the corridor, and into the little used North Wing. The steward's office was the third room to the left, and she stood before the closed door for a moment. Was this the best idea? Probably not, but she needed counsel from someone, and Aunt Mary refused to consider telling the earl the truth.

She knocked three times, so quietly the man in the room might not have heard. But she heard a faint voice, took a deep breath, and pushed the door open, peering inside.

"Mr. Seath, have you a moment to speak with me?"

He looked surprised, then pleased, a reaction she hadn't expected.

"Come in, my dear. Come in."

He stood at her entrance, and motioned to a chair beside his desk.

Even though the office was crowded with papers and books, the desk was clear. Her father's desk had been the same.

"Today is the momentous day. My felicitations on your wedding."

"Thank you," she said, sitting where he indicated and folding her hands in front of her.

"You're troubled," he said. "What is it?"

"I can't marry an earl, Mr. Seath. It's not done."

His smile dimmed a little as he sat back in the chair and pressed his fingertips together.

"A great many things about the Earl of Denbleigh aren't done, Miss MacDonald. I agree, this is an unusual situation, but the earl is an unusual man."

Mr. Seath's gaze was too pointed, as if he saw beneath her stated fears to the real truth.

"I know nothing about being a countess. I don't know the etiquette, I don't know how one dresses. I'm woefully ignorant."

"Anyone would expect you to be," he said, surprising her. "But you will have people to guide you. Your aunt, for one, who has an eminently practical head on her shoulders. Myself, if you would allow me the privilege of doing so. As to your clothes, that could be solved by looking through a few magazines, or consultation with a seamstress."

He waved one of his thin and fragile hands in the air. "You've the manners of a countess now, Miss MacDonald. I've never heard but the best of you."

She stared down at her hands, red and chapped from weeks and months of work. She had calluses in places she was certain no lady would ever have calluses.

"Gloves, my dear," he said. "Until your hands have resumed their normal appearance."

Did everyone have answers for everything? Couldn't they see it was impossible?

"What do I talk to him about?"

"What do you talk to him about now?" Mr. Seath asked.

Ghosts and his boyhood, and things he hadn't discussed with other women. Was that what he wanted from her, a little unusual conversation? Well, he would certainly get it by marrying a maid.

Her secret burned in her chest. The wish to share it with another human being, someone who wouldn't ignore the situation like Aunt Mary, was unbearable. But she didn't want to burden the steward. The poor man didn't look as if he had enough strength to keep breathing through the day.

"My mother had the wasting sickness," she blurted out, then stopped, horrified.

He didn't say anything, and she wondered if she should continue. Mr. Seath had always been kind to her, and she wished to reciprocate, if she could.

"I made a tea for her every morning and evening," she said. "It helped with her appetite. Can I do the same for you, Mr. Seath?"

For a long moment he simply regarded her, his eyes flat.

"I could ask why you think I'm ill," he said. "But we both know that would be foolish, don't we?"

She couldn't answer. All she did was look at him, trying to share her feelings without words being said.

He stood, circling the desk to stand at the small window.

From there he looked even more affected by his illness, as if he were shrinking inside his clothes. The cuffs of his shirt covered half his hand, and his coat hung loosely from his shoulders.

"I did not mean to be so personal, Mr. Seath."

"Do you know, you are the only one who has dared to say a word to me," he said, turning to look at her.

His smile was oddly sad, and because of it, she stood and walked to the window, placing her hand on his sleeve. Wordlessly, they stared at the view of the MacCraig Forest, and beyond to the bog.

"I've been giving a lot of thought to mortality, Miss Mac-Donald. What measures a man's life? What is the mark of a life well lived?"

"To leave the world a better place than you found it?" she asked, remembering some of the philosophy she'd read in books from Ballindair's library. "Or perhaps it's simpler, Mr. Seath. To do whatever you do as well as you can."

He turned his head. "And you think you're not equipped to be a countess, Miss MacDonald?"

She dropped her hand, took a step back, prepared to give him reasons why she shouldn't be the Earl of Denbleigh's bride, but he continued.

"I never married," he said. "My spouse was Ballindair. My brother. My children. My soul-consuming interest."

She had no words to say. Instead, she only felt a deep and abiding pity for the man.

"Rank, privilege, status, these are all things we've made up, Miss MacDonald. They don't mean anything. They're not real."

They were as real as anything she knew.

"You have all the seeds within you for greatness. Simply reverse the role you've been living for the past year. Instead of taking orders, give them. Remember what it was like to feel slighted and never do so. Recall how it felt to be toiling anonymously, and make sure you see the people around you. Perhaps having been a maid, Miss MacDonald, you'll be the greatest countess of them all."

Her eyes swam with tears, and she blinked them back.

"Everyone has such great hopes for me," she said. "I'm the only one who knows the truth of the situation."

"Or perhaps you're simply being harder on yourself than anyone else," he said. "Perhaps we see the truth better than you."

She nodded, willing to let him win this argument.

"I'll go and make that tea now," she said.

He nodded, smiling again. A sweet and somber smile tugging at her heart.

"And afterward, go and prepare yourself to be a bride."

At the door, she paused, and asked him the one question she'd come to ask.

"Tell me something about marital law," she said.

"And what makes you think I know anything about marital law?" he asked.

Surprised, she could only look back at him. "I think you know a good bit about everything, Mr. Seath."

His laughter was scratchy sounding, as if he'd rarely had a chance to use it.

"A charming woman offers to make me tea and tells me I'm wise. I truly thank you for coming to see me."

He held up his hand, his fingers nearly skeletal. "Ask your question, Miss MacDonald," he said. "If I do not know the answer, I shall endeavor to discover it for you."

She should excuse herself now, go and make his tea, and have another maid bring it to him. Instead, she did the very worst thing she could possibly do. She asked him for the truth.

"If a man or woman is married under a false name," she asked, "is the union legal?"

His gaze was steady.

"I cannot think it would be, Miss MacDonald. But I will consult with others before I render my judgment, shall I?"

She nodded, and escaped before he asked her any more questions.

Chapter 18

RULES FOR STAFF: *Be respectful of the housekeeper's position and obey her dictates. Show the same respect for the majordomo and steward.*

Instead of being married at the kirk where they attended Sunday services, the tradition was for the Earls of Denbleigh to be wed at the small chapel attached to Ballindair's East Wing. The décor of the chapel was plain, as if the Murderous MacCraigs, having decided their souls needed saving, dispensed with any trappings of their wealth—just in case God saw it and demanded a greater tithe. The benches in front of the wooden slab of the altar were hard and plain oak. No cushioned backsides for the MacCraig penitents.

The four stained-glass windows—the only concession to a religious atmosphere—weren't of a spiritual theme, but demonstrated a few MacCraig lairds in the act of attempting to impress God. One laird washed the feet of his clan members. Another raised a sword against a large green monster—Satan or a mythical Highland creature? One tender scene showed a laird cradling his son with one hand, the other holding a sword pointed toward the earth.

The plate on the rough-hewn wood altar was hammered silver, two large discs resembling ornate coins. Jean wasn't certain what they were used for, and this wasn't the time to ask.

No guests had been invited to this wedding, but the staff of Ballindair occupied the pews. She would have preferred the ceremony be done in secret. The fewer people who witnessed this farce, the better.

The earl was wearing a kilt. Of course he'd be wearing a kilt. She just didn't expect the oh so proper and English-sounding Earl of Denbleigh to look like a Murderous Mac-Craig. With his black hair tumbling across his forehead, his tailored jacket and red and black tartan kilt, he didn't look very English—or as proper as he'd appeared on his first day back at Ballindair.

He was quite handsome, so much so that several of the women in the congregation could be heard to sigh.

The idea of bedding him, of even being next to him naked, filled her with a dry-mouthed terror. But beneath it was anticipation, warming and growing, trying to hide and woefully bad at it.

What did she know about bedding any man, let alone an earl? Let alone *this* earl?

Morgan's hand felt warm, large, and strangely comforting. She placed her fingers on his palm and had a fleeting vision of grabbing his hand and racing from the chapel.

She didn't dare look at the altar, for fear it might catch fire. God could not be happy about this day.

Behind her, in a place of honor, sat Aunt Mary and Catriona. Her sister had insisted on a new dress, and the seamstress and her staff labored long into the night to finish it. No doubt Catriona was the object of everyone's stare. Jean had never seen her look so beautiful. She should be the bride. From the gaze eating through her back, evidently her sister felt the same way.

Aunt Mary was beaming, her happiness evident for anyone to see. Not only had her nieces ceased to be maids, but she'd been elevated in stature, simply because she was now related by marriage to the Earl of Denbleigh.

Mr. Seath was the only one who wasn't smiling, and she knew why.

She met his gaze once. Strangely, he only nodded back at her. He'd not told anyone she'd come to him, or the question she asked. If he had, she wouldn't be standing next to a tall and strong and handsome man, lying to God and all those assembled.

It was a wonder the ghosts of Ballindair weren't present, especially the French Nun, moaning and groaning, or the Herald, issuing dire warnings of future disaster.

The Presbyterian minister nodded somberly at them, then escorted them to a small desk where Morgan signed his name before handing the pen to her. Her difficulty breathing wasn't because the corset was laced tightly in order to fit her into the beautiful wedding dress. No, it was a guilty conscience and a healthy dose of fear. Fear of God, and fear of what might happen should anyone discover the truth.

The marriage ceremony was accomplished in a matter of minutes. She stood beside Morgan, her hand trembling in his. She repeated everything she was told to say, in a voice low enough not to be overheard by the assembled staff.

Only one bad moment occurred, when the minister called her by name. She blinked at him, feeling as if she stood on a precipice above Hell itself. Morgan looked at her curiously. She'd only shaken her head and repeated the vows under a name not her own.

Aunt Mary didn't appear worried. Neither was Catriona.

Was she the only one who cared that tonight she'd indulge in sin?

And was that a shiver of anticipation?

His wedding to Lillian had been an Anglican service, with the whole of her family in attendance. His father had been dead a year, and he alone except for friends. Andrew was in attendance then, too.

At Ballindair, however, there was no trace of the Anglican service. The very Presbyterian minister officiated, scowling at him the whole time. After they repeated their vows, but before leaving the altar, Morgan withdrew the clan brooch from his pocket and pinned it on the collar of Jean's dress. The red and black pattern of the MacCraig tartan looked good against the yellow fabric.

He nodded to Andrew, who stepped forward and bowed to Jean. In his hands was a replica of the first MacCraig sword ever carried into battle. By accepting the sword, as every MacCraig bride had—with the exception of Lillian—she acknowledged her entrance into the clan.

Andrew had agreed to do this duty for him, but his carefully expressionless face indicated his disapproval. So far as Morgan was concerned, as long as he didn't voice his concerns, he could dislike this marriage all he wanted.

He didn't want the kind of relationship Andrew had with his wife. She spent what she wanted, lived how she wanted, and was free of his interference in her life. Periodically, Andrew would return home, to greet the newest addition to his brood, or plant another child in his wife's belly, before returning to London once again.

What kind of marriage would he and Jean have? They were still strangers, but he'd thought he knew Lillian, only to be startled by her true nature.

Jean spoke her mind and was very firm when she wanted

to be, witness her protestations about their marriage. He still wanted to smile when thinking of her four objections.

He knew three things about his wife. She was intensely loyal to those she loved—witness her attempt to protect her sister, and that she'd never told him the housekeeper was her aunt. She was curious about a great many things, especially the Ballindair ghosts, and had never been kissed. If she had, she wouldn't have worn that look of startled awareness in the garden.

He watched her take up the sword in both hands.

"You're now a MacCraig," he said, in a voice loud enough to carry to the back of the chapel.

Not one person murmured or spoke.

The pipes swelled again, as they had when she entered the chapel, nearly sweeping every thought from her head. She bent to retrieve the sword, grateful her aunt had instructed her on the MacCraig wedding ceremony.

Once she straightened, Catriona stepped to her side, took the sword, then stepped back, leaving her and Morgan looking at each other.

He offered his arm, and she placed her hand on it and allowed him to lead her away from the altar.

"Your Ladyship . . ."

Jean stopped, not because of the oddness of the label, but because Morgan had laid his hand over hers.

A little boy with black hair and wide blue eyes was standing in the aisle, looking up at her. In his hands, he held a small pillow, and on the pillow rested a rusty horseshoe.

Abruptly, he thrust the pillow at her. Morgan gripped the horseshoe before it slipped to the ground.

"It's for luck," he said, handing it to her.

She almost laughed, but contained herself. Bending down, she thanked the little boy, and he bowed to her, an arm at his waist. How long had someone made him practice that?

Standing again, she gripped the horseshoe with a sweaty hand. She'd need more than luck. Perhaps it wouldn't be amiss to say a prayer for divine intervention and forgiveness.

As they moved out of the chapel, Morgan stopped and grabbed two small drawstring bags from the shelf by the door. After handing one to Jean, he opened his, revealing hundreds of coins.

Gathering up a handful, the two of them walking again, he scattered them over the chapel steps and out into the courtyard.

"Is this for luck, too?" she asked, doing the same with her coins. Children clambered around them, the adults laughing and talking as they bent to retrieve as many coins as they could.

"It is," he said. "The tradition is, whatever we give out will be returned to us throughout our marriage."

She threw more coins, hoping they'd do something to offset the lie she'd just uttered.

Chapter 19

RULES FOR STAFF: *Be punctual in rising and dutiful when seeking your bed.*

Was she supposed to sit here, like a good little countess, and wait until Morgan came to take her virtue? Did women simply wait for the man? If she were brave, daring, and shocking like Catriona, she would go to the Laird's Tower.

Could she do that? Did she even want to?

This whole business of a wedding night was a chore, something to be done before the rest of her life might proceed, a turnstile over which she must jump.

Should she feel differently because she knew she wasn't truly married?

Perhaps Morgan wasn't going to come to her at all. Perhaps he'd changed his mind. Perhaps Mr. Seath had told him she wasn't who she claimed to be.

Very well, she should count Morgan's absence as a blessing, then. She would not be living in sin. She would not be perpetrating fraud against the earl or the inhabitants of Ballindair.

And she most certainly wouldn't be the Countess of Denbleigh.

She stood, walked a path from the door to the fireplace and back to the door again.

Did men go through the same thing? Surely not. Surely a man's first adventure at lovemaking was eminently easier. Were they afraid?

She honestly doubted Mr. Seath had said anything. She knew her aunt and Catriona had kept silent. Of them all, she was the only one tempted to tell the earl the truth, and as the hours passed, she realized it would be a hideous scandal to admit her identity now.

Did he intend to make her wait?

Had she misunderstood? Should she go to his room? That would be the act of the sacrificial lamb, wouldn't it?

Your Lordship, I am here to divest myself of my virginity.

No, if he was going to take her maidenhead, he would have to come and fetch it.

She sat, folded her hands in her lap, her knees together, her feet perfectly aligned. *There, the proper pose of a countess.* Is that how they sat all the time? She relaxed a little, enough so her elbows touched the arms of the chair.

Tilting her head to one side, she surveyed the door and willed him to come to her.

Another quarter hour, and he still hadn't arrived. Was she supposed to be asleep? Was she supposed to be awakened by Morgan, as if he were the prince in his French fairy tale? That hardly seemed right, either.

What a pity they couldn't handle this matter with more practicality. He would come to her door; she would let him in, and they would be about this business of making her a wife.

What a pity she couldn't just offer up her virginity to him

on a silver salver with a card attached. *From your wife to my husband.*

He would examine it, then store it somewhere where he could take it out to periodically look at it.

What would virginity look like—a small gold star, perhaps? Or a little statue of Aphrodite?

If she listened to Catriona, she would think being with a man was all instinct. There had been something intrinsically wrong with her younger sister lecturing her about lovemaking.

"You don't need to worry," Catriona had said earlier that night. "I'm sure the earl is a kind and generous lover."

Shocked, she'd wordlessly stared at her sister.

"According to Andrew, the earl cut a wide swath through the women in London. Not as wide as Andrew, of course."

Jean remained silent because Catriona had managed to steal the words from her mind.

"I promised Father," she finally said. "I promised him I would look after you."

"And you have. Perfectly," Catriona said. "You've been as maternal as any mother hen."

"I haven't," Jean said, shaking her head. "I haven't, if you know anything about lovers. If you know enough to discuss a man's prowess."

Catriona faced her, hands on her hips. "What shall I do, sister? Lie to you?" She fluttered her lashes and pasted a simpering smile on her face. "I am as virtuous as you, dear Jean. I have never lain with a man. I have never known the meaning of passion. I do not scream a man's name when he brings me pleasure. I do not like to have my breasts suckled. And I don't enjoy kissing."

Once again Catriona had shocked her.

"Are those lies good enough?" Catriona smiled, a genuinely sweet smile.

If her sister could manufacture that expression so easily, how many other times had she been deceived by her?

"Anything I'd say would sound foolish, Catriona. I'm only sad you gave yourself away so freely."

Amazingly, Catriona's expression was one of humor.

"I agree," she said. "I was going to only settle for an earl, but my sister tricked me. I was left with a mere mister."

When Jean remained stunned and silent, Catriona bent to kiss her on the cheek, then left the room.

Two hours had passed. What was the reason for Morgan's delay? Was there some ritual a new bridegroom had to endure? Another horrible thought occurred to her: They wouldn't be coming to her room in a procession, would they? Morgan, Andrew, and the piper?

She went to find her cloak. Anything to make her feel less mentally and physically exposed as she felt at the moment.

The seamstress had provided her with a nightgown and matching wrapper, the color a pale yellow and the fabric entirely too diaphanous. Now, with her cloak, she felt a little more proper.

How much longer was she going to have to wait?

She opened the door of the Countess's Suite and stood there, staring down the empty hall. Should she go to him?

She stood outside her room for several minutes. If she turned left and went down the main staircase, she could intersect the corridor leading to the Laird's Tower. If she turned right, she could take the stairs to the Long Gallery.

The French Nun better not whisper a warning to her tonight, when it was days too late. The time for advice had been when she tried to save her sister, an act for which she'd only been punished.

Catriona hadn't wanted to be saved, and that was the true irony of this entire situation.

* * *

For an hour Morgan argued with himself. This marriage needed to be different from the beginning. He was not going to be a doting husband. He was not going to be enamored with his wife to the exclusion of his common sense. He was not going to be in love.

No, this union was for an entirely different purpose.

He expected absolute loyalty from Jean, as well as fidelity. That was not too much to ask, given he'd raised her in status and his wealth was at her disposal.

He had no intention of going to her room like some besotted idiot, grateful for her compliance. He was not going to be eager. Perhaps it would be better if he dispensed with the wedding night entirely, poured himself one of his favorite whiskeys and read a good book.

No, it would be better if she came to him. However, given her stricken look at their wedding, he had his doubts that she would.

Would she consider bedding him to be payment for his kindness and generosity? He doubted that, too. Otherwise, she wouldn't have argued against the marriage.

He waited another hour before he was certain she wasn't going to come to him, then went to the Countess's Suite. After the first knock, he was annoyed. The second had him irritated. When he opened the door, it was to find his new bride wasn't where she was supposed to be. She wasn't waiting for him in bed. She wasn't even in the room.

Damned if his wife wasn't missing.

Clouds scurried overhead, revealing a full moon, then hiding it, then exposing it again like a maiden flirting behind a fan. The tops of the trees, emerald turned to ebony by night, shivered in the restless wind.

If ghosts were ever abroad at Ballindair, tonight should have been the night. But all was quiet, silent enough that Jean heard approaching footsteps.

The moment had come to confront her husband. Not quite a husband, though, was he? What, then, did she call him? Paramour? Lover? Not that, either.

Two places were special to her at Ballindair: the library, and here, in the Long Gallery. He'd claimed the library, rightfully so, and since he'd found her with such ease, she needed to cultivate another place, a more secretive location to hide.

"What are you doing here?" Morgan asked, stepping out of the shadows.

"Tell me about your wife," she said.

"You're my wife."

She clenched her hands tightly.

"Tell me about your *other* wife."

"That's hardly a suitable topic for my wedding night, is it? To discuss one wife with another?"

"Why did you divorce her?"

He didn't speak for several moments, but she could hear him walking toward her. She straightened her shoulders, clasped her hands tightly in front of her, and steadied herself.

"I don't look like any of those women," she said, waving one hand to the line of portraits. She didn't have blond hair or beautiful blue eyes. She was tall, and rather large in the chest, but her hair was a plain brown, as were her eyes.

"Must you?"

He took a few steps forward, and she moved sideways.

"Are you afraid of me?"

Startled, she turned her head to address his black shape. "Of course not."

"Then why do you tense whenever I come near you?" he asked.

"Perhaps I'm wondering if you're going to kiss me again," she heard herself saying. What on earth made her say that?

"I only kissed you once."

"Yes," she said.

"We could be kissing instead of talking," he said, moving still closer.

"Perhaps they're not mutually exclusive," she said. "Could one not kiss, then talk? Or talk, then kiss?"

"Talking of Lillian does not put me in the mood for kissing."

She turned and faced him fully. "Why not? She was your wife. Were you forced into the marriage?"

"I was not."

"Then you must have felt something for her at the beginning of your marriage, didn't you?"

"I felt a great many things for Lillian. Do you want the whole horrible story? Do you want me to divulge everything so you can investigate it, examine it, then approve or disapprove?"

"It isn't my place to approve or disapprove," she said.

She turned and walked deeper into the shadows.

"I was naive when I met her. Not necessarily young," he said. "But I was naive about women, I suppose."

"Is that a detriment for men? Being naive about women?"

"It was a detriment for me," he said. "Especially with a woman like Lillian."

"Why did you divorce her?"

"Did you know it was relatively easy for a man to divorce a woman? It's much harder for her to do the same."

She didn't want a lecture on the law.

"Why did you divorce her?" she asked again.

"She was unfaithful to me. Not once, but many times. Enough times there were wagers as to the exact number of her lovers."

Silence stretched thin between them. She could hear the sigh of the wind against Ballindair, as if nature decried the confession of its laird.

"Why?" she asked, giving in to her curiosity.

"Why did I divorce her? I've just given you the answer."

She shook her head. "No, why was she unfaithful?"

"Why is anyone unfaithful? Because they wish to find from others what they can't find in their own bedrooms, perhaps. Or she loathed me for some reason and wanted to punish me for it."

"Are you so loathsome?"

His laughter, disembodied and cloaked in shadows, was an eerie response.

"I never thought so. But perhaps I am. If you contact Lillian, I'm certain she could give you a list of all my flaws and faults. She no doubt has informed the rest of society about them."

"Doesn't she suffer the same way you do?"

"I don't suffer," he said.

"Oh, but you do. If you didn't suffer for your own actions, we wouldn't be standing here now. We wouldn't be married. Honor would not have propelled you to do something so blatantly idiotic as to marry me."

"Now you sound like Andrew," he said.

That comment stung. "Evidently, Andrew was not able to dissuade you from making an unwise marriage."

"First of all, you want to know about Lillian, and now you're declaring this marriage unwise. Hardly the wedding night I expected."

She didn't have a rejoinder for that.

"Were you ghost hunting again?"

"I wasn't ghost hunting," she said. "I was trying to escape you."

"Why?"

"I'm frightened," she said.

"Of me?"

"Partly," she admitted. Wholly, in reality, but she wasn't going to expose the extent of her fear. "I'm not as beautiful as your wife was."

"You don't know what Lillian looked like."

"Wasn't she beautiful?"

"Perhaps, but you're my wife now," he said, his tone brusque. "I would prefer if you would cease referring to Lillian as my wife. She hasn't been my wife for two years. And even before that she didn't exactly behave in a wifely manner."

"Did you share a bed?"

"Another question I didn't expect," he said. "Why should I go to her bed when it had been well populated by a dozen or more men? Men, I might add, I knew well."

"That must have hurt," she said, "to know your friends were betraying you."

Again he moved toward her.

"I asked myself many times," he said, "if they were truly friends."

"She doesn't seem to be suffering," he said as he came closer. "To use your word. The divorce hasn't changed her behavior."

Then she could feel him standing behind her. She shivered. "Are you going to divorce me?"

"If you're unfaithful, probably. I divorced one wife, I can divorce another. Granted, Scotland and England would probably reel in horror. Have you plans on being unfaithful?"

"Shouldn't I bed someone first, before I entertain thoughts of adultery?"

"You realize, of course, that I'll know if you're telling the truth about being a virgin?"

"You can tell?" she asked. "How?"

He didn't say anything for a moment. "Very well, you're not as beautiful as Lillian. But does outward beauty matter as much as a woman's character?"

She laughed, unwillingly amused.

"You'll pardon me, Your Lordship, if I don't give any credence to that remark. If you had to choose between a beautiful woman and a plain one—"

"I chose the plain one."

Another sting of words.

"I've never bedded anyone. I don't know anything about it. You will find me massively inept. I haven't, in your parlance, traveled excessively."

"Thank God."

He turned her to face him.

"Do you think I want you experienced? Do you think I want anyone to have kissed you but me? Do you think I want a harlot in my bed?"

"How do you know no one else has ever kissed me?" she asked. "Perhaps I've been kissed by dozens of men."

"Have you?"

"Of course not."

"You say that with great conviction. It's a habit of yours."

"I didn't know you'd been in my vicinity long enough to notice my habits," she said.

"I've been around you more than anyone at Ballindair," he said, a comment that startled her. "You might even say you've been a companion of sorts."

"Have I?"

"And when I wasn't around you, I found myself thinking of you a great deal. You're a very interesting woman, Your Ladyship."

"You mustn't call me that," she said, taking a step back.

"Countess," he said, taunting her. He followed her, matching her retreat. "Your Ladyship."

"Has anyone told you what a prig you can be, Your Lordship?"

"Not in the last hour or so," he said. "I find it odd it's my bride who insists on doing so."

"Your bride has just had certain facts made clear to her," she said. "I am to be eminently grateful you've married me, plain as I am. I don't have the beauty of my sister, or Lillian, but I haven't sent anyone fleeing in fright, either."

"That's not what I said at all."

"Isn't it?"

"Are you deliberately instigating an argument, Jean? Do you think if you make me angry enough, I'll avoid you on our wedding night?"

She turned to face him.

"As a ploy, madam, it has worked. I dislike the idea of bedding a quarrelsome woman." A moment later he said, "Do you want me to leave?"

"Yes," she said, fervently and simply.

Suddenly, he was gone, only the muffled sound of his footsteps in the darkness reassuring her that he hadn't been a ghost.

Chapter 20

RULES FOR STAFF: *Be prompt at all meals, except when required to be at your duties.*

This marriage had started out all wrong.

She'd questioned him about Lillian and his honor. Then, when he insulted her, entirely by accident, she acted offended. Worse, she'd been hurt.

Why hadn't she been in her room? Why wasn't she waiting for him there? Why had he gone in search of her? For that matter, why was it necessary for him to search for her?

Did she think to escape him?

Did she think he was a brute who would force himself on her? She'd said she was afraid. Dear God, did she think that?

He'd been a very inept seducer, however, hadn't he?

She'd banished him, but he'd as much as summoned his own banishment.

Morgan stopped in the middle of the corridor leading to the Laird's Tower. Perhaps she *had* been frightened.

This would never do.

He couldn't leave her alone tonight, of all nights. Had he ever seduced an innocent before? Never, which left only one: Jean, ghost huntress, debater, former maid, and a woman who said the most surprising things.

Why shouldn't he bed her? She was legally his wife. He was legally her husband. Granted, they didn't know each other well yet, but that would come, wouldn't it? Though not if they remained separate, each aloof from the other.

He turned, intent for the Long Gallery once again, seduction in mind.

Jean stood in the Long Gallery, listening. Would the French Nun refuse to appear before her now, simply because she was married? Did she only counsel those single women who'd lost their hearts to the Murderous MacCraigs?

Surely she wasn't so idiotic as to expect advice from a ghost?

Then from whom?

Catriona would laugh merrily to know she'd been left alone on her wedding night. Or that she'd sent her husband away. And she dared not go to her aunt. Aunt Mary would only say, "For heaven sakes, Jean, be a little more practical."

Hadn't she proven to be practical? Especially during that last year in Inverness? She was the one who kept everything together, especially on those days when Catriona indulged in fits of weeping. What good were tears?

Then why was she brushing away her own now?

What exactly was she supposed to do?

She shouldn't have asked those questions about his wife— about Lillian. She shouldn't have told him she was afraid.

She shouldn't have sent him away.

Was there a scale, somewhere? One measuring the levels of fear a human experienced? If a scale did exist, with one being the lowest level of fear—a placid acceptance of all that life brings—and ten being screaming and running away, then what she felt right now was a seven, or perhaps a six. Nothing like those days in Inverness, when she'd endured a nine. Being without prospects, money, charity, friends, or hope had been daunting indeed.

Everything had changed, however, hadn't it? A thought lasting until she saw Morgan striding down the Long Gallery. She didn't need light to know there was an intent and determined look on his face.

Her fear level rose to eight.

She looked absurd standing there, the moonlight streaming over her dark cloak. She hadn't fastened it; in between the folds he could see the hint of her nightgown. She looked ethereal, like a ghost of herself.

Foolish woman.

His pulse raced, no doubt because of their argument. He'd always liked a good debate.

How long had it been since he'd bedded a woman? Long enough. He didn't have to deny himself any longer, did he?

"Do virgins feel lust?" he asked, stopping in front of her.

"I beg your pardon?" she asked, blinking.

He didn't ask again; he knew full well she'd understood him the first time.

"You seemed interested in me when I was naked. Was it lust I saw on your face?"

Lillian had seduced him; Jean had no concept of the idea. She didn't realize how lovely she was, standing in the moonlight, the illumination enough that he could discern the frown on her face.

A prickly bride.

"I have no intention of answering that question."

"Let's say it was lust. Couldn't you feel it again?"

She blinked at him.

"You think I insulted you," he said.

"It's not an opinion, Your Lordship. You did."

"Morgan."

"I'm not your first wife."

That comment was surprising.

"No, you certainly aren't."

"If you'd wanted a beautiful wife, you shouldn't have insisted on this marriage."

He was not about to respond to that comment. "Are you really afraid?"

She turned her head, an answer without words.

He placed his hands on her shoulders and drew her toward him. Pressing his lips against her ear, he whispered, "Don't be afraid of me, Jean."

"I'm not exactly afraid," she said. "I'm cautious. Unprepared. Unschooled."

"Virginal."

She nodded.

He turned her, grabbed her hand and left the Long Gallery.

It was time that inconvenient virginity was done away with; the sooner the better.

She was not foolish enough to try to escape, but his strides were longer than hers and her slippers kept falling off.

In the corridor she said, "I won't run away, but I can't keep up with you. Or am I to leave my shoes as a trail for the maids to follow in the morning? Like your French story?"

He turned and looked at her. She pulled her hand free and bent to put on her slippers again.

Standing, she said, "If I agree to go with you to your suite, will you let me do so without dragging me there?"

A look slid over his face, too quickly for her to decipher

it. But he immediately bowed his head in acknowledgment of her words.

"Forgive me," he said. "I didn't mean to be boorish."

"Don't be ridiculous," she said. "You weren't boorish. Perhaps a little eager," she added.

His smile took her aback.

"I'll be damned if I know how to act at this moment," he said. "I never envisioned a wedding night like this."

"I never envisioned a wedding night," she admitted.

"Surely that's not true. Didn't you see yourself marrying?"

She shook her head. "No, I didn't. I did see myself attending Catriona's wedding, being a doting aunt to all her children, but as for myself, no."

He looked at her and frowned.

She'd said something wrong, something that had irritated him. Instead of speaking, however, he simply turned and led the way to the Laird's Tower. Not once did he look back. She felt not unlike a mongrel pup who'd found a hint—the barest hint—of a meal and a place to rest for the night.

"Shall I feel grateful you've decided to bed me?"

"If you wish," he said, his voice reverberating against the stone of the tower.

She halted on the steps, one hand gripping her nightgown and cloak, the other holding onto the banister.

"Were your ancestors called the Murderous MacCraigs because they killed people or because they incited others to violence?"

At the top of the stairs he turned and looked down at her, his smile causing her heart to beat faster.

"Have I incited you to violence, Jean?"

He incited her to something, but she wasn't exactly sure what it was.

Her hands were trembling, her face felt too hot. She'd

never had any training in flirting. Nor did it come naturally to her, as it did to Catriona. Tonight, of all nights, she should feel soft and feminine, intriguing, a little mysterious. Instead, her fear level remained at an eight.

If he kissed her, perhaps she'd feel better.

She eyed him as she climbed the rest of the stairs.

"May I ask you something?"

He turned back and glanced at her. A nod was her only encouragement.

"Does a woman experience pleasure in the marriage bed?" She didn't look at him when she spoke, but at the floor. "Is that proper?"

"You ask the damnedest questions, Jean."

Still, she didn't look at him, moving beyond him to stand at his sitting room door.

"It doesn't seem quite right if a man is the only one to enjoy the act, does it?"

"Shall we adjourn to the library so you can seek out a book on the subject? Or talk to one of your ghosts?"

"I doubt if there's a book on the subject," she said.

"You've already looked."

She wasn't going to answer that. "And they're more properly your ghosts," she said. "And they've given me no advice at all. Not even the French Nun, and I half expected her to counsel me to run as far and as fast as I can from you."

"Why? We're married. You're not in danger of becoming a fallen woman."

He swung open the door and made a gesture with his arm for her to precede him. She did so, forcing herself to take a deep breath. Her fear level was now an eight and a half or perhaps a nine.

Without being coaxed, she strode into his bedchamber, removing her cloak and throwing it on the nearest chair. Seconds later her wrapper joined the cloak.

Again, without a word or an action on his part, she climbed up on the bed and sat on the edge, her hands clasped demurely on her lap. She stared straight ahead, wishing the mirror on the wall wasn't aligned so she could see herself as she sat there. In the moonlight, she looked unearthly pale, except for the twin spots of color on her cheeks. Her hair, however, looked exceptionally well.

"If women didn't enjoy it, I doubt my wife—" He stopped himself. "—Lillian would have engaged in it."

She nodded, wishing he hadn't brought up Lillian again.

"I'm not going to ravage you," he said.

"Pity," she said. "If you did ravage me, it would be over soon. We'd be done with it."

He didn't say anything. When she turned her head, he was staring at her with the most interesting look on his face.

"Are you angry?" she asked.

He shook his head. "Surprised, perhaps. Confused, of a certainty. I never expected to be urged to hurry on my wedding night."

"Oh, I'm not asking you to hurry," she said, feeling the fear level rise one notch. "But it would be better if it was done with, don't you think?"

"Perhaps," he said, coming to stand before her. "If that's how you feel, we should perform the expurgated version of the wedding night." He reached out and unclasped her hands, taking both of them in his larger ones.

"You're a virgin?" he asked solemnly.

She nodded, just as serious.

"And you want this done rather quickly?"

She nodded, a little less fervently.

He gently pulled her from the bed until she was standing in front of him, placed both hands on either side of the curved neckline of her nightgown, and ripped the garment in two.

"You're trembling," he said softly.

It would be foolish to pretend otherwise, so she only nodded.

She was standing there naked before him, and he was looking at her with the same intensity and regard she'd once studied him.

She forced herself to stand straight, hands down at her sides. Let him look his fill, then. She certainly had.

A small smile graced the corners of his mouth.

"You call yourself plain, Jean?"

What did he expect her to say? Compared to Catriona, she was.

"I've never seen a woman less plain."

She wanted to ask him if his experience with women was so extensive, then realized it would be a foolish question indeed. It might bring Lillian back into the room.

Besides, Morgan was tall, strong, and handsome. Of course he had a great deal of experience.

His hand reached out and gently cupped her breast, his thumb sliding over her nipple. Her indrawn breath made him smile.

"I didn't touch you," she said.

His laughter was disconcerting. "No, but you wanted to."

Her gaze flew to his face. How had he known that?

He stepped back and began to remove his clothes. He had no hesitation in doing so, and appeared to relish her wide-eyed stare. First his shoes, then his jacket, shirt, trousers, and underclothes were removed and tossed to the other side of the room.

Did he think to have a maid in his wife? Was she supposed to pick up after him?

There was a great deal about marriage she needed to know, and it looked as if she was going to get an education right this moment.

He stood in front of her, one particular physical item of interest growing as she stared.

"Why does it do that?"

His laughter filled the room.

"It's his way of greeting you," he said.

"Do you always refer to it as though it's someone else?"

He grabbed her, wrapping his arms around her and pulling her close.

"What a delight you are, Jean," he said, kissing her temple.

He'd effectively trapped her with her arms in front. She snaked her hands between them and wound them around to his back.

His skin was so very warm. Before she had time to further muse on the different contours of their bodies, he was kissing her.

Every thought flew out of her head.

All she could do was feel—the soft and hard texture of his lips, the heat of his inquisitive tongue, and the sensation of the top of her head lifting up to the ceiling.

Was this passion? Or was he right, and she'd been feeling lust all along?

Her fingernails scored his back, and he made a sound in his throat.

Shamed, she murmured an apology against his lips.

He pulled back and looked at her, his eyes glittering.

"Why?"

She only shook her head.

He took another step backward, and she wanted to apologize again. Was he going to leave now? Had she hurt him, or done something wrong?

Her hands flailed in the air, coming to rest against her thighs. Her body was warm, as if he'd somehow conveyed his heat to her. Her skin felt prickly, and her breath was coming too fast.

She wanted to do something and didn't know what.

"Dear God, you're lovely," he said, his voice sounding choked.

He reached out a hand to touch her shoulder, then trail down her left arm. The other measured the contours of her right breast.

"You have magnificent breasts," he said. "And that damnable uniform didn't give a hint of you."

"I believe that's the intent," she said.

His laughter startled her again. Was she supposed to make him laugh so often, especially on their wedding night?

Now, one large hand cupped a buttock, while the other pressed flat against her abdomen.

She shivered.

"Everything about you is perfect," he said. "You're the most beautiful creature I've ever seen."

She'd never known words could warm her from the inside out.

Her hand reached out and pressed flat against his chest, wanting to make him feel the same.

"You are," she said softly.

He was a statue come to life, Roman or Greek, did it matter? He was a warrior, and she could easily envision him holding a shield and a spear. Or perhaps it was more correct to say he already held a spear, one pressing insistently against her.

She smiled at her own impropriety. Then he was kissing her again, but this time the room swirled around her. No, that was him as he put his arms around her.

Suddenly, she was on her back. How had he managed that?

Before she could comment, he was on the bed, leaning over her, kissing her again, and her hands had no place to go but trail through the hair on his chest.

"I wish to God you weren't a virgin," he said, kissing her throat.

Shocked, she drew back.

"Do you want me experienced?"

His expression was suddenly thunderous. "You'll not lie with anyone else, Jean. Ever. You're my wife. Do you understand?"

"Perfectly, Your Lordship. Must you call me 'wife' in that tone? As if I'm vermin? Or Lillian?"

Abruptly, he was standing beside the bed, glaring down at her.

"You're right, this marriage was a mistake."

As she watched, naked and stunned, he stalked to where he'd tossed his clothing, grabbed it and left the room.

She fell back on the bed, staring up at the tester. Her lips were still tingly. Her body still felt his touch, but Morgan had left her.

Surely, this wasn't a normal wedding night? This was the second time he'd stalked off. Was that a usual reaction from a bridegroom?

Should she return to her room? Should she go in search of him?

Was the peerage so different? She couldn't understand why he'd been so offended. All she'd done was ask a question. Was she not supposed to ask questions? Was she supposed to be docile, submissive, and subservient?

In other words, was she supposed to behave exactly as she had as a maid?

She sat up, looked around for her cloak, and realized she'd left it in the sitting room. Naked, she peered around the door.

Morgan wasn't there. She sighed heavily as she donned her cloak and left the Laird's Tower, her destination the one place he would go in the middle of the night.

A few moments later she stood in front of the library door. The fact it was closed indicated he was inside.

She should retire to the Countess's Suite. Anywhere but be

here, on a wedding night that wasn't a wedding night. What a very strange night indeed. She'd sent him away with a command, then he'd walked away on an insult. Perhaps they were destined never to come together.

Was it a sign? An omen that she wasn't supposed to be even his pretend wife?

Yet he'd kissed her. He'd touched her as no man had ever touched her.

According to her aunt, she should thank Providence circumstances had brought her any husband, even a false one.

Slowly, she pushed open the door, to find Morgan seated at the desk in a nimbus of light from the oil lamp. His gaze was fixed on the door as if he'd expected her to arrive any moment.

"My name is Jean," she said, as if they'd never been introduced. "I'm not Lillian. I wish you would not confuse me with her."

He didn't speak. Nor did his gaze leave her.

A bare-chested Morgan was even more intimidating than he'd been in his kilt and jacket. Now, she could really envision him as one of the Murderous MacCraigs, especially with that look on his face.

"Did you at least put on your shoes?" she asked.

He frowned at her.

She shrugged at his silence. "I didn't wear mine, either," she said, coming around the edge of the desk. She held out one foot and both of them stared at it. "Do you think this means I'm a hoyden?" she asked. "I've never gone anywhere barefoot before."

She sat on the corner of the desk and leaned closer to him. Should she confess she wasn't wearing anything beneath her cloak, either?

"I don't know if you would take the word of a former maid," she said. She held up her hand to forestall his comment. "But I promise never to bed another man as long as you are alive, Morgan."

"Do you have plans for my imminent death, madam?"

"No," she said. "But I don't want to promise I would never bed another man for the rest of *my* life. What if you were killed?" she asked, pushing back the hideous idea of Morgan's death. "I would have to obey that vow forever. That hardly seems fair."

He shook his head.

"Are you always so rigorously honest, Jean, even to your own detriment?"

"No," she said, regretting it was the truth. "I'm not. But when is honesty ever detrimental?"

"When I suspect you of plotting my death."

"Of course you don't," she said. "I don't think you're angry at all. I think you're just a little bit frightened."

She couldn't determine the look on his face. It wasn't anger. Nor was it amusement. Perhaps it was confusion or bewilderment. Truly, she wasn't adverse to confusing Morgan. He'd done that from the moment he insisted on marrying her.

"Am I supposed to be frightened of you?" he asked.

She considered the question for a moment. "Good heavens, wouldn't that be something? An earl and a maid, and the earl is quivering in his boots." She craned her neck for a view of his feet. "But you're barefoot, too."

He shook his head.

"Are you coming back to our bed?" she asked, then amended the comment. "Your bed." She looked around the room. The library was in shadows. She liked this room and knew every cranny of it.

"There's a settee upstairs," she said, "if you would prefer not to go that far."

"Are you suggesting I couple with you in the library?"

"I don't think I'd like the desk," she said, looking at the

surface. "It's leather, but there are all those brass nail heads. And it wouldn't be comfortable on my back."

He didn't say a word.

"What shall we do?" she asked, genuinely confused. "Shall I go back to my room? Shall we pretend not to be married? I don't mind, except I do wish you hadn't seen me naked."

"You've seen me naked," he said, in a calmer voice than he'd spoken earlier.

She nodded.

"We could both forget," she suggested.

"Or we could simply dispense with this damn wedding night."

Abruptly, he stood, grabbed her wrist and pulled her unceremoniously from the room.

He was muttering to himself, but she couldn't understand the words. The very fact that he was irritated was a good sign. She could cope very well with Morgan in that state since she'd had the most practice with it. His tenderness and praise had confused her, had opened up something in her heart that swelled even now.

She raced to keep up with him, making a mental note that whenever he dragged her somewhere it was easier when she was barefoot.

Halfway down the corridor he stopped and backed her up to the wall. Only one lone light was illuminated, leaving the rest of the corridor in long shadows.

He towered over her like a mountain.

"Am I supposed to be afraid of you?" she asked, putting her hands on his shoulders.

"God, no," he said, leaning in to kiss her.

Her hands reached up to bracket either side of his face, and then she didn't know anything for some moments. His mouth was warm, his tongue insistent.

No one told her she could become delirious with a kiss. Not one person had ever warned her a kiss could heat her body to this extent.

"You're naked under the cloak," he said, his voice hoarse.

She nodded.

When he pulled away, she made a moan of discontent, but then her cloak was open and his mouth was on her breast.

Surprise kept her silent. This was passion, she was certain of it. Her body felt as if it were liquefying. She would become nothing more than a puddle in a moment, a stain on the crimson runner.

Wherever his mouth touched, her skin quivered.

Why couldn't she breathe?

His lips left her breast for her mouth, a fierce, possessive, and shocking kiss, an explosion of taste and color urging her to surrender.

He opened his mouth, inviting her in, and her tongue found his, darting in and out, teasing and daring, brave as she'd never been brave with any man.

He made a sound in the back of his throat, and she pressed against him, wishing she didn't have the cloak shielding her nakedness. Wishing, too, he was as naked as she.

He pulled her closer, thrusting his tongue into her mouth, tasting her. She was suddenly dizzy, as if his kiss was a narcotic, some drug that lessened her resistance and made her compliant to Morgan's will.

Her breasts ached, dampness pooled between her thighs, and she felt the same tingling emptiness that had accompanied every thought of him for days now. She wanted to be touched in a shocking way. Another kiss and she'd ask him to remove his clothes. At the sight of him, she'd toss off her cloak and join him in nakedness.

Suddenly, they were racing back to the Laird's Tower.

She grabbed her cloak with both hands, glancing at him

as they ran. His face was bronzed, his look intent.

A laugh caught in her throat when he took her hand at the top of the stairs. She was out of breath, feeling as if the world had turned itself upside down.

When he kissed her again, she held onto him for balance, loving the shape of his mouth, his hot breath.

How had she lived before being kissed?

Then he was naked and they were on his bed again, the distance from the door to his bedroom crossed in a fog of feeling. When he trailed kisses between her breasts and down to her stomach, her breath came in choppy pants.

She felt like herself and yet more than herself. Herself times ten, perhaps, as if she were both older and wiser than she'd been this morning. Her fear level had dropped to a two or a one, or maybe it was naught.

Instead of gasping in horror, or being shocked when his fingers slid in her intimate folds, her legs widened to give him access. When he found her slick and wet, he made a murmur of appreciation.

Another lesson learned, passion was a good thing between husband and wife.

She wanted, needed, to do something, so she raised up and linked her arms around his neck, bringing his head down for a kiss. She nibbled on his bottom lip, then laved it with her tongue. Breathed into his mouth and gently sucked the tip of his tongue.

She rained kisses along his jaw, down his throat. He lifted himself over her, bracing himself on his forearms.

"I wish you weren't a virgin," he said again before sliding into her, an invasion so shocking her eyes widened and her hands gripped his shoulders, nails biting into his skin.

She might have made a sound if he hadn't kissed her at that moment.

The delight of his kiss and his touch gave way to a pinch

of discomfort, a feeling of being stretched and invaded. She wanted suddenly to stop it, to demand he leave her. Instead, he raised himself, surging back into her, unknowing or uncaring about her pain.

Where had the passion gone? It had disappeared in an instant to be replaced by *this*. Tears welled in her eyes. How long was he going to do this?

An endless time, hours, or days, or perhaps only moments later, he lifted himself off her. She rolled to her side, drawing up her legs.

Catriona had lied to her.

This hadn't been pleasurable at all.

She lay as quiet as possible, wondering when she could go back to her room.

Suddenly, Morgan left the bed, returning in a few minutes to sit on the edge of the mattress.

"Turn over, Jean," he said, touching her arm.

She shook her head.

"Turn over," he said again, gently pulling her to lay on her back.

She closed her eyes, pretending he wasn't there.

"Was it very painful?"

The question surprised her, enough that she opened her eyes and looked at him. Did he honestly care?

"Not very," she lied.

"I'm sorry. I hear it's like that for a virgin. At least it's over."

Dear God, did he want to do it again? She closed her legs tightly.

He placed a wet cloth against the juncture of her legs, surprising her again.

"Morgan . . ." she began, then faded to a stop as he began to bathe her. The warm cloth was oddly comforting as he insinuated it between her legs.

"Next time will be better," he said.

Next time? When did he plan to do it again?

His head dipped and he kissed her stomach. She flinched, tried to draw away, but he simply placed one large hand on her hip to keep her in place.

Then Morgan MacCraig did something she'd never expected, had never prepared for, had never imagined. He kissed her in a place she'd never thought to be kissed. She raised up, a hand fisting in his hair, but he calmly reached out and entwined his fingers with hers.

She lay back, closing her eyes, feeling the most incredible heat throughout her body. Embarrassment of a certainty, mixed with another sensation.

She pulled her hand free.

"Morgan," she whispered.

He did something with his fingers, gently stretching her.

She tensed, expecting him to enter her again, but all he did was use his tongue to stroke against her, long, lingering touches that made her shiver.

Grabbing the sheet with both hands, she tried not to move. Was it allowable to move? He was using his tongue in magical ways, stealing her breath.

Time narrowed. Slowed. Stopped.

Her heart pounded as a bubble of pleasure traveled from her center throughout her body.

Morgan's hand stroked her hip, gripped her buttock, claiming her as his mouth drove her insane.

She began to make inarticulate noises. Pleading with him, begging him either to stop or never to stop, she wasn't certain. Her hands left the sheets and flailed in the air. Then he pursed his lips, pulling gently on one particular spot, and her hips arched upward, her eyes closing at the surge of feeling. She bit her lip, held captive by the sensations. She was surrounded by colors, bright, wicked shards of light dancing in her mind.

Her hands gripped his shoulders. She moaned, and he murmured against her, the sound tipping her over into bliss.

Jean woke, to find herself alone in the earl's bed. Morgan, she corrected.

She sat on the edge of the bed, her legs dangling.

Once again she saw herself in the mirror on the opposite wall, and this time she winced. Her hair was a cloud around her head; her face was pink. Her lips were too full, and her eyes wide.

She should've drawn up the sheet around her, but instead she sat looking down at her own naked body as if it was a sight she'd never seen. In a way, she hadn't. She was as surprised by her body's reactions as by the events of the night before.

Where was Morgan? Was he avoiding her? Had he arisen early on purpose? Was he wanting to be away from her?

What was she to do now? Her days as a maid had been carefully orchestrated and scheduled. She woke, she washed, she dressed, then went to an early breakfast before inspection and being assigned her chores.

Very well, she could dress and find breakfast. As to her chores, that was a mystery, wasn't it?

Morgan returned to the Laird's Tower, knowing if he didn't, Jean might very well go in search of him.

Besides, he had visions of waking his surprising bride up in the most delightful way. But when he entered his bedchamber, she was sitting on the edge of the bed, a frown on her face.

Before he could greet her, she looked up, saw him, and grabbed for the sheet and wrapped it around her nakedness.

He wished she hadn't done that. But he could always strip it from her.

"Leave your hair down," he said.

Her hand went to the length of her hair, falling below her shoulders.

"It's not proper," she said.

"Who decides what's proper and what's not?" he asked, coming to stand in front of her. His fingers threaded through her hair.

A flush began in her chest and traveled up her neck to bloom in her cheeks.

"Do I embarrass you?" he asked. When she didn't answer, he merely asked her again.

"Is it entirely proper, everything we've done?"

He knew exactly what part of their lovemaking she was talking about, and although he wished to smile, doing so might hurt her feelings. Her innocence was charming and something to be guarded.

He placed his hands on her shoulders, gently smoothing them down to her wrists.

"Nothing we do together, Jean, is wrong."

She wouldn't look at him. Instead, she stared at her knees, covered by the sheet.

"It felt wrong," she said softly, shaking her head from side to side.

"You didn't like it?"

Her face flamed as she raised her eyes. "I liked it very much. It just felt wicked."

He smiled. "I restrained myself a great deal last night," he said. "I promise you, the next time I enter you, you'll feel only pleasure. No more discomfort."

She nodded, as if understanding. "That's why you wished I wasn't a virgin," she said.

Was she going to remember everything he said?

Perhaps her directness was part of her appeal. She didn't pose, and she didn't flirt, and she didn't do so many other things he was accustomed to women doing. Or perhaps it would be fairer to say: Lillian doing.

He leaned in to kiss her, smiling when she made a sound in the back of her throat.

The day was still early, and he was a new bridegroom. He began to remove his clothes. When he was done, he tumbled his wife back on the bed.

Perhaps he could show her, by example, just how wicked they could be.

Chapter 21

RULES FOR STAFF: *No relative or friend shall be allowed in the house at any time.*

"**Y**ou need to settle yourself," Andrew said. "This isn't painful."

He smiled reassuringly at the young maid seated on the overstuffed burgundy chair near the fireplace. The juxtaposition of her dark blue uniform against the richness of the upholstery interested him creatively.

The girl had knocked on the door to clean his room, and instead became the perfect subject.

"What's your name, my dear?" he asked, more in an effort to reassure her than because he cared.

"Donalda, sir," she said, her voice trembling. "Please sir, I need to be about my duties. Mrs. MacDonald knows how long it takes to clean each room. She'll be looking for me now."

He waved his hand in the air, dismissing the housekeeper.

"I shall just tell her I've absconded with you because I needed a subject for a portrait."

He wouldn't begin with his oils until the sketch was perfect. Besides, he'd only brought a few canvasses along with him, never thinking he would stay this long in Scotland.

But the entertainment value here was priceless. Not only was Morgan's behavior fascinating, but the new countess was proving to be vastly amusing as well. As for the other recreation, he smiled, thinking of Catriona. Poor puss, she didn't know how to handle her elevation in rank.

She was ignoring him, and the give and take of their play was engaging.

All in all, he was enjoying himself a great deal more than he'd expected.

The little maid—what was her name again?—perched on the edge of the chair, wringing her hands nervously despite his admonition for her to remain still. If she wasn't going to cooperate any better than that, he might as well dismiss her. But he never liked to lose, especially when the battle was joined with a woman.

He put down the stick of charcoal, turning away from his sketch to smile at her.

"I shall speak to the housekeeper on your behalf, my dear. Please, don't concern yourself with anything."

"But, sir," she said, "it's not proper."

She glanced toward the open door. She'd insisted on that. Nothing would come of it if someone objected to her being in the room alone with him.

He wasn't about to be shamed into a union with a maid. He was happily married and not likely to change. His wife suited him well, and she was an excellent mother to their brood.

Not once had she complained about his frequent absences, even when he informed her he was going to Scotland. Over the years, she'd learned there were two matters that captured his attention: the health of his children and the funds required to maintain his home. Beyond those subjects, he didn't involve himself with domestic drama. She, in turn, remained silent about his activities.

"Shall I call for one of your companions, then?" he asked.

She looked terrified at the idea. "Oh no, sir, that would bring Mrs. MacDonald up here for certain."

He wanted to finish the damn sketch, and if the woman was going to give him a problem, after he'd already completed half of it, then the entire day would be a waste.

Ignoring her protest, he stood and went to the bellpull, tugging on it once.

Jean was certain she would be blushing for the rest of her life. Just as certain as what she'd done with Morgan hadn't been common knowledge. If it was, how could anyone stay away from lovemaking? Everyone she knew would be seeking out partners, in order to experience what she'd felt.

Or was that kind of passion limited to marriage?

Or could it be only Morgan?

What a conundrum, to have all those questions and no one to ask.

Perhaps she'd been too hard on Catriona. After last night, this morning, and a few hours ago, she was beginning to understand why lovemaking held such an allure.

It might well be addictive. Opium was supposed to steal a man's soul. Could passion steal a woman's?

She'd left Morgan sleeping—he deserved his rest. Her face flamed again. She needed to bathe and change. Or brush her hair, if nothing else.

Thankfully, she didn't pass anyone as she crept back to the Countess's Suite. Whatever would she say to them, looking as she did? Her face was chafed in spots, and her hair a riotous mess of tangles. She'd lost her nightgown at Morgan's hands, and beneath her cloak she was naked again.

She washed and dressed, running a brush through her hair

before arranging it in a bun. There, she looked proper and decorous, if one could ignore the dancing look in her eyes. She couldn't keep from smiling, either.

No one had ever told her she would feel so *good*. Oh, she was a little sore, but overall she felt wonderful, glorious, incredible, and wasn't that a surprise?

Catriona sat at her vanity, staring at herself in the mirror, disliking what she saw. Her nose was too large for her face. Or maybe her mouth was too small.

She turned her head slightly to the side so she could view herself in a three-quarter pose. The new hairstyle she'd decided on was a great deal more flattering than the one she'd been forced to wear as a maid.

But she couldn't say very much about the seamstress's ability. The poor thing just needed more helpers, that was all. The woman had taken an inordinately long time to hem the dress she wore now, a rather plain thing originally planned for Jean.

"And I shall need a few more day dresses, Anne," Catriona said, addressing the seamstress.

Her aunt stood behind her, her mouth pursed in disapproval.

"Jean will need to augment her wardrobe first, Catriona," she said.

Catriona turned and smiled sweetly at her aunt.

"Is it not true Jean is my sister?" she asked.

Aunt Mary nodded once.

"Is it not true her husband is an earl?"

Another nod.

"Then I am the sister-in-law of an earl, am I not?"

This time her aunt didn't nod, merely folded her arms and stared at Catriona.

"While you, dear Aunt, are still of the servant class."

"You'll have to wait," Aunt Mary said after a long moment.

"This dress will do for now," she said to the seamstress. "But you've finished a few more day dresses for Jean, have you not?" she asked.

The woman looked to her aunt when she'd asked the question, then nodded.

"Then I shall need another one of those," Catriona said. "Or would you have me attired in a maid's uniform, Aunt?"

Her aunt grudgingly nodded, and while Anne went off to do Catriona's bidding, Mary went to stand at the window, ignoring her niece.

Perhaps it was just as well she was wearing her sister's clothes, Catriona reflected. Once she was properly attired, no one would notice poor Jean. She'd be known as the Plain Countess.

She sent a blinding smile in her aunt's direction, but Aunt Mary didn't look in the mood to be charmed.

No matter, just as long as her aunt understood the situation had indeed changed. She was no longer subject to her orders. If anything, Aunt Mary would have to listen to her.

What a wonderful situation, as promising as marrying an earl without the bother of a husband. A man could be so cloying, especially once you bedded him. This way, all she had to do was appeal to Jean, and her sister would give her whatever she wanted.

But it was a pity she wouldn't be a countess. Everyone she'd asked had agreed the earl had chosen the wrong sister.

She couldn't help wonder how Jean's wedding night had gone.

Would Morgan be enamored of her sister, enough to return to London? According to Andrew, Morgan had no intention of socializing again. Surely that would all change now that he'd become a bridegroom once more.

Or was Morgan hesitant to introduce Jean to society? Perhaps he was a little bit ashamed of her since Jean had been a maid. Even worse, Jean was plain, a little gawky, definitely insecure, and lacking womanly graces.

She herself needed to be in London, Catriona thought, not stuck here at Ballindair.

She'd avoided Andrew for days, because he'd treated her with too much familiarity, expecting her to come to his bed whenever he wished it. Whenever he smiled in her direction, she'd pointedly looked away. Even at the wedding yesterday, she pretended not to see him.

Perhaps she'd been a little too rash. It was one of her failings. However, she could always charm herself out of any situation. She would just have to ensure she did it this time, too.

The seamstress knocked, and when her aunt hesitated, Catriona waved her hand toward the door. Whatever her aunt was going to say was lost when the woman knocked again.

Instead of the seamstress, however, two girls stood in the corridor, each looking panicked.

"He wants another maid in the room," one of the girls said. "He's got Donalda in there, and he says he's going to paint her."

"Andrew?" Catriona asked, standing. "He's painting Donalda?"

After their first encounter, he'd never once asked to paint her. And now he was painting Donalda? The girl was plain, as plain as Jean, with dull black hair and a pointed nose. Why was Andrew painting Donalda?

Her aunt turned to her with a severe look. "Mr. Prender," she corrected.

Catriona allowed herself a small smile, but she didn't modify her comment.

She surveyed herself in the mirror, pleased with what she saw, and followed her aunt out the door.

*   *   *

What on earth was wrong? Jean heard the sound even through the closed door.

Someone was crying.

She left her room, hoping her aunt would not assign a maid to her suite. She could tend the rooms herself. Very well, perhaps a countess didn't do that sort of thing, but she didn't want to be in the awkward position of having one of her former companions intimate with all the details of her new life.

She suddenly realized that the staff at Ballindair had more privacy than the earl and his family.

Perhaps, if her aunt insisted on someone serving her, they could hire a woman from Inverness. Someone who hadn't known her when she was a maid.

She stopped at the landing, staring down the corridor toward the guest rooms. Her aunt, two maids, and Catriona were congregated outside Mr. Prender's room.

Catriona was attired in one of the new dresses made for Jean, who saw it had evidently been hemmed for her, since it wasn't dragging on the ground.

Pushing back her annoyance, she moved toward the group.

The two maids turned and looked at her, with varying expressions on their faces. One of them—Anice—was amused by the circumstances. The other frowned at her, as if resenting her elevation and new status.

"What you're doing isn't proper," Catriona said, pointing her finger inside the open doorway.

Her sister lecturing anyone on propriety was a little humorous. Aunt Mary, however, did not look at all amused.

Suddenly, Donalda burst out of the room, tears streaming down her red face.

"I'm not a slut like some," she said, turning to Catriona.

Mr. Prender was standing in the doorway, looking carefully nonchalant.

Catriona looked from Donalda to Mr. Prender, her eyes narrowed as if trying to decide whether anything had happened between them.

Perhaps because of knowledge gleaned from her wedding night, Jean was abruptly aware of the charged atmosphere between her sister and Mr. Prender. She knew, without a doubt, they'd been lovers, and probably still were.

"Has Mr. Prender taken advantage of you, Donalda?" her aunt asked, stopping the girl in the hall.

Donalda was still crying, but she shook her head.

At least there wouldn't be any fear of an unwanted child.

If Catriona became pregnant, what would happen to her? Did the peerage consider an unmarried pregnant woman a pariah? Was she shuffled off into obscurity? Or must she pretend to be a widow?

If her sister insisted on indulging in such reckless, abandoned behavior, she might find herself in that position.

Jean strode forward, nodding at her aunt and placing her hand on Catriona's arm, urging her into the sitting room. She nodded to Mr. Prender, who took her lead and walked farther into the room of his own accord. Only then did she gesture toward her aunt. When the four of them were in the room, she closed the door.

Let the maids guess at what transpired inside this room.

She turned to Mr. Prender and said, "Could you explain what has happened here?"

Catriona began to talk, but Jean deliberately turned away from her sister. There were times when Catriona was simply too self-absorbed to be relied on for information.

"I was only painting one of your maids," Mr. Prender said.

Jean took a step back from him, folded her hands in front

of her and regarded him somberly. She really didn't like the man. For the whole of the ceremony yesterday, he'd had a smirk on his face, as if he thought the wedding was beneath him. Now, he had the same expression, as if amused by their consternation.

"I take it Donalda did not wish to be painted," she said.

"Donalda is a flirt," Catriona said.

Jean didn't even turn to look in her sister's direction.

Donalda was a slender girl with a perpetual look of worry. Her nose was long, her chin too sharp, and her black hair thin to the point of being able to see her scalp.

She couldn't imagine anyone less of a flirt than Donalda. The girl was in tears most of the time. Life at Ballindair did not agree with her.

"If I erred, Countess," Mr. Prender said, "then please forgive me."

He bowed from the waist, a curiously insulting gesture.

She turned to her aunt. "Why were the other girls here?" she asked.

Aunt Mary frowned at Mr. Prender, and when she spoke, her attention was still on him.

"Donalda insisted on another maid as chaperone. The girl took one look at the situation and came and got me."

Jean turned to Catriona. "And why are you involved?"

Her sister placed one hand flat against the placket of her borrowed dress.

"Everyone knows I'm only concerned, of course. I came to see if I could smooth out the situation," she said, her gaze flirting with Andrew's.

Did Morgan have any other properties? Somewhere Catriona could be sent? Perhaps she might even be convinced to take on the role she herself had been offered. What a silly notion. Catriona couldn't be bothered to clean anything, let alone supervise those who did. Now, if a position involved being fitted for clothes or staring longingly in the mirror at herself, then she would be perfectly suited for it.

Or perhaps they could send her to an outlying cottage, in the company of a paid companion or chaperone. Someone who would guard Catriona's virtue—what was left of it—and prevent her from giving another man the look she was currently sending Mr. Prender.

Jean felt as if she should stand between them in order to protect her sister from Mr. Prender's gaze—that of a love-starved dog.

Dear heavens, what a difference a day made. Yesterday, she'd been ignorant. Today, the veil of innocence had been stripped from her, and she understood only too well the meaning of those looks.

Did she look at Morgan in the same manner, as if she were starving and he was a roast?

Something fluttered in her stomach. Perhaps she was feeling a bit of hunger herself. That thought drew her up so sharply she fixed a stern gaze on both Mr. Prender and her sister.

"Leave Donalda alone," she said to Andrew. She turned to Catriona. "Leave Mr. Prender alone," she said, not caring that Aunt Mary gasped behind her.

If that was too much plain speaking, they would simply have to accept it. At least everyone knew she was aware of what was going on, and now Aunt Mary did, too.

Between the two of them, perhaps they could convince Catriona to act in a more respectable fashion.

Andrew smiled at her before turning his attention toward Catriona again.

"Perhaps your sister might agree to be my model. I've grown tired of the Scottish landscape."

Jean regarded him in silence.

If the two of them wanted so desperately to be together, let it be in public.

"In the Great Hall," she said, and turned to her aunt. "Somewhere that isn't private. No corners, curtained alcoves, or shadowy recesses." She glanced at Catriona. "Somewhere crowded."

Aunt Mary nodded. For as long as Mr. Prender painted her sister, she would ensure that her aunt sent all manner of maids and footmen, perhaps even grooms and farmhands, traipsing through the Great Hall.

Mr. Prender's smile slipped a little.

The look he gave her was considering, as if he were gauging how much charm would be needed to sway her from her decision.

Jean folded her arms. "That's the only circumstance in which I would agree to allow you to paint my sister," she said. "And I would appreciate it if you would not waylay any of our maids in the future."

He raised one eyebrow but didn't speak.

"Very well, Countess," he finally said.

She pasted a smile on her face as he bowed again.

How on earth could Morgan abide him?

"Aunt Mary will accompany you to your room," she said, gesturing toward her sister. She didn't want Catriona remaining behind in Mr. Prender's suite.

It was, perhaps, a good thing that her sister didn't give voice to the thought flashing in her eyes.

She should warn her, Jean thought, that such an angry expression had a deleterious effect, and might permanently mar her looks. Instead, she opened the door and nodded at the three maids, who stepped back from the doorway, and gratefully left the group behind.

Chapter 22

RULES FOR STAFF: *No gossip will be allowed concerning the family.*

Ballindair was a thundercloud. Streaks of lightning, in the form of various personalities, were making their presence known in his home. Weeping maids, raised voices, and a clanking, banging boiler made for a rapidly approaching storm.

He'd spent most of his morning in a thoroughly unsatisfactory meeting with his steward. The man was ill, but refused to talk of it. In the face of his pride, Morgan remained silent.

In addition, Andrew had taken up painting in the middle of the Great Hall. He had a pedestal erected, something that looked to Morgan remarkably like a catafalque. On this structure, his sister-in-law half sat, half reclined, in a pose more odalisque than respectable.

When he gave his list of complaints to the housekeeper, all she did was stare at him.

"Are you paying attention, Mrs. MacDonald?"

Had he lost all conversational ability? Was the house-keeper going to ignore everything he said simply because they were now related by marriage? Would she be so foolish?

"Of course I'm paying attention, Your Lordship," she said in a clipped voice. "Jean has already passed on to me her concern about the boiler. We are having one of our men look at it. As to Mr. Prender, Jean thought it best he paint Catriona in a public place."

"Jean did?" he asked, feeling a curious confusion. Was Jean behind the storm of his home? "Tell me, does she have anything to do with Seath's illness?"

Now she looked surprised.

"How did you know, Your Lordship?"

He shook his head. "Know what?"

"Jean has been making him tea every day. And a good strong broth. It seems to be helping him."

"Where is my wife now?" he asked cautiously. Was she stirring up some additional surprises for him?

"I believe she's in the Laird's Garden," Mrs. MacDonald said, looking at him as if he were the most surprising aspect in all of this.

He left her then, before she could sense his utter and total confusion.

This morning he'd awakened Jean with a kiss. She'd turned to him, eager and willing, giving herself to him with a freedom that awed him. A week of marriage had left him feeling . . . happy.

For the first time in a very long time, he found things about which to laugh. One night he'd sat with Jean and to-gether they'd read an idiotic book entitled *The Ghosts of Ballindair,* a tome no doubt commissioned by one of his an-cestors in need of some way to spend his money.

They'd argued about some of the superstitions listed in the book, especially those pertaining to the Murderous Mac-

Craigs. The debate had ended in laughter, which ended in loving.

He was teaching Jean chess, and the disbelief with which she greeted the rules amused him: "What do you mean, my knight can't move that way?" or "Why is the knight allowed to jump and the bishop can't?" or "You know I don't speak French. What does *en passant* mean?"

More than once he'd found himself talking about London with her. Not his disillusionment, but the work he'd done in Parliament. He described his favorite places, only to have her counter that Scotland was the equal of any sight to be found in England. Then she'd kissed him, and proceeded to show him just how "well-traveled" she was becoming.

Now she was missing again.

He went in search of his wife.

Andrew watched Catriona as she lay on her back, eyes closed, a soft smile gracing her full lips. They'd escaped from the Great Hall for a well-deserved interlude in his rooms. He suspected they weren't fooling anyone. If the staff of Ballindair was like other establishments, their affair was already common knowledge.

One corner of her lips curled up in a half smile as if she ridiculed his thoughts.

She was like a cat, intensely herself, self-reliant, and not needing anyone. She'd allowed him to spirit her away because it served her to do so. Did she have an itch needing to be scratched? Would she have done so if there was another man nearby? Or if she hadn't seen him smile at one of the maids this morning? She was not jealous as much as she was possessive, a trait that he recognized because it was in his own nature.

He was feeling the same way right now.

Catriona hadn't appeared impressed with either his size

or his skill at lovemaking. After the first night, she'd thanked him prettily, then said nothing further.

He was in the curious position of being fascinated by a woman who wanted nothing to do with him unless it was on her terms.

Although she was beautiful, he'd had other beautiful women. Her body was lush and inviting, and she'd learned some tricks. She made no pretense of being educated, and only laughed merrily when he quoted poetry to her.

"Don't tell me words. Give me actions. Don't promise me. Produce."

No doubt his fascination with Catriona was because there were no other willing women about. The majority of Ballindair maids were plain creatures. Or perhaps they only looked plain next to Catriona.

She was purely amoral, and since he'd often considered himself to be the same, he wondered if that was why he couldn't get enough of her. Perhaps she was his female counterpart.

If he took her to London, she'd probably leave him the moment she had a more advantageous offer. But the fact that he even thought of taking her back to London surprised him. He was the one who'd always said good-bye first.

Catriona, however, was like a burr in his flesh.

She stretched slightly, curling her hand beneath the pillow, and opened her eyes, smiling at him.

He rolled over close to her, thinking perhaps they could spare another few minutes.

The air was sweet and balmy, heady with the scent of flowers planted in borders beside the walk. Jean didn't know what they were called, but she enjoyed watching their bright pink blooms sway in the breeze.

What a pity the garden was restricted to the laird and his

family. Everyone should be able to walk along the gravel paths through the labyrinth of hedges and trees. Just as she was forming a request to Morgan to open up the garden, she stopped, surprised. There, sitting on a bench at the juncture of two paths, was Mr. Seath.

His eyes were closed, his hands flat on his thighs and his head tilted back. A ray of sun caught him, bathing the man in an ethereal glow.

Each time they met, he shared a little more of his life with her. Each time she brought him the tea she'd made for him to calm his stomach, she shared a little of hers as well.

He was as pale as death, even in the glow of the sun. His features were even more pronounced, as the illness stripped away everything and left only the essential parts: a long, bony nose, high cheekbones, and wide forehead. Even his wrinkles were gone, a testament to the voracious hunger of the wasting sickness.

His garments hung on him like a child playing make-believe in his father's clothes. The cuffs of his shirt nearly covered the tips of his fingers; his trousers hung in folds from his legs. His throat, with its prominent Adam's apple, was a frail stamen rising from his collar.

Tears peppered her eyes, and she blinked them back, a restraint long practiced with her mother. Her crying would not help him. Her pity would not take away his pain. She knew that only too well.

Quietly, she approached the steward. Would he mind her company? Or had he sought out this space in the Laird's Garden to be alone with nature and with God? She was debating about retreating when he opened his eyes.

"Just what this day needed," he said faintly. "Another flower in the garden."

Her laughter bubbled free. "I've never been called a flower," she said. "What type might I be?"

"A rose?" Before she could answer, he shook his head. "Not a common rose, my dear, but a wild rose, one unexpectedly sweet."

He regarded her solemnly for several minutes, during which time she drew closer, then sat beside him on the bench.

A smile curved her lips, and she was grateful for his foolishness. A flower, indeed.

"A flower with a sense of its own self," he said. "It doesn't try to have many petals. It says accept me as I am. I am different. I am unique."

Her laughter made him smile.

He pointed to a flower bed not far from where they sat.

"See those pink flowers?"

She nodded. "Are they wild roses, then?"

"Indeed they are. And growing late this season, as if they know how much I love them."

She studied the flowers for a few moments. He thought her a wild rose.

Was he saying, in his very tactful way, that she was caught between two worlds? Neither a weed nor truly a rose. Neither maid nor truly a countess.

Her life had been easier as a maid. She'd had the rules explained to her, taught to her, and repeated every day. As a countess she was constrained by a set of unwritten rules. She was supposed to know not only what to do, but what not to do.

Or was she feeling caught between two worlds today because of her conscience? Was being a wife the most difficult pretense of all?

Every night, she'd told herself to bar Morgan's entrance to her room, but she never did, welcoming him with a hunger that surprised her. On those occasions when she'd gone to the Laird's Tower, she told herself she should claim fatigue, illness, her monthly time. Anything but become ensnared even deeper in a lie.

She should leave before dawn, not sleep with him all night, cuddled against his warmth, feeling his skin against hers even in her sleep.

Passion, or perhaps Morgan, was a net trapping her, yet she was doing nothing to free herself. When he touched her, she felt some unknown part of herself take over. The woman he summoned loved the stroke of his fingers, laughed when he tickled her, sighed when he entered her, and sobbed her pleasure.

Every night, they loved, and every morning she told herself she wasn't his wife. Oh, it felt that way. She felt as if she had the right to stroke his hair back from his brow, and kiss the corner of his lips, or capture his earlobe between her teeth and tug gently in play.

To distance herself from thoughts of Morgan, she asked, "Are you feeling better today?"

"I'm not." But the tone in which he said those words was not querulous or complaining. He said it merely as a simple statement. A comment with so little emotion that it might have been a remark about the weather.

She turned her head to look at him, wishing she had some words to ease him in some way. All she had was a silly tea, but she would brew a pot of it now if he wished.

He reached over and placed his hand on top of one of hers. She put her other hand on his, feeling his cold skin, as if his body was preparing for the grave.

She looked down at their joined hands, feeling tears again. Sometimes she couldn't stop them when they came. Sometimes they were there before she knew it, the past rising up to envelope her in a fog of emotion.

"Did your mother die very long ago?"

"Two years," she said.

"It was very painful for you, wasn't it?"

She nodded. "I miss her every day," she said.

She looked down at their joined hands. How long had it been since she'd allowed herself to truly cry? Too long, perhaps, because the tears began to run unchecked down her face.

Sweet man, to care so much for her pain, when it was her mother who'd suffered.

Toward the end, she and Catriona had only heard moans and cries from their parents' bedroom. Her mother had wept to die, pleading with her husband to help her.

But she didn't say that to Mr. Seath. Instead, she gripped his hand even harder.

In the next moment, she found herself engulfed in a hug. Her head was on his shoulder and she was weeping in earnest, great gulping sobs for her mother, and for her father as well.

Her arms encircled him, feeling the frailty of his body, knowing the same fate faced him. Perhaps some of her tears were for this kind and gentle man.

She allowed herself a few minutes of grief before pulling away, embarrassed. When he handed her a handkerchief, she took it gratefully, blotting at her face.

Her right hand was still gripping his, and she was gratified to note his touch felt warmer.

She wanted to do something to help this dear man. What could she do?

"What is your real name?" Mr. Seath asked.

All thought simply evaporated.

She turned her head slowly and looked at the steward. His expression hadn't changed, and in his eyes there was a calm understanding.

Fear iced her stomach, banishing her grief.

He knew. Somehow, he knew.

Chapter 23

"**I**s it MacDonald?"

She shook her head. "No," she said, sighing. "It's Cameron."

He nodded. "Ah, I remember talk of a Dr. Cameron. Quite a scandal. I recall mention of two daughters."

She folded his handkerchief, then folded it again. She couldn't look at him. Her earlier sorrow had been replaced by something cold and sharp like terror.

"That's why you wanted to know, of course. If a marriage was legal."

She managed to nod.

"It isn't, of course, but you knew that."

Once again she nodded.

"And, so, you came to Ballindair not long after," he said.

She nodded. "No one wished to have anything to do with us," she said.

"How very difficult for you," he said.

Difficult enough they'd nearly starved to death. Without Aunt Mary's intervention, they might well have. Or Catriona would've achieved her goal of becoming a rich man's mistress.

Hardly what their father would have wished for her.

They sat in the quiet for a few minutes, the peace of the garden and Mr. Seath's silent acceptance washing over her.

Evidently, he wasn't going to say anything. But how did she live with her daily guilt? How did she push away the feelings she was coming to have for Morgan? It was one thing to lie to the Earl of Denbleigh, another to lie to Morgan, a man who considered himself her husband.

"How are you finding your new life?" he asked.

She wasn't appreciably happier. In fact, she might even say she was markedly miserable. She was enchanted by her husband, fascinated by their lovemaking, confused, and beset by a dozen emotions.

"None of the maids approve of me," she said, grasping at the most idiotic thing to say.

His chuckle surprised her. She turned her head to look at him.

"Did you expect them to? People are people, my dear. You've risen from their ranks to be their employer. Don't you think they're wondering what you will do next? You're suddenly in a position of power. They worry. They think, did she like me when we worked together? If she didn't, will she use it against me?"

She gently extricated her hand from his. "I would never do any of those things."

"Then prove it."

She frowned at him. "How do I prove something I wouldn't do?"

"By giving them a picture of who you are. Have you shown them who their new countess is?"

She told him of the episode of Mr. Prender's room.

He nodded. "That's a good start, but you need to carry your actions further. Ensure Donalda wasn't harmed for her experience. Have you talked to her?"

She shook her head.

"She may well have felt intimidated by you even before you married the earl, simply because of your relationship with the housekeeper. She comes from a very poor family and desperately needs this job. Did you know that?"

Again she shook her head.

"Then let me tell you, my dear," Mr. Seath said.

Jean listened to Donalda's story, feeling more and more regretful as she did. She'd worked beside the girl for months and never knew any of what Mr. Seath was telling her now. Not once had Donalda ever confided in her. Not once had she ever complained. Yet she'd never been curious enough to ask Donalda anything about her past.

"She's afraid of losing her position. If she does, it might put her whole family in jeopardy."

Being a countess—being a responsible countess—was not as easy as everyone thought it should be. So far, she'd made a mess of it. All she'd done was weep in the garden, daydream of her husband, and be childishly annoyed by the actions of her former coworkers.

"You'll need to tell the earl, of course," he said.

"About Donalda?" she asked, turning to him.

"About you," he said with a smile.

"How? 'Your Lordship, not only have you married a maid, but you've married Jean Cameron. Yes, *that* Jean Cameron. If you thought scandal had touched you before, it is nothing to what people will say now.'"

"Do you think the earl cares that much about scandal?" the steward asked. "If he had, would he have divorced his wife? Wasn't that a scandalous act in itself?"

"In his case," she said, "it was the lesser of two scandals."

"A matter of degrees," he said.

She nodded. "I don't think he anticipated the reaction of society, Mr. Seath. I think it caught him by surprise. People can be exceptionally cruel, especially to those who've stepped beyond the boundaries of society. My sister and I had done nothing, but we were treated with the same degree of horror people felt for my father. They didn't see his actions as merciful, but rather, merciless."

She looked up at the sky. "Can you imagine what society would do to Morgan once they discover who I am?"

"Perhaps it's a good thing you're not married then, my dear," Mr. Seath said.

Surprised, she turned to him.

"Without a legal marriage, he'll be able to claim you as a dalliance, a misalliance. The whole thing could be passed off as a jest, perhaps. But what will happen to you when the day comes and the truth is known?"

The question startled her.

She thought of a suitable answer, discarded it, thought of another, and ended up saying, "I don't know."

"Is that why you haven't told him?" he asked. His smile was infinitely kind.

She glanced away.

"A way will be revealed to you," he said. "I have only confidence in you. You think you're an improper countess. I can think of no one better. You're exactly what the earl needs."

She very much doubted that.

"You must understand, my dear, what kind of man your husband is. He might brave scandal for the sake of doing the right thing, but he has a great deal of pride. Even more, he holds himself to a higher standard than most. He believes he must be the epitome of all that is just and good about Scotland. He has his family's earlier reputation to live down and his father's heritage to achieve." Mr. Seath shook his head. "The boy in the man will not allow any alterations in what he believes is true, even if it means accepting a falsehood."

She didn't speak, despite her curiosity. There were some things, perhaps, she shouldn't ask. Questions that would not be considered proper, even from a new wife.

However, Mr. Seath continued, as if he realized she was constrained by her own sense of propriety. "I've spoken of Donalda," he said. "The earl's father was instrumental in creating the poverty they experience now. Have you heard of the Clearances?"

She nodded. Tales had spread far and wide, along with newspaper accounts about how some lairds had pushed people off their property, finding it more advantageous to raise sheep than allow the crofters to continue to rent and farm the land.

"Morgan's father gave me orders to do the same for an entire area of Ballindair land."

"And Morgan doesn't know?"

Mr. Seath shook his head. "The earl has not expressed any desire to know about the workings of the estate. Even so, I doubt he would tolerate any ill words spoken of his father.

"Donalda's family still lives in a small cottage not far from here," he said. "I took it upon myself to make the arrangements. I've not told the earl what I've done, but I could not sit by while people starved."

She nodded, understanding.

"I would prefer you not tell him," he said. "Of course, it is entirely within your power to do so. That, I can understand."

"Shall we agree to keep each other's secrets, then?" she said. "You have one of mine, and now I have one of yours."

He reached out, patted her hand and smiled at her. A reprieve, and only that, because one day soon she knew she'd have to tell Morgan the truth.

In an extemporaneous gesture unlike her, she reached over and hugged Mr. Seath, wishing she could infuse him with her own health. He hadn't upbraided her for her secret. Nor had he looked at her with contempt. For that alone, and even if she hadn't come to feel a great fondness for him, she would have been grateful.

Jean pulled back, turning her head to see Morgan standing on the path. Instead of approaching them, he turned and walked in the other direction.

She frowned in his direction.

Was he jealous? Could he be that foolish?"

She stood, bent and kissed Mr. Seath on the forehead, surprising both of them, before heading in the direction Morgan had disappeared.

Jean found Morgan in the library, the third room she visited since beginning to search for him. When she asked the maid if she'd seen the earl, Molly hadn't even looked in her direction, merely shook her head.

Mr. Seath's words came to mind. She stopped, wondering what she could say to ease the situation. Not a word came to her. Instead, she thanked Molly, and when the maid turned and looked at her in surprise, she began to understand.

Her behavior from this point on would form the foundation of her relationship with the staff. Gradually, they might come to respect her. But only if she demonstrated respect first.

She entered the library, knowing Morgan was there almost immediately. The room seemed changed with his presence. When she climbed the curving iron staircase, she saw his shoes first, then his trousers.

He turned and glanced at her disinterestedly, as if the book he held was of monumental importance and she less so.

"You can't possibly be jealous of Mr. Seath, Morgan."

He turned to face her, his features frozen into a mask, his eyes flat and cold.

"Perhaps it's your upbringing," he said. "Although I was given to expect better from you. My wife needs to be above reproach. Meeting a man and sitting with him in a garden, unattended by anyone else, is not acceptable behavior."

She took a few steps toward him, stopping only when she was an arm's length away.

"Even if the man is desperately ill? Or haven't you noticed that?"

He didn't answer, merely put the book back on the shelf. She took another step closer.

"Also, Mr. Seath is old enough to be my father."

He glanced at her. "I've seen many unions, madam, between an older man and a younger woman."

"I'd thought your accent was fading, but when you're angry, you sound very English."

He didn't even look at her.

"Mr. Seath is dying, Morgan. Can you not see that? Can you not have some pity for the man?"

"I am not speaking of my steward, madam. But of my wife."

She took a step backward, away from him. "How disagreeable you sound, as if I were some onerous responsibility of yours. Something you had to care for that annoyed you. My wife. My brass urn. My chamber pot."

"What were you talking about with him? Why was he embracing you?"

He was the one to close the distance between them now. How very tall he was—nearly half a head taller than she. It annoyed her to have to tilt back her head to look up at him.

But it further irritated her to see the narrowed and suspicious expression in his eyes.

"We were congratulating ourselves on our ruse, of course," she said. "That no one knew of our great and momentous love. We're going to escape together and run away to Paris, to live a life of unbridled ecstasy." She folded her arms. "Of course, any idiot could see Mr. Seath can barely stand. As a lover he, no doubt, would be somewhat lacking."

Morgan's cheekbones were a dull bronze color now. Good, let him be as angry as she was.

"I do not take jests about fidelity well, Jean."

"I doubt you take jests at all, Morgan," she said. "Life is not all about duty and honor and privilege," she said. "And wealth," she added for good measure. "It can also be about fun. About joy. About amusement. About the lighter things of life."

"I find your lecture odd given you were weeping in his arms."

Dear Lord, how long had he been standing there?

"Do you find me excessively boring?" he suddenly asked.

She blinked at him. "You?"

He nodded.

"I wouldn't have used the word boring to describe you, Morgan. Infuriating, perhaps. Annoying, of a certainty. Not boring."

He folded his arms in front of his chest. "I do not want to have to wonder about my wife's actions, madam."

She shook her head. "Well, Morgan, you are going to wonder about me. You are even going to worry about me, I daresay. Because I'm a human being, and can't be placed in a jar for you to study. I walk. I talk. I think. I speak. None of which is under your control. You will have to trust me."

"Trust doesn't come easy to me."

She marched toward him and punched him in the chest

with her finger, before saying between clenched teeth, "I am not Lillian."

A corner of his lip turned up, as if he mocked her protestation.

"See you don't behave as she did, then."

She narrowed her eyes and stared at him. "You can be insufferable," she said. "Perhaps Lillian had a reason for her infidelity."

They both stared at each other, Jean horror-struck by what she'd just said. She hadn't meant it, but she knew from his expression that if she tried to explain, he wouldn't accept her words. Perhaps it was better for her to simply leave the room before she made a worse mess of things.

She descended the staircase and left the library, intent on her room. Praying, too, that Catriona wasn't there, her aunt would leave her alone, and no domestic catastrophes required her presence. What she wanted was to simply sit in a corner and pretend she was a ghost of Ballindair.

Better a ghost than a live and troubled human being.

Chapter 24

Morgan wasn't sure what bothered him most—the fact that Jean had been crying and was comforted by his steward, or the fact that she hadn't told him what they were discussing.

Had she confided in the older man that she was miserable in her marriage? Had she told Mr. Seath she regretted their union? Had she even ventured an opinion that he was a lamentable lover?

She'd called him insufferable.

Lillian had used the word enough times that it pinched now.

He knew well enough his steward was ill. Plus, the man had shown enough loyalty to the MacCraigs over the years that Morgan didn't suspect him of trying to lure his wife away.

But there were different kinds of adultery.

Why did he mind that she might have confided her thoughts to another man? Because she should have come to him. Why hadn't she?

I am not Lillian.

The comment whipped at him, as if each word was equipped with a barbed tail.

He'd been nearly insensate in Jean's arms. He'd been sotted with joy over her response to him. He'd felt mighty, and eager, boyish, and skilled. Right now he felt none of those things. Only foolish, because coupled with that thought was another—he'd brought it on himself by accusing her.

Or by caring too much.

Catriona stretched, feeling remarkably well, considering she'd been engaged in very strenuous sex for the last hour.

"You're a remarkable lover," she said, turning her head and smiling over at Andrew. "But I'd wager every woman you bed tells you that."

He kept his eyes closed, but his smile had a certain wickedness to it.

She propped herself up on one elbow and trailed a path up his bare chest with two fingers. "Have you had very many lovers? I would say a good hundred or more."

"I've never taken the time to count them," he said, his smile broadening.

Her fingers trailed along his lips, tracing their contours.

"But I thank you, nonetheless," he said, "for such praise. Perhaps I should get it in writing and just hand out critiques of my performance."

"No doubt it would shorten the time between meeting a woman and getting her into your bed."

He opened his eyes, turned his head and smiled at her. "Oh, but those are the most delightful moments. The chase, my dear, is sometimes more fun than catching the quarry."

She leaned forward and kissed the tip of his nose, answering his smile with one of her own.

"You are a great deal of fun, dear Andrew."

He turned his head and closed his eyes again as she sat up.

"Are you going to pose for me later?" he asked.

"Is that a euphemism?" She laughed. "If that's what you wish."

He slit open one eye. "Because you have nothing better to do with your time?"

"I have no wardrobe for anything else," she said, shrugging.

It was his turn for laughter. "I do believe I've met my match. A thoroughly amoral woman. Have you always been that way?"

"I'm not certain I like the term amoral, Andrew," she said, frowning. "It doesn't seem proper, somehow. Is it considered amoral if I simply know what I want and choose to go after it?"

He rolled to his side and studied her. "Even your back is beautiful," he said as she stood to slip on her shift. "There's nothing wrong with knowing what you want or in choosing to go after it, my dear. What's not so proper, perhaps, is the fact that I do not doubt you'd push anyone out of your way to achieve it."

She turned and knelt on the bed, uncaring the shift was so thin it gave him a perfect view of her. Let him look his fill. She liked when Andrew's eyes sparkled with lust.

"I'm not quite that vicious," she said. "I just don't want anyone standing between me and what I want."

"What you want, my dear? Dare I hope it's me?"

She smiled.

"Your watch has been stolen, dear Andrew. It's loss is a burden to you, since it was the last gift given you by your father."

He frowned at her, turned, and reached for his watch

where it sat on the bedside table. He dangled it by its chain in front of her.

"I haven't lost it at all, Catriona."

She palmed the watch, raising her hand to pool the chain in her hand, and gently pulled it from him.

"Oh, but you have," she said. "And the culprit must be punished."

He frowned at her, awareness dawning in his eyes. "Is that entirely necessary?"

"Donalda called me names, Andrew. She needs to be taught a lesson." She stood, looking down at him. "Or perhaps that's what you think of me. That I am a slut."

"Why do I think you won't come back to my bed unless I accuse the girl of theft?"

She smiled, glad he understood.

"What if I think the price is too high?"

"Do you?" she asked, slowly removing her shift. She stood in front of him naked, beautiful, and knowing it.

He laughed, reached for his watch, then for her.

Night came too quickly for Jean.

With night came the prospect of dinner. With dinner came the idea of sitting at a table with Morgan, Catriona, and Andrew.

She didn't think she could bear the presence of any of them tonight, most especially Morgan.

She'd been married a week. A week, and she'd managed to offend her husband so much that he hadn't spoken to her all day. If he'd sought her out, she had no knowledge of it. She hadn't been hard to find. She'd stayed in her room.

This afternoon she'd gathered up her courage and gone to the library, hoping he'd still be there. She'd planned an apology, reciting the exact words over and over again until they were firmly fixed in her mind.

I'm sorry I was with Mr. Seath, Morgan. Although I consider him a friend, I can see where our being together might be misinterpreted.

Would that be enough of an apology? She wasn't going to grovel.

The point was moot, because Morgan wasn't in the library. Nor did she go in further search of him.

She should tell him the truth, let him do the worst. She could, with any luck, obtain a position somewhere. As a maid, true, since it was all she had any experience doing, unless someone had a need for a slightly less than virtuous quasicountess. But there was Aunt Mary to consider, and even though her aunt had advised her to keep silent, Aunt Mary didn't deserve to be dismissed. Her aunt loved every inch of Ballindair almost as much as Mr. Seath. It was there in her education of the maids, in her lectures as to the art and beautiful objects scattered around the castle.

She needed to consider Catriona, too, on a ruinous path and unstoppable. She hadn't the slightest idea what to do about it.

Night brought yet another problem. Was Morgan going to come to her room?

Could a wife ever refuse a husband? What woman in her right mind would want to refuse Morgan? A woman who was, perhaps, confused, daunted, and more than a little apprehensive.

How could Lillian have strayed? Was the woman a fool? Or did she want something from Morgan he couldn't give her? Love, perhaps? Affection? Or an even more basic emotion: respect.

Jean sat in her room staring at the bellpull, summoning up her courage. She stood, walked to where it hung and jerked it once.

When Betty, one of the younger maids, appeared at the

door, Jean gave her a note, forced a smile to her face and said, "Would you please convey this to the earl, Betty?"

The girl nodded, without a curtsy or a comment.

Frankly, she didn't care if anyone ever curtsied to her, and she could dispense with all that Your Ladyship nonsense. It was disconcerting, however, to still be treated as if she were invisible.

Her note had been simple and to the point: *I am not feeling well enough to join you for dinner.* Morgan would simply have to accept her illness. Would it stop him from coming to her room?

She wasn't going to sit here and wait for him.

He'd done as much as compare her to Lillian, and in such a lordly tone that she knew he'd done it on purpose. He could be the great Earl of Denbleigh with anyone else, but she was no longer a maid.

Wasn't that what Mr. Seath had wanted her to know? Whatever happened from this point forward would be as a result of her behavior. People were allowed to have memories, yes, but it was her responsibility to supplant better memories on top of the poor ones they might have. Let the maids see her as the Countess of Denbleigh, not as a maid.

At the same time, let Morgan see her as Jean and not Lillian.

No doubt Lillian would've gone to him with some cajoling remark, even attempted to seduce the man. Well, she wasn't going to do that. She didn't want to have anything to do with Morgan MacCraig right at the moment.

The more she thought about their encounter, the more annoyed she became. The more time that passed, the more determined she was to refuse him admittance into her room and her bed.

Her stomach growled, reminding her that all she'd had to eat today was a scone at breakfast. She wasn't in the mood for another bout of being treated as if she were invisible by one of the maids, so she ignored her hunger, a habit she'd learned in Inverness.

Instead of readying herself for bed, she tugged on her skirts, worked at the tapes of her hoop until it was free, and let it drop to the floor. Stepping over the collapsed monstrosity, she grabbed the material of her skirt, now too long and dragging on the floor, opened the door of her sitting room and sailed into the corridor.

Another thing—the ghosts of Ballindair owed her an apology, especially the French Nun. If it hadn't been for her, she wouldn't have been in this situation to begin with. She wouldn't have collided with Morgan. She wouldn't have had to explain her presence in the Laird's Tower. She would have melted into the sea of other servants and never been noticed.

A thought brought her up short: She would have still gone in search of Catriona.

Very well, perhaps the ghosts didn't owe her an apology.

Everyone expected her to be so grateful to be a countess, to be the wife of a wealthy man, a titled man, a peer. Why hadn't anyone said to Morgan: "You're to be congratulated, sir, on your new wife." Very well, she wasn't beautiful, not like Catriona. She was tall and slender with great bulbous breasts. Whenever one of her dresses had to be altered for Catriona, her sister made the remark that she could have folded her arms inside the bodice and still have plenty of room left over.

She asked questions, and wasn't content to simply allow herself to be taught and told by others. Why had God given her a mind if he hadn't wanted her to use it?

Perhaps they would say something like: "Congratulations, Your Lordship, on your new wife. She has a sparkling wit, a rapacious mind. What insightful questions she asks! What cogent logic she expresses!"

There, that sounded better, didn't it?

She was lacking in knowledge of flowers, musicals, or watercolors, and her needlework left a great deal to be desired. Nor did she speak French.

She had, however, been a good maid.

Perhaps someone could congratulate Morgan for that: "Every bit of furniture around her is polished to perfection, Your Lordship!"

Oh bother.

Instead of going to the Long Gallery, she headed for the West Tower, a place she'd never been before in her ghostly excursions. Even though full night had descended on Ballindair, she wasn't afraid. She'd never been afraid in the castle. Granted, there were probably more reasons to be frightened of corporeal bodies than spiritual ones, but she felt safe at Ballindair, as if the castle had welcomed her from the beginning.

Wouldn't it be nice if Morgan could do the same?

It was one thing to marry her because of his sense of honor. But was she supposed to live in this narrow little box in Morgan's mind? She couldn't meet with Mr. Seath—Mr. Seath!—in the garden, lest someone think it was scandalous. What else couldn't she do?

Oh, she didn't even want to know.

The West Tower was the most difficult tower to access. Furniture was stored there, as well as armaments. Evidently, the MacCraigs had been excessively bloodthirsty in the past. They could cover every single wall at Ballindair with knives, dirks, swords, and shields, and still have weapons left over.

Aunt Mary had insisted that even the storerooms be cleaned from time to time, but she had never been assigned the West Tower. Only the most skilled and experienced maids were allowed to touch these artifacts.

Strange, that most of the ghosts of Ballindair weren't involved in warfare. Instead, they centered around a Mac-Craig's treatment of a lover or a wife.

Jean went down a set of darkened stairs, making her wish that she'd had the foresight to bring a lantern. Most of Ballindair corridors were lit by gas lamps. An expensive luxury, she'd been told, but the Earls of Denbleigh deserved no less.

At the bottom of the steps she hesitated.

Instead of turning left, toward the West Tower, she turned right and headed for the kitchen. At this time of night there was still activity inside, and every single person stopped what he was doing and turned to look at her.

There, that was a sign, if nothing else, of her change in station. Before, no one would have commented, or even noted, her appearance.

By her marriage, she was no longer friends with the staff of Ballindair. She was, instead, the person to be served, and possibly ridiculed, when the staff relaxed or the work for the day was complete.

Each of them looked at her, resentment evident on their faces. She could almost hear their thoughts: *What's she going to make me do now? Doesn't she know I'm tired and want to go to my bed?*

Diane, a maid of all work, came forward.

"Yes? What do you want?"

She and Diana had gossiped about the laundress, had laughed at various jests a footman had told, had marveled to each other about the treasures kept in Ballindair's rooms. Now, the girl was looking at her as if she were a stranger. Worse, an enemy.

How foolish she'd been. She couldn't serve herself. Doing so would only give rise to more gossip.

Acting like a maid, she was, for all she married the earl. Is she going to clean the scullery next?

"I'd like a candle, please," she said, giving no further explanation.

Should she ask for something to eat? No, she had no intention of fueling the fire of gossip. No doubt they already knew she wasn't in the dining room. She could only imagine what stories they'd tell.

Begging for a scrap, she was. Don't the earl let her eat with him no more?

Diane nodded, retreated to the storeroom. When she returned, she had a beeswax candle—another sign of Jean's rise in status—inserted into a small silver candlestick. Diane held out a matchbox and the candlestick, and Jean took them both with a nod.

"Thank you," she said, before turning and leaving the room. If she were brave enough, she'd stand just outside the door and listen to what they said about her. But she wasn't that courageous, so she walked back to the base of the tower, lit the candle, and slowly made her way to the second floor.

The West Tower was the first one built at Ballindair. Several changes had been made to the other towers over the years, but here the windows were mere arrow slits, letting in only a faint stream of moonlight.

Everywhere she looked, crates and trunks were stacked on top of each other, and several objects, too large to be crated, were covered in sheets.

She sat down on a crate, holding the candle in her left hand and arranging her skirts with her right.

The problem with ghosts was they were always invisible or nearly so. Sometimes, she was certain she'd felt a ghost pass by, or experienced a physical sensation that had no observable cause.

After several moments she said, "Why should anyone believe in ghosts, really? It's not as if there's substantial proof of you. When you tell another person you've seen a ghost, he looks at you oddly. And another thing, why doesn't everyone become a ghost? Is a ghost someone who was miserable in life? Or someone who precipitated his own death? Or, perhaps, someone who regretted the deeds of the past?"

No one answered her. Nor did anything move.

She looked around her at the shadows.

"Do ghosts live in heaven? Are they given permission to return to haunt the living? Or do they live here, at Ballindair? If so, why can't we see ghosts during the day? Must you sleep as well?"

In the next moment the air felt a little chilly, enough so she could see the breath in front of her face.

She studied the candle's flame, amazed to find her hand shaking just a little. She steadied it by gripping her wrist tight and resting the candlestick on her knee. Because she was staring so fixedly on the flame, when she looked away all she saw was a bright white glow against the darkness. A figure shivered and shimmered.

She blinked, and the room swirled around her. As she opened her mouth to speak to the ghost, the room tilted, her head felt absurdly light, and she was sent tumbling to the floor.

Chapter 25

Jean hadn't been feeling well enough for dinner, but she was evidently feeling well enough to leave her room.

When Mrs. MacDonald met him at the door of the Countess's Suite, having been summoned with some degree of haste by a maid he'd encountered, Morgan folded his arms, stared at the woman and said, "Where is my wife, madam?"

She looked a little surprised by his question, which only made him repeat it.

"Where is my wife? Why is she never in her room?"

The housekeeper just blinked at him.

"I'm sure I don't know, Your Lordship."

"Do you always lose your maids with such alacrity, Mrs. MacDonald?"

She drew herself up and looked at him in a rather queenly fashion. "I do not, Your Lordship. However, Jean is no longer a maid. She is your wife."

"Then she should behave like a wife."

To his surprise, Mrs. MacDonald took one step back, away from him.

Had he suddenly become contagious?

"I will endeavor to find out where Jean has gone, Your Lordship. Shall I send her to the Laird's Tower?"

"Simply find her, Mrs. MacDonald," he said, further annoyed by that question. Did she think he'd sought out his wife simply for entertainment? No, his reason for being here was more important than that.

She nodded once, then turned and left the room.

As he sat in Jean's sitting room, he realized she hadn't made an imprint on the room at all. No personal possessions dotted the top of the bureau. Nothing sat on top of the vanity. Did she even have any personal possessions?

At Ballindair he was surrounded by those things he needed to guard and protect for succeeding generations. Had she nothing at all?

What had he given her in the short time they'd been wed? The clan brooch at their wedding, but then he'd immediately suggested she give it to Mr. Seath to place in the strongbox.

He stood and walked into her bedroom, going to the armoire. He had no right to rifle through her belongings, a thought that made him hesitate for only a moment.

He opened the two drawers to find they were only partially filled with threadbare undergarments. After opening the doors, he was unsurprised to find only three dresses there. Her wedding dress, a uniform, and the dress she'd worn yesterday morning.

Lillian had so many clothes, another room had been given up to them, a series of armoires holding day dresses, evening dresses, corsets and pantaloons made in France, laced festooned creations that had cost him a fortune.

He closed the armoire doors, disturbed and curiously

unable to define what he was feeling. If Jean had married him for his wealth, she'd yet to solicit him for funds. Why the hell hadn't she come to him and asked him for jewelry? Or a monthly allowance?

Why exactly had she married him?

She hadn't wanted to, that much had been clear from her impassioned speech on the eve of their wedding. Nor had she been a cheerful bride. Instead, she'd looked on the verge of tears several times during the ceremony.

What had she said? *You need to find someone of your own rank, Your Lordship. Someone who would be thrilled to be a countess.*

She hadn't appeared overjoyed to be a countess. Whenever he called her "Your Ladyship," she flinched. He'd never seen her give anyone an order. She hadn't wanted to change anything at Ballindair to suit her. She wasn't suddenly interested in traveling to London, Edinburgh, or Paris. Nor had she asked for anything for Catriona or her aunt.

Why the hell had she married him?

When Mrs. MacDonald returned, he'd ask the status of his wife's wardrobe. Perhaps he should import someone from Inverness. And cloth—did they have enough and in the patterns Jean preferred? He'd have to meet with Mr. Seath and have the man purchase a wagon full of the stuff. Anything she wished. And he'd have the strongbox brought to him, so he could retrieve the MacCraig brooch. And money, he'd give her money.

Maybe that would be an inducement for her to remain in her room.

Mrs. MacDonald didn't even knock on the door, merely opened it.

"Do you presume upon your relationship with my wife?" he asked, annoyed on Jean's behalf.

"I beg your pardon, Your Lordship?"

"You will knock, Mrs. MacDonald, every single time you come into this room. Just because Jean is your niece does not negate her right to privacy. Do you understand?"

She nodded swiftly, her face changing to a pink hue.

She was not going to treat Jean as if she was some scullery maid. He pushed the thought out of his mind that she'd been a scullery maid once, by her own admission.

He'd been a boy once, yet he would bridle if anyone treated him that way now.

"Have you found her?" he asked.

"We haven't, sir—" she began, only to be interrupted by a girl's excited voice.

"Come quick, ma'am, come quick. She's dead, she is!"

Morgan would forever remember Mrs. MacDonald's terrifying composure.

She raised both hands, palms parallel to the floor, and lowered them slowly, as if to calm the girl's hysterical utterance by gesture alone.

Surprisingly, it worked.

"Who is dead, child?"

Even he knew the answer to that question. He shot an impatient look at the housekeeper.

"It's Jean, ma'am." The girl sent him a frantic glance, curtsied, and corrected herself. "Her Ladyship, ma'am. She's dead, she is!"

"I'm sure she isn't," Mrs. MacDonald said, still exhibiting an unearthly tranquility. "Have you found her?"

He wanted to shake the woman.

"Yes, ma'am. In the West Tower, ma'am. With all the crates and trunks. It was Rory who found her, ma'am. Near burned to death."

Mrs. MacDonald glanced at Morgan, and only then did he see the frantic worry in her eyes. His estimation of her rose a notch.

"Very well, we shall see for ourselves."

In a reproachable violation of manners, he preceded the housekeeper and maid out the door. Later, he'd apologize. For now, he was intent on reaching Jean.

The West Tower, that's what the maid said. He began to run.

When you were a little boy, did you ever go hunting for ghosts? Jean's question on that night in the Long Gallery. What had he answered? Something about being in the West Tower. Even as a boy, he had been forbidden to play in the West Tower. Too many dangers lurked among the crates and trunks. Too many armaments that could injure him, not to mention the two cannons stored there. The MacCraigs were nothing if not prepared for famine, siege, and war.

The tower was the perfect place for a boy to play, to pretend to be one of his murderous ancestors. When he'd gone there in direct disobedience to the rule, he was found out, of course, and summoned to the library, to stand before the massive desk and listen respectfully to his father's lecture.

"Have you no idea of the dangers that might befall you?" his father had asked.

Morgan hung his head, staring at the floor.

"I want your promise you'll not go there again."

Dismayed, he stared at his father. When asked for his oath, he gave it, knowing he'd never break it. A MacCraig kept his promises. A MacCraig never broke an oath.

He had. One of the more important: *Until death us depart.* But Providence or serendipity had given him a second chance in the form of his new marriage.

He raced up the steps of the tower, pushed past the crowd of people at the narrow door, and saw Jean crumpled on the floor.

For a moment he couldn't move. The air smelled not of smoke but of flowers, a scent he couldn't define. A silver candlestick was on the wooden floor, a scorch mark forming an arrow point to where the candle lay a short distance away, extinguished.

His feet finally began to move, and he said something or did something or made some gesture—he wasn't sure what—but people parted to allow him to enter the overcrowded circular room.

Her hair was spread around her head, the black cloak parted at the knee. He patted it back in place, then raised a trembling hand to her cheek before lifting her into his arms.

She couldn't be dead. Jean couldn't be dead.

Chapter 26

RULES FOR STAFF: *Staff are allowed to eat only after the family has partaken of meals, and only those items allowed by the majordomo, housekeeper, or steward.*

"**I**f you stayed in your room nights, madam, none of this would have happened."

Jean opened her eyes to find Morgan bending over her. No, he wasn't bending over her. He was carrying her. And he was surrounded by people, a great many people.

"What happened?" Was that faint and tremulous voice hers?

"That's a question I was just about to ask you," he said.

How odd she felt so dizzy.

She lay her head back against his arm, closed her eyes and pretended she was asleep. This was a dream, nothing more. She was not surrounded by the staff of Ballindair as Morgan carried her through the corridor.

"What's the last thing you remember?" Morgan asked when they reached the Laird's Tower.

His face was an odd pale shade, his chin firmed, his expression giving her pause. Was he angry at her?

Reaching out, she placed one trembling hand against his cheek.

"You can't do this anymore," he said. "You have to stay in your room."

"I have to stay in my room? Am I a prisoner?"

He gave her a narrow-eyed glance. "Of course not."

"But I have to stay in my room."

He mounted the steps to the Laird's Suite, turning at the landing.

"That will be all, Mrs. MacDonald. I'll see to my wife."

Her aunt was there, too? How many people had witnessed her faint?

He entered the suite, still carrying her, and sat her down gently on the edge of the bed.

"If you hadn't been hunting ghosts, Jean, this wouldn't have happened."

She stared down at her dress, pleating the fabric between her fingers. "I rather think it was a case of not eating anything, more than exploring."

His glower got worse.

"I know you didn't join us for dinner, but I thought it a ploy to annoy me more than anything else. Didn't you have a tray in your room?"

She shook her head.

"Why are you acting like a child? Or are you truly ill?"

"I'm not a child," she said, her own irritation growing. "Very well, perhaps it was a ploy. Not to ignore you," she said, holding up her hand. "Just to avoid you."

"Why?"

That was a difficult question to answer, wasn't it?

"You don't think I'm capable of behaving with any honor. It isn't simply a province of men, you know."

Now, all she saw was confusion on his face.

She balled up her hands into fists and raised her gaze to the ceiling. "You thought I had an assignation with Mr. Seath."

"I did not. You misinterpreted."

Her eyes widened. "I didn't misinterpret anything, Morgan. You came close to accusing me of having an affair with the man. You thought I was Lillian."

He moved to the bureau, the same piece of furniture behind which she'd hidden a few weeks ago. He studied the mirror over it as if he'd never seen his face before. Then she realized he was looking at her in the reflection.

"Do you think I'm like Lillian?"

"I've never met anyone less like Lillian," he said.

She forced a smile to her face. "Because she was beautiful, of course."

He shook his head. "Because she wouldn't have allowed a steward to touch her, let alone champion the man."

"He's very ill. Why haven't you done anything about it?"

There was that look of confusion again.

"What would you have me do, madam?"

She didn't like the tone in his voice.

"I would have you give him a helper, an assistant. Have someone else do the brunt of his work. The man hasn't long to live, Morgan."

"Oh? Are you now a physician?"

"I have some acquaintance with his illness," she said. "But it doesn't require anyone with training, Morgan. All you need to do is look at the man. Or talk to him. You're just like Catriona. Concerned only with yourself."

His face became a frozen mask.

She slid from the bed, reeling from a wave of dizziness.

"You are sick. Damn it, Jean."

She suddenly found herself in his arms again. This time she grabbed his shirt with both hands, closing her eyes and wishing the room wasn't spinning so fast. They were in a vortex, a whirlpool like the one she'd once seen on the edge of the ocean. She could almost taste the salty brine on her lips, feel her hair thick and sticky.

Was she hallucinating?

"I think I saw a ghost," she murmured faintly.

"You could have seen the Pope, madam, for all I care at the moment."

How very Scots he sounded. She'd have to tell him that, when she could reason it out better.

His heart was thudding fiercely beneath her ear. For all its rapid rhythm, it was a curiously comforting sound. She pressed herself against his chest, then realized he was lowering her onto the bed.

If he wanted his way with her, she was just going to have to decline. Either that, or faint in the middle of lovemaking.

Morgan had never, in his entire life, fed another human being. The annoyance he felt at Jean for not eating was fading beneath the sheer logistics of it all.

First he had to prop her up on the pillows. Secondly, he had to ignore her protests, which was easier said than done. Jean could be very persuasive when she wished. Worse, she fixed a look on him as quelling as his father's. Despite his worry, however, he was inclined to smile from time to time, which surprised him.

He spooned a little of the soup, carried it to her mouth with a napkin beneath the spoon to catch any errant spills, and praised her when she took a sip.

Jean was a querulous patient.

She stared up at the ceiling between spoonfuls as if to chastise him for being too slow. Since he was new at this, he decided to ignore her.

"I can only have gruel?" she asked.

"It isn't gruel, as you well know. It's chicken soup. A very good chicken soup, I might add."

She was looking at the ceiling again.

"After you've had your soup, and your stomach has had a chance to adjust to food, we can go on to mutton."

She wrinkled her nose. "I don't like mutton," she said.

"That's too bad," he said. "You're having mutton, with a little jelly on the side if you're good."

She looked at the ceiling again.

He followed her glance. All he saw above him was the pattern of gathers in the canopy over the bed.

"What are you doing?" she asked.

"I'm trying to find out what you find so favorable in the ceiling," he said, still staring upward.

She poked him in the ribs. "Are you going to continue to feed me, or let me starve?"

"I think you were doing a very good job at that. Who goes for two days without eating?"

"It wasn't two days," she said, but her voice lacked conviction.

"However long it was, it was foolish."

She only shrugged.

"Do you really think I'm like your sister?" he asked.

She looked down at the sheet. He wasn't going to speak until she answered him.

"You both seem to be extraordinarily interested in yourselves," she said after a moment had passed. "To the exclusion of everyone else."

He didn't know how to answer that.

She sighed heavily and looked up at the ceiling again.

"Do you do that on purpose in order to annoy me?" he asked.

"I've found," she said, "that it doesn't take much to annoy you."

He sat back, spoon in his hand forgotten. She took it from his grasp and began to feed herself. She wasn't looking so pale now.

When the knock on the door came, he called out. A moment later two maids entered, each of them carrying a small portion of Jean's meager possessions. She set the spoon down and stared at him.

"What are you doing?" she asked.

"I've decided," he said, feeling very despotic, "if you won't take care of yourself, someone shall have to. I had a choice. Hire a nursemaid for you or do it myself."

She glanced at the two girls, then back at him. Yes, he'd spoken in front of the staff, but it had to be done.

He studied both of the maids. "Anything you hear in this room is not to be discussed with anyone else. Is that understood?"

The two girls nodded, carefully keeping their gaze from Jean.

After they'd left the room, she frowned at him.

"Do you think that's going to alter their behavior?" she asked, evidently annoyed. "They're going to whisper what they heard and saw all over Ballindair."

She wasn't looking at the ceiling now. She wasn't looking at anything. She leaned back against the pillow and closed her eyes, and he was chagrined to see one tiny tear travel from the corner of her eye down her cheek. She brushed it away impatiently.

"Do you care so much about what they think of you?" he asked.

"I didn't think I would," she said, not opening her eyes. "Isn't it funny, but I find I do. I didn't know very many of them all that well. But we were all maids together. And now I don't seem to fit in anywhere."

He took the bowl and spoon and placed it on the tray table beside him.

"I thought the same thing in London," he said. "Neither fish nor fowl. I was still an earl, but I had shocked everyone by my actions."

She opened her eyes.

"Did you care so very much about what they thought of you?" she asked.

"I didn't think I would," he said, repeating her words with a smile. "But I found I did, very much."

"Did it hurt?"

Now that was a question no one had asked him. Did it hurt? Surprisingly, he found himself telling her the truth.

"Yes," he said. "I expected people to understand. What I'd done was preferable to enduring Lillian's infidelity. Instead, I wasn't viewed as noble as much as scandalous."

"People see scandal where they will," she said softly.

Her gaze was on the window and the view beyond. He wondered what she was really seeing. Something that made her sad, or at least pensive.

"They will take the most noble of actions and twist it around until it's evil," she said.

He had the most curious wish to tend to her. To care for her as he never wanted to do before for another person.

He wanted to know everything there was to know about her, an interest he'd never felt before for another human being. She divulged very little of herself and only on a reciprocal basis.

Another thing he'd never done, share himself.

Had he always been so restricted in his speech and emotions? With everyone, perhaps, but Andrew. And even with Andrew he'd had pockets of secrecy, things he'd never shared with anyone but Jean.

"You said you thought you saw a ghost," he said. "Was it just any ghost? Or a certain one?"

Again she had that far-off gaze.

"I think it was the French Nun," she said. She turned her head to look at him. "I think I just made out her shape."

"Any words of wisdom from the old gal?"

Her fleeting smile summoned his own.

"Things like: 'Don't trust the MacCraigs?' No, nothing."

"Did she at least moan or groan?"

"She shimmered. She looked like moonlight. Or the reflection of the sun on the surface of a loch."

He brought the plate of mutton closer. Like it or not, she was going to eat some of it, then he was going to tuck her in and remain at her side.

The fact that he was being so protective should have worried him. Instead, it felt oddly right.

Chapter 27

When her parents were gone, Jean had assumed the role of mother for Catriona. Or, at the very least, wise elder sister. But no one had cared for her in so long, as Morgan was now, that it brought tears to her eyes.

He startled her by removing his shoes, sitting on the edge of the bed and moving to her side. Before she could protest or even ask what he was doing, he extended his arm behind her back and pulled her close to him.

"You were trembling," he said.

"An extra blanket would do," she said.

He didn't have a response to that, merely shelved his chin on top of her head. She allowed herself to place her hand against his shirt and tuck her head against his chest.

His heart beat steady and loud. If she closed her eyes and allowed herself to relax, she might fall asleep right here.

"I thought she was going to offer me advice," she said.

"Who?"

His voice rumbled against her cheek. What a lovely voice he had. The longer he was home, the more his voice sounded normal, not English at all.

"The French Nun," she said.

"What kind of advice? If not stay away from the Murderous MacCraigs, that is?"

The amusement in his tone made her smile sleepily.

"You realize, of course, that Ballindair's ghosts are probably a figment of an ancestor's imagination," he said. "My family was known as the Murderous MacCraigs for generations. They had a good reason to spread the tales of a ghost or two."

She glanced up at him. "The better to scare their enemies?"

"Exactly."

"Except they aren't warrior ghosts. Just the Herald, and no one ever hears from him. They're all poor women, weeping at the way they were treated by MacCraig men. That would hardly impress an enemy."

"Oh, they weren't all that bad."

"The French Nun is an example of how bad one of them was."

She waited a few minutes, then asked the question bothering her since the maids appeared. Her parents had shared one room all her life, but her father hadn't been a peer. Nor had they lived in a place like Ballindair.

"Is it entirely normal for us to share a room?"

"Nothing has been normal about this marriage from the very beginning. I see no reason to attempt to replicate normalcy at this late date."

She frowned at him. "What if I gave you my word I won't go in search of Ballindair's ghosts?"

After the episode in the West Tower, she was giving a

great deal of thought to ghost hunting only during the daytime. Having the entire staff at Ballindair watch as she was carted off to bed had been embarrassing.

"I wouldn't believe you," he said.

"How very insulting," she said. "It's true, then."

"What is?"

"You don't respect me."

A moment of silence passed. "Why would you think that?" he asked.

"I find myself suddenly fatigued." She moved away, lay back against the pillows and closed her eyes.

"Am I supposed to apologize for my presence, and take myself off to the sitting room?"

She didn't answer him.

"This is our bed, madam," he said, in that insufferable tone of his.

He left the bed. When he didn't say anything else, she slitted her eyes open to find him removing his clothes. He smiled in her direction, which made her clench her eyes shut.

A few moments later she heard the splash of water from the bathing chamber.

If anyone should sleep in the sitting room, it should be her. This was his bed. No, their bed, evidently, from this point on.

Would they grumble at each other all night long?

She stifled her smile. Even when they disagreed, it was strangely exciting.

When he entered the bedroom, her eyes widened.

"I do not sleep in a nightshirt, madam. Besides, you've seen me naked before."

She only nodded, moving her gaze to the night-darkened window with some difficulty. Morgan really was beautiful.

He moved to the other side of the bed, reached out and pulled her over.

"You're on my side," he said.

"What if that's the side where I'm most accustomed to sleeping?"

"I'm the husband. I choose."

"Now, that is autocratic," she said. "Did Lillian simply agree to that?"

"I didn't sleep with Lillian. And you agreed not to bring her up again."

She nodded. She had.

"Must you call me madam? It's very off-putting."

"Perhaps I say it to keep reminding you that you're married."

"I think it's because you don't remember my name," she said. "It's an easy name. Only one syllable. You could even make half a noise and I might think it's my name."

He was laughing.

She bit back her own smile, and frowned at him when he got into bed.

Although she was feeling less dizzy, she was still a little weak. Was she supposed to go to sleep fully dressed?

She had a few alternatives. Number one, she could get out of bed and undress herself. She might be a little unsteady on her feet, but it wouldn't take long. Or she could always ring for a maid and be the Countess of Denbleigh. No, she didn't want to do that.

Number three, she could ask for assistance from Morgan, which might lead to other activities, and she wasn't feeling up to it right now.

Was a wife allowed to say no to a husband? Especially one as autocratic as Morgan?

She might well have the opportunity to find out.

She slid her feet out of the bed, wishing the mattress wasn't so high. Slowly, she stood. All she had to do was unbutton her dress, remove her skirt and bodice, and place them somewhere neatly.

Before she could even unbutton the first button, Morgan was there, standing in front of her, naked. Her eyes darted to his shoulders and stayed there, but then slid to the base of his throat and down his chest, then resolutely up to his chin.

She must keep her gaze on his chin.

"Is it permissible to say no to a husband?"

He'd nearly finished with her bodice and was attempting to unfasten the button on the waistband of her skirt.

"Are you asking me if it's a societal rule? Or if I'm some kind of ravening beast who insists on having my husbandly rights every single night?"

"Perhaps a bit of both," she said.

"I haven't the slightest idea what the societal rule is," he said. "As for me, I believe I have my baser needs under control. Before our marriage, I was not very 'well-traveled.'"

"I don't believe you," she said.

His head jerked up and he stared at her.

"No one who looks like you would have any difficulty coaxing a woman to your bed."

"I was a husband, Jean," he said. "I was attempting—even if my wife was not—to maintain my vows."

"And afterward? You were divorced for some time, were you not?"

His smile was curiously warming.

"I'm trying to decide why you think I've had such success with women."

"If you haven't," she said, "I haven't the slightest idea why not. You're a very good lover."

Was he blushing? His cheekbones were oddly darker, but it could just be the shadow on the side of the bed.

"I'm your only lover."

"Women just know these things," she said airily, which only prompted his laugh.

"You're an innocent," he said.

"Of the two labels," she said, "I prefer madam. At least it makes me sound as if I have some experience and some sense."

"I think you have a great deal of sense," he said. "Except in the bedroom."

Her eyes widened. "Would you have preferred me to come to you educated?"

"If anyone is going to educate you," he said, finishing with her petticoat, "it's going to be me."

"But not tonight," she said firmly.

His smile was challenging, but she was reassured when he nodded.

"Do you think it's possible I'm with child?"

That certainly got his attention. He stepped back, his hands dropping.

"It would be too soon, wouldn't it?" she asked.

He still didn't answer.

"Would you be happy to have a child?"

Still, no response.

She finished removing the rest of her garments herself, stopping only when she got to her shift. She should sleep in something. Even if he slept naked, it was no excuse for her to do so.

She walked to the armoire where the girls had put her clothing and withdrew a nightgown. When she turned back to him, he was looking at her, his eyes following her every movement.

"Yes," he said slowly. "I would be happy to have a child."

She only nodded in return, and retreated to the bathing chamber.

When she returned to the bedroom, the room was darkened. Morgan had extinguished the gas lamps on the wall, and the only light was from the Highland night spilling in through the open curtains.

He was asleep, or pretending to be, for which she was grateful.

She crawled into the bed, stood again to gather up the material of the nightgown, then sat once more. After a great deal of moving about, she got most of the material smoothed over her legs so it wasn't one great huge lump of fabric.

"Are you ever going to settle down?" he asked.

"You have the most amazing voice," she said in response. "It makes me feel all warm inside."

"If you intend to spend the rest of this night celibate," he said, "it would be better if you didn't give me any more compliments. Or tell me my voice warms you."

"Am I not supposed to say things like that?"

"Not if you don't want me to reciprocate."

A few minutes of silence passed between them, her curiosity building.

"What would you say? If you reciprocated, that is?"

He made an impatient sound.

"I would tell you that you have the most beautiful breasts I've ever seen."

"Oh."

"And, if I hadn't known you were a virgin, I would have thought you a houri."

She didn't know how to take that comment at all. "Are you calling me a whore?"

Abruptly, his hand rested on her waist and he rolled her to her side so she was facing him. He was so close she could feel his breath on her cheek.

"Not a whore, a houri," he said. "An alluring woman."

"Have you seen very many?"

"Houris?"

"Breasts."

"My share," he said, his tone amused. "Before my bout of celibacy, that is."

"And before you were a husband."

"Yes."

"Do you miss it?"

"Being a bachelor?"

"Yes," she said, a sibilant whisper in the darkness.

"Ah, but look what I've gotten for giving it up. A ghost hunter enchantress."

"You shouldn't say things like that, Morgan."

"Why not? You're my wife."

"Your words make my stomach flutter."

"And you want to be celibate tonight."

"I believe it's best, don't you?" she asked.

"I think it's better if I don't answer that question," he said.

She only saw the dark shape of him before he kissed her cheek, then her nose, then her lips. His mouth lingered and she was the one to deepen the kiss.

"You're very tired," he said.

"Am I?

"And still feeling the effects of your faint."

"I think it's you," she said. "Whenever you kiss me I feel a little dizzy."

He made another sound in the back of his throat, and she wondered if she'd offended him somehow.

In apology, she leaned forward and kissed him some more. She should say good night now. She should turn over and attempt to sleep, although how she was going to sleep with him right next to her, all naked and warm, she didn't know.

He pulled her closer until she was lying next to him, her head on his arm. She placed one hand against his chest, her fingers splayed, then willfully exploring.

"Jean," he said. "Didn't you want to sleep?"

She drew her hand back. "Of course," she said, feeling chastised.

He followed the line of her arm down to her hand, grabbing her fist and kissing her knuckles.

"Touch me," he said, and it wasn't a command as much as a request.

They weren't going to make love, but she could certainly touch. Perhaps she could give him as much pleasure as he did when he stroked and caressed her.

Her hand flattened against his chest again, then slowly rubbed up and down. His abdomen was flat and muscled, inciting her touch. She wanted to go farther, but she stopped her explorations to lean forward.

Slowly, her mouth found his in the darkness. Not strictly a touch, but something she needed to do, wanted to do. Kissing Morgan was a pleasure she felt to her toes.

"Go to sleep, Jean," he said, and his voice sounded harsh. The stroke of his hand along her back, however, was tender.

She rolled over. A few minutes later she turned her head. He was on his back, one arm over his head. A rigid pose, except for that arm. As if one part of him wanted to escape the boundary he'd established for himself.

The longer she knew him, the more he charmed her down to her toes. Were husbands supposed to do that?

She turned again, facing away from him. A moment later he moved closer. His hand touched her shoulder, and she could feel the warmth of his palm through the thin linen of her nightgown.

His hand trailed down to her elbow, coming to rest at her wrist. Since her hand was flat against her chest, so was his now.

His fingers moved from her wrist to the tip of her thumb. Then they were slipping into the placket of her nightgown, gently stroking her skin as if to test if she was awake.

She moved her hand and pressed it against his, holding it in place.

Now was the time to speak, to again let him know she was too fatigued. But surely he could tell how fast her heart was beating. Warmth was pooling between her thighs even now. How traitorous her body was. On a hierarchy of control, Morgan was given more precedence than her own will.

When had that happened?

When she'd first seen him, naked and proud, a statue of a man. A work of art created by God.

She rolled over again, annoyed at the nightgown that kept getting twisted. She still held his hand, keeping it low against her waist.

In the darkness, she addressed him. "Can you not sleep?"

"I find it very difficult to sleep next to you," he said, his voice carrying a surprising note of humor. "I'm like a boy around you. Should I apologize?"

"Morgan," she said. Just the sound of his name, like water over river stones. Like the sigh of breeze through the trees. A name belonging to Scotland.

Here, in the quiet of the night, with just the two of them, secure and inviolate in this great wide bed, was the perfect moment to tell him, to divulge all, to confess her duplicity.

She released his hand and placed her palm against his cheek. Would he repudiate her?

Speak the truth, Jean. Tell him who you are. Tell him this marriage isn't legal. Tell him you've brought him as much scandal, if not more, than Lillian.

Tell him, and he'll send you away. Tell him, and Catriona will no longer be the sister-in-law of an earl, but a castoff. Tell him, and Aunt Mary will be punished for her silence as well.

Tell him, and the world, so peaceful and dear at this moment, will once again be a dark and terrifying place.

Tell him, and any feelings he might have for you, couched

in lust or unwilling affection, would vanish in the blink of an eye.

Dear God, forgive her, but she didn't want to leave him.

One day he'd find out. Would he forgive her then? Or would he hate her for never telling him?

The thought lasted until his mouth touched hers. She opened her lips, inhaling his breath, tasting his tongue, deepening the kiss. A short time ago she'd never been kissed, and now she sank into the mindless pleasure with only a dim protest from her conscience.

He touched her and all she could think of was how he would make her feel. Foolish woman, to trade scruples for pleasure. To want the fleeting joy of Morgan's loving more than the honor of her own character.

Was it wrong to love Morgan MacCraig? To lie with him even though she knew she wasn't truly his wife? If so, then she was truly damned.

Jean didn't wear scent. Otherwise, he might think himself intoxicated by it. Nor had she mesmerized him. Not in the darkness with only the faint shape of her to be seen. But he could feel her well enough, as his palm pressed against the sheer linen of her voluminous nightgown.

What had possessed her to wear such a thing?

Perhaps he could convince her it was easier to come naked to their bed.

He could imagine her look if he said that. She'd pinken up, her gaze would dance around the room, and her hands would grab at her skirt, then rest at her waist, then press against her bodice.

Little wren indeed.

More like a secret cardinal.

He deepened the kiss, imagined her lips growing redder even as he felt the talent of her tongue dueling with his.

Who would have known that beneath the plain plumage lay a woman graced by God with the most majestic body he'd ever seen?

Her legs were a league long, ending in shapely ankles and feet. Her hips were gently curved, her abdomen flat and adorned by a strangely alluring navel. He'd kissed her there, and she'd shivered and smiled. A few minutes later she wasn't smiling, but moaning.

The memory of her response to him made him hard whenever he thought of it. Now, having been in that condition for more than an hour, he was ripe for her plucking.

He sat up, pulled her to him and, grabbing the placket of her nightgown, simply ripped it from her.

"Morgan!"

His name, but no other protest. Nor did she think to shield herself from him as he rent the garment into pieces. She simply lay there, making him wish he'd lit the lamps. All of them, in splendid debauchery, the better to see Jean.

He'd been celibate for a fair amount of time, that's what it was. His condition had nothing to do with the fact her breasts lured him, sight unseen, their nipples thorny against the pad of his thumb.

After throwing the remnants of her nightgown to the floor, he leaned over her and gave into another temptation, a deep and drugging kiss.

He pulled away with difficulty, pressing a kiss against the plump curve of her breast, then licking an erect nipple. Her indrawn breath might have made him smile at another time, but right at the moment he was mindless with need.

Her body lured him to kiss it, to suckle those magnificent breasts, to stroke his fingers between her thighs and play with her tender folds. He wanted to nibble on her buttocks, roll over on his back and have her ride him until he was gasping and covered in sweat.

He'd never been as inflamed about a woman.

Both hands pressed against a breast, directed her nipple to his lips. His lips ringed it, licked at it, inciting another gasp from her when he sucked hard, then bit gently.

Her hands were beating a tattoo against his shoulders, her torso turning toward him as if to give more of herself to him.

He rolled to his back, and with less care than he'd given any woman, he pulled her onto him.

"Are you ready?" he asked.

She didn't answer. The only sound was an inarticulate murmur. A protest? Damn it, not now.

He thrust his fingers between her thighs, felt her wetness, and almost stopped to say a prayer of thanks to a merciful God. Grabbing her waist, he raised her high enough that he could enter her.

She moaned.

He bit back an oath, took two deep breaths, and stilled, still gripping her waist.

What the hell had he done?

What words could he possible offer her? He'd been little more than a rutting animal. She hadn't wanted to make love tonight, and he'd tried to take her anyway.

He lifted her off him, but her hands slapped at him. Her head flew back, the mass of her hair tumbling over her shoulders.

"I'm sorry, Jean," he said, trying to explain.

Then his little wren shocked him by gripping his cock with both hands. Using her knees for leverage, she rose up, seating herself on him as if she'd done this forever. As if she'd always ridden him, demanding that he surrender.

He closed his eyes and felt her clench around him. In that instant, and with no more finesse, he erupted into her.

The wren had taken down the eagle.

Chapter 28

For two weeks Morgan lived an almost idyllic life. At night his every libidinous desire was fulfilled by a woman who was as passionate as she was charming. Jean constantly surprised him, made him smile, and occupied a great many of his thoughts.

He'd given her the MacCraig clan brooch after retrieving it from the strongbox, but she'd only put it in a little casket on top of the bureau. He'd met with the seamstress, who confessed that her time was being spent on Catriona's garments. She would be more than happy to inform his sister-in-law that Jean's clothing came first. He also gave her instructions to order whatever fabric she needed; expense was not a concern. If Jean had agreed to fittings, he didn't know of it.

Twice, he'd brought up the subject of an allowance. The

first time, she appeared surprised when he explained that she needed her own money. The second time, he merely informed her that Mr. Seath would provide whatever she needed. She only raised one eyebrow, but didn't ask any further questions.

Once he had her possessions moved into the Laird's Tower, he expected her to be underfoot all the time. He steeled himself to be annoyed or at the very least irritated by another person's constant presence. Jean, however, was proving to be elusive during the day. Nor was she often to be found in the Laird's Tower.

Twice, he'd found her in the garden, industriously scribbling. When he questioned her, she looked embarrassed and he let the subject drop. When she wasn't in the garden, she was to be found flitting about Ballindair like a frantic moth. Once, he asked about her and was told she'd gone to the stables. When he arrived there, he was informed that she'd left for the home farms.

He visited those childhood haunts he'd avoided up until now, read a great deal, and went through his father's papers, a chore he found surprisingly compelling. His father had recorded his daily activities in a series of journals, and he was going through them one by one.

The only disruption to his life came when he received another letter from his solicitor in London. Lillian was once again petitioning for the house in Paris. Once again he wrote the man and told him that she could badger him all she wanted, he was done with her demands.

One unexpected benefit of his marriage was that he was no longer disturbed by the repudiation of his peers. In fact, he barely recalled London.

He found himself anticipating night, knowing Jean would return to the Laird's Tower from her mysterious occupations during the day.

More often than not she begged off from dinner, claiming fatigue, a headache, a lack of interest in food—a bevy of reasons he finally understood after encountering Catriona and Andrew at dinner. They purred and clawed at each other like two cats in heat, a demonstration of lust that might have been amusing if it hadn't been so inappropriate.

Andrew was married, and his behavior distasteful. Catriona might have once been an innocent, but it was all too obvious she was Andrew's enthusiastic and unrepentant mistress.

Jean's antipathy for the evening meal was suddenly understandable.

A solution occurred to him, one that would ensure that his wife would at least eat dinner. He'd had dinner brought to their sitting room, and Jean was both surprised and pleased.

This morning she managed to rise, wash, and dress without waking him, a feat he found remarkable given that he'd always been a light sleeper. When he walked into the library, he was surprised to find her seated at his father's desk, earnestly writing in a brown leather journal. She didn't look up when he entered, or even glance in his direction when he stood in front of the desk, waiting. She merely waved to the corner of the desk.

"Put it there, please," she said, adding a soft, "Thank you."

"I've not brought you a cup of tea," he said.

Her head jerked up.

Strangely enough, she looked embarrassed.

When she closed the ledger, he was only more curious. "What are you doing?"

Her face flamed but she didn't answer.

"Chronicling your encounters with Ballindair's ghosts?" He sat on the edge of the desk, amused. "Is that it?"

"It would be a worthwhile endeavor."

Left unsaid were the words he nevertheless heard: an endeavor more worthy than any of yours. Perhaps he was being unfair. Jean didn't criticize.

He wished, sometimes, that she would be more vocal about certain things. Her sister's behavior, for example. Catriona needed female guidance before she ruined her life. As it was, she was acting in a manner guaranteed to bring about censure.

Jean didn't correct her sister. Nor did she complain about her. Where another woman might castigate, she observed. He had the strangest feeling she was doing the same with him.

"Do you think me without purpose?" he asked.

She surprised him by putting the ledger down, sitting back in his father's chair and regarding him seriously.

"You spend a great many hours simply inspecting Ballindair, Morgan. Saying hello to the staff. Enjoying the day. But there's so much more you could be doing."

Suddenly, he felt much as he had as a boy, in this very room, the sting of criticism as painful now as it was then.

Standing, he looked down at her. "What would that be?"

Her eyes softened, and for a moment he thought that expression was directed at him. "You could seek out Mr. Seath," she said. "He needs assistance. You could hire someone to help him."

She'd suggested that before, and he hadn't acted on it.

"I doubt he'd be pleased at my interference," he said.

She let out a sigh, and this time he had no difficulty interpreting he was the recipient of it.

"The man is ill, or haven't you noticed?"

He nodded. At least a nod was civil, unlike the words that sprang to his lips. He took a deep breath, then managed to maintain his composure.

"I've been involved in Ballindair since my father's death, madam. I'm aware of all that needs to be done."

"Are you?"

Was she questioning him?

It seems she was, because she continued. "Or has Mr.

Seath merely kept you informed of what he's already done?"

"Isn't that the nature of a steward's job?"

She took another breath, put down her pen and stood.

He thrust a hand through his hair, eyeing her with some caution. With her pink cheeks and flashing eyes, Jean looked to be in a temper.

She stepped closer, poking him in the chest with an ink-stained finger.

"That's just it, Morgan, can he perform his job?"

"Then it's time he was replaced." Even as he said the words, Morgan knew he'd never strip the man of his post. William Seath had served Ballindair and his father admirably.

When he said as much to her, she only nodded.

"He's been loyal to Ballindair, Morgan. It's time you were as loyal to him."

A dozen remarks flew to his lips, silenced by only one thing—surprise. What other woman would have championed the steward with such fervency? None of his acquaintance.

"What would you have me do?"

"Do what he's done all these years. Tally the daily figures, inspect the crops, horses, and cattle. Meet with the stable master and the overseer of the home farms. Give the weekly allocation to the housekeeper, approve the quarterly bonus, inspect the buildings, approve the uniform allowance, order cloth and supplies."

"How the hell do you know so much about what he does?" he asked, amazed at her knowledge.

At first she looked as if she wasn't going to tell him, then she sat down at the desk once again, staring at the leather-tooled blotter.

"I've been bringing him his ledgers and reading the reports for the last week," she said. "He's been too ill to leave his bed."

He hadn't known. Worse, he hadn't made it his business to know.

He sat on the corner of the desk once again.

"That isn't a compilation of your encounters with Ballindair's ghosts, is it?"

She shook her head. "I was always good at sums," she said. "I thought I would tally the month's figures for Mr. Seath."

Her words embarrassed him, an emotion with which he thought himself familiar, especially over the last year. This, however, was different, as if he'd failed in some elemental duty, or failed her.

His wife had as much as accused him of being a dilettante, and perhaps he had been. He hadn't understood the situation. Nor had he visited his steward, a man who'd faithfully carried out the duties of his office with more diligence than the Earl of Denbleigh.

This library had seen some of his earliest failures, revealed to his father. Now, it seemed, to his wife. He didn't like to fail. He didn't like the heat at the back of his neck or the uneasiness in the pit of his stomach. Nor was he enamored of the thought that he was being shamed in a way no one had managed in either London or Edinburgh.

His wife had done what he hadn't. Without a word, without a complaint, silently and cheerfully, she'd taken on the responsibility he'd blithely ignored.

He extended his hand, and she looked at him, confused.

"The ledger, Jean," he said. "I'll take it to Seath. While I'm there, I'll see if he could tolerate an assistant."

"You'll hire someone, then?"

He shook his head. "I'll help him for as long as it's needed."

They exchanged a long look. She handed him the ledger, and he stood, tucking it under one arm.

At the door, he turned back to look at her.

He'd entered into this marriage for a variety of reasons, and had been prepared to be a proper husband. He hadn't known then that Jean was no ordinary woman.

"You were a very good maid, weren't you?" he asked.

Her blush deepened. Did the question embarrass her?

"I tried to be," she said. "Why do anything without it being your best?"

"Thank you," he said, and wasn't certain why he was thanking her. Perhaps it was because she'd called him to task. Or perhaps because she'd expected more from him, and in doing so, demonstrated her trust in him. She believed in him, although she'd never uttered the words. By her actions, by her look right at this moment, she conveyed her certainty that he would act in a decent and honorable way.

No one else had ever given him that unconditional acceptance.

Jean watched as Morgan left the library. Once the door closed behind him, she folded her arms on the desk and lay her head down.

This was misery.

She couldn't do it.

She had to do it.

How, though? How did she go one day to the next knowing the life she was living was a lie? She was no more married to Morgan than Catriona was married to Andrew. The only difference was the world didn't know it.

She'd never considered she would fall in love with the very surprising Earl of Denbleigh.

He'd been pleasant and personable to everyone at Ballindair. The maids sighed after him. The footmen, stable lads, and farm boys used him as an example of how to act. He allowed her the freedom to say whatever she wished, witness her comments a few moments ago.

She'd expected him to dismiss her words, to be angry. Instead, he'd looked thoughtful for a moment, then simply nodded and asked for the ledger.

Not an autocrat at all, but a man capable of learning, and being kind, witness the night he'd fed her, warmed her, then loved her, the joy of that coupling still causing her to sigh. And all the nights since, when she'd lost herself to their lovemaking.

She moved until her cheek rested on the back of a cooler hand. Perhaps it would be just as well if she didn't think of the last fortnight right now.

She was too close to tears, and for once her sorrow had nothing to do with the past.

Standing at the doorway of Seath's sitting room and looking at the man propped up in bed, Morgan felt the bite of shame.

He should have known about Seath's decline.

He'd never seen anyone's appearance change so drastically in two weeks. Seath was now cadaverlike, the spark of life within him blazing defiantly through his bright eyes.

Because of his length of service to the MacCraigs, and due to his elevated stature as the steward of Ballindair, Seath's accommodations were large, the suite equal to one occupied by important guests.

Morgan crossed the room, moving to sit on a straight chair beside Seath's bed.

Jean had seen, had known, and had cared. How much of the steward's duties had she taken on while he acted like a self-indulgent ass?

Perhaps she was right, and he was more like Catriona than he was comfortable acknowledging.

Mr. Seath struggled to sit upright, but Morgan placed his hand on the other man's shoulder, easing him back against the pillow.

Had someone been assigned to care for the man? Why wasn't anyone at the door? Or in his suite, to fetch what he wanted? He knew he could at least ensure that someone was at Seath's side at all times.

"Your Lordship," the steward said, in a voice so frail Morgan had to lean forward to hear it. "Forgive me. I fear you see me at my worst. Could we meet tomorrow, instead?"

Even now Seath's pride prevented him from acknowledging the truth of his illness. Or perhaps it wasn't pride, but fear. He might have felt the same if he stared Death in the face.

"No," Morgan said, placing the ledger on the side of the bed. "I want nothing from you but for you to rest."

Seath glanced down at the ledger. A faint smile wreathed his grayish lips.

"She told you."

Morgan nodded.

"She's an exceedingly stubborn woman, Your Lordship," Seath said. "She would assist me no matter what I said."

"I have experienced a little of that obstinacy." The two men shared a smile. "Have you the strength to teach me what I need to know?" he asked, clasping the man's trembling hand in his own.

The older man closed his eyes and lay like that for a moment. Death was too close, waiting at the threshold or perched on the windowsill.

"I can think of no one better suited to care for Ballindair," Seath said, opening his eyes.

The steward smiled again, an expression piercing Morgan with regret.

"What can I do for you?" he asked, feeling inept and powerless. "I'll summon a physician."

Seath raised his hand off the bed. For a moment it hovered in the air, trembling, before it fell back to the sheet.

"Her ladyship has already arranged for a physician, sir," he said in a faltering voice. "There is little he can do, however."

"You'll outlive us all," Morgan said.

Seath's glance was filled with gentle chiding, enough that Morgan didn't say another word.

The awkward silence was broken by Mrs. MacDonald's strident voice.

"Mr. Seath, we have a situation."

Morgan looked up at the ceiling, a mirror of Jean's expression, caught himself and sent Seath a rueful smile.

Mrs. MacDonald was upon them before he could stand, hide behind the armoire, or do something equally furtive to escape her.

Chapter 29

RULES FOR STAFF: *Your person and your appearance shall, at all times, mirror the high standards of Ballindair.*

How the hell had he been talked into mitigating a dispute between his housekeeper and his best friend?

Morgan stood at the doorway of Andrew's room, Mrs. MacDonald beside him. Next to her was a sobbing maid and two of her friends.

"Your watch is missing," Morgan said.

"Not exactly," Andrew said. "I believe my watch was stolen."

Morgan pushed back his irritation. Andrew wouldn't have offended him so greatly without good measure. Even so, he wished his friend had come to him rather than make a public pronouncement, involve Mrs. MacDonald, and accuse one of the maids.

The staff at Ballindair was known for its honesty. He would tolerate no less. Besides, being a thief guaranteed dismissal, and work was not that plentiful in the Highlands that anyone would willingly turn their back on employment.

"Are you certain it's been stolen?" Morgan asked. "Could you not have simply misplaced it?"

"We've looked everywhere, Your Lordship," Mrs. Mac-Donald said. "The watch is not to be found within Mr. Prender's suite."

"Then there's nothing more to be done," Morgan said. "You'll need to search the servants' quarters."

She nodded once, looking as unhappy as he felt about that pronouncement. If Andrew's watch hadn't been stolen, and the search revealed no sign of it, they'd all have to deal with an irritated staff.

A Highland servant and one from London were a great deal alike. They had a sense of their own worth coupled with a certain arrogance. The employer who offended his servants could guarantee himself boiler problems, inedible food, and clothing with too much starch.

Not to mention all the glowering and grumbling could get on one's nerves.

He'd once attended a country weekend at the Duchess of Marsham's home. Her majordomo, a man imported from London, had gotten his nose out of joint. Undoubtedly for some imagined infraction, since the duchess was known for her cordial nature. All weekend the man could be heard sniffing and grumbling at the maids, directing the footmen hither and yon, and generally making life miserable for the guests, all with perfect decorum.

Morgan could only imagine what the staff at Ballindair would do.

Mrs. MacDonald turned, and with the three upstairs maids in tow, headed for the servants' stairs.

"I hope to God there's no truth to your accusation," he said, turning to Andrew.

Andrew's face, normally amused even in repose, reflected a gravity Morgan had rarely seen.

"What will happen to the thief?"

"Shouldn't you have thought of that before you made your accusations so public?"

"It was my father's watch, Morgan," Andrew said.

He nodded, remembering it well.

"Do you have anyone in mind?" he asked, not liking the feeling he was getting.

Andrew merely shrugged. "It was someone," he said.

"I hope you realize this is no game, Andrew. Nor is it a way to convince a maid to come to your bed. She'll be fired."

Andrew only nodded, turned and entered his room, closing the door behind him.

Morgan stared at the closed door for a moment. Should he challenge Andrew? Or call off the search? No, it was too late for that.

Andrew had been his friend for years. But he'd seen him less in the last two weeks than he'd seen Mrs. MacDonald, and he avoided her when he could.

When they did meet, their conversation was stilted. Andrew wasn't interested in anything regarding Ballindair, Morgan's heritage, or Scotland.

Instead, he seemed determined to bring up the past on every occasion. Morgan didn't care to occupy his time with reminiscences of Lillian or London.

The past was the past, his mistakes glaring and immutable. Focusing on those, however, would draw his eyes away from the promise of the future, and the enjoyment of the present.

The boy he'd been was fading like a specter. He was no longer that child. His life had been marked by both successes—such as his work at the distilleries—and failures, such as his marriage.

He could do nothing about disappointing his father. Nor could he re-create those days of innocent joy when the world was at his feet and he believed he could effortlessly achieve his father's greatness.

The challenge was to make something of his life as it was now, neither based on his father's expectations nor his own childish ones.

He had the sudden, uncomfortable thought that Andrew belonged in the past, and wouldn't be a friend to the man he now truly wished to be.

"I didn't do it, Mrs. MacDonald. I swear. I'd never take anything belonging to someone else. I swear."

Donalda's voice kept rising in tone and strength, accompanied by tears. Not only was she weeping, but so was every other maid at Ballindair. They knew Donalda's circumstances only too well. Banishment from Ballindair meant certain starvation for her family.

Mary MacDonald nodded, sadness filling her heart. Of all the girls on staff, Donalda was the easiest to manage. She'd always taken direction well, had endeavored to please, and was a hard worker.

Mary hated this part of her position.

She looked down at Mr. Prender's watch in her hand. They'd found it below Donalda's pillow, as if the girl had kept it close to marvel at the intricacy of the gold case and the diamonds sprinkled over the face.

If the girl had truly stolen the watch, she'd have hidden it in a better place, planned to take it to Inverness to sell. The proceeds would've kept her family in food for a year. Instead, the watch had been too easily found and now she must be dismissed from Ballindair.

There was no other choice.

Mary looked up to find her niece standing at the end of

the hall. Catriona smiled, nodded at her, then disappeared down the main staircase, giving Mary the impression she was utterly pleased with what had just transpired.

The housekeeper wanted to cry.

"I didn't do it, Mrs. MacDonald,"

Mary had her doubts as well, but the rules were there for a reason. If she kept Donalda on, her own credibility would be weakened. Nor did she think it would do any good to appeal to the earl for clemency, not when the theft involved his friend.

She was, however, going to remember Catriona's pleased and self-satisfied expression.

How foolish did Catriona think everyone was? Did she think brownies washed the linens in Mr. Prender's room? All of them, with the exception of Jean, and perhaps the earl, knew she was spending all her free time with Andrew Prender. They were not discussing literature or the goings-on in London in his room.

Regrettably, she'd have to dismiss Donalda. But there must be something she could do for the family. Because of Mr. Seath's worsening condition, she didn't feel right going to him for assistance.

There was only one person who could help: the new Countess of Denbleigh.

When she was a maid, Jean had been given a task and expected to perform it to the best of her ability. Her work, as she'd been lectured, was a demonstration of both her diligence and her attitude.

Every morning, she'd begun her day with a challenge to herself. How could she be better at her tasks than the day before? How could she learn more, do more, and be more valuable in her position? Even the laundry had been a learning experience.

The life of a maid was less complex and, strangely, more rewarding than the life of a countess. The seamstress was in the process of making more clothes for her than she'd ever owned. She had jewelry—Morgan had insisted she keep the MacCraig clan brooch, and several pairs of earrings belonging to his mother. To her great dismay, he had settled an amount of money on her, money that was even now sitting in the drawer of the bureau. What did she need to buy? All she had to do was look around her and her every wish was fulfilled.

Yet the art and the treasures of Ballindair meant nothing to her. Perhaps she would have felt more of an acquisitive glee if she hadn't cleaned those statues, dusted those gilt frames, and polished that silver.

The only thing she prized about being a countess was sharing Morgan's bed. But for the ability to touch him, love him, and share her thoughts with him, she would happily go back to being a maid.

The man she was on her way to see would have been pleased if she did. Or if she'd never married Morgan.

Andrew had set up his chair and easel on the west lawn, having evidently tired of Catriona as a subject. Perhaps the mountains in the distance lured him more than her sister, or, like the rest of them, he was simply tired of Catriona's machinations.

The day was bright and sunny with not a cloud in sight, which might explain why he was taking advantage of the respite from rain and painting here.

She studied him for a few moments, then resolutely made her way in his direction. She didn't like Andrew Prender, a confession she'd not made to another soul. There was something grating about the man. Every time he addressed her, she had the impression he was laughing at the fact Morgan had married a maid.

Or perhaps he simply thought her beneath him.

Jean wished the seamstress had finished with another one of her new dresses. As it was, she was wearing the same thing she'd worn the day before. Soon, it would become like a uniform. If not similar in style to her maid's attire, then worn as often.

At least the dress wasn't a solid color, but an emerald stripe with a small contrasting ribbon of brown. The bodice buttoned up the front, and the buttons were rosettes carved from bone.

Andrew looked up as she approached, put his brush down in the tray of the easel and smiled a welcoming smile.

She wished she could accept the sincerity of it, but she didn't trust the man.

"I am indeed gifted today," he said. "A clear sky and the Countess of Denbleigh come to see me herself."

She didn't bother smiling in return. She wasn't that much of a hypocrite.

Evidently neither was Mr. Prender, because he didn't stand as she neared him.

"Why did you single out Donalda for punishment?" she asked.

Polite conversation was all well and good, but she had no desire to discuss the weather with him. All she wanted to do was find out if Aunt Mary's suspicions were correct.

His eyes widened at her attack. "I don't know what you're talking about, Countess."

"You needn't continue addressing me in that fashion, Mr. Prender," she said. "I'm only too aware of your opinion of me. You can either call me Jean or simply nothing at all."

He remained silent.

Had she angered him? Good. She'd been angry ever since learning of Donalda's dismissal.

"Is it your aim to punish Donalda?" At his look, she added,

"The girl who's been dismissed for the theft of your watch."

"I don't know the girl," he said, his attention focused on the squiggly lines on the canvas in front of him. "Are you thinking I should excuse her for the theft?"

"I'm thinking you orchestrated the theft," she said. "But I don't know why. I doubt Donalda's the type to interest you, Mr. Prender. Did she spurn your advances in some way? Are you still angry that she didn't wish to be painted?"

He turned his head and smiled at her. A perfectly agreeable smile if you didn't notice the sharp and avaricious gleam in his eyes.

"I much prefer your sister, Jean," he said.

She took a step back, his words washing over her. What had she expected? For him to act the part of gentlemen?

"You don't like me, do you, Countess?"

"Am I expected to, Mr. Prender, after that remark?"

He stood, then came closer. She didn't retreat, but remained where she was, fisting her hands in her skirt. They were similar in height, so she looked him straight in the eye when he was close.

"Are you like your sister, Countess? If so, I can understand why Morgan might be captivated."

She could feel the warmth in her cheeks. She might not be versed in the ways of the peerage, but she knew that kind of comment was frowned upon in polite conversation.

She took a step back, ceding the ground. "And you, Mr. Prender, are you so captivated by my sister you would harm another?"

He smiled at her. "How very virtuous you sound, Countess. Perhaps Morgan isn't that fortunate after all."

She didn't want to be here, and she didn't want to converse with Mr. Prender any further. Besides, she already had her answer.

Turning, she left him, all the while feeling his gaze on her back. Could she ask Morgan to hint that Andrew's stay as a guest had come to an end?

She couldn't very well send Catriona away. What was she going to do about her? Her sister didn't care whom she hurt, including Donalda.

Donalda. That situation must be rectified. She wished Aunt Mary had talked to her before banishing the girl. But she'd been with Mr. Seath, and Aunt Mary hadn't wanted to disturb her reading to the ill man.

Instead of returning to the castle, she walked through the south courtyard to the stables. When she requested a carriage, the stable master didn't hesitate, and when she told him her destination, he nodded, giving her an approving grin.

"A poor thing's been done today, I'm thinking," he said. "A poor, poor thing. I sent a wagon to take her home."

Had he done so on her aunt's orders, or had he simply made the decision himself? She smiled at him, grateful.

"Do you care to inform me about your charming conversation with Andrew?"

She turned to find Morgan leaning against the stable door, his arms folded in front of him in a nonchalant position. But she was coming to know him. He was feeling anything but calm at the moment.

His eyes flashed fire.

"I'll just ready the carriage," the stable master said, wisely removing himself from the scene.

"Your hair is tumbling down," he said, his voice tight.

She felt for her bun, only to realize it had, indeed, come loose.

"No doubt Lillian was groomed to perfection," she said.

"Why are you mentioning Lillian?"

"Because whenever I've done anything to annoy you, you think about her. Such as right now. You're wondering if you can trust me."

He unfolded his arms and strode across the floor, halting directly in front of her.

"Was I doing that?" he asked.

"You were."

He neither refuted her comment or agreed with it.

"Are you accusing me of lusting after your friend?" she asked. Disbelief held her in place, staring at him. "I haven't the slightest interest in Andrew. He's obnoxious and a boor."

"What did he do to you?"

The question was asked quietly, but his voice held a world of menace.

"He did nothing."

"He didn't proposition you?"

She laughed. "Of course he didn't."

"Andrew's been known to be direct to beautiful women. He didn't insult you?"

For a moment she thought it was a jest. But after searching his face, she realized he was serious.

"I'm not beautiful, Morgan."

"Of course you are," he said. "You're too pale, normally, but the moment your face gets a little color, you're remarkably attractive."

She was blushing even now.

"You can't think to be jealous," she said.

He waved his hand in the air.

"I'm not jealous. Call me protective, if you must. I won't have you insulted."

She blinked at him, uncertain what to say. His irritation felt, strangely, like a warm blanket he'd wrapped around her.

"What did he do? Why were you meeting with him, and where are you going?"

"Come with me," she urged. "Come with me and I'll answer all your questions."

To her surprise, he didn't hesitate, except to tell the stable master to inform Mrs. MacDonald they were going to be away for a time.

"Where are we going?" he said after they'd settled into the carriage.

"A girl was dismissed from Ballindair."

"For theft," he said, nodding.

"What do you know about her?"

He frowned. "Nothing. Should I?"

She nodded. "You should, I think. Don't you see the people who serve you?"

"I try not to," he said, to her surprise. "Sometimes, all those people, set to obey your slightest whim, are oppressive. Sometimes, all you want is a little privacy, so you pretend someone isn't standing there, waiting for you to ask for something or send them on an errand."

She'd never considered that.

"Nor did I particularly like being dressed by someone else. Or having my buttocks grabbed to ensure the fit of my trousers wasn't too tight."

Startled laughter escaped her.

He smiled. "My valet even tried to adjust my inseam, but only once."

"Perhaps he was only impressed by your manly dimensions," she said with a smile.

No doubt his look was meant to be quelling, but she couldn't help but laugh again.

"Why are you going to see her?" he asked a few moments later.

"I'm going to bring her back to Ballindair. A wrong has been committed."

"And you're going to make it right?"

She nodded.

"Tell me about her," he said, settling back against the seat.

"She's been in service at Ballindair the last two years and

is the sole support of her family, which numbers three," she said, reciting the information Mr. Seath had provided her. "A younger brother, her mother, and her father who was injured a few years ago and can barely walk."

To his credit, Morgan asked, "What will happen to her family if she's not employed?"

Before she could answer that the situation would be dire, indeed, for the entire family, Morgan tapped on the driver's window and gave him the signal to stop.

At her look, he said, "A bit of my past. Do we have time?"

She nodded.

"Then come and see," he said, and leaving the carriage, held out his hand for her.

She dismounted, taking care as she descended the steps. Following Morgan, she wondered what had put that smile on his face.

Chapter 30

RULES FOR STAFF: *You are allowed one tallow candle per week, a ration of soap per month, and a towel.*

She'd never walked this far on her half day off, but now Jean wished she had. From here she could see the shadowed mountains in the distance and the wider body of water. She'd have to ask Morgan what it was called.

Heather perfumed the humid air, and a line of dark clouds marched toward them, threatening another afternoon of rain.

Below, on the slope of the glen, nearly at the edge of the water, she saw a whitewashed long house, obviously deserted. The thatch roof was in pieces and the door stood ajar.

This was the desolation Mr. Seath had talked about; this was what the 8th Earl of Denbleigh had wanted and designed. There, on the heather covered hills, were the undulating flocks of sheep, black-faced and sturdy, eating their way across the earth.

Morgan was walking toward a sycamore tree that sat by

itself in the middle of the glen. She followed, taking care to avoid the worst of the brambles and nettles, and an occasional hole in the ground leading to some animal's burrow.

"What is it?" she asked, reaching him.

His palm pressed against the bark of the tree. Above his fingers something glittered in the bright sunlight. Several coins had been hammered into the bark.

"It's a wishing tree," she said, amazed.

He nodded, his fingers trailing over the coins.

"My father and I did this first one," he said, pointing to the lowest coin. "When I was a boy."

She kept silent, hoping he would tell her more.

"Every year on my birthday," he said.

She counted them. "There are only ten."

He nodded again. "That's when I went away to school." He pointed to another coin all by itself, high above the others. This coin hadn't been hammered as deep into the bark.

"On the day I was leaving Ballindair, I asked the coachman to stop," he said. "I hammered it in myself with the heel of my boot."

He grinned at her, the expression transforming his face. In that instant she could almost see him as he'd been on that long ago day.

"You didn't want to go?"'

He shook his head. "I didn't want to leave Ballindair or my father."

"You loved him very much," she said.

"He was the most honorable man I've ever known."

Knowing what she did about his father, she kept silent.

A few moments later they returned to the carriage.

Once inside, she faced the window, marking the location of the tree in her mind. Perhaps they would come back here again one day, and she'd have the opportunity to hammer in her own coin.

"What did you wish for when you were a boy?" she asked.

"What did I wish for?" he repeated, looking startled at the question.

He sat opposite her, his back to the horses, and regarded her with such a vague glance she knew he was recalling the past and not seeing her.

"I suppose I wished for the things all boys do." He looked away, as if suddenly embarrassed. "That last year," he said, "I wanted to stay at Ballindair."

"Didn't you like school?"

He sat back, smiling. "I enjoyed learning. I had a tutor at home, but it was nothing to all those minds assembled in one place. I could ask questions of anyone, not simply my father."

"Was your father proud of you?" she asked.

He continued looking out the window as he spoke. "I suppose he was."

"Did he never say?"

He turned to her. "Why are we discussing my past, when you're so reticent to speak of your own upbringing?"

"Because my upbringing in Inverness was nothing to living at Ballindair," she said.

He only nodded, as if he agreed with her.

For several minutes they didn't speak. She folded her hands, pretending an interest in the passing scenery. In reality, she was thinking about her own wish.

In Inverness, she'd wanted to survive. She wanted food, heat, and some sort of future.

When first coming to Ballindair, she wanted a way to accept her role, to cope with her circumstances.

Now? A way to tell the truth, to stop living the lie. To make Morgan understand and accept what she'd done and make it right, somehow. Wasn't that the most foolish wish of all?

The coachman evidently knew his way, because he drew to a halt several minutes later.

When he opened the door, he cautioned, "I'm sorry, Your Ladyship, Your Lordship. I can't go no farther."

Stepping out, Jean was assaulted by the grimness of the landscape. The verdant glen had given way to gray, brown, or tan, with an occasional startling note of green. As if the earth wanted to remind a visitor this was not a stark and alien land after all.

A whitewashed long house, similar to the deserted one she'd seen earlier, sat shelved on a steep hill, bracketed by gorse, rocks, and clumps of purple heather. A serpentine path led to it, winding around boulders that looked as if they'd been tossed there by a giant, querulous child.

She waited until Morgan was beside her to start walking toward the cottage.

"What are they doing living in such a desolate place?" he asked. He scuffed the toe of his boot in the rocky ground. "I doubt this would grow anything. Why did they choose this place?'

"Mr. Seath gave them the cottage," she said. "Or the use of it, at least. They had no other place to go."

She argued with herself for a moment before telling him the rest. "Your father evicted them, so he could put sheep in their place."

He halted beside her on the path and stared at her as if she'd suddenly sprouted two heads. He didn't move, even when she continued walking.

"Where did you hear that?" he asked when he caught up with her.

"From Mr. Seath," she said.

"You can't be right," he said. "You must have misunderstood."

She stopped, held onto her skirts with both hands and stared down at the gravel path.

"You don't have to believe me," she said. "I can understand if you don't. But Mr. Seath was given orders to evict twenty families. He was able to move eleven of them. Four of them decided to immigrate. Two went to live in Inverness, and he lost track of the other three."

She glanced up at him to find his jaw squared, his blue eyes flat and cold.

"My father wouldn't have done that. He wouldn't have evicted his own crofters."

"Your father was a human being. Only a man, capable of making mistakes. Don't imagine him as something he wasn't."

"I haven't imagined him," he said stiffly.

"Then you're not looking at him with an adult's eyes," she said, as kindly as she was able. "When you're a child, a parent can never do anything wrong. But when we grow up, Morgan, we begin to see our parents as people. We begin to understand they make mistakes just like we do. We begin to see them as fallible. It's important to do so, I think. So we can begin to forgive them."

"I have nothing for which to forgive my father."

His lips were thinned and there was color on his cheeks, as if he blazed with unspoken words.

"Define honor, Morgan."

"Sorry?"

"Define honor," she said. "What is honor to you?"

"I hardly think it's necessary for me to explain how I feel."

"I think you define honor as perfection. An honorable man is someone who does all things perfectly. I don't know anyone like that."

"A man of honor is someone who obeys his own code."

She smiled. "What's a man's code? Does every man have

his own secret code? Isn't that anarchy? Shouldn't you sub-scribe to a community code? Something other people could agree upon? Something less selfish?"

He folded his arms.

"You're saying my father was selfish?"

"I don't know. Perhaps he was."

Morgan's eyes swept over the glen, taking in the deso-lation. For a few moments they both pretended an intense regard for the moor, the shimmering river winding through the hazy glen, the shadow of the mountains in the distance, and the approaching storm.

"Perhaps your code is just as flawed," she said softly.

He glanced at her.

"You divorced Lillian, a thoroughly shocking thing to do."

"No less shocking than her bedding every man in London."

"Exactly," she said.

His eyes narrowed. "You're a very cunning conversation-alist, Jean."

"Am I?" she asked, pleased. She headed back up the path, Morgan following.

He still looked angry.

She shouldn't have said anything. Who was she to con-demn his father?

"Why?" he asked.

She glanced at him.

"Why are you going to bring her back? Regardless of her poverty, she shouldn't have stolen from Andrew."

She shook her head. "I don't believe she stole Andrew's watch," she said. "Neither does my aunt," she added, recall-ing Aunt Mary's conversation.

I think Catriona's at the heart of this, Jean. She looked sly as a fox, she did, with that little smile of hers like she was pleased with the whole thing.

She walked back to where he stood.

"I don't trust Andrew," she said. "And I don't trust my sister."

"You think she had something to do with this?" he asked, looking surprised.

"Yes," she said, feeling disloyal and relieved at the same time. "Catriona is not above using others to her bidding. For some reason, I think she wanted Donalda sent away. What better way than to prove the girl guilty of theft?"

"What's to stop Catriona from accusing her again, if what you say is true?"

She slapped her hands down on either side of her skirts. "Nothing," she admitted. "Or perhaps simply because I'll be watching her."

She turned and began walking up the path again, not once glancing back to see if he followed her. But she heard his footsteps, and let out the breath she was holding.

Today was a day of revelations, wasn't it? Yet the greatest of them remained hidden. Who was she to criticize anyone when her own character wasn't sterling?

Her mother had always told her that secrets fester. They were like starter for bread dough: fermenting in the darkness. Or was her true identity a secret? Wasn't it simply a lie?

Chapter 31

Up close, the cottage was larger than it appeared from the road. Efforts had been made to shore up the sides of the structure, and the thatch had been replaced with new grass.

Two sheep grazed contentedly nearby, making Jean wonder if they'd migrated from the larger herd. Did Donalda's family survive on purloined mutton? Smoke floated in gauzy tendrils from the hole in the thatch and hung against the cloudy sky a moment before dissipating.

From inside came the sound of laughter, so alien to what she thought they'd encounter that she glanced at Morgan.

He strode past her to knock on the door. To Jean's surprise, Donalda came to the door. For once, she was not in the Ballindair uniform of dark blue dress and white apron. Instead, she wore a plain white top and a dark green skirt.

Seeing the earl standing behind her, she bobbed a curtsy, then turned and called inside the cottage.

"Mam, it's the MacCraig and his wife."

Not once did Donalda look directly at her, and Jean honestly couldn't fault her for that. If what she suspected was true, and Catriona had orchestrated her termination, then she would be viewed as the enemy.

Donalda stepped aside to allow Morgan to enter. He greeted Donalda's mother, a shorter, older version of her daughter. Her hair, as black as Donalda's, was arranged in a bun at the nape of her neck. Her smile was accompanied by a wariness in her gaze conveying only one message: Strangers brought trouble.

A boy, looking to be about four, pushed his way past her skirts, staring up at Morgan. There, the source of the laughter, a smile still on his face and in his blue eyes.

"You be the MacCraig, then?" he asked.

Morgan nodded, his answering smile nearly as charming as the boy's.

The interior walls of the cottage were rough, the chinks between the stones filled with crumbling mortar. From where she stood, Jean could see holes in the roof, the gray skies promising rain that would turn the hard-packed dirt floor to mud.

Even in Inverness her circumstances had never been as dire.

The lone window opened up to the darker hill and its shadows. Yet touches of beauty caught her eye. A table and two chairs were pushed up against the wall, a bouquet of heather in a crystal vase acting as centerpiece. A bureau served as pantry and washing area, the ewer and basin sitting atop it made of Ballindair porcelain.

Donalda stepped in front of her mother, her gaze meeting Jean's.

"Mrs. MacDonald gave me that," she said. "And the

dishes, too. When the earl's men burned our home." She glanced at Morgan. "We'd nothing left but the clothes on our backs."

"Donalda."

Jean turned toward the source of the voice, and realized part of the cottage had been sectioned off for another room. A man stood there, supporting himself on two crutches carved from tree branches. Someone had drawn a stick figure on the side of one crutch, and she glanced at the little boy, wondering if it was his handiwork.

The man's face was long, as if pulled down by the weight of his troubles. His nose was hooked, his chin pointed. Yet for all the imperfections of his features, he had kind eyes, humor lurking in their blue depths.

"You'll be polite to guests in our home," he said, the strong burr reminding Jean of her own father's voice.

"We don't mean to disturb you," Morgan said. "But we've come to speak to Donalda."

For a moment fear flashed over the girl's face, but then her features settled into a firm resolve. She nodded just once, forced a smile for her parents, then led Jean and Morgan back outside the cottage.

Once they were a little distance away, Morgan asked, "Did you steal Andrew's watch?"

Donalda only blinked at him, no doubt surprised by the directness of the question.

She grabbed the material of her skirt, stared up at him and shook her head. "No, Your Lordship, I didn't. I'd never take anything that wasn't mine."

He glanced back at the cottage. "Have you told your parents, then?"

"Not yet." She stared down at the ground. "I couldn't find a way to do it."

Jean stepped forward, placed her hand on Donalda's arm. "Then there's no reason to. We want you to come back to Ballindair with us."

"I'll not be called a thief," she said.

"No one will call you a thief," Jean said.

Donalda looked to Morgan for confirmation, a gesture to be expected. Still, the girl's distrust stung.

"No one will," he repeated.

Donalda took a deep breath, nodded, then placed both hands against her reddened cheeks.

"I've left my things there," she said, pointing to a large boulder. "I didn't want Mam to see me with the bundle. She'd know for sure I'd been turned out."

She looked up at Morgan again. "I lied, sir. I told her you'd let me come for a half day and sent me home in the wagon. I'd not been able to come home for an age because of the distance."

He only smiled at her. "I think a white lie is acceptable in this case, Donalda."

He left them, returning to the cottage, no doubt to explain that Donalda was needed back at Ballindair. If Donalda's mother was like other females in Morgan's presence, she'd melt at the sight of his smile.

"Why?" Donalda asked, turning to Jean. "Why are you being kind when we both know it's your sister who planned this?"

"Because you're innocent," Jean said, turning and walking back toward the carriage.

She would tell the truth when she could, perhaps to make up for living the bigger lie.

Once back at Ballindair, Morgan took his leave, making his way to the lawn where Andrew was still painting the scenery. The sky was darkening ominously. Was Andrew going to sit in the rain and paint a Highland storm?

He stood watching him for a moment, well aware the other man had already noted his presence. A sign of their discord, that Andrew didn't turn and wave, or call out to him.

This moment had been coming for months, maybe years.

He needed to mark the day on a calendar somewhere. Perhaps he should take up his father's habit of journaling. What, exactly, would he write?

On this date, I put away childish things. Or: *Today, my life was revealed to me as never before.*

Perhaps he'd never been willing to see what was in front of his eyes. That had been his excuse with Lillian. He'd told himself he hadn't been looking for her infidelity, but it was glaringly apparent from the first days of their marriage. He simply hadn't wanted to admit it until he'd been made a laughingstock.

And his father? *What is honor?* Jean's question and his effort to define it had left him floundering.

His conversation with Jean had sparked another question. Why had Andrew argued so vociferously against his marriage to her? Had he known that Jean was one of those rare people who saw clearly and spoke the truth? Had he worried she might see through him as well?

Morgan approached his boyhood friend.

The noxious mixture of paint, turpentine, and some mixture Andrew used to prepare his canvas overwhelmed any hint of flower, blooming bush, or fresh breeze. How did the man tolerate the stench?

He stopped at Andrew's side. "I think it's time for you to leave," he said.

"I've overstayed my welcome, then?" Andrew asked, turning his head to look at Morgan, his smile not meeting his eyes. "Is it your wife, Morgan, that's done this to us?" He didn't put down his brush, but continued shading the side of a particularly odd looking bush. No, it was a tree.

"Jean has nothing to do with this. This is just between you and me."

"As it's always been."

"As it's always been," Morgan said.

Andrew carefully wiped off the brush, then placed it in its holder.

"Did you bed Lillian, Andrew?"

"Would I do that to a friend?"

"Did you?" Morgan asked.

"She was a bitch in heat, Morgan."

"And you were just one of her mongrels, is that it?"

"Do you really think that of me?"

"Until today, I would've said no," Morgan said. "Until this moment, I would've argued with anyone who dared suggest it to me."

"And now?"

Morgan wasn't sure what he felt, but it wasn't surprise, curiously, or disbelief. Had he always known?

"Don't look at me all lordly, Morgan. I don't have the same rigid concept of honor you do."

Since he wasn't exactly certain what that meant anymore, Morgan remained silent.

Andrew stood. "I'll be gone by morning. That is, if you'll loan me a coach. Or do you want me to walk away from your grand castle?"

"I'll do anything, including giving you the damn carriage, if it means you'll be gone."

"You'd toss aside our friendship for a woman?"

"For Lillian? No."

Morgan left before his anger could make him say something that would only escalate this confrontation. There was a time to fight, and a time to walk away.

He walked away.

* * *

Jean sat on the chair in the sitting room, smiling at the seamstress as she scurried out of the room, followed by the two young girls who assisted her. All three wore harried expressions, as if they wished for a few more hours in the day.

Catriona had appropriated the Rouge Room, the name coming from the color of the pale red draperies and the bed curtains. Beneath Jean's feet was a carpet of beige, woven with blowsy pink flowers. The furniture was larger than in the Countess's Suite, the vanity easily accommodating a woman in full skirts sitting at the bench seat. Two armoires sat side by side. Had Catriona given orders to move furniture from another room? Or had she chosen this suite because it could accommodate her growing wardrobe?

The room smelled of sandalwood, no doubt from the potpourri dishes on the vanity and bureau. Ever since childhood, Catriona had been sensitive to odors, one of the reasons she'd been excused from scullery duty.

How many dresses was her sister having made? Perhaps, on another day, she'd care enough to ask, but there were weightier matters to discuss.

Catriona came out of the bedroom, patting her hair into place. She was attired in a new dress, a striped blue fabric.

Before she could speak, Jean said, "When you were a little girl, people used to stop Mother in the street and tell her what a lovely child you were. You've only grown prettier, at least on the outside."

Catriona smiled. She always liked being complimented.

"I don't think, however, that you've given as much attention to your character as you have your hair or your wardrobe."

Jean sat back in the chair, folded her hands on her lap and regarded her sister somberly.

"I've brought Donalda back to Ballindair," she said. "I

don't want any other accusations made against her. Whatever problems you had with the girl, you're not to attempt to get her into trouble again. Is that understood?"

A flush colored Catriona's cheeks. "How very countess-like you sound, sister."

"Is that understood, Catriona?"

Catriona abruptly sat on the chair opposite Jean, her skirts billowing.

"Everyone knows a thief isn't to be trusted."

"She isn't a thief," Jean said.

Catriona studied her for a moment, then said, "Andrew told."

"On the contrary, he didn't have to say a word. Your actions speak for themselves."

"She'd been beastly to me, Jean. She called me a name and she tells stories."

"What kind of stories?"

Catriona looked away.

"That you've been sharing Andrew's bed? Everyone already knows."

Catriona stared directly at her. "You didn't."

Jean nodded. "I did," she said.

"Why didn't you say anything?"

"Because I didn't know what to say," Jean admitted. "Or maybe I didn't want to believe it."

Catriona's smile altered in character, turning a little sad. "Haven't you learned, Jean, that wanting something *not* to be doesn't make it so?"

For a moment they were simply sisters again, holding onto each other in a world gone mad.

Jean leaned forward, clasping her hands together. "I see nothing good coming from this situation, Catriona. Sooner or later Andrew will leave, and what will become of you? You'll just be a memory to him."

"I don't care, Jean. It's not as if I love him."

Before her marriage, that statement would've shocked Jean to her toes. Now, she understood.

"You enjoy his lovemaking," she said.

Catriona looked startled by that comment. "I would ask you the same about the earl, but I can see I don't have to," she said.

Jean could feel warmth bathe her face. "Morgan is very kind," she said. "A very thoughtful person."

"A man will do a great many things simply to get a woman into his bed and keep her there," Catriona said. "Andrew will do anything for me."

Perhaps it had been avarice that led her sister astray instead of passion.

"Are you willing to trade your body for whatever you can acquire?"

"It's my only asset, Jean. What else would you have me use?"

"Is it too much to want you to act in a decent manner?"

Catriona smiled. "You're lecturing me? You became a countess because you were found in the earl's bedroom."

Jean closed her eyes and took a deep breath. It was too late to wish Catriona to be an innocent. Too late for a great many things. She opened her eyes and looked at her sister.

"The world will judge you harshly, Catriona," she said, feeling as if she'd aged ten years in the last five minutes. "They won't know of your past or your grief. They won't realize you're afraid."

Catriona looked as if she wanted to say something, then subsided in silence.

"All they'll see," Jean continued, "is a greedy, grasping woman."

"I don't care what they see," Catriona said.

But in her face was a shadow of the child she'd been, the sister Jean had tried to protect.

"I won't let you be a spider at Ballindair," Jean said. "Trapping people in your web."

Catriona laughed merrily. "How foolish you can be, Jean. Is it becoming a countess? You were so much easier to deal with when you were a simple maid. You've become so virtuous. Tell me, have you told Morgan who you are?"

Jean stood, wanting to take herself off someplace to hide. Strangely, the first location that entered her mind was the sitting room in the Laird's Tower. Morgan might be there.

He might question her about this meeting, but he might also open his arms, allow her to lean her head against his shoulder and simply be comforted for a while.

As Jean left the room, the truth struck her with the force of the blow. As much as she might dislike what her sister had said, of the two of them, Catriona was more honest.

Night was so damned late in coming in Scotland. When Catriona hinted that she might come to him, Andrew waited patiently, until it seemed dawn would arrive before full darkness.

Tonight, she'd arrived, undressed in front of him, and let him take her to his bed. An interlude of madness, and so much more than lovemaking. At times he could swear his soul left his body to tangle among the clouds. Then, lonely for her presence, it would fly back into his body again.

Perhaps he should take up poetry.

"Come to London with me," he said, pulling Catriona on top of him. He laughed as she tossed her head back and forth, sending her blond curls dancing across his chest. "I'm leaving tomorrow."

"Are you?" she asked, almost disinterestedly.

"I'll set you up in your own lodgings," he said.

Instead of answering, she traced a path of freckles across

his shoulder to the base of his throat, interested in his physical imperfections.

He'd never felt this way for a woman.

"I'm asking you to be my mistress," he said.

Her look held nothing of surprise or joy. Instead, she looked bored.

"I've never made that offer to a woman," he said, annoyed.

"I suppose there must be a time for everything."

Irritation seeped through him along with another emotion he wasn't comfortable at identifying. Who was he to feel fear at a woman's reaction? Once he was back in London, he could have any woman he wanted, one each night for months to come.

None of them, however, would be like Catriona.

"Does that mean you won't?"

She climbed off him, moving to sit on the edge of the bed, uncaring for her nakedness. Of course, any woman with a body like hers shouldn't mind. Her blond hair tumbled down her back, and he wanted to stroke it.

He wanted her again—improvidently, imprudently, insanely.

"Well?"

She turned to face him, a half smile gracing her well-kissed lips.

"Shall I come to London with you?" She'd placed a fingertip against the edge of her smile, as if considering the matter. "I really don't know, Andrew," she said. "Shall I?"

He looked away before he begged.

"What kind of lodgings?" she asked.

"A town house, perhaps," he said. "In a fashionable square. I'm a very wealthy man." He slid his hand down her arm. "And, if you have a child, I'll support him as well."

She looked at him speculatively, as if gauging the truth

of his statement. Did he need to take her to see his banker?

"A carriage," she said, and he knew he'd won.

Once he got her back in London, this insane fascination would ease. He'd be able to see what she was, simply a woman with beauty and a willful personality. If he tired of her, he'd suggest several friends who might want to take over her care.

"A carriage," he said, smiling.

"And a generous sum for shopping. I detest wearing the same clothes over and over."

He nodded, agreeing, happy again.

And damned glad to see the last of Scotland.

Chapter 32

〜〜〜

RULES FOR STAFF: *Seniority is granted those with more than five years service.*

How had Seath done it all those years?

Morgan tucked the ledger under his arm and made for the stable. According to the timetable the steward had given him, the quarterly inventory for tack, animals, and feed was due. After that he had to address the seamstress's concerns about fabric, additional clothing for the staff, as well as talk to the manager of the dairy operations to ensure the problem with low milk production was a temporary matter and not a possible concern.

Even if he subtracted the home farms, the sheep, the woods, the various fishing endeavors, and the stables, Ballindair itself required a huge outlay of funds and time.

He didn't begrudge the money spent on his ancestral home, but he was exhausted from merely trying to keep up with Mr. Seath, let alone outstrip any of his steward's accomplishments.

How had Jean done it for a week?

He'd been an ardent bridegroom then, and had kept her up half the night. In the morning, when he'd wondered idly where his bride had gotten to, she was performing tasks that would fell an ordinary man.

At the moment, he felt regrettably ordinary.

And not a little ashamed of himself.

These weeks at Ballindair had felt curiously expectant. He knew what he'd been waiting for now—his life. Who was he? What did he want to accomplish, now that he couldn't follow in his father's footsteps? Twin questions he hadn't asked since London. What stunned him was the realization that the answers didn't come quickly or with ease.

He heard a squishing sound, looked down at his pristine boots—self-polished since he didn't have a valet—and sighed. A reminder, then, to look where he walked. That advice was good for the rest of his life, too.

Up until now, he hadn't given all that much thought to what his steward had done. Had he been blind? Evidently so, and in more than one area.

"Is it true?" he'd asked Seath on returning from Donalda's cottage. "Did my father clear out the crofters for sheep?"

The man looked even paler on being asked the question. He stared at the far wall as if he wished to be anywhere but his sick bed.

Morgan reached out, placed his hand on the man's arm. "Why?"

With a sigh, Seath turned and looked at him. "Your father was a very careful man about Ballindair," he said.

Morgan nodded. Lessons of frugality had been taught him since he was a boy.

"But surely Ballindair is in no financial danger?" If so, he would simply transfer some money from the distilleries.

Seath shook his head.

"Then why would he do such a thing?"

"Your father was a difficult man in many instances, Your Lordship. Everything, to him, must pull its own weight. If the income from harvesting the trees was lacking, then we stopped cutting them until wood brought us a better price. If the fishing production was not as good one year, then he brought the boats in."

"And the crofters?"

"Sheep were more profitable."

There was that faraway look again.

"So he replaced people with sheep?" Morgan asked.

Seath nodded.

All his life, he'd held up his father as the epitome of honor and decency. Yet in that one act, the 8th earl became human.

Jean was right. He'd been looking at his father through the eyes of a child.

"Thank you for your honesty," he said, standing. "Thank you, also, for trying to make right what you could. What happened to the families?"

Mr. Seath smiled weakly. "We have, perhaps, a sight more footmen than we need, Your Lordship. And the dairy maids hardly need to number ten. But it was all I could do."

Morgan nodded, thinking of Donalda's father and brother. He explained the situation to Seath, surprised when the man began to smile.

"The man would make a good boatman," Seath said. "He doesn't need legs for that. Fishing is good this year. And the lad could be trained, in time, in a skill at Ballindair."

Another of his tasks today, to find a place for the family. A place close enough so Donalda's father could walk home after work. Perhaps they could build something, past Strath

Dalross, near the river. A comfortable little cottage to make up for the one that had been burned one night.

Smiling, Morgan continued walking and planning.

The last time Jean had seen Morgan was when she was dressing for the day.

At least, that's what she'd intended on doing.

He'd grabbed her from behind, wrapping his arms around her and nuzzling her neck where her wrapper had fallen open.

For a moment she allowed herself the luxury of indulging in his touch and the kiss he gave her when he spun her around.

Morgan, naked in the dawn's light, was a sight to behold.

She stood on tiptoe to press her cheek against his. His skin was warm, his morning beard scratchy. Tears pressed against her eyelids and threatened to fall.

Her hands wrapped around his shoulders and she hugged him, wishing she had the power to stop time. If she did, she'd choose this moment of silence and need.

"Thank you," he said.

She drew back.

"For what?"

He frowned. "I don't know if I can explain it," he said. "Thank you for being you."

"A strange compliment," she said, "but I'll take it."

He kissed her in response, and for a few moments thought flew right out of her head.

When they separated, she smiled at him, feeling as if the world was a bright and beautiful place. That sentiment warmed her all morning, up until the time she reached Mr. Seath's room.

"You just missed the earl," he said faintly. "He's off to the stables."

If anything, the steward looked more ill than he had a day

earlier. Dark circles lay beneath his dull eyes. His hair was lank against his head,

"Is there any family we can summon for you?" she asked, sitting beside his bed.

The time had come, perhaps, to make preparations. His faint smile was an acknowledgment of her thought.

"Ballindair has been all the family I ever wanted or needed." His smile faded. "That's sad, isn't it? To have a love for a building. A structure cannot hug you or hold you, or touch your hand."

She moved the chair closer, sat, and reached out and took one of his hands, clasping it between her own.

"Has the physician given you anything for the pain?"

"There's nothing more he can do," Seath said.

They sat in silence for a few moments.

"I'm proud of him," he said. "The earl. Morgan. He's taken on the burden of Ballindair."

She nodded.

"He has it within him to be a great man."

Again she nodded.

"You'll need to tell him, of course," he said, his voice faint.

"I know," she softly said. Her secret was always with her, keeping pace with her, walking side by side and whispering to her in the early morning hours.

"You were a good maid, Jean."

She smiled. "I was a good maid."

The steward kept journals about the purchases and expenditures on Ballindair's behalf. He'd also told her that throughout the years, he'd kept notes that might be relevant to succeeding generations.

Had he written about her? What had he said? Just the bare facts of the situation? Or would he append his own thoughts? *On this date, wed to the 9th Earl of Denbleigh, one single woman, once resident of Inverness and upstairs maid.*

"You'll be a good countess."

She shrugged.

"Is it that you don't believe in yourself? Or are you afraid of the future?"

The future was frightening for both of them, wasn't it?

"If the earl sends you away, then he's a fool."

"He probably will," she said. "He would have no reason to keep me."

He only smiled weakly, and she could tell he'd exhausted himself.

She rearranged his pillows, reached for the cup of tea she'd brewed him earlier, and helped him drink the last of it.

"Is there anything I can do?" she asked. Weeping in front of him wouldn't be wise, but it was hard to push back her tears.

"Stay with him, if you can. He needs you more than he knows."

"If I can," she said. What she didn't say was that she needed Morgan as well. Or perhaps Mr. Seath already knew, because he only patted her hand.

When the time came, she would sit vigil with him, praying to ease his pain. For now, she stood and bent over the bed, surprising them both when she kissed him on the forehead.

The time would be soon.

Nodding to Tom, the young man assigned to care for the steward, she left Mr. Seath's room, to find her aunt pacing in the hall. The older woman was dressed in her usual manner of dark blue dress, white apron, and lace cap resting on her coronet. The only changes in her demeanor were her clenched hands and a decided look of worry.

"Do you know where Catriona is?" Aunt Mary asked in greeting.

"I haven't seen her this morning," Jean said, moving away

from Mr. Seath's room so as not to disturb him. "Have you checked with the seamstresses?"

Aunt Mary shook her head. "They haven't seen her, either."

That was strange.

"I don't think she's here. She's not in her room, and she isn't anywhere to be found," her aunt said, a wrinkle deepening above the bridge of her nose.

Jean stared at her in dismay. "Where do you think she is?"

Had her words sent Catriona fleeing from Ballindair? If so, it would be the first time her sister had paid any heed to what she'd said.

"Mr. Prender is also gone."

Jean understood immediately. "And you think she's gone with him?"

Aunt Mary nodded, and told her in a whisper, "The earl sent him packing. He left this morning without a word to any of us or a tip to the maids." The frown returned in earnest. "And left a mess."

Jean had a sinking feeling.

"She's my sister's girl, and she's not been raised to be a strumpet."

They shared a look. Although the words weren't said, they both knew Catriona hadn't acted in the manner she'd been raised.

"Where was he bound?" Jean asked.

When Aunt Mary only shook her head, Jean sighed again. "Never mind. I'll ask the stable master."

"She's ruined if she's gone with him," her aunt said.

"I'll find her," Jean said, patting her aunt on the arm, then went in search of Morgan.

Chapter 33

"The trains don't run every day from Inverness to London," Morgan said.

Jean nodded, grateful for that at least. "But you think he's taken her to London."

He sat back against the carriage seat and studied her.

"I'm not so sure it's a case of abduction, Jean."

"I know," she agreed.

The idea they might save Catriona from her own rashness was foolish. However, they could certainly prevent her from making matters worse. Once society learned of her decision to accompany a married man anywhere, her reputation would be forever sullied.

The best they could hope for was to intercept Catriona before she appeared anywhere publicly with Andrew.

She leaned her head back against the high seat, trying

to forestall her tears. One escaped and she brushed it away impatiently.

Suddenly, Morgan was there beside her, sweeping her skirts out of the way and pulling her into his arms. She wasn't the type to cry. She grew annoyed at weepy women. But she grabbed his jacket and buried her face inside it, hating the situation and loving the smell of him.

"Catriona has brought you nothing but shame," she said a moment later. "I'm sorry for that."

"What more can anyone say about me?"

A great deal, if the truth was known. Now was not the time to tell him, however, when they were racing toward Inverness to save her sister. Now was not the moment, when he was so kind and concerned.

Less than a quarter hour had transpired from when she'd told him about Catriona missing and the carriage being ready. Morgan had been willing to stop what he was doing to help her, and she'd forever remember that.

"Catriona was always a sweet girl," she said. "She smiled a great deal, and went out of her way to be charming."

"She probably learned early on her appearance mattered more than anything else."

Jean closed her eyes, resting her head against his chest and finding the position remarkably comfortable.

"It's not uncommon," she said. "Women have no occupation, other than being wife or mother. We're to be personable and helpful. Even the rules for maids accentuate our appearance. We are to be attractive, clean, and tidy."

"There are rules for maids?"

Surprised, she lifted her head and looked at him.

"Didn't you know? We were given to understand the Earl of Denbleigh had dictated those rules himself."

His face clouded for a moment. "It wasn't me. Perhaps my father did so. Are there other rules?"

"There are thirty-six of them," she said.

An eyebrow arched upward. "That many?"

"Would you like me to recite them?" she asked. "That is another rule. We have to memorize them." She sighed into his chest.

"If I'm ever tremendously bored, you can. Perhaps we'll address the issue when we return to Ballindair."

Before she could answer, there was a noise at the driver's box.

"I see them, sir. MacDuff is driving them hard."

"Can we catch them?" Morgan asked.

"He's got our best pair, sir. But the landau is heavier than the barouche."

"Pull over, Guthrie."

She reached out and touched his sleeve. "Are you going to quit, Morgan?"

"Of course not," he said. "We're just going to go about the chase in a different manner."

He opened the half door and descended the carriage.

She followed, watching as he and the driver worked on the harness of one of the lead horses. Before she knew it, the horse was free and Morgan was on it, gone in a clatter of hooves and dust.

She stared after him. Evidently, she was supposed to remain here, while he rescued her sister. Was a countess supposed to remain docilely behind?

Oh, dear Lord, she didn't know.

"Guthrie," she said, remembering the man as a kind and personable sort, "why aren't we following him in the carriage?"

"I'd have to let loose Sally to make it balanced. The other two might be able to carry the load, but I'll not ask it of them. And I'll not ask the three to pull the carriage unbalanced, neither."

She strode ahead to the lone lead horse. "Is this Sally?"

He nodded.

She stood in front of Sally as the horse bobbed its head at her. Cautiously, she raised her hand and petted it on its long nose, the very first time she'd ever touched a horse.

"I need your help," she said, leaning close to whisper so Guthrie couldn't hear. "I need to get to Morgan. Can you take me there?"

The horse raised its nose and whacked her on the chin. She stood back, eyed Sally, and decided the answer had been an enthusiastic yes.

"Will you let loose Sally," she said. "And help me mount her, please."

Guthrie didn't look the least convinced of her equestrian talents. She wasn't going to tell him she'd never ridden before, but how hard could it be? People got on a horse, directed the animal to a certain location, and the horse did all the work.

"Sally's not a riding horse," he said, his mouth set in a mulish line. "She's a carriage horse. She's used to pulling in tandem."

Morgan had done just fine.

"If you'll remove the harness, please, Guthrie, and help me mount."

"Are you sure? It won't be a pleasant ride."

Since she had nothing against which to measure it, she doubted she'd mind all that much.

"I'm very sure," she said, stepping out of the way.

Guthrie eyed her attire with some misgivings.

She stared down at her skirt, realizing what was making him pause. How on earth could she ride a horse with a hoop?

"Give me a moment," she said, and strode behind the carriage. With only the birds, field mice, and an occasional eagle as her witness, she removed her hoop. Grabbing it up from the road, she collapsed it as much as she could and tucked it in the space beneath the carriage seat.

She rejoined Guthrie, who pretended not to notice her skirts were now trailing on the ground. She wasn't acting very countesslike, but she wasn't a real countess, was she?

Pasting a smile on her face, she eyed Sally with what she hoped was confidence, and proceeded to mount her first horse.

Thank God for MacDuff. When the man had seen him riding after them, he slowed the carriage. Morgan saw Andrew peering out the window, and after spotting him, draw back.

Now, Morgan dismounted, waiting for Andrew and Catriona to leave the carriage. If they didn't exit on their own, he'd go in and get his sister-in-law—his foolish and self-absorbed sister-in-law.

Andrew opened the door, stepping down from the carriage with his customary smirk, an expression Morgan decided he'd seen just too damn often of late.

"What is it, Morgan? Feeling a need to rescue a damsel in distress?" He gestured with one hand toward Catriona as she peered out of the carriage. "There's no need. Catriona is coming with me of her own accord."

"I'll speak with you, Andrew," he said.

Andrew turned and said something to Catriona, then strode toward him.

"Are you about to make us walk to Inverness, Morgan? I never thought you to be so ill-mannered."

"She's not your usual conquest, Andrew. Leave her be."

Andrew smiled. "I will agree she's not like Lillian, no. Lillian was a true slut, Morgan. Before she's finished, she'll have bedded most of London."

Morgan didn't comment. Andrew might well be right.

"She was so damn needy, you know? She needed attention, Morgan. She wanted affection or love or something passing for it."

"You know this how? From your vast experience with women?" He managed a smile. "You've misjudged this time, Andrew. I'm not letting you take Catriona."

"Can you stop me?" Andrew raised his fists.

The picture of Andrew, so much shorter, willing to fight him, might have been amusing at another time. Now, it just annoyed him.

"No," Morgan said calmly. "I'm not going to fight you for Catriona. Nor am I going to fight you about Lillian. I find I don't much care. You weren't the first lover she had and you certainly weren't the last."

Slowly, Andrew dropped his fists and took a deep breath.

"That's good, then," he said.

Morgan's fist shot out before Andrew could protect himself, the blow so hard it shuddered up Morgan's arm.

Andrew stumbled back and nearly fell, but righted himself at the last moment. He bent over, hands braced on his knees, shaking his head as if to clear it. As he straightened, he cradled his jaw in one palm.

"I thought you said she wasn't worth it," he said, his words garbled.

"She isn't," Morgan said. "That's for making Jean cry."

He walked to the carriage, reached in and grabbed his sister-in-law none too gently by the arm. Once outside the carriage, he turned her to face him.

"You have a choice to make. And you need to make it now."

Catriona pulled away, rubbing at her arm where he'd grabbed her.

"It was my decision to go with Andrew."

"I understand that," Morgan said. "I'm offering you another choice. To go and live with my aunt in Edinburgh. You'll be chaperoned and taught the ways of society." Before she could protest, he raised his hand. "I know, you were both educated properly in Inverness. I know you're not a maid. If you accept my offer, my aunt will teach you what you need to know in order to take your proper place in society as the sister-in-law of an earl. As inbred as society is, being related to me will advance you far more than anything Andrew can do for you."

"Even if you're a scandal, Morgan?"

He smiled, admiring her courage, if nothing else. "You'll find that a whiff of scandal will only make people more curious about you, Catriona. While they may wish to excoriate me, they'll look at you with different eyes."

He took a step closer to her. "If you go with Andrew now, Catriona, you'll never be more than what he makes you. Is that the choice you want to make?"

She didn't answer for a moment. Did she think herself in love? How did he convince her Andrew wasn't worth the effort? Today, he might want Catriona. Tomorrow, however, his eyes might linger on another woman.

"Catriona," Andrew said, approaching them. He stretched out his hand to her. "Come with me. We'll have a lovely life together."

"He's married," Morgan said. "Did he tell you that?"

She nodded.

"I love you," Andrew said, a remark that had Morgan frowning. How many women had heard Andrew's avowal?

"Will you live the life you choose, Catriona?" he asked her. "Or the life Andrew chooses for you?"

She smiled, then, and Morgan marveled at her beauty. Catriona would be well received wherever she went.

"Catriona, please," Andrew said.

Perhaps Andrew did feel something for Catriona. A

pity, since he had a wife and five children waiting at home. Andrew needed to visit his family more often.

Catriona turned, and without a backward glance, placed her hand on Morgan's arm.

"Jean said you were kind," she said. "But I thought she was saying that because you were her husband and she had to."

His laughter surprised them both. "I doubt Jean would say anything just because she had to."

"She really will make quite a good countess," Catriona said.

He nodded. "I do believe you're right."

Before he could say more, screams interrupted them.

He turned to see his countess, the irrepressible Jean, bent over the neck of a horse, her hands clenched in its mane. He couldn't decide who was more terrified, the wide-eyed horse or Jean. But since he was married to the latter, he went to her rescue.

Chapter 34

$\sim\sim$

RULES FOR STAFF: *None of the equipment, service, tools, or equipage belonging to the family is to be used by the staff.*

"**A**re you feeling better after your equestrienne adventure?" Morgan asked, entering the sitting room.

Jean felt warmth suffuse her face, which didn't displease her all that much. Morgan had said she was beautiful with a blush. Silly man.

"I am," she said. "But you needn't have treated me like I was an invalid. I'm perfectly fine. Only a little sore. And Sally? Has she recuperated as well?"

"Sally's none the worse for wear. Guthrie's been cooing to her all evening, and has given her an extra ration of feed."

"I can just imagine what he's saying to the poor horse. 'Never mind, Sally, I'll never let the nasty woman on your back again.'"

Morgan's laugh had a booming sound that filled the room and made her smile.

"And Catriona? Safely on her way?" he asked.

"She couldn't wait to leave," she said. "I think she was afraid you'd withdraw your offer. Does your aunt know what to expect?"

"I sent along a letter of introduction, enough money to see her through the end of the year, and a warning to Catriona. If she doesn't behave, she'll be forced to do good works with my aunt. My aunt is very strong on good works."

"And Andrew is no doubt in Inverness by now," Jean said. "Good riddance to him."

He came to stand in front of her, reaching for the empty cup she held.

"My footman," she said, as he placed it on the nearby table.

He didn't respond, merely lifted her out of her chair and sat again, with her in his arms.

She made a sound of surprise, but settled back into place quickly enough. A remarkable experience, sitting on Morgan's lap.

"I'm not ill," she said, leaning her head against his shoulder.

"I know," he said. "I just wanted to hold you."

She was silent after that surprising announcement.

"Thank you," she said. "For what you've done for Catriona."

"I was thinking about sending her to my aunt before she decided to leave with Andrew. I should have mentioned it earlier."

They sat companionably for a moment.

"I do respect you," he said, startling her again.

She raised up and looked at him.

"I've been thinking about what you said, about trust and respect being paired. I think you're right. And I wanted you to know I do respect you."

She waited, but when he didn't say anything else, she asked, "Do you trust me?"

"Yes," he said, and the word was so quickly spoken she knew it was true.

Turning, she placed her hands on either side of his face, reached up and kissed him. Sometimes, he shaved twice a day, but today he hadn't, and the bristly feel of his whiskers against her palms was curiously arousing.

She wanted to thank him for being a gentle lover, for teaching her about passion, for giving her pleasure. She wanted to thank him for his kindnesses, not just to Catriona, but also to her. He'd never ridiculed her, even in her silliest moments, or when she'd gone exploring for ghosts. Instead, he'd shared the adventure with her.

Morgan was not the arrogant boor she'd thought him at their first meeting. Instead, he was a complicated, intense man who sought to achieve his father's honor, never realizing he'd surpassed the 8th earl in decency, caring, and responsibility. For the last few days, he'd been the steward of Ballindair, and when his daily duties were done, he'd spent time with Mr. Seath.

She'd believed him to be autocratic, and now she knew that the man who'd first come home to Ballindair had been in pain. She folded her arms around his neck, placed her cheek against his and wished she could remove those memories, as well as any of his doubts.

He deserved someone to love him, and she did. He deserved someone to honor him, and she did. But he also deserved someone to be honest with him, and she'd not yet done so.

He pulled back and kissed her, and tears peppered her eyes beneath closed lids.

She loved his kisses, loved everything about him. Even when he annoyed her, he charmed her.

Standing, she stood and stretched out her hand to him. Without a word, they went into the bedroom, and in the light of the Highland night, she removed her clothes. When he would have moved to help her, she shook her head. She wanted to come to him naked, to bare everything of her body since she couldn't share her mind, her past, or a great many of her thoughts.

When it was done, when the clothing was neatly folded and placed on a chair, she pulled down the counterpane of the bed and knelt there, reaching for him.

First, his shirt, and once that was done, she placed her hands flat against his chest. How magnificent he was. Muscles ranged from his corded neck all the way down to his broad and long feet.

"You'll have to do the rest," she said, pointing to his trousers.

He only smiled and rid himself of his clothing.

The light in the room should have shamed her. She should have kept beneath the covers instead of letting him look his fill. But as she touched him, she could feel his eyes on her.

She reached out and held that part of him that fascinated her. She knew he liked her to explore him, with her fingers and her mouth. Now, she dared herself to make his eyes darken and his breath come fast.

A powerful man, one momentarily in her thrall.

Her hands moved from his beautiful cock to rest on his hips.

"May I touch you?" he asked, his voice a husky burr.

"Where?" she asked softly, her words a mere breath of sound.

"Here," he said, placing one finger against her shoulder.

"I suppose that would be acceptable," she said primly.

She sat back on her heels, pulling him closer. When he mounted the bed to kneel in front of her, she reached around him to squeeze his beautiful muscular buttocks.

The finger he'd placed on her shoulder moved to trace a path to the base of her throat and from there to rest between her breasts. Slowly, as if asking permission, the finger moved to the left, over the curving slope of her breast to rest against her nipple.

She would have cautioned him that she'd not given him permission to touch her there, but his finger slowly twirled around the nipple, causing heat to blossom deep inside.

She closed her eyes, the better to experience the sensation, an awakening, perhaps. A dampening, readying herself for him.

His kiss made her lose her concentration, until all she could think about was him. She wrapped her arms around his shoulders, breasts against his chest, her cleft pressing against his length.

Suddenly, she was on her back and he was over her, kissing her ear, her throat, her breasts, an exploration conducted with lips, mouth, and gentle whispers as he lingered over select locations.

Smiling, she threaded her fingers through his thick hair, her heart expanding with an indescribable joy.

His fingers danced among her swollen folds, her legs widening instinctively. He tasted her then, his tongue darting, circling, teasing.

"Morgan." His name sent chills through her.

"Jean." He kissed his way back up her body, whispered her name in her ear. "Jean," he said again.

Time elongated, then narrowed to frame only the two of them. If the world outside this bed existed, she neither felt nor saw it. Only Morgan with his teasing smile and intoxicating kisses, who touched her with slow fingers, as if fascinated by the sensation of skin against skin.

When he entered her, so slowly she almost screamed at the restraint of it, her hands gripped his shoulders, then his waist, then his buttocks to pull him to her.

He refused to hurry, however, torturing her with need.

She made a helpless murmur and won a quick kiss for it. She placed her palm against his cheek, before gripping his shoulders with insistent hands, anchoring him in place by a touch gone suddenly dominant and needful.

She wanted the moments to last forever. Let her forever recall the touch of his tongue, the tenderness of his kiss against each eyelid, his soft breath as he nuzzled the hair at her temple, then kissed the curve of her ear.

Her mouth opened against his skin, her tongue tasting him.

The bedchamber became an oasis of shadows, a place of whispered promises, grazing kisses, and the touch of his fingers gliding over her skin. Her fingers clenched on his upper arms, then shoulders, before grasping his back as he entered her. Her breath caught on a sob as her forehead ground against his shoulder, her eyes tight as her body responded, knowing him, trusting him, as he led her into a land of pleasure.

For a few moments she was lost in the movement, the hot, slick feel of his body thrusting into hers: torso to breast, hip to hip, thigh to thigh. She lifted up, wanting more, needing more, until she felt something give, an abrupt surrender that poured molten bliss into a hundred places in her body and melted her bones.

She murmured his name, and he clenched, emptying himself into her with a throaty growl that ended with a kiss.

Were those her legs or his? And whose hand lay possessively between her breasts, fingers splayed? Lost in the throbbing aftershocks of passion, she didn't care.

Morgan smiled at her when she opened her eyes. Embarrassment warmed her. When the blush traveled to her cheeks, he laughed, raised his head and kissed her.

She was reminded of the first time she'd seen him. If she'd

known then what she knew now, she might well have grabbed him and kissed him soundly. She did exactly that, kissing his smile.

The light revealed the teasing glint in his eyes, the tousled black hair, the sheer beauty of his shoulders and chest. She leaned to the side to get a glimpse of his buttocks, smiling at herself.

"And just what are you looking at?" he asked, brushing a kiss across her nose.

"Your lovely backside, Your Lordship."

Before this moment, with his smile coming wicked and amused, she might never have confessed to such a thing.

"Never the likes of those breasts of yours, Your Ladyship."

She smiled back at him, feeling his equal in this moment, captivated by passion, and perhaps a little bemused by it.

When they loved again, it was sweet and simple, she rising and falling away, him setting the slow and silky rhythm. When pleasure seeped through her, it was with grace and delicacy, a reminder that passion can have a pure edge, and one not so needy.

Delight unfurled where they joined, and deep inside petals of bliss traveled outward. Her legs trembled, her fingers tingled, her breath hitched even as her blood surged through her body.

On a sigh, she surrendered, becoming nothing more than a feeling, a color, a wisp. Only Morgan kept her from disappearing.

She wrapped her arms around him and sighed again, holding him with tenderness and quiet joy.

Loving him, as she'd never loved another.

Chapter 35

With Catriona gone from Ballindair, the castle became an almost enchanted place. Or perhaps it was Andrew's absence that was responsible for Morgan's pervasive feeling of relief.

If it rained, he blessed the fact it would aid the crops. If it remained sunny, he took pleasure in the Highland summer day. Nothing could disturb his ebullience, unless it was the condition of his steward, a man he was coming to admire more each day.

Or perhaps the whole of his existence was made better by the presence of one woman, his surprising wife. Even thinking of her made him smile, and when he caught himself doing that, he laughed, and focused once more on his tasks.

When gloaming swirled at the base of the trees, and

waning sunlight sparkled through the highest branches, Morgan would put down his ledgers, dismiss any visitors to the library, and nearly sprint to the Laird's Tower.

They'd not given up the habit of eating dinner in the sitting room, and it was a cozy prelude to a night promising passion and wonder, surprise and delight.

He'd never felt this way before, and it amazed and amused him. At the bottom of those feelings was another: caution. Jean was, with every smile and comment, beginning to wrap herself around his consciousness and embed herself in his mind. Perhaps she was even stealing little bits of his soul.

Whatever was happening was new and too difficult to reveal. But even the cynical part of him was being won over by a woman's laugh.

He found himself winding around her at night, as if she were his pillow. When he awoke one night, it was with a curious sense of discomfort. Jean wasn't beside him in the bed. He listened for a moment, but no sounds came from the bathing chamber.

He sat up, lighting the lamp beside the bed.

Annoyed, he grabbed his robe and made his way into the sitting room, the lamp an impromptu lantern.

She wasn't there, either.

Had she gone ghost hunting again? What could those damn ghosts give her that he couldn't?

He put down the lamp and dressed, then made his way to the Long Gallery by the glow of moonlight. When he discovered the chamber empty, he was more worried than annoyed. She'd fainted in the West Tower, which was the second place he visited.

She wasn't there, either.

As he passed the kitchen, he saw two crying maids, each comforting the other, followed by a young man blinking rapidly.

He reached out, grabbed the lad's arm and asked, "What is it?"

Please, God, don't let Jean have been hurt.

The young man belatedly realized who Morgan was and jerked to attention. "Begging your pardon, Your Lordship. It's Mr. Seath."

Morgan suddenly knew where Jean was.

A crowd of people surrounded the steward's door, parting for him as he approached. He stood in the doorway for a moment, then crossed the small sitting room to the bedroom.

William Seath lay on his bed, his emaciated frame propped up on two pillows. His hair had been brushed back from his forehead, his features appearing even sharper in death. An odd glow surrounded him, until Morgan realized it was the lamp beside the bed casting a yellowish hue throughout the room.

Yet the man was smiling, his face serene, without the lines of fatigue and pain that had marred his appearance for so long.

Mrs. MacDonald sat on one side of the bed, Jean on the other. She was speaking softly, and it was a moment before Morgan realized she was praying aloud.

Her hand lay over Mr. Seath's in a comforting touch.

The windows were open, the better to allow Mr. Seath's soul to leave Ballindair.

He came to stand beside Jean, reaching out to clasp her shoulder. She didn't turn or look up at him, only sagged against him as if needing his support.

"He was a good man," Morgan said, feeling his throat tighten. "A very good man."

Mrs. MacDonald nodded, tears streaming down her face. She made no effort to hide her grief. Nor would he have asked her to do so. To hell with those damn rules for staff.

"Why didn't you wake me?" he asked.

"Tom came and got me," Jean said. She placed her free hand against his where it rested on her shoulder.

If she were another woman, or William Seath another man, or even if he had been the same man he'd been upon returning from London, he would have said something about the impropriety of the Countess of Denbleigh visiting a man—even an ill one—alone in his bedchamber.

But he only smiled, and said, "I'm glad you were with him." He looked at Mrs. MacDonald. "Have the mirrors covered," he said, "and the clocks stopped."

The housekeeper turned surprised eyes to him.

"He was like a member of the family," Morgan said. "What we do for our own, we should do for him."

She nodded, and began giving instructions.

"And the bell, sir?"

He gave his assent. A man from the staff would stand before Ballindair and ring the heavy bell signaling a life's end. Those who heard it would know they'd lost someone of importance at Ballindair. They would be invited to participate in the service to both mourn William Seath and encourage his soul to rest.

"Did he have any family at all?"

"No," Jean said, looking up at him. "Ballindair was his family."

He nodded. "Then we'll act the same," he said.

When Jean stood, he took her into his arms in full view of the staff remaining at William Seath's door.

Jean and her aunt were preparing to sit vigil with William Seath. His body had been washed and then dressed again in his dead clothes. Only then was he laid in his coffin. Because he was so emaciated at the time of his death, only two of them were needed for that task.

If he'd had any family, the task of watching over the body

would have fallen to them, but there was no shortage of volunteers for the hours ahead.

Her aunt opened her Bible, preparing to read aloud from it, when Morgan entered the Clan Hall where the bier had been erected.

"I'll sit with Jean," he said.

Aunt Mary merely nodded and slipped out of the room without a word.

Morgan moved a chair to sit beside her. Perhaps it would have been more proper for him to be on the other side of the coffin, but she was grateful for his proximity.

"You were very fond of him," he said.

She nodded, unwilling to tell him not all her tears were for the steward. Instead, she was feeling selfishly melancholy at the moment.

The time had come.

What would he say? Worse, what would he do?

There was every possibility he would simply walk away. Or he might commend her honesty at the same time as he banished her to a different life, one away from him.

Regardless of what he might do, she had to tell him who she was.

"You once asked me how I knew Mr. Seath's condition was so dire," she said, speaking softly in deference to the occasion.

He nodded.

"My mother had the same wasting sickness," she said. She clasped both hands in front of her, squeezing tightly. The pain made her concentrate on the feeling in her hands, and not the mists of the past rising to envelop her. She didn't want to think of those days. She didn't, yet she must.

"She became ill very sudden," she said. "Because my father was a physician, he knew the symptoms well. He told us she hadn't long to live."

He placed his hand over hers. She looked down at their hands, wishing she could absorb some of his heat. She was cold, from the inside out.

"The end didn't come soon enough," she said. "Each day was agony for her. Then each hour. Even the air against her skin was too much. Sometimes, we could hear her praying to die."

How many times had she heard her mother weeping? Or those long, agonized moans indicating the morphine wasn't helping?

On that last morning, her father had come into the kitchen, looking pale and drawn. He'd aged in the intervening weeks, the lines of suffering reminding her of those on her mother's face.

That morning his eyes had looked haunted, and he simply stood in the middle of the room. When she had gone to him, followed by Catriona, he extended his arms around both of them, lowering his head to whisper, "My girls."

That was all he'd said.

Looking back, she didn't think it was a cry for help or a plea for forgiveness. He had simply acknowledged the moment as the last guilt-free one he would have. Then he left them, returning to the bedroom he'd shared with his beloved wife.

What had happened next had never been in any doubt. Her father came downstairs to the sitting room an hour later. He faced both Catriona and her, saying very calmly, "I have ended your mother's misery."

An excess of morphine had simply stopped her breathing.

He'd not attempted to escape his crime, but reported himself to the authorities.

"As a physician," Jean said to Morgan in the Clan Hall, "he'd always attempted to save lives. In that instance, he willfully took one."

Not once, however, had he ever seemed to regret his act. Instead, a sense of calm and peace had come over her father as he awaited his punishment.

"What happened to him?" Morgan asked.

"They hanged him for what he'd done," she said.

She'd never said those words aloud. Aunt Mary knew the story, of course, and after her father surrendered to the authorities, everyone in Inverness had known.

Her father had adored her mother, to the extent of destroying his own life to help her.

Her father had never expected either Catriona or her to forgive him. And he'd also been prepared for the authorities. He hadn't tried to evade them or the consequences of his deed. Instead, he went to the gallows wearing a small smile, the guard had said. The last word on his lips had been their mother's name.

The power of love was frightening.

Love made people behave in ways that were improvident. Love ruined reason. Love was like a cancer, encompassing everything in its path.

And she'd caught the disease.

Morgan didn't move, his hand still covering hers.

"I'm sorry, Jean."

She glanced over at him. In his look was only compassion, not censure. Perhaps she'd be able to recall that expression later, when it was gone.

"It was a very great scandal," she said. "Both Catriona and I were known as the Murderer's Girls."

People had avoided them at the shops and in the street. They'd been shunned by their neighbors, and any friends who'd remained through their mother's torturous illness.

The greatest kindnesses had come from strangers: a guard at the prison who arranged a place for them to wait where they didn't have to view their father's hanging; a woman who asked if they were hungry on the way to Ballindair, then shared her dinner with them.

"I don't remember any scandal involving the MacDonalds," he said, frowning.

Here it was. The moment she'd dreaded ever since marrying him.

"My name isn't MacDonald," she said. "Nor is Catriona's." She took a deep breath, a little difficult given that she could barely breathe. "It's Cameron. Jean Cameron."

He nodded. "I remember the case," he said. "Dr. Cameron. I think they called him something else."

"A great many names." She was not going to recite the list of calumnies they'd uttered about her father.

"I'm sorry, Jean."

In that instant, she realized he still didn't understand.

She leaned close to him, lay her head against his shoulder and closed her eyes. He smelled of something wonderful: the scent of his soap or simply him? She didn't want to move, but to stay here forever, in just this place, within his comforting arms.

But to do so would be to cheat him of the truth, and it was something she owed him.

She pulled back, keeping him from reaching for her by the simple act of placing her hand against his chest.

"I'm the one who's sorry," she said.

"For what?" His eyes softened. "Do you think I would blame you for your father's actions, Jean?"

"You came home because of scandal," she countered.

"I came home because it was time to come home."

Her smile felt bittersweet; did it look so to him?

"You lectured me on honor, Morgan. It was the reason we married. You wanted to be honorable above all else."

"And you questioned the meaning of honor, if I recall."

She forced herself to meet his gaze as she struggled to get her voice under control.

"I've brought you shame and dishonor, Morgan. We're not married. My name is Cameron, not MacDonald, and neither the law nor the kirk will say it's a true and honorable marriage."

He didn't say anything for a moment, but a muscle flexed in his cheek. She wished he would speak all those thoughts burning in his eyes. Let them out and let her deal with them as well as she could.

He sat back as if he couldn't bear to touch her. She clasped her hands in her lap again, intently staring at her whitened knuckles. She had borne many things in her life; she could endure this, too.

In the silence, she could barely hear herself breathe. She was trembling, freezing, even though the afternoon was temperate and leaning toward warm, the sun a glowing disk in the sky.

Help me.

Perhaps God judged her wanting at that moment, because Morgan spoke.

"What do you propose we do about the situation?" His voice was cold, as if he'd caught her chill.

"If you were a man like Andrew, I'd suggest this episode would enhance your reputation. You could even claim the entire idea of marrying a maid was just a grand jest."

He didn't say anything, and a second later she looked up to find him staring at her. Morgan could be very intimidating when he wished to be.

"You could say I was a partner in your little scheme." She remembered Aunt Mary's words. "A strumpet."

His face tightened. "You were a virgin, Jean. I didn't imagine that. Would you sacrifice your reputation for the sake of my honor?"

"People don't care about a maid's reputation, Morgan." When he didn't speak, she continued. "I have no funds. I could always go into service again, I suppose. Will you allow my aunt to give me a recommendation?"

He looked at her as if she was something beneath his shoe. Her fingers danced along the edge of the placket of buttons on her bodice. Should she offer to reimburse him for her clothes?

"What are you talking about?"

"I couldn't go back to being a maid at Ballindair." She forced a smile to her face. "Even the ghosts would be scandalized."

He stared at her.

She looked out over the Clan Hall. "I've always been better suited to be a maid than a countess," she said.

Standing, she placed a hand on Mr. Seath's coffin, patting it gently.

Wordlessly, she turned and left the Clan Hall,

Jean could only remember one time when she was as miserable, but unlike that time, there would be no sound of a rope being pulled tight, or the muffled echo of a body dropping from a noose.

No, this death wasn't of the physical form but of the spirit.

Chapter 36

A cloud hung over the castle at the death of William Seath. Ballindair's steward had been a much respected and beloved personage.

Or perhaps the dour mood was due more to the Earl of Denbleigh's incessant glower. Or the Countess of Denbleigh's refusal to see anyone, having retreated to her suite and remaining there, secluded.

For whatever reason, the weather mimicked the mood of those within Ballindair. A whistling wind sent the branches of the nearby trees fluttering like a scandalized matron's fan. Black-bottomed clouds scuttled overhead and the air felt heavy with rain.

Morgan used the library as his den, as restless as an old lion facing its mortality, pacing back and forth before the window. For two days, he'd handled what business needed to be transacted, gave orders, inspected inventories, and answered questions, but all the while, his mind was focused on a certain set of rooms on the second floor.

Jean had moved her belongings out of the Laird's Tower and back into the Countess's Suite.

He'd let her. He hadn't said a word or lifted a hand to prevent her. Why the hell not? he wondered. Perhaps he could claim surprise. Or confusion, again. Or a dozen other emotions he couldn't recall ever experiencing except around her.

Almost immediately, however, he knew he'd made another mistake.

He'd gone to the Countess's Suite three times, and three times she ignored his knock. She wouldn't listen to him, and even returned the notes he sent her, unread. The last time he'd gone to the suite, just this morning, he caught the glance of a passing maid, her look of pity reminding him of London.

This was not, however, London.

Andrew was wrong. Perhaps he didn't care about what his staff thought, or the whole of Scotland. Throw London into that category, and the world, while he was at it. But he cared very much about the opinions of one particular person: the wren, the ghost hunter, the maid, and his wife, the Countess of Denbleigh.

A woman who wasn't his wife, after all.

For the first time, he understood why Jean had argued so vehemently against their marriage. Why, also, she'd looked so horrified when he gave her a sum of money.

She didn't consider herself married.

She didn't think of herself as the Countess of Denbleigh.

She knew she wasn't his wife.

If his father was alive, what would he say to this situation?

Morgan stopped, staring out the window. Most of his life, he'd cared about his father's opinion. He'd worked like a demon at the distilleries in order to prove himself worthy of the great man's approval.

Now, he didn't care a jot.

Something odd had happened to him since coming home to Ballindair. Instead of finding only the memory of a better time, he'd found purpose.

He knew every expenditure for his home. He knew the exact number of people he employed, and most of their names. He knew if they were married, where they lived, what their salaries were, and their stories. He knew the groom and the maid who planned to marry in the spring, about Mrs. MacDonald's insistence that all her maids be able to tally their own sums and read and write. He knew the West Tower had a roof leak and that everyone at Ballindair was heartily sick of mutton. He knew the exact acreage he owned, how many fish were caught, the number of cattle and sheep, and every single crack in the foundation.

Because of a man he'd come to admire, and mourned now, he'd learned even more about himself. He might have held the title, but he'd never been Laird of the MacCraigs until the last month.

His mood had mellowed and warmed. He felt like smiling all the time, at least until the last few days. He had even done something he'd never have done a month ago—he sent instructions to his solicitor to sign over the Paris house to Lillian. Perhaps she only wanted to find a measure of peace for herself, something similar to what he'd found at Ballindair. Let her live there and be happy.

As far as his own happiness, Providence had delivered a surprise to him, right to his doorstep, to his very person, when Jean had blinked down at him on the floor of the Laird's Tower.

Here, I give you a woman to challenge your thoughts of

all women. Here is one who hunts ghosts, speaks bluntly, and fascinates you beyond measure.

Jean had confused him, pushed him to the edge of incompetence, and amused him. She'd nudged him into looking at those facets of his life he'd heretofore cherished: his father and the concept of honor.

What had she said? Something about beginning to see his father as a fallible human being, someone who made mistakes. He saw that now, and also something else. His father had obeyed a code, but it was one he'd devised for himself. The world had simply flowed around it, like a burn cascading around a boulder.

His sister-in-law was, surprisingly, the same kind of person. Centered in herself, with no apologies to anyone. Catriona did what she did because she wanted to do it.

His father had always appeared contented with his life. So, too, Catriona. Was that the secret to happiness? To live for oneself, and to hell with anyone else?

He couldn't live that way, not when he cared, very much, what one particular person thought. Someone who was refusing to speak to him, see him, or even listen to him.

He continued pacing, startled when a shaft of sunlight illuminated the window. The dark clouds parted, revealing a sky of brilliant blue.

Leaving the library, he approached the housekeeper's office, a small chamber beside the kitchen where Mrs. MacDonald settled her accounts and planned for the week ahead.

"Mrs. MacDonald," he said, opening the door the way the housekeeper had so often, without notice or knock. "You and I have to talk."

Jean sat in the Countess's Suite, unattended and unbothered. Her aunt was her only visitor, and her words were bracing, rather than compassionate.

"You're grieving for him," she said.

She had only nodded, not explaining that she mourned twice: for Mr. Seath and for her short marriage.

Morgan had said nothing when she had her things moved from the Laird's Tower. Nor had any of the maids. No one had sent her any sidelong looks, either.

Catriona was in Edinburgh, but she wouldn't have been a great source of comfort anyway. Her sister had always tended to her own problems first, exactly the way she herself was acting now.

"There are things to do, Jean," her aunt had said. "Things requiring your participation."

When she looked at her aunt, the older woman held up her hand to forestall her words. "Whatever your issues with the earl, they can wait until later."

Jean nodded.

"For now, it's important you lead the women to the grave site."

She frowned. "We're having the funeral today?"

Her aunt jerked her head toward the door. "When will you be ready?"

"An hour," she said.

"I'll send Betty to help you," her aunt said.

Perhaps it was a clue to her distraction, but she didn't think to stop her until after the door had closed.

She had no mourning. There hadn't been time to dye any of her new dresses, either. Besides, Catriona had appropriated half of her wardrobe.

"I'm going to Edinburgh," her sister had said. "You'll just be here."

Since she couldn't argue with that comment, Jean had turned over three of her new dresses, leaving her only one, plus her wedding dress. The yellow of the wedding dress would be a little glaring on such a somber occasion, so she opted for the dark blue with the white lace collar and cuffs.

On this day, of all days, she shouldn't be concerned about her attire.

She missed Mr. Seath. She wanted to seek his counsel, listen to his stories of Ballindair and the 8th earl, and the adventures Morgan had gotten himself into as a boy.

Would he have approved of her honesty, even as late as it had come?

She stood, thanked Betty for helping with her hair, and stared at herself in the mirror. Her face was flushed, her lips pink, her eyes sparkling. For all her desolation, she looked pretty.

She was a fallen woman now. An unmarried woman who'd had congress with a man. A harlot who was finding it difficult to regret the past weeks.

Betty left the room, leaving the door ajar.

Jean stepped into the hall, listening to the silence. The castle was in mourning for one of its own, the absence of sound as solemn as tears.

She bent her head, composed herself to see Morgan, and went to lead the procession of women. Only the men would go into the churchyard. The women would stand at the gate and wait for them.

The utter stillness of Ballindair struck her as she descended the curving staircase, went through the foyer and to the iron-banded front door. No one hastened to open it for her, and it proved to be a difficult task to move.

Finally, she was through, to be greeted by a day as lovely as she'd ever seen in the Highlands. A sky so blue it rivaled Loch Tullie for purity hung over the glen of the MacCraigs, hued with purple and pink, and spots of yellow on deep green.

She could smell the scent of heather wafting on the gentle breeze, along with, surprisingly, sandalwood.

When she looked around and saw the mass of people, she

took a deep breath, preparing herself to take her place at the front of the gathered women.

Except that Morgan stepped out of the crowd to greet her, holding out his hand. He was wearing a kilt again, his black jacket setting off the colors of the MacCraig plaid. He'd never looked so handsome. Nor had she ever longed for him as much.

Slowly, she placed her hand in his.

His smile should have warned her, but she was left in ignorance until he walked with her to the open courtyard, then turned her around.

Aligned in a horseshoe shape in front of Ballindair was the entire staff. Her aunt stood at the head of the maids. Footmen, stable boys, gardeners, those who worked in the farms and outbuildings all stood there solemnly regarding Morgan.

She would have thought it the Laird's Greeting but for the occasion. There was only one thing missing, however: Mr. Seath's casket.

"Isn't there to be a funeral?" she asked.

"No," Morgan said, startling her. "Not today. We're having another type of ceremony. The minister is in the chapel, waiting."

He turned her to face him.

"Marry me, Jean MacDonald," he said. "Or Jean Cameron. Or whatever your name might be. Marry me before God and our people."

She blinked at him. In his eyes was a warmth she'd never thought to see.

"I'll have this marriage blessed by God and the law," he said. "So you can never say it's illegal."

She took a step back. "I won't be used, Morgan."

He frowned at her.

"I won't be used to atone for past sins. Or because you're afraid of scandal."

He smiled, a curiously wicked smile. "There'll be scandal aplenty for the whole of Scotland to hear about," he said, reaching out and grabbing her hand to gently pull her toward him.

He lowered his head and spoke next to her ear. "I can hear the whispering now. 'Did you hear about the Earl of Denbleigh? One of the Murderous MacCraigs? He captured one of his maids and wouldn't let her go. Made her live with him the rest of her days. When their children were born, they were all bastards, poor dears, but he wouldn't relent.'"

"Morgan," she said, pulling back and looking up at him in shock.

"Jean, married or not, you'll live with me at Ballindair." He shrugged. "I'd prefer you were my countess, but if you're set on remaining a maid, I'll make sure Mrs. MacDonald knows you're to have only one duty."

She could barely breathe, let alone speak, but she managed to frame the question. "And what would that be?"

Evidently uncaring about the interested staff of Ballindair, he kissed her gently on the forehead, nose, and then softly on the lips.

"To be my love."

She looked up at him, her hand flat against his chest and her heart full.

"Oh, Morgan."

"Say yes. Say you'll marry me."

She began to smile. "I'll marry you, Your Lordship."

"And be my love?"

"How can you doubt it, my darling Morgan?"

There, in full view of the staff of Ballindair, he pulled her into his arms. Dimly, she registered the cheers before Morgan kissed her again.

A few moments later Morgan MacCraig, 9th Earl of Denbleigh, took Jean Cameron, maid, into the chapel and before the staff of Ballindair made her a countess in truth.

In the Highlands, ghosts were common. If a visitor asked a group of ten Highlanders to tell him a tale, eight of those would relate a firsthand account of meeting a ghost in person. Sometimes the stories incited a chill. Occasionally they amused the listener.

At Ballindair, the French Nun was known to try to prevent the fate that had befallen her from happening to another woman. For nearly two hundred years she'd flitted among Ballindair's rooms, occasionally viewed by a foolish maid or a man with less prudence than lust.

The Green Lady lamented her short life, and wished she'd chosen more wisely. The Herald played his pipes and was rarely heard, for all the talk to the contrary.

Now, the curtain in the Long Gallery shivered, solidified to become a familiar shape, that of a human form. As his body lay in the Clan Hall, the spirit of William Seath lingered at Ballindair, the place he loved most in all the world.

This new ghost, strong and powerful as he hadn't been in the last months of his life, stood at the window, surveying his domain and witnessing the celebration of love and life in the courtyard below. If a ghost could be said to smile, he did.

In the next moment, sunlight streamed into the room, dissipating the illusion.

The sound of cheers banished the silence. A sense of joy, along with the scent of wild roses, filled the room. Then the Long Gallery was truly empty, if only for a little while.

Author's Note

The rules for staff were adapted from actual rules issued to servants in the nineteenth century.

Whiskey/whisky has always had two spellings. Whiskey is an American and Irish spelling, while whisky is most definitely a Scottish and Canadian spelling. Since I'm an American author writing about Scotland, you can imagine my conundrum. I've settled for whiskey, and my apologies for not using the more proper Scottish spelling.

The Anglican wedding service (dating from 1549) reads:

> *I take thee N. to my wedded wife, to have and to holde from this day forwarde, for better, for wurse, for richer, for poorer, in sickenes, and in health, to love and to cherishe, til death us departe: according to Goddes holy ordeinaunce: And therto I plight thee my trouth.*

The poetry mentioned in Chapter 10 is "Answer" by Sir Walter Scott.

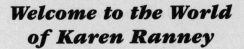

Welcome to the World of Karen Ranney

Turn the page to find out
what other wonderful romances
Karen Ranney has in store for you.

A Borrowed Scot

Who Is Montgomery Fairfax?

Though she possesses remarkable talents and astonishing insight, Veronica MacLeod knows nothing about the man who appears from nowhere to prevent her from committing the most foolish and desperate act of her life. Recently named Lord Fairfax of Doncaster Hall, the breathtaking, secretive stranger agrees to perform the one act of kindness that can rescue the Scottish beauty from scandal and disgrace—by taking Veronica as his bride.

Journeying with Montgomery Fairfax to his magnificent estate in the Highlands, Veronica knows deep in her heart that this is a man she can truly love—a noble soul, a caring and passionate lover whose touch awakens feelings she's never before known. Yet there are ghosts in Montgomery's shuttered past that haunt him still. Unless Veronica can somehow unlock the enigma that is her new husband, their powerful passion could be undone by the sins and sorrows of yesterday.

A Scottish Love

Shona Imrie should have agreed to Gordon MacDermond's proposal of marriage seven years ago—before he went off to war and returned a national hero—but the proud Scottish lass would accept no man's charity. The dashing soldier would never truly share her love and the passion that left her weak and breathless—or so she believed—so instead she gave herself to another. Now she faces disgrace, poverty, and a life spent alone for her steadfast refusal to follow her heart.

Honored with a baronetcy for his courage under fire, Gordon has everything he could ever want—except for the one thing he most fervently desires: the headstrong beauty he foolishly let slip through his fingers. Conquering Shona's stubborn pride, however, will prove his most difficult battle—though it is the one for which he is most willing to risk his life, his heart, and his soul.

A Highland Duchess

The beautiful but haughty Duchess of Herridge is known to all the *ton* as the "Ice Queen." But to Ian McNair, the exquisite Emma is nothing like the rumors. Sensual and passionate, she moves him as no other woman has before. If only she were his wife and not his captive . . .

Little does Emma know that the dark and mysterious stranger who bursts into her bedroom to kidnap her is the powerful Earl of Buchane, and the only man who has been able to see past her proper façade. As the Ice Queen's defenses melt under the powerful passion she finds with her handsome captor, she begins to believe that love may be possible. Yet fate has decreed that the dream can never be—for pursuing it means sacrificing everything they hold dear: their honor, their futures . . . and perhaps their lives.

Sold to a Laird

Lady Sarah Baines was devoted to her mother and her family home, Chavensworth. Douglas Eston was devoted to making a fortune and inventing. The two of them are married when Lady Sarah's father proposes the match and threatens to send Lady Sarah's ill mother to Scotland if she protests.

Douglas finds himself the victim of love at first sight, while Sarah thinks her husband is much too, well, earthy for her tastes. Marriage is simply something she had to do to ensure her mother's well-being, and even when her mother dies in the next week, it's not a sacrifice she regrets.

She cannot, however, simply write her mother's relatives and inform them of her death. She convinces Douglas—an ex pat Scot—to return to Scotland with her, to a place called Kilmarin. At Kilmarin, she is given the Tulloch Sgàthán, the Tulloch mirror. Legend stated that a woman who looked into the mirror saw her true fate.

Douglas and Sarah begin to appreciate the other, and through passion, Douglas is able to express his true feelings for his wife. But once they return to England and Douglas disappears and is presumed dead, Sarah has to face her own feelings for the man she's come to respect and admire.

A Scotsman in Love

Margaret Dalrousie was once willing to sacrifice all for her calling. The talented artist would let no man interfere with her gift. But now, living in a small Scottish cottage on the estate of Glengarrow, she has not painted a portrait in ages. For not even the calming haven in the remote woods can erase the memories that darken Margaret's days and nights. And now, with the return of the Earl of Linnet to his ancestral home, her hopes of peace have disappeared.

From the first moment he encountered Margaret on his land, the Earl of Linnet was nothing but annoyed. The grieving nobleman has his own secrets that have lured him to the solitude of the Highlands, and his own reasons for wanting to be alone. Yet he is intrigued by his hauntingly beautiful neighbor. Could she be the spark that will draw him out of bittersweet sorrow—the woman who could transform him from a Scotsman in sadness to a Scotsman in love?

The Devil Wears Tartan

Some say he is dangerous. Others say he is mad. None of them knows the truth about Marshall Ross, the Devil of Ambrose. He shuns proper society, sworn to let no one discover his terrible secret. Including the beautiful woman he has chosen to be his wife.

Only desperation could bring Davina McLaren to the legendary Edinburgh castle to become the bride of a man she has never met. Plagued by scandal, left with no choices, she has made her bargain with the devil. And now she must share his bed.

From the moment they meet, Davina and Marshall are rocked by an unexpected desire that leaves them only yearning for more. But the pleasures of the marriage bed cannot protect them from the sins of the past. With an enemy of Marshall's drawing ever closer and everything they now cherish most at stake, he and Davina must fight to protect the passion they cannot deny.

The Scottish Companion

Haunted by the mysterious deaths of his two brothers, Grant Roberson, 10th Earl of Straithern, fears for his life. Determined to produce an heir before it's too late, Grant has promised to wed a woman he has never met. But instead of being enticed by his bride-to-be, Grant can't fight his attraction to the understated beauty and wit of her paid companion.

Gillian Cameron long ago learned the danger of falling in love. Now, as the companion to a spoiled bluestocking, she has learned to keep a firm hold on her emotions. But, from the moment she meets him, she is powerless to resist the alluring and handsome earl.

Fighting their attraction, Gillian and Grant must band together to stop an unknown enemy from striking. Will the threat of danger be enough to make them realize their true feelings?

Autumn in Scotland

Betrothed to an earl she had never met, Charlotte Haversham arrived at Balfurin, hoping to find love at the legendary Scottish castle. Instead she found decaying towers and no husband among the ruins. So Charlotte worked a miracle, transforming the rotting fortress into a prestigious girls' school. And now, five years later, her life is filled with purpose—until . . .

A man storms Charlotte's castle—and he is *not* the reprehensible Earl of Marne, the one who stole her dowry and dignity, but rather the absent lord's handsome, worldly cousin Dixon MacKinnon. Mesmerized by the fiery Charlotte, Dixon is reluctant to correct her mistake. And though she's determined not to play the fool again, Charlotte finds herself strangely thrilled by the scoundrel's amorous attentions. But a dangerous intrigue has drawn Dixon to Balfurin. And if his ruse is prematurely revealed, a passionate, blossoming love affair could crumble into ruin.

An Unlikely Governess

Impoverished and untitled, with no marital prospects or so much as a single suitor, Beatrice Sinclair is forced to accept employment as governess to a frightened, lonely child from a noble family—ignoring rumors of dark intrigues to do so. Surely, no future could be as dark as the past she wishes to leave behind. And she admits fascination with the young duke's adult cousin, Devlen Gordan, a seductive rogue who excites her from the first charged moment they meet. But she dares not trust him—even after he spirits them to isolation and safety when the life of her young charge is threatened.

Devlen is charming, mysterious, powerful—and Beatrice cannot refuse him. He is opening new worlds for her, filling her life with passion . . . and peril. But what are Devlen's secrets? Is he her lover or her enemy? Will following her heart be foolishness or a path to lasting happiness?

Till Next We Meet

When Adam Moncrief, Colonel of the Highland Scots Fu-
siliers, agrees to write a letter to Catherine Dunnan, one of
his officers' wives, a forbidden correspondence develops and
he soon becomes fascinated with her even though Catherine
thinks the letters come from her husband, Harry Dunnan.
Although Adam stops writing after Harry is killed, a year
after his last letter he still can't forget her. Then when he
unexpectedly inherits the title of the Duke of Lymond, Adam
decides the timing is perfect to pay a visit to the now single
and available Catherine. What he finds, however, is not the
charming, spunky woman he knew from her letters, but a
woman stricken by grief, drugged by laudanum and in fear
for her life. In order to protect her, Adam marries Catherine,
hoping that despite her seemingly fragile state, he will once
again discover the woman he fell in love with.

The Highland Lords: Book One
One Man's Love

He was her enemy, a British colonel in war-torn Scotland. But as a youth, Alec Landers, earl of Sherbourne, had spent his summers known as Ian, running free on the Scottish Highlands—and falling in love with the tempting Leitis MacRae. With her fiery spirit and vibrant beauty, she is still the woman who holds his heart, but revealing his heritage now would condemn them both. Yet as the mysterious Raven, an outlaw who defies the English and protects the people, Alec could be Leitis's noble hero again—even as he risks a traitor's death.

Leitis MacRae thought the English could do nothing more to her clan, but that was before Colonel Alec Landers came to reside where the MacRaes once ruled. Now, to save the only family she has left, Leitis agrees to be a prisoner in her uncle's place, willing to face even an English colonel to save his life. But Alec, with his soldier's strength and strange compassion, is an unwelcome surprise. Soon Leitis cannot help the traitorous feelings she has when he's near . . . nor the strange sensation that she's known him once before. And as danger and passion lead them to love, will their bond survive Alec's unmasking? Or will Leitis decide to scorn her beloved enemy?

The Highland Lords: Book Two
When the Laird Returns

Though a descendant of proud Scottish lairds, Alisdair MacRae had never seen his ancestral Highland estate—nor imagined that he'd have to marry to reclaim it! But the unscrupulous neighboring laird Magnus Drummond has assumed control of the property—and he will relinquish it only for a King's ransom . . . and a groom for his daughter Iseabal! Alisdair never thought to give up the unfettered life he loves—not even for a bride with the face of an angel and the sensuous grace that would inflame the desire of any male.

Is Iseabal to be a bride without benefit of a courtship? Though she yearns for a love match, the determined lass will gladly bind herself to Alisdair if he offers her an escape from her father's cruelty. This proud, surprisingly tender stranger awakens a new fire inside her, releasing a spirit as brave and adventurous as his own. Alisdair feels the heat also, but can Iseabal win his trust as well as his passion—ensuring that both their dreams come true . . . now that the laird has returned?

The Highland Lords: Book Three
The Irresistible MacRae

To avoid a scandal that would devastate her family, Riona McKinsey has agreed to marry the wrong man—though the one she yearns for is James MacRae. Had she not been maneuvered into a compromising position by a man of Edinburgh—who covets her family's wealth more than Riona's love—the dutiful Highland miss could have followed her heart into MacRae's strong and loving arms. But alas, it is not to be.

A man of the wild, tempest-tossed ocean, James MacRae never dreamed he'd find his greatest temptation on land. Yet from the instant the dashing adventurer first gazed deeply into Riona's haunting gray eyes, he knew there was no lass in all of Scotland he'd ever want more. The matchless lady is betrothed to another—and unwilling to break off her engagement or share the reason why she will marry her intended. But how can MacRae ignore the passion that burns like fire inside, drawing him relentlessly toward a love that could ruin them both?

The Highland Lords: Book Four
To Love a Scottish Lord

Hamish MacRae, a changed man, returned to his beloved Scotland intending to turn his back on the world. The proud, brooding lord wants nothing more than to be left alone, but an unwanted visitor to his lonely castle has defied his wishes. While it is true that this healer, Mary Gilly, is a beauty beyond compare, it will take more than her miraculous potions to soothe his wounded spirit. But Mary's tender heart is slowly melting Hamish's frozen one . . . awakening a burning need to keep her with him—forever.

Never before has Mary felt such an attraction to a man! The mysterious Hamish MacRae is strong and commanding, with a face and form so handsome it makes Mary tremble with wanting him. Already shadowy forces are coming closer, heartless whispers and cruel rumors abound, and it will take a love more pure and powerful than any other to divine the truth—and promise a future neither had dreamed possible.

The Highland Lords: Book Five
So In Love

Jeanne du Marchand adored her dashing young Scotsman, Douglas MacRae, and every moment in his arms was pure rapture. But when her father, the Comte du Marchand, learned she was carrying Douglas's child, Jeanne was torn from the proud youth without a word of farewell—and separated not long after from her newborn baby daughter. Jeanne feared her life was over, for all she truly cared about was lost to her. Can the power of love prevail?

Once Douglas believed his lady's loving words—until her betrayal turned his ardor to contempt. He cannot forget even now, ten years later, when destiny brings her to his native Scotland, broken in spirit but as beautiful as before. His pride will not let him play the fool again, although memories of a past—secret, innocent, and fragile—tempt him. Can passion lead to love and forgiveness?

After the Kiss

Margaret Esterly is desperate—and desperation can lead to shocking behavior! Beautiful and gently-bred, she was the essence of prim, proper English womanhood—until fate widowed her and thrust her into poverty overnight. Now she finds herself at a dazzling masked ball, determined to sell a volume of scandalous memoirs to the gala's noble host. But amid the heated fantasy of the evening, Margaret boldly, impetuously shares a moment of passion with a darkly handsome gentleman . . . and then flees into the night.

Who was this exquisite creature who swept into Michael Hawthorne's arms, and then vanished? The startled yet pleasingly stimulated Earl of Montraine is not about to forget the intoxicating woman of mystery so easily—especially since Michael's heart soon tells him that he has at last found his perfect bride. But once he locates her again, will he be able to convince the reticent lady that their moment of ecstasy was no mere accident . . . and that just one kiss can lead to paradise?

My True Love

Anne Sinclair has been haunted by visions of a handsome black-haired warrior all her life. His face invades her dreams and fills her nights with passionate longing. So the beautiful laird's daughter leaves her remote Scottish castle, telling no one, to search for the man called Stephen—a man she does not know but who fights in war-torn England, a place she has never seen. Stephen Harrington, Earl of Langlinais, never expected to rescue this unexplained beauty from the hands of his enemy. And yet, when their eyes first meet, he feels from the depths of his soul that he should know her . . . that he needs to touch her, and keep her by his side forever. For unknown to both of them, they are in the center of a centuries-old love . . . a love that is about to surpass their wildest dreams.

My Beloved

They call her the Langlinais Bride—though she's seen her husband only one time . . . on their wedding day, twelve years ago.

For years naïve, convent-bred Juliana dreaded being summoned to the side of the man she wed as a child so long ago. Now her husband, Sebastian, Earl of Langlinais, has become ensnared in his villainous brother's wicked plots—and has no choice but to turn to his virgin bride for help.

Juliana now finds herself face-to-face with a man so virile and so powerful that she's fascinated by him—just as he asks her to go against everything she holds true. Sebastian never counted on being enchanted by the beauty of this innocent angel he intended to keep as wife in name only—and he dares not reveal to her the secret reason why their love can never be . . .

Upon a Wicked Time

Tessa Astley is everything a duke should want in a wife. A breathtaking beauty with a reputation that is positively above reproach, she desires nothing more than the love of her husband, the man she's long pined for.

Only Jered Mandville doesn't want a soul mate, just a proper duchess hidden away on his country estate to beget heirs. He certainly doesn't see a place for his bride in his decadent life in London.

Tessa won't let her fairy tale slip through her fingers. She'd do anything to win Jered's heart. So Tessa starts a campaign to win her husband's heart by invading his home, his reckless adventures, and his bed—all to prove to her cynical duke that even a happy ending can be delightfully wicked . . .

My Wicked Fantasy

Mary Kate Bennett was married too early, widowed too young, and left to fend for herself without a penny. Her path was never meant to cross with Archer St. John's, except for a terrible carriage accident with the wickedly handsome Earl of Sanderhurst. Mary Kate awakens in a mysterious lord's bed to a life more luxurious than she could have ever imagined, facing a man she's never met before, but instinctively knows . . .

The whispers about Archer follow him wherever he goes. Had the reclusive nobleman murdered his unhappy countess? When Mary Kate enters his life so unexpectedly, the bold earl is convinced that she has all the answers he has been searching for. So why can't he think of anything else besides her decadently red hair, her luminescent skin, and the feelings this vibrant, spirited beauty evokes within his masculine soul?

Their love can be a fantasy, or it can be strong enough to entwine their destinies forever.